ANCESTRY

ANCESTRY

Simon Mawer

Other Press
New York

First published in Great Britain in 2022 by Little, Brown

Copyright © Simon Mawer 2022

Production editor: Yvonne E. Cárdenas

Typeset in Sabon by M Rules

1 3 5 7 9 10 8 6 4 2

Library of Congress Cataloging-in-Publication Data
Names: Mawer, Simon, author.
Title: Ancestry / Simon Mawer.
Description: New York : Other Press, [2022]
Identifiers: LCCN 2022018926 (print) | LCCN 2022018927 (ebook) |
ISBN 9781635423198 (hardcover) | ISBN 9781635423204 (ebook)
Subjects: LCGFT: Novels.
Classification: LCC PR9120.9.M38 A53 2022 (print) |
LCC PR9120.9.M38 (ebook) | DDC 823/.914—dc23
LC record available at https://lccn.loc.gov/2022018926
LC ebook record available at https://lccn.loc.gov/2022018927

To Naomi Lulham (1832–1908)
and Ann Scanlon (1827–1907),
who would otherwise be forgotten

So we beat on, boats against the current, borne back ceaselessly into the past.

F. SCOTT FITZGERALD,
The Great Gatsby

Preface

What is the past? I don't mean personal memory – I mean the distant past beyond living experience. History is the way the past is *told*, an altogether different thing. But what *is* this past? In what does it consist? In one sense, of course, we carry our past within us, in the nucleus of every cell in our bodies – that acronymic DNA that we have been bequeathed and that, in turn, we cut and shuffle and deal out to our children like so many packs of cards. But there are other things besides. There may be family stories, memories that are handed down, soon to become distorted out of all proportion or simply fade and be forgotten. Then there are the artefacts, the scratchings of pens on fading documents – census entries, birth certificates, perhaps even a diary or a collection of letters. Other than those traces, is the past anything more than quaint old buildings that we treasure far beyond their material worth and the objects that sit in museums – this pewter bowl, that rusted cutlass, these gems, those pieces of pottery – to be glanced at indifferently by schoolchildren on field trips? But a past that only consists of the artefacts is like a skeleton unearthed in an archaeological dig. Where is the flesh and blood? Who were the people? What did they feel? Where have they gone?

Part 1

Suffolk, 1837

The beach was an escape. A long, empty strand, a smear of sand and shingle beaten by waves and stretching away into the haze of distance. Nothing much but marram grass grew there in the shifting surface, along with sea kale and sand couch and a creeping bindweed with pale pink trumpet flowers. But out to sea? A glimpse of sails, tan sails bending towards the south. People going miles and miles. To where? To the ends of the earth, wherever they were.

The two boys walked along the shingle for a while, hoping to find something, anything, that they might have. Sometimes you discovered things washed up. Bits from ships. Wood and stuff. Useful, maybe. When there was a wreck, then all the people from the village would be out looking. Kids wouldn't get a chance. Like the previous year, after that great storm when there were twenty ships cast up and wrecked. But on a day like this, with the sun in the sky and a fine, cool breeze from off the water ...

"Over there!"

It was something, sure enough. Below the shingle, on the flesh-coloured sand, a mass of grey just where the waves broke. Not a rock. There were no rocks round here. Maybe a dead seal. You saw seals often, their heads bobbing in the water, like people swimming almost. Or maybe it was an old coat. A coat'd be useful once the salt had been washed out of it.

They ran, stumbling, down onto the sand, and stopped.

A head. Seaweed for hair. White skin and a barnacle beard. A single, glaucous eye glaring up at the sky. One foot was buried in the sand, the other moved with the breaking of the waves, as though the man was beating time to some tune that only he could hear.

"He's dead," Isaac whispered.

"What'll we do?" his brother Abraham asked.

"Go and tell someone, do we'll get into trouble."

They didn't move. The eye stared. There was sand in the earhole. A hand lay like a dead fish beside the face. Mauve lips. Blue nails.

Abraham put out a foot and pushed.

"What you doin'?"

"Just seein'."

"That's insulting the dead."

"I'm not insulting him. I don't know him. He's just dead." He crouched down and pushed his hand in among the folds of sodden cloth.

"Hey! What you doin' now?"

"Just seein'."

The cloth clung to his fingers as he felt around inside. It was like groping in the guts of some dead animal, a rabbit, maybe. Except they were warm whereas this was cold: the chill of the grave. Then his fingers found something tough, some different thing among the cold cling. He pulled his hand out to see. It was a leather purse, like a mermaid's purse, one of those egg cases they sometimes found along the beach. The curate, who called himself a student of God's natural wonders, had told them they were the egg cases of sharks. But inside this purse, no embryo dogfish. Instead, when Abraham pulled it open, there were two gold coins, gleaming in the sudden sunlight.

The boys breathed deeply. A woman's head on one side; on the other, a shield. "That's the Queen," said Isaac, trying to take one.

Abraham snatched it back. "Them's mine."

"Them's not yours, them's 'is."

"Them's gold and them's mine." He took one of them and put it to his mouth to bite it, not because he knew why but because he'd seen that done, at the market in Lowestoft. There was the taste of salt but nothing more. Except the hard touch of metal. "Gold," he repeated.

"That's theft, that is."

"No 'tisn't. That's salvage."

Isaac was stumped. "What's salvage?"

"It's where you find something and it's yours. Finders keepers, like."

"Where d'you learn that?"

"I heard people say it. Boat people."

Isaac pondered the matter. "What'll happen when you try to get the worth of it? They'll know 'tain't yours. You'll be done for thievin'. Could be sent to the Demon's land."

Abraham pondered the possibility. Did he believe in demons? People went to the demons, it was said, arrested for thieving and sent away forever to the other side of the world where the demons lived. Demon's Land. But was it true? Were there really demons? People said you had a guardian angel sitting on your shoulder and looking over you and he'd never seen one of them either. He shrugged demons and angels away and crouched beside the figure whose guardian angel had clearly not been paying attention when most needed.

"Let's see what else's there." Emboldened by familiarity, he rummaged among the clothes but there was nothing further of interest, just some sodden papers in an inside pocket, the ink all blurred. The two boys stared without comprehension at the ruined writing before stuffing the pages back.

"He's got a belt."

They undid the buckle and tried to pull at the belt for a while, but nothing moved, the weight of the corpse, half embedded in sand, holding the belt fast. When they dug into the sand to free a leg they discovered no boot, only a foot as white as chalk, toes like pebbles. Boots would have been useful. "Maybe he'd took 'em off to swim." Abraham had heard of people doing that. You had to do that, it seemed, or the boots dragged you down. But he didn't know. Neither of them knew because neither of them could swim. And neither had boots.

"What'll we do now?"

They looked round, along the stretch of beach running down the narrowing lines of perspective to the north and south. You could just make out the masts of ships at Lowestoft. Closer, fishing boats were drawn up on the shingle where figures moved about their fishing business, oblivious to corpses or children mucking about on the sand half a mile away.

"We got to tell someone, do we'll get into trouble."

"Our father then."

"He'll lather us."

Isaac was the nervous one, the one who always felt the heavy shadow of his father. He contemplated the lathering they'd get from their father – for what? Just for being and doing. You didn't get lathered for a *reason*. "Not if we show him the money."

Gold. Cole. How would he get the worth of it? Abraham didn't know how much, but he did know that it was more money than their father would earn in a month and more.

"That's my money."

"It's ours," said Isaac, "or I'll tell."

They made their way back through the dunes and the low cliff, across the grassland that had once been common grazing but was now enclosed by the local gentry, towards the cluster of cottages beyond the tower of St. Edmund's Church.

First thing they did was find a place – a crack in the wall of the cottage – where they could hide the purse for the moment. Then they could go looking for their father, who was working with others digging out a drainage ditch. It wasn't good to disturb their father when he was working but they did it nevertheless – this was big news, news that would stir the village. "Hey, Fa, we found a dead 'un," is what they said. What Abraham said, in fact, his voice shrill but supported by Isaac repeating the same thing.

The men, all three of them, deep in the ditch, mired with mud, stopped.

"What you say?"

"A dead 'un. A body."

Their father leant on his spade and wiped sweat from his forehead. "Where's this?"

"On the beach."

"Man, is it? You touch it?"

"No."

He nodded, stuck his shovel in the mud and clambered out of the ditch. "Best not touch it. Might bring fever. Best go and see."

The most exciting thing to happen in Kessingland since the big storm, that's what people said. Down on the beach a crowd watched as a local doctor and an officer of the coastguard splashed through the shallows – the tide was flowing – to examine the body. A stir of interest as the clothes were opened. A gasp at the sight of a white leg. A muttering and not a few prayers as arms and legs were lifted and the corpse was released from the grip of sand and carried to the church by half a dozen men of the village. A group of women – the usual busybodies – attended to the winding. The word had got around that he was German, washed across the German Ocean* to end up on this miserable shoreline. Poor soul, people said, so far from home. There was no money on him to pay for a wooden coffin, so they buried him in the shroud. A dozen and more watched as the parson – the Reverend Lockwood – intoned doom-filled words over the gaping grave:

"Man that is born of woman hath but a short time to live and is full of misery. He cometh up and is cut down like a flower; he fleeth as it were a shadow ... "

From the boundary wall of the churchyard, Abraham and Isaac watched this strange ritual, with the lowering of the corpse and the solemn tossing of a handful of earth, like the earth itself devouring its creatures.

"Earth to earth, ashes to ashes, dust to dust."

Mud to mud, the rector might have added but didn't.

"That'll happen to us one day," Abraham said. In his own case, as it happened, he was wrong; but he was right about other things – like the fact that the people were mistaken about the German (if he was a German) having no money for a coffin, because they didn't know about the two gold coins, secreted now in the outer wall of the cottage, did they? Isaac thought they would rot in hell for what they had done, robbing a dead; but Abraham only laughed. Hell was what they learned about in church and Sunday school – eternal fires

---

* The North Sea was commonly known as the German Ocean until the First World War made German references unpatriotic.

and devils and pain – but at least it was somewhere else rather than here. At least it wasn't the drudgery of rising at first light and working through the mud all day and eating turnips and bread, and fish if you were lucky, and going to bed as the sun went down, as though the night meant the end of life. What did they have to lose, taking their chances in hell?

Kessingland

Kessingland – the land of the watercress beds – was not an easy place to live. Forever threatened by flooding rivers and the encroaching sea, it wasn't much more than just water and mud, dissected by ditches dug by the ancestors who had come from Holland two centuries earlier (but Abraham knew nothing of them). The same ancestors had also thrown up dikes to keep the water at bay, and built lifting pumps that constantly worked, driven by the wind off the German Ocean. So life there was mainly mud, or, when the summer came and the thin crust dried out, dust. The rest that was not mud and dust was rain and the smoke of the cottage where Abraham lived with his parents, John and Mary, and four brothers, the family scratching and gouging an existence out of the land as agricultural labourers.

It could be the start of a Dickensian novel, couldn't it? *David Copperfield*, maybe. The same part of the world, the same shoreline life. Or *Great Expectations*, with a shocking discovery in the marshes. So what difference does documentary evidence make to the story? Because these people are not fictions. Abraham Block and his brother Isaac, their parents John and Mary Ann (née Wright), were once as real as you and, presumably, me. Following a daughter, Martha, who died at only a month old, and Isaac who was born in 1828, Abraham was their third child, born in 1831 and baptised on 6 March.

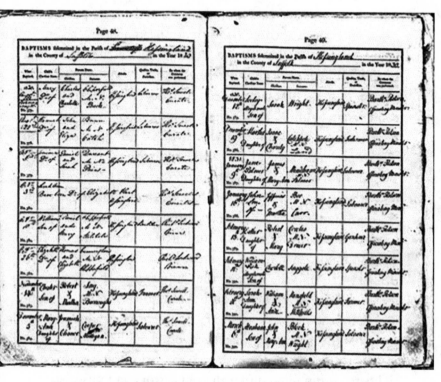

Extract from baptismal registration of Kessingland, 1830/31

There he is in the register of baptism, his name beautifully inscribed along with his parents' at the bottom of the right-hand page. Ironically, they themselves couldn't read, but still, there they are among all the other names of men and women who no longer exist but who once lived and loved, felt pain and happiness and sorrow in this impoverished corner of East Anglia.

*

After the brief excitement of the drowned man, life went on. Their father argued with their mother over things the boys didn't comprehend. Sometimes he hit her. Sometimes he hit them. That was the way of the world. His mother bore three other boys after Abraham and then she died, as people did often enough in those days, of nothing much – a fever, an ague, an influence, a miasma coming out of the water that saturated the land – and there was another funeral, with the parson intoning the same words as he had over the unknown drowned man and the congregation looking on with the same resignation at the sight of a wooden box being lowered into the ground and covered with sodden earth.

Thus by the age of seven Abraham was motherless, growing up with his four brothers more by luck than good judgement, chasing his older brother Isaac through a handful of years towards adult life. School took up little of their time (neither Abraham nor Isaac learned to read or write) and got little in the way of the other things, the daily things that mattered, useful things like gathering rushes for rush-lights or scavenging along the beach, or fishing, illegally, in the ditches that dissected the landscape. They were often hungry because they were children of the dispossessed, country people stripped of rights to common land that their ancestors had possessed for centuries.* That also was the way of things.

Quite soon another mother came, a half-mother, "stepmother" the father said, although what this new woman had to do with steps they couldn't comprehend. She came to look after the youngest, William and James, and then she too was pregnant and duly gave birth. So there was yet another baby in the cottage, the stepmother cooing over the

---

* By a succession of Inclosure [sic] Acts passed through Parliament from 1773. In reality, legalised theft.

new brother – half-brother, stepbrother – and more or less indifferent to the others. The birth was all muddled with other things that happened at that time, the two older boys starting work, the same work as the father for a fraction of the money and all their monies taken away by the parents anyway, so Isaac and Abraham never saw anything of it. "You've got to pay your way now you're old enough," was all the father said. And it was true. By ten years old, children were grown up enough to dig, to lift, to pull, to cut, to do whatever the landlord needed, the landlord being a vague figure never seen but at a distance.

Abraham thought of the gold coin, his gold coin that lay, sly and promising, within the leather purse snuck in that crack in the cottage wall. He and Isaac had even closed it over while doing work that the father required, the same time as he was repairing the thatch for winter. "You boys make up some daub," he said. "Make yourselves useful." So the boys had mixed up mud and straw and filled in the holes and cracks, and so hid the treasure away. And when the daub was dry they plastered it over. Safe as houses.

"Mark the spot," Abraham had said to Isaac, "else we forget. When I go, I'll need that coin."

Isaac laughed. "Where'd you go, bor?"

"Far away from here as I can."

"Why, bor?"

"To see the world." Which sounded fantastical but surely had possibilities, seeing that, while his family worked in the fields, digging potatoes and turnips and cutting wheat if they were lucky, the sea bordered the parish on the east and the port town of Lowestoft was but an hour's walk north. You could sit on the edge of the dunes and stare out at the water to the horizon on a clear day, see ships, hear gulls, feel the distance; at night you could watch the stars wheel overhead.

So the boys grew and the sovereigns grew, two coins becoming, in imagination, a hoard, while the unknown sailor – German? Dutch? – rotted in his unmarked grave and metamorphosed into a mystic benefactor who wanted only good things to happen to the two boys. Abraham spent time there among the gravestones, looking not at his mother's but at the anonymous mound that covered the man he had never known in life, the cold, marble flesh, the beard, the clutching hand, the single, staring eye. That eye haunted him. What had it seen? Pirates and shipwrecks? Strange, exotic shores, naked savages, cannibals, human sacrifice? Marvels to put against the slow and monotonous march of the seasons in Kessingland on the edge of the German Ocean, where the sailing ships passed by and cared not a sovereign, not even a farthing, about the poor webbed-footed creatures who scraped a living on the flatlands, the smee, the smeath, the levels below the sea.

"Where will ye' go, then, bor?" they asked when he boasted.

"I'll go, I'll go … away. That's where I'll go. Away." You could see the frustration in his face. He didn't know anywhere, that was the trouble. He barely saw books except the Bible and couldn't read what he did see. He didn't know places, couldn't tell the name of anywhere beyond Lowestoft, except Lunnun maybe, but the big city was no more than hearsay. German he'd heard of because of the ocean that ate at the coastline, and Dutch, which may have been the same thing.

"How'll ye' get there, Abram?" they'd ask, and he knew the answer to that:

"By boat."

"An' where'll ye' get that boat, bor?"

"My uncle," he'd reply with pride. His uncle, his father's younger brother, one of twins and cleverer by far than any of them, had done that – gone from Kessingland to Lunnun to work in the docks. Real work where you earned a wage.

This Uncle Isaac, after whom Abraham's brother was named, had visited once or twice, coming from Lunnun by coach and recently, wonder of wonders, by steam train. That was something, wasn't it? When he had gone to the city all those years ago, Uncle Isaac had had to walk, but now he could afford a train ticket to Yarmouth – indeed two, because on the second visit he brought his new wife with him, Aunt Lydia, who had airs and graces and turned up her nose as she entered the cottage. Perhaps it was the smoke from the fire or perhaps it was the smell. You couldn't tell, not smelling it yourself.

Uncle Isaac

Uncle Isaac was a bigger man than Abraham's father and, though four years younger, seemed older in a way, louder and more demonstrative, talking most of the time and all the while gesturing strongly as though swatting flies and poking people's eyes out. The two men sat either side of the fire smoking and drinking small beer while the boys listened from the shadows. "There's no future for the lads here, John," Uncle Isaac'd say. "None whatever. What are your wages, then? Eh? Twenty pence a day? They could earn twice that in the docks, more if you've got a trade."

The father shook his head. "What's good enough for our father and his father before him is good enough for my boys."

Uncle Isaac laughed. "You don't even know who your father is, John. Nor if he's the same one as mine."

The father hushed him. "Them boys'll hear," he warned.

The boys lurked, breaths held.

"Theys should know, shouldn't they?" said Uncle Isaac. "It's the plain truth. If they're old enough to work, they're old enough to know that their grandmother was no better than she should have been."*

---

* Their grandmother Elizabeth Block, born 1774, contrived to have ten children all born outside wedlock. Four of them, including Isaac, were by the same man, one Thomas Pain (or Payne). John Block ("Base son of Elizabeth Block" in the baptismal register) does not have any father named.

"You talk bad of the dead. And the woman you owe your life to."

Uncle Isaac laughed again. "Look, brother—"

"Half-brother. Go on, say it."

More laughter. You didn't hear much laughter, only when this uncle came here. "We don't know, do we? We don't know what went on beneath the bedsheets."

"Bedsheets, is it? That what you got in Lunnun, then? Bedsheets."

As though bedsheets were some kind of blasphemy.

"Yes, we got bedsheets. And good food in our bellies. And so can your boys have if they come to the city. I'm telling you this, brother: that Abraham," he turned, pointing, his face lit only by the rush-light and hanging in the shadows like a lantern-man. "He's a small enough bugger but he's got a brain on him."

"Didn't learn his letters."

"So he can always learn that if he puts his mind to it." He raised his voice to the boy. "What do you want to do, Abraham? Dig ditches and plough fields all your life?"

To be asked a question by an adult – an abstract question about wishes and desires – was startling. The boy's mind scrambled for words. "I want," he said. "I want ... to go away. See places."

"There you are, John. He wants to see places, not stay here with his face stuck in the mud and not enough food in his belly. Already a little runt. Why don't you let him come to me and we'll sort him out with a real job? A trade, something useful."

"And see places," said Abraham, in case the point had been missed.

Uncle Isaac laughed. "On the ships then. Why not. You been afloat, boy?"

"No. But I watch 'em."

"You watch 'em. Hear that, John? Your son watches ships, and dreams."

"There's no affording dreams here."

"Bet there's not on your wages, even less on his. Let his dreams come true, you old bastard! Let him come to London, work in the docks a bit, see the big ships. Maybe he can get a place on one of them. They're looking for young lads who wish to go aloft. I'll bet he can climb like a monkey, can you boy? Eh?" He glanced at Abraham and then turned back to his father. "And he'd earn good enough money, even indentured."

Abraham dared to ask: "What's indentured?"

"Indentured is slavery," his father said.

Uncle Isaac laughed. "No more slavery than his life here. If you're indentured, you sign on as an apprentice, boy. You learn. They give you keep and put money in your pocket. And at the end of the time you've got a seaman's ticket. And a future. Imagine that."

And then the conversation changed and he was telling stories about ships setting off for distant places. A place called America. A place called China. A place called Stralia. Ships going all over, not ships like those you saw from the shoreline here, beating against the wind and heading for Lowestoft or Yarmouth, but big ships that rounded the world. Those were what he saw in the port of Lunnun. Not bloody fishing boats stinking of fish but big ships smelling of spices and fruits from all over. "Lemons, you seen lemons? Or oranges?" He'd brought oranges, just to show, two of them that they divided up and tasted. "There," Uncle Isaac said, watching them. "Taste the future. Better 'an turnips, in't it?"

Guardians

Time passed in the way that time does, both slow and fast at once, as though time itself is malleable. The time of Kessingland was slow, excruciatingly slow, the time of the seasons, the cold of winter, with frost and chilblains and a poor fire and little food, through the relief of spring to the growth of summer when there was food on the plate and work enough to be had and the illusion of plenty that would betray you with the scarcity of the next winter. That was all there was to Kessingland time, season after season, year after year, time emerging from some unknown past and traipsing off into the future, when Abraham's father would die just like his mother already had and he, Abraham, would become an image of his parent, and sire children just as his father had done and condemn them to this narrow, flat land, bound by rivers and the German Ocean, just as he had been condemned.

That was Kessingland time.

Time elsewhere – Abraham barely heard whisper of this – moved with remarkable speed, bringing all the different times of the country into one single time, racing along as fast as a train, synchronising station clocks throughout the land and culminating in the universal adoption of Greenwich Mean Time. And that kind of time came with a summons before the Board of Guardians, fine men in stiff collars and black jackets and striped trousers, men with side whiskers and moustaches and the solemn expressions of prophets. The Reverend Lockwood was one of them, the man who had buried Abraham's mother as well as the stranger washed up on the beach.

Abraham attended with his father, the pair of them awkward and over-awed by all the attention.

"John," the Reverend Lockwood said, "we have your best interests at heart." Which was a consolation, given the solemnity of the meeting. It was to do with poverty, of course. Being poor was what you were, your irremovable and irredeemable fate, an aspect of your being; and these were the Guardians of the Poor, whose legal and perhaps even God-given responsibility it was to watch over the poor. "I think you know this, do you not?"

His father screwed up his cap and admitted as much. The vicar nodded approvingly. "In the past, when there was no work, the parish granted your family outside relief. At other times you and yours have worked well and have not been a burden on the parish. But now things are changing. In their wisdom those who rule over us all have seen fit to bring the relief of the poor into a more modern form. Outside relief is coming to an end and inside relief is what will be offered families such as yours when you fall upon hard times, such as now. Of course, you know of the workhouses. There is, for example, the workhouse at Oulton."

"We don't need no workhouse. I got enough for the moment. My lads, they work. It is just now, in the winter ..."

"Indeed, John, indeed. That is precisely why we have called this meeting, to preclude your having to come cap in hand to the parish, because I regret to say that in the future the parish may no longer be able to assist you and other folk in the manner that it has in the past."

"Get on with it, man," one of the august gentlemen muttered.

Lockwood closed his eyes for a moment as though in sudden pain. "We are impatient to help you, John," he said. "And so we have this proposal for you, that one of your boys, perhaps this very fellow here, should cease to be a burden on you and on the parish."

"What, you'd send him to the workhouse?"

"Nothing to do with the workhouse, John. Nothing whatsoever. We wish to give him an opportunity, to raise him out of the Slough of Despond—"

"The what?"

"The hopeless cycle of poverty in which you find yourselves. Give him, and you, a chance in life."

John Block frowned. "He's to become a servant?"

"Indeed no. But to take up an apprenticeship."

"That's slavery."

"It's nothing of the kind."

"And who'd have him? He can't read or write, can barely do his sums."

Mr. Lockwood sighed. "That is hardly his fault. And the mercantile profession is obliged to take on young men as apprentices whether or not they can read and write. I am talking of his going to sea."

"To *sea*? You mean this here Abraham, going to sea?"

"Indeed I do. *We* do. What could be more appropriate to a lad born but a mile from the sea? This gentleman" – he indicated one of the group – "is important in the coal trade at Lowestoft. He has influence and can arrange to have young Abraham indentured aboard one of the colliers plying between here and Newcastle."

The gentleman in question nodded thoughtfully, as though at the uttering of a profound truth. "With Messrs. Charlton

23

and Ramsay," he said portentously, as though calling on Old Testament prophets. "The *Bedlington*."

The boy's father seemed angry. Confused, as well. He looked from Lockwood to the other gentlemen at the table, then down to his young boy. "What's wrong with the dry land, helping his family here? That's what he's for."

"John, you have another four sons to help you out ... or to become a burden on the parish when none of you can find work. I'm offering a way out for one of them. Take a little of the weight off your shoulders and give him a future. Let us find out what he himself thinks."

All eyes turned to the boy standing beside his father. "Well, lad?" one of the other gentlemen demanded. "What do you say? Want to learn a trade? Want to go away to sea? Want to see the world?"

Abraham Block, a mere fifteen, a mere five foot three, fresh-faced and excited but trying his best not to show it, looked back at them. He didn't know it but his stare appeared insolent, bearing within it, as it did, a faint smile. That expression came not from any disdain for these important men but from the fact that he knew what would happen to him. He'd be lathered by his father and shut away on bread and water for a week and made to work in the house for his stepmother and generally made to look a fool. And be laughed at by his brothers – the runt of the family who was always in trouble, the one who made an idiot of himself by daring to hope to run away to sea.

"Yes," he said.

The *Bedlington*

The walk to Lowestoft along the shore of the German Ocean. Gulls crying. Ships out to sea, beating against the winter wind. In his pocket was a letter from one of the gentlemen to a certain Edward Charlton, master of the *Bedlington*. Of course, he couldn't read it; he'd been told that was what the slanting pen-strokes signified and that this is what he should present to the right man at the port of Lowestoft. So he went, wearing a threadbare jacket and patched trousers, and carrying his whole world in a bundle of cloth. On his feet the only boots he had ever worn. He started out at the crack of dawn, walking across the dull flatlands where peewits outnumbered men, over rivers where wherries slid through waters brown with the silt of East Anglia, to Lowestoft where people stared at him as though he had come from Africa.

"Where you going, bor?" they asked, grinning.

"I'm goin' to sea," he told them and they laughed, as though going to sea was something fantastic, the stuff of dreams and fantasies. He may have been the runt of the litter but he was tough with it. And indifferent, harbouring the memory of that talk with Uncle Isaac and confident of the sovereign in his pocket. At the bridge in the centre of town he asked for directions and they pointed at the obvious, the forest of masts, as bare as winter trees, in the outer harbour. The stench of fish went with a cloud of shrieking gulls. A coal-wharf gave a further clue, piles of the black stuff on the quayside and grimy ships unloading.

"*Bedlington*?"

Someone pointed. He walked along the quayside, stepping over ropes that he would come to call springs, avoiding bollards, avoiding cables, avoiding doing anything that might pitch him arse over tit or, worse, over the edge into the depths where the water sucked and slithered between the hulls of ships. The *Bedlington* was one such, moored to the quay, with a single gangplank out and a crewman sitting on a bollard smoking.

"Got a letter for the master."

The sailor looked him up and down and smoked. Only then, a good time having elapsed, did he hold out his hand, as though his gesture and the taking of the letter was nothing to do with Abraham's original statement, as though he, a man, had done nothing in obedience to what a boy might have said. He looked the letter over and sucked on his pipe a bit more. Abraham wondered whether he could read. Reading was a strange thing, the deciphering of the shapes and figures to make words out of them. Abraham knew something of it, the sounds of some of the letters, and he could mouth a word or two. P-I-G. H-E-N. But it was how you put them together fast that evaded him. Yet the sailor nodded, as though he understood plain enough even though there was so little written on the outside of the letter, just what Abraham had been told: *Edward Charlton, Esq., Master of the* Bedlington, *at Lowestoft.*

"Wait there." The sailor took the letter, leaving Abraham on the quayside stripped of the one thing that justified his presence here in the alien world of the port – the letter he couldn't read. He waited. Gulls screamed. Fish stank. The tide ebbed. There was this feeling of helplessness, but also of acceptance.

He couldn't put it into words because he didn't have many: powerless but resigned. What will be will be. A shrug.

"What you doing, bor?" a man asked, passing by.

"Waitin'."

That seemed a good enough answer. Waiting for the tide. Waiting for the wind. What goes round comes round.

A while later – how long? minutes? hours? – the sailor reappeared and gestured Abraham aboard. He crossed the gangplank gingerly, balancing as the sailor hadn't needed to, and stepped onto the deck. This was his first time on a ship, the first time to feel the movement that came through the wood even in the shelter of the harbour, the feeling that this construction of beams and planks was somehow alive, sensitive to the slightest shift of the medium beneath her and the air around her, that she was only tied to the solid land by a few ropes and that her real life was free and far away.

"Mind yer 'ead."

But he didn't need to duck, slipping as easily as an eel into the wooden innards of the vessel. The sailor knocked at a closed door as low as the entrance to a cottage.

"Come!"

The door was opened onto the main cabin, where the master of the *Bedlington* sat behind a table, the stern windows at his back and light all around him so that he might have been a god. He was writing – that magical art – before he looked up. "What's your name, boy?"

"Abraham Block, sir."

"I hope you're not a blockhead, boy." His voice was strange, the tones of Tyneside. Abraham struggled to understand.

"I don't think so, sir."

"You've been recommended to me by one of my clients. What do you know of the sea and ships?"

"Nothing, sir, but what I've seen from shore."

"And yet you are to be indentured aboard my ship and we're to make a seaman out of you, is that it?"

"That's what I hope, sir."

"Five years, boy. Do you know what that means?"

"I know years, sir."

"It means you'll start a boy and end up a man on board this ship. It means you'll work for me when we're afloat and be a burden on me when we're ashore. Let's just hope that's not too often. It means you live on the *Bedlington* and maybe die on the *Bedlington*. The sea is an unforgiving world. If you do something stupid you can be dead in an instant. If you fall overboard, as like as not we'll never see you again. Do you understand that?"

"Yes, sir."

"Sure as hell you don't, not yet. But you will, boy, you will. At least your mother's not come with you, to snivel over you and ask me to look after you."

"My mother's dead, sir."

"That's good, boy, because now your mother is the *Bedlington*. She's the only hinny'll keep you safe."

"Yes, sir."

The man frowned. "You know hinny?"

"Yes, sir. When a stallion covers a donkey, that's a hinny."

A laugh. "You're a real farm boy, aren't you? Where I come from a hinny's a woman, young man. Something you're too young to know about, I'll be bound. But you'll learn, no doubt, just as you'll learn seamanship – the hard way."

They signed the documents at the custom house by the bridge, or at least Charlton signed and Abraham Block put his mark – an uncertain X – in the presence of the assistant chief customs officer. A five-year indenture aboard the *Bedlington*, to end on 30 November 1852.

Abraham Block's entry in the register of indentures, 30 November 1847

Block. It's a good surname for a sailor. Tough, indomitable, hinting at things obstructed, trials faced, troubles borne, loads hoisted by block and tackle. And "Abraham," the name of the patriarch, father of the great monotheistic religions, as single-minded as the religions themselves, a man with enough grim determination to sacrifice his own son to a dreadful god.

Abraham or Abram? Both appear in the records, but never *Abram* when he is directly responsible. *Abraham* then, although he'd never have been able to tell how his name was written. No reading, no writing, no perspective on the world beyond what he had been told or overheard or seen for himself, which wasn't much until that moment when he signed on for the first time.

First Voyages

On the third of December the *Bedlington* was warped out of Lowestoft harbour to beat against the winter northerlies up the east coast towards Newcastle. Abraham Block's life at sea had begun. A life governed by bells and brutality. He lived in the fo'c'sle, crouched in the gloaming that came through the companionway, slinging his hammock in a few feet of space among men who cursed and laughed and spoke a language he didn't understand. They called him a fucking ploughboy, a fucking landlubber, a fucking bilge-rat stealing their rations and giving nothing in return, a fucking cocksucker. The place stank like a pigsty but he soon came to accept that and the fact that he and they stank just as much. He discovered in himself a resilience he didn't know he possessed. He knew seasickness. He knew cold – salt-cold, which is the bitterest cold of all. He knew raw hands from heaving on halyards and sheets, he knew the scrubbing of decks and the polishing of brass fittings. But he didn't know hunger. He knew waking in the small hours for the morning watch, he knew being bullied and being lusted after, knew the sting of the bosun's starter across his back, but at least he had regular food. He discovered tacking and jibing, wearing and going about. He learned the names of sails and their uses, the difference between sheets and shrouds and that neither were for wrapping corpses. He discovered that nothing was a "rope" yet so much was made of rope – halyards, sheets, cables, springs, shrouds, stays. He came to understand the strange geometry of a sailing ship, the sudden rotation of the entire world around the fixed point of the vessel when going about. He learned how to take a bearing on the lights of another vessel at night and how to warn the coxswain if the bearing stayed constant. "Dead easy, lad. If she stays on a constant bearing and if the cox'n don't do summat about it, you're goin' to collide. And if we collide, you're dead. We're all dead."

He heard men talk in strange accents – the curious convolutions of Tyne and Wear mainly – and heard of foreign places and new customs. He learned to smoke a pipe and chew a quid. He learned to box the compass and sight with a sextant. He learned what the crew members said about women and what they intended to do with them when they got ashore. He learned that there were those who thought his own arse would do for the time being. He learned to shut up and listen.

Not only that, he carried with him, on that journey into his future, one-sixteenth of my genes. Of course, he wouldn't have considered looking beyond his own immediate fate – the apprenticeship some unnamed man had arranged on this unknown ship – but nevertheless there he is, with his genes and his . . . what? I wonder what else he is bringing with him, what of those intangible, unmeasurable things that run through families – memories, stories, myths and legends that pass down the generations, unconsciously as well as consciously. He lived on another planet, distant in both time and space from the one you and I occupy. But he found freedom of a kind. No longer was he bound to that small stretch of muddy land behind the storm beach at Kessingland. No longer was he obliged to dig and shift and cut. No longer did he go hungry through the winter months. Instead he slung a hammock in the narrow spaces of the fo'c'sle and ate with a dozen weather-beaten men who had seen the world, or at least some of it. And he began to see some of it himself. You can pick over the bones of a sailor's life by following his ship through the reports in *Lloyd's List* and the *Shipping and Mercantile Gazette*. There are sailing dates, sightings at sea, landfalls, cargoes: all details meticulously recorded for anxious owners and fearful relatives.

In the early days of the next year – 1848 – the *Bedlington* went "foreign" for the first time, to Amsterdam, taking six days across the German Ocean with fifty chaldrons of Newcastle coal in her hold.* Thus Abraham came to know what foreign was. In Amsterdam he drank *jenever* for the first time and by the end of the evening was blind drunk. The newspapers don't record that, but surely it happened, his companions laughing at his antics, then laughing even more when he was vomiting in the gutter outside the tavern. The next evening they took him to a whorehouse. He went with trepidation, feeling himself on the verge of adulthood, uncertain but eager to learn. "You'll be all right here, lad," one of the men reassured him. "They's got doctors inspecting them so they're clean enough. You'll not catch nothing."

He never imagined that you could catch anything from fucking. Animals didn't seem to catch anything (he thought of cows back home, of pigs, of sheep), so why humans? But

---

* A chaldron was a measure of coal equivalent to 53 cwt (Newcastle chaldron) or 28 cwt (London Pool chaldron). I'll bet there were a few disputes over that.

his shipmates knew better. "Pox, crabs, clap, there's all sorts around," he was warned. "Wash your prick with seawater afterwards. Does wonders."

When it was his turn he was shown into a small room at the back of the building, a dark, wooden cell little more than a hutch, ripe with a smell like rabbits. In the shadows a woman hitched up her skirts and bent over for him to do it like a stallion covering a mare. He had a sudden, slippery sensation of release, something that up to now had only been achieved with his own hand in the secrecy of his hammock; and that was it. She was wiping herself and straightening up and eyeing him with amusement.

"Your first time, was it lovey?" Lovey. Her English was guttural, gleaned from hundreds of clients, hundreds of lovies. He admitted that it was. "Sweet," she said, and suddenly put out her hand to stroke his cheek, a human gesture that he had not felt since the death of his mother eight years earlier. But still he had to pay her from the precious store of coins that had come from the sovereign found on the drowned man all those years ago.

The next day they put out from Amsterdam back across the German Ocean to Seaham in County Durham. From Seaham to Shields. From Shields back to the Netherlands with more coal, but this time to Helvoet. From there to Dordt to load cargo for the return to Shields. The *Bedlington* was just one among thousands of ships plying back and forth across the German Ocean, the time of passage depending on the wind: anything from two days to a week or more for a crossing.

Thus winter migrated into summer. The pitching desert of the sea metamorphosed from angry to calm, from storm to still.

He grew to know the movements of the ship, the smells, the sounds, the way she pitched when close-hauled, the way she rose and fell when running before the wind, her ugly roll on a beam reach. He knew the meanings of all those words that had seemed so strange when first he came aboard. He began to become a seaman.

Back to Holland, to Dordt again, with fifty-three chaldrons of West Hartley Main coal, then to Rotterdam and back north to Stockton. On to Newcastle to load more coal (fifty-five chaldrons) and back to Rotterdam. A regular workhorse. Nine crossings of the German Ocean in the year, battering into winds, pitching against the seas, sailing by night and day. Times waiting for the right tide or the right wind. Times playing cards and losing what little of the sovereign was still left. Times tacking the ship, mooring the ship, warping the ship. Loading and unloading. Sometimes docking for repairs – a sail breached, a line parted, a plank stove in – but then casting off and battening down and getting on with it, running with the tide, running with the wind, beating into wind, back and forth, back and forth, summer and winter, sun and rain. The sour taste of vomit in his mouth. The perpetual damp of salt. Summer heat and winter cold. Salt on the lips and the skin, on the tongue and in the tears. Salt everywhere. Salt cod, salt herring, salt beef. Salt vegetables. Salt smarting the eyes. Salt in the brain. And then the words overheard in Rotterdam in November between the master and the first mate as they were loading timber. "London, Mr. Finch. Once we're clear of the Hook we set a course for London."

Word went round the ship – London. The anticipation among the crew was palpable. London. The biggest port in the world, the greatest concentration of sail in the world but also the longest approach, from the shoals and mudflats of the estuary all the winding way to the Tower, through the great meanders of the river, through the powerful tides and the fluky winds and traffic. "London's a bastard," one of the crew said. "Good quim in London," said another.

London

The crossing went well – overnight running before a cold easterly. They were in the great maw of the Thames at dawn, among the other vessels anchored near the Nore lightship waiting for the tide. It was a grey morning where sky and sea seemed almost the same substance, sculpted by the breeze, shifting with the motion of a ship at anchor. There was a tension around the vessel, tempers as taut as halyards. The motion brought on sickness even if you had your sea legs. More ships in sight than Abraham had ever seen. Signal flags flying like bunting at a parade. Thames barges pitching and shoving. A tug chuttering against breeze and tide, paddle wheels thrashing against the water, funnel throwing smoke and sparks into the air.

"Is it on fire?" Abraham asked and men laughed at his naivety. "It's a fucking steamboat, boy. A steam tug. Pulls the fucking boats in and out of harbour."

"Why not us?"

"What you mean, why not us?"

"Why don't they tow us in?"

"Cost, mate. Simple as that. It costs too much to hire a tug to do the job in a couple of hours, so we have to spend two days or more doing it. Simple. Our labour don't cost nuffin'."

Time of frustration, jostling with others in the tideway, searching for the right wind, lying at anchor for hours at a stretch awaiting the turn of the tide, anchoring at night with lights lit and other ships all around like stars in a universe that was never still. When the tide and wind allowed, they moved into the narrows of the Sea Reach with some sail set, tacking awkwardly up the stream, the mate and the coxswain matching each other for blasphemy as the wind shifted. The river closed its banks around them, mudflats and marsh giving way to occasional villages, a small town, a church tower, a fortress. Standing beacons marked shoals. Steamboats puttered across the river, belching smoke and noise. Abraham looked around him, knowing a new form of excitement that was different from the thrill of the deep sea – the thrill of the mariner coming to land, edging towards the largest city in the world that still couldn't be seen but created a great afterglow in the western sky long after the sun had gone down – the mimic sunset of gaslight.

They anchored in Gravesend Reach and waited for the next dawn. Bumboats came around, touting for trade. Fruit, vegetables, gin, girls. "Chousers," one of the men said. But goods were bought and a girl's skirts were lifted to show what she had on offer. There was laughter and catcalls until the mate came on deck and bawled them out. "She's feeble-minded!" he shouted. "Can't you see that? A poor, blighted child!"

They talked about it later, when they were off watch. "He's got one of his own," someone said of the mate.

"Got one what?" Abraham asked.

"An idiot. His daughter. Gets poked by half the village."

"How do you know?"

The man shrugged. "Everyone knows it."

At dawn they raised anchor and caught the tide once more. Their course veered with the convolutions of the river, at times with the wind, at times against it, the agonising crab-progress of a ship in narrow straits clutching at a fluky wind. Gravesend

Reach to Northfield Hope to Fiddler's Reach, going by the lead all the time. Then the Long Reach, where they caught a favourable breeze that gave them way even as the tide turned and got them to anchor off a cluster of buildings called Erith. Ships passed them on the ebb tide, an East Indiaman pulled by a steam tug. Snows, brigs, brigantines with short sails set. "It's easier going out than in," the mate told Abraham. The master, Charlton, rarely addressed a word to him but the mate did, gave him useful information, tried to do what they ought to do with an apprentice: teach him. "Easier going out than in because in the city the ebb tide is longer than the flood. It'll last for a good seven hours here, leaving us with only five of flow to work with. And less the further in we go."

They had a book beside them at the wheel, Abraham noticed. A book that held the key to all this going about and pausing. The mystery of the printed word that he had never learned to decipher. But he heard the names called out as they went: Rand's Reach, Erith Reach, Barking Reach. Halfway Reach seemed some kind of progress, but "Halfway going out, not halfway going in," the mate said, dashing his hopes. Then Gallions Reach, Woolwich Reach with the Royal Arsenal buildings on the south shore, Bugsby's Hole, Blackwall Reach, the Isle of Dogs.

On the south bank there were the lawns and pillars of a palace and a great hulk moored there: a three-decker shorn of her masts and flying a red ensign at her stern. "Sailors' hospital," said one of the men who knew these things. "*Dreadnought*. Ship of the line once. Fought at Trafalgar." He shrugged. "Now look at her."

They went about, coming up through the wind and heading into Limehouse Reach. The city itself crowded ahead: wharves, piers, moored ships, churches, warehouses all competing for attention. A forest of masts, as though trees themselves had somehow taken root in the river and returned to their original, living state, waving in the winter wind. Boats queued up to berth, ferry boats cut across the river, barges worked their way against the tide with the indifference that familiarity brings, a harbour-master's wherry darted to and fro, chivvying shipping like a sheepdog herding sheep. The harbour-master himself stood in the stern-sheets with a loudhailer, demanding attention. His voice came faintly through the sound of the water, the wind in the rigging and the alien noises from the shore. For Abraham Block it was his first view of the city that was to become the nearest thing he ever had to a home. He was astonished.

They passed the night at anchor in Limehouse Hole in sixteen feet of water and woke to a cold, still morning. Fog skulked around the wharves. Ships clung to the shore like lice to the flanks of a great inert beast. They kedged the *Bedlington* in and moored at Bell Wharf Tier, the outermost of a dozen vessels. There would be days to wait before unloading. Abraham was set to scrubbing the decks. Cold, raw fingers but at least the exertion brought some kind of warmth. The mercury fell. Mr. Finch, the mate, showed him. "That's freezing. Thirty-two degrees. Now we're five degrees below freezing. Twenty-seven."

"Why isn't it all froze, then?"

"The river? Nah, it takes time. Days and days of real cold. Last time it did that was 1814. I remember my father telling me you could cross from one side to t'other. They had market stalls on the ice and all sorts. But it'll not happen now. River's too fast nowadays. Now you get back to your work, young fella. Keep warm that way."

On the third day, when all the tasks that might have occupied his time had been completed, he had the gall to ask

Mr. Finch (not the master, never the master) for permission to go ashore.

"Go ashore? What for, boy? They'll eat you alive."

"To see my family. My uncle."

"Lives here, does he? Whereabouts?"

"Lunnun, sir."

The man laughed. "Of course, London. I meant, where in London? It's the biggest city in the world, boy. You need to know where."

"Dunno, sir. They told me Orchard Row."

"Could be anywhere, Orchard Row."

"It's in Lunnun."

"I meant, anywhere in London. There are many places with the same name. It's a big city. They run out of new names."

"Somewhere near the docks," he said. And then a memory, a distant, strange memory of what had already become a distant, strange time, came to his mind: "Stepney, that's what he said. Orchard Row, Stepney."

Stepney

He stepped across the decks of the ships in the tier, then onto the jetty and up onto the quayside. Ashore. The ground shifted beneath his feet as though he were still afloat, as though he were still full of gin.

Coal-whippers were at work on the quay, heaving bags from the hull of a collier. Coal dust was in the air, and the acrid, sulphurous smell of burning. You tasted it on the tongue as much as smelled it in your nose. Smoke smudged the air above the buildings, fusing with the morning fog and hanging like rags above the roofs. He climbed steep stairs and went through a narrow alley into a space where trolleys rattled. He didn't understand the narrowness of this place. He'd been brought up in the open space of Suffolk, the alluvial flats, the open skies, and now he'd had a year of the vast expanses of the sea, encircled by the horizon and overwhelmed by the sky. But here the limits of the world were cliffs of buildings gathered round and pressing in on him.

"Excuse me—"

Men shrugged and walked past, pushing carts. There were others looking strange – Chinamen, dark-skinned blacka-moors, men with long ringlets, all sorts. Stalls, some kind of market. Men shouting, calling prices.

"Excuse me—"

It was his insignificance that amazed him, that in all this noise and bustle no one took any notice. "Excuse me—"

"What?" It was a woman selling matches. She turned and looked him up and down, trying to figure out what type of customer he might be and deciding he was no customer at all. "What you want, dearie? Not going to waste my time, are you?"

"The church," he said.

"Church? There's churches all over. There's St. James, St. George, St. Paul. I know 'em all."

"Stepney Church."

"You a matelot? Proberly you mean St. Dunstan's." She pointed through the buildings, gave directions, names – Back Lane, Albert Square, Commercial Road, Arbour Square, 'Eaf Street – names he wouldn't recognise if he saw them because he couldn't read. He walked in the vague direction, through caverns measureless to man, populated by more people than he had seen in the whole of his life. And not just people but animals – dogs and horses, a cavalcade of horses breathing steam out into the cold air, dogs picking over litter, pigeons fluttering, and beneath everything, beneath the litter, beneath your feet, beneath the horses' hooves, rats scurrying. There were familiar smells – horse piss and horse shit, human shit, rotting vegetables – blended with smells he was only beginning to discover – the pungent smell of spices, the sour stench of vinegar, the stink of a tannery. The streets ran between cliffs of buildings. Pubs, factories, warehouses, a covered market, a church, shops, houses all slammed together as though by some ill-tempered child playing with pebbles and mud. In one place the street went under arches and a steam engine chuttered overhead, belching smoke like those steamers on the river, but dragging carriages after it. He stood and stared while people pushed past. Beyond the railway arches was a wide road where

42

wagons trundled past, carts, wagonettes, handcarts, carriages, every imaginable vehicle. Men crossed the road, dodging the traffic. Whistles blew. Whips cracked. Shouts rang out. He walked along the pavement, past children begging. One of them had a broom and was offering to sweep a clean way through the debris across to the other side. An omnibus went past with people on the roof wrapped tightly against the cold. Someone gestured. A curse or a salute? In the last year he had learned to interpret the world of the sea and ships but this new, urban world was beyond him. He stopped someone at random and asked, "Orchard Row?" and the man pointed overhead, to a painted sign on the corner building. "Can't you read?"

He couldn't, neither the mood of the place, nor its sounds and sights, nor even the sign itself which said – he could just spell out the letters – *O-R-C-H-A-R-D R-O-W.*

"No, I can't. Not really."

The man shrugged and walked on. Abraham looked along the street at a row of houses as uniform as beads on a string. There was a pub on the corner, the Royal Duchess. He pushed open the door and went into the fug of smoke and beer.

"Block?" the landlord said when Abraham asked. "You mean Isaac Block?"

"That'll be him. I'm his nephew."

The landlord laughed. "Comes in here when the wife isn't looking. Where you been, boy? Been foreign?"

"Come from Rotterdam."

"Apprentice?"

"Yes."

The man nodded. "What'll you have?"

"Got no money."

The man laughed. "Apprentices never have no money. On the house."

"A beer."

43

Beer was drawn and a measure of whisky poured into a tumbler. "Dutch courage," the landlord said and called to one of the drinkers, "This here's Isaac's nephew, going to confront his aunt."

There was laughter. Abraham drank. The bitter cool of beer and the sharp flash of the whisky.

"Don't tell your aunt, though," the landlord warned. "Else there'll be all hell to pay. You'll find them at number seventeen."

Abraham finished his beer and went outside, fortified against the cold and against the anxiety he felt.

You have to discard a century of concrete history in order to see Abraham Block make his way up that street looking for number seventeen because Orchard Row is no more. The buildings are no more, the street plan is no more, nothing of Orchard Row remains, not even the name, which transmuted in the middle of the nineteenth century from "Orchard Row" into "Old Church Road." Maybe the assonance between the two names helped give rise to the change, there being no longer any evidence of fruit trees hereabouts but plain evidence of St. Dunstan's Church still standing at the top end, surrounded by a small park that is the last vestige of the village that Stepney once was.

Under its new name the street itself lasted until the winter of 1940/41 when high-explosive bombs obliterated the houses at either end. Then came the postwar period when developers changed the face of London far more than did the Luftwaffe, overriding the street pattern itself so that nowadays "Old Church Road" remains only in part, as an isolated loop of dull 1960s housing that no longer connects either to Commercial Road at the south end or Stepney Way at the north.

Thus in November 1848, Abraham Block, a man who no longer exists, walked along a street that no longer exists towards a house that no longer exists: number seventeen, a narrow terrace house, brick-built in the Regency period, one window on the ground floor, two on the first, the front door stepped right on to the pavement. There was a brass door knocker cast like a fist holding a ball.

He stood on the step. He told himself he was a sailor. He'd crossed the German Ocean. He'd been foreign. He'd been drunk on gin and he'd smoked a pipe. He'd chewed tobacco. He'd had a woman more than once since that first time in Holland. He was a man. And yet he was anxious, standing outside that indifferent door on an indifferent street in the largest and most daunting city in the world, waiting to confront a family member for the first time since leaving home. He lifted the door-knocker, hammered it down and waited.

Sounds within, of someone approaching. A woman's voice through the door. "Who is it?"

Aunt ... he couldn't remember her name, if it was her. The publican had warned him. Fearsome. "It's Abraham," he called. "Abraham Block." A name to be proud of. A serious, tough name. Block and tackle.

There was noise inside, of bolts being drawn. The door opened a fraction and a face peered out. Suspicious eyes. A sour trap of a mouth. It was not a face, or even part of a face, that he recognised, but then he had last seen her years ago – five, six? A lifetime. "Yes?" the face said.

"Is my Uncle Isaac here? Isaac Block? I'm Abraham."

The door opened further. The woman – shawled against the cold – stood back a fraction and looked him up and down. "What brought you here? Sailor are you?"

"More 'an a year now. Been all over. Holland, mainly."

She sniffed. "You'd best come in."

He edged through into the narrow space and followed her out to the back where there was a dank kitchen and back door that gave out on to a narrow yard. "I hope you're not looking to stay," the woman said – what was her name? It came to him in a flash – Lydia, Aunt Lydia. If this was indeed the same woman. Did he recognise her from the aunt he had last seen all those years ago when he was a child skulking in the shadows of the cottage and listening to the talk of adults? "We have lodgers, you see. The rooms are taken."

"I'm on the *Bedlington*, docked at Bell Wharf."

"So what are you after?"

"I just wanted to see my uncle."

"Well you'll have to wait. He gets off shift at six. I suppose you'll be wanting something to eat."

"I wouldn't mind . . . "

She put out some bread and a smear of dripping, with water to drink. While he ate she watched, as though watching might make him consume less. Her conversation was as begrudging as her offering of food – no more than the occasional observation about life in the city and the cost of everything and how everyone wanted something for nothing these days. Only one subject seemed to arouse real interest – the morals of sailors. Sailors were everywhere round here, being so close to the docks. And they didn't have no shame. All those days spent at sea with nothing to do with their time or their money and then they come ashore and think they can buy everything and anything. "I hope you haven't learned any of their disgusting ways, young Abraham Block. Although I don't see how you can avoid it, living with them. You should see what they get up to, and the women what encourage them. Gin and fornication, that's what it is. I hope you never do anything like that."

She watched him blush, which confirmed her worst fears. "Wouldn't surprise me," she said. "I know you Blocks well enough. It's in the blood, isn't it? From your grandmother Elizabeth."

"My grandmother?" He remembered some talk between his father and his uncle. Something half-recalled, half understood. Not knowing who their father was. Or who their fathers were.

"Yes, your grandmother, boy, who had ten children and all of them born on the wrong side of the blanket. Elizabeth Block, she was."

"Wrong side of the blanket?"

She laughed without humour. "Bastards, boy, bastards all ten of them. Including your father and your uncle."

It was a relief when the opening front door announced the arrival of her husband, who didn't seem much different from the uncle Abraham recalled from his visits to Kessingland, a man who laughed at the sight of his nephew and punched him in the shoulder and called him a fine fella-me-lad and remarked on how he'd grown and how was he doing?

"I'm an apprentice seaman."

"Ha! Didn't I tell your father that? Get away from Kessingland and see the world. Learn a trade, that's the future. What's your ship?"

"The *Bedlington*."

"Ah, I know the *Bedlington*. Ketch, isn't she?"

"Schooner."

"Schooner, of course. Standing at Limehouse Stairs."

"Bell Wharf."

"Same difference. She's a collier, isn't she?"

"She carries coal, yes. But this voyage came with timber, from Rotterdam."

"Rotterdam," Isaac repeated, turning to his wife. "You see, woman. A mere sixteen and already he's seeing the world."

"Seventeen, Uncle."

"Seventeen, then. John Block's little son and here he is come to London from Rotterdam. And what you doing now,

47

young Abraham? Are you here to stay? You must stay with us. Prepare a bed for him, Wife."

The woman pinched her lips. "He can't stay. I've explained. We've no room, what with the lodger."

"Nonsense. He can sleep on the floor here in the parlour. Imagine what my brother would think if we turned his son away!"

There was, of course, no need for this hospitality dispute. Whether or not he liked the idea of sleeping on the floor, apprentices were kept tightly bound to their ship lest they be tempted away to other vessels. Abraham had to be back on board the *Bedlington* that evening. But in the meantime he could stay for a frugal supper at the Orchard Road house, with Aunt Lydia silent in her disapproval and Uncle Isaac full of enthusiasm and bonhomie and tales of the docklands. Thus were the fragile ties of kinship maintained in that century of change, creating some kind of tenuous link between Kessingland and London.

The Sailor Returns

Abraham continued his apprenticeship on the *Bedlington* for a further year, carrying coal from Newcastle to France throughout 1849, visiting Rouen four times (an entry up the meanders of the Seine almost as difficult as the Thames) and Boulogne three times. And then, at the end of the year – on Boxing Day to be exact – the *Bedlington* put into Lowestoft.

There would have been a certain sailor's swagger as he stepped ashore at his home port. He'd seen the port of Rotterdam and heard Dutch spoken, he had been to Boulogne and Rouen and heard French, to London and been part of the greatest city in the world. Most of what he saw around him in Lowestoft were fishing smacks and fisher folk, people familiar to him when he was no more than the young son of a farm labourer, while here he was, returning from abroad. People knew he was a sailor from his weathered complexion, his sailor's ducks, his dark blue pea-jacket, the narrow-brimmed tarpaulin set back on his head, indeed the whole manner with which he held himself.

"Where you been, bor?"

"Been foreign."

"What vessel?"

"The *Bedlington*, out of Newcastle."

He walked the hour to Kessingland, unsteady on his feet at

first but soon enough walking fast. Long strides for a small fellow. Easy through the frosted fields. He told himself that his rolling gait was because he was used to walking on a heaving deck but in fact it was as much an affectation as anything. He was fit and strong and felt master of all he saw – the low, waterlogged fields, the drainage ditches slated with ice, the pollard willows, the small cottages with their thatch and their patched walls.

The sailor returns. It sounds like a genre painting by Augustus Egg or Arthur Hughes – a young lad, his kitbag over his shoulder, a steady smile on his lips and a hopeful gleam in his eyes, returning home after two years away ... to find what? What has changed? Abraham left his four brothers with their father, his second wife Sarah, and her child. Now only three remain, the father and the twins, William and James, now twelve years of age. Seeing them there in the shadows of the cottage with their old father is like stepping back into the past, a dark, enclosed past with no horizon. They look at him with wide eyes, as though at an envoy from another world.

"So what are the others doing?" he asks.

His father seems slower, greyer. "George is in Beccles, in service. Training to be a footman."

"A footman," Abraham repeats, as though footman is something disgraceful. "And Isaac?"

"Isaac passed on."

"Passed on?"

"Died."

Silence. Isaac gone and he never knew. The peat fire smoulders, giving out little heat. The smoke stings his eyes. Salt stings your eyes but it is a different sting which isn't going to turn you blind. "What was it that did for him?"

His father shrugs a life away. "Fever."

"A fever."

"Nothing to be done."

"Of course not. And the wife?"

"She's in service. A scullery maid. Lives in."

Abraham looks around the narrow room, as dark and low as the 'tween-decks of the *Bedlington*, but somehow without any hope. At least the *Bedlington* promises a foreign port, a cargo, a voyage to another country. "Glad I got out," he says.

Abraham at the churchyard, thinking of death. Death on land is different from death at sea: it leaves a trace. They lost a man from the *Bedlington*, midway between Newcastle and Boulogne, a Tyneside man called Ben whom everyone liked when they thought about him at all. He was taken by a rogue wave. One moment he was there, hauling on a sheet, next moment he was gone, vanished without a trace. There was the cry of "Man overboard!" and someone threw an oar into the water to mark the place, while the coxswain put the helm up to bring the ship about, but it took a good fifteen minutes to turn her around and bring her back, more or less, to where it must have happened. It was another fifteen minutes before they found the oar, but not Ben. The man wasn't even a swimmer. He'd just disappeared. No memorial, no grave, nothing to mark his going, just the commotion of the sea and a floating oar pulled out of the water, and a prayer said by the master, reading from the ship's prayer book and giving a solemn tone to the words so that he sounded just like the Reverend Lockwood back in Kessingland:

"We therefore commit his body to the deep, to be turned into corruption, looking for the resurrection of the body, when the sea shall give up her dead."

But there at Abraham's feet in Kessingland graveyard was the physical evidence of Isaac's going: the heaped turf of a pauper's grave and the knowledge that his bodily remains were there, mere feet below the surface. The rest of him, the essence that made of the body a living being, where was that? Abraham had no answer. Abstract thought doesn't sit well with illiteracy, yet Abraham surely considered his future as he stood there looking at his brother's grave. Going away to sea had seemed a good enough choice but he now thought bigger than the east coast of England and a small stretch of northern Europe. There were greater fish in the sea.

Within a few months he had jumped ship and deserted his indenture with the *Bedlington*. The fact is there in the register of apprentices: a red line struck through the original entry and a fateful addendum written across in red ink: *Deserted 6.6.50.**

The ship he deserted to was the *Gipsy Queen*, captained by a man named White. She was a schooner like the *Bedlington* but despite also coming from Shields, with the *Gipsy Queen* there would be few tedious runs up and down the east coast. She traded further abroad, to the Baltic, to the Mediterranean. In March 1850 Abraham Block set off on his first voyage to Kronstadt and St. Petersburg.

---

* Visible on the register entry shown on page 29.

Block or Black?

In the records there's something fishy about Abraham Block, a vagueness of detail about his age and even his name. Sometimes Block becomes Black. Occasionally his birth year shifts between 1834 and 1831 to suit circumstances. And he signs on for that second indenture on the *Gipsy Queen* a few months before his first indenture on the *Bedlington* is officially cancelled. For the second indenture he gives a false age and possibly a false name. Was that to confuse the authorities, so that they wouldn't catch up with a deserter? The official register records *Abraham Black* aged fifteen, the indenture to run for four years until 22 March 1854. But *is* it "Black"? The handwriting is ambiguous:

Indenture on the Gipsy Queen, *1850. Abraham in the centre*

Black or Block?

It's hard to tell. The age is certainly wrong: in 1850, Abraham Block was nineteen years old, not fifteen – the baptismal register of Kessingland shows that he was christened on 6 March 1831. So is it even the same person who took on an indenture on the *Gipsy Queen* in March 1850?

You nose around the documents, straining to decipher handwriting, trying to figure out abbreviations, worrying over the people behind the entries. Was Abraham Black actually Abraham Block?

In the early nineteenth century, British ships were obliged by act of Parliament to carry a certain number of apprentice sailors. The aim was to ensure a supply of skilled seamen for the Royal Navy should Britain once again find herself at war. Ship owners hated the law. It obliged them not only to take unskilled boys into their crews and teach them their trade but also to clothe and feed them even when the ship was in port and the normal crew would be laid off. Who wants a useless kid hanging around when there's no work? But you'd be stuck with an apprentice until his indenture – usually five years – was over.

A ship the size of the *Gipsy Queen* would have been obliged to take on only a single apprentice, yet it may be that Abraham had provided a neat way round the law – he was by now a seaman with two years' experience. Was he perhaps a phoney apprentice to be kept on the books to make it look like the *Gipsy Queen* was obeying the letter of the law? He might even have been offered an ordinary seaman's wage as long as he went along with the myth of being an apprentice, and as long as he accepted the deception that he was a mere fifteen years old.

Lies come home to roost. A couple of years later, in 1853, Abraham Block is admitted to hospital. We'll come to that all in good time but the point here is that there is no doubt or ambiguity about his identity then. On the hospital records his details are all there: Abraham Block, apprentice on the *Gipsy Queen*, nineteen years old, 5ft 5in tall, born Rushmere (a hamlet of Kessingland), Suffolk. He's still lying about his age (he was actually twenty-one at the date of admission) but everything else is in order. It's him.

Wanderer

As befits her name, the *Gipsy Queen* was a wanderer. She was a schooner, fore-and-aft rigged and light on her feet. With a full head of sail and a fair wind she was as graceful as a seabird dancing across the ocean; close-hauled, she heeled over and pitched against the waves with a grim determination that her looks might have belied. Her landfalls and departures can be traced through the pages of *Lloyd's List* and the *Shipping and Mercantile Gazette*. From London, in November 1850 she sailed north to Shields. There she spent a month in port being copper-bottomed before loading with coal (151 chaldrons) and heading for the Mediterranean and the Black Sea.

Sailing to Byzantium. What would it all have meant to Abraham, the illiterate Suffolk farm boy? No classical education. Not a word of Latin or Greek. No knowledge of the Romans or the Greeks, the Byzantine Empire or the Ottomans. Passing the Pillars of Hercules but seeing only mountains; sailing past Sicily but seeing only bleached hillsides adorned with scrubby grey-green vegetation; rounding the Peloponnese but seeing only a headland; sailing through the Hellespont but seeing only cliffs and a choppy, narrow sea.

Beyond the Sea of Marmara lay Constantinople and the Golden Horn, the Sublime Porte. Names that meant nothing to him. What would he have made of it all? Out of his miserable stock of money he'd have bought things, something carved in olive wood, perhaps, or a piece of beaten brass. Or maybe a length of multicoloured silk to make a lady's jacket that Aunt Lydia would never wear. What else would he have done? Drunk raki, smoked a narghile, smoked cannabis, smoked opium, paid a few *para* for a whore, maybe even had a young boy in a bagnio in Pera, who knows? He was a sailor, adrift in a world he had never imagined and couldn't comprehend.

From Constantinople the *Gipsy Queen* made her way through the Bosporus into the Black Sea. At Burgas they took on maize and wheat before heading home. By July 1851 she had passed Malta and was at Gibraltar, running the straits while the wind funnelled through the narrows and combined with the current as though to keep the ship out of the ocean. By August she was making landfall at Queenstown in southern Ireland. From there, after a short turn around, it was back towards the Mediterranean and the Black Sea. London must have seemed a long way away. Almost the whole of 1852 was spent between southern Ireland and the eastern Mediterranean, three voyages in all. She visited Corfu and Constantinople, Ibraila on the Danube and Odessa. She battled the meltemi winds of the Ionian and the fluky breezes of the Black Sea. Her brand-new copper bottom kept her clean and sharp.

Abraham Block was far from anywhere he might have called home.

Naomi

The year is 1849 and Naomi Lulham is travelling by coach and four from Hastings to Frittenden near Tonbridge where her mother's relatives live. She has no idea that Abraham Block exists, never mind that he is at this very moment on the German Ocean heading towards the port of Boulogne.

The strange trajectories of men and women across time and space – in retrospect people who are going to meet seem destined to do so but at the moment, carried along in the flow of time, they have no idea of each other's existence. What does a sailor working his way between Newcastle or London and Amsterdam or Boulogne have to do with a young woman travelling north from the south-coast town of Hastings? Indeed, an illiterate sailor working before the mast on a Newcastle collier is almost beyond her comprehension. She has been to school. She can read and write; probably more important than that, she can cut and sew for, like her older sisters, she is an able sempstress. She is bright, attractive, skilled in manoeuvring her way round people and impatient of life in Hastings where she has lived all her seventeen years. She doesn't want to end up a fishwife. She wants to follow her older sister Mary (the only one of her eight siblings to have escaped the town) and see the outside world, explore the biggest city on earth, explore possibilities and people.

After a few days in Frittenden being cosseted and cautioned by her aunt, she is impatient to continue her journey northwards to London, this time by the newly opened railway from Tonbridge. She is leaving behind everything she has known – her mother (her father died five years ago), her seven siblings and Hastings itself, which is even now expanding into the new world of sea-bathing and holiday-making. The only known thing that lies before her is her sister Mary, whom she has worshipped ever since, as a four-year-old, she watched her getting married in All Saints Church, saw her and her about-to-be husband standing at the altar among the candles, looking like saints preparing to rise into the heavens.

Rail

Tonbridge railway station was startling, the most remarkable sight Naomi had ever seen. So many people all together. Men and women of the third class crowded behind railings like sheep in a pen, jostling, laughing, complaining; the "quality" walking up and down quite freely while the train lay there like a great beast – a dragon, she thought – with its head heaving and sighing and blowing gusts of smoke and steam into the air. The sulphurous smell of burning coal scorched the senses. That went with dragons well enough. Brimstone and fire. So many grand people in this hell, the gentlemen with tall hats, the ladies in beautiful crinolines, some with parasols, one carrying a dog. The ladies all seemed to float, while the gentlemen strode. Something fantastic about it all.

Her Frittenden aunt had insisted that she travel second class, first being out of the question on account of the cost but third being beyond the pale. "In third class you never know what might happen to you. All manner of things men and women get up to."

"What manner of things, Aunt?"

"Never you mind. And even in second class be sure not to smile too much, my dear. You may give the wrong impression."

But Naomi couldn't help smiling. She knew how well she looked in her bonnet and her best skirt, the stiffened one decorated with bows of taffeta that she had sewn herself. Why shouldn't she smile? For a while she stood, uncertain but smiling, among the milling people, until one of the officials took her case away to stow it on the roof and showed her where to mount the carriage. The interior was hardly luxurious – bench seats of plain wood – but it was more spacious than the coach in which she had travelled from Hastings. Other passengers entered the compartment, men handing women up, skirts crushed, hats doffed, strangers edging past her knees, nodding and apologising. A young man came and sat beside her. There were four to a bench and he was pressed against her, his right leg against her left, his right arm awkwardly in his lap so that it would not touch her.

"So sorry, ma'am," he said, smiling.

He was good-looking, she thought, so she smiled back, just as her aunt had warned her not to. "That's quite all right."

Acknowledging him gave her just a moment's opportunity to examine him but she couldn't do that for too long or it would look exceedingly rude, or perhaps even familiar. He had a light moustache and the pale suggestion of side whiskers. An open, interested face. Decent, surely. Was it possible, she wondered, to tell a man's character from his face? This remarkable form of transport, throwing dozens and dozens of complete strangers together, brought the question to mind. There she sat, with a total stranger pressing thigh against thigh and she had no idea what his intentions towards her might be. Maybe this would be one of those moments that she had read about, a moment when your life changes.

Were the others in the compartment watching her? She felt sure they must be. She tried not to blush.

"Goin' to London, are you?" the man asked. The question startled her. Did he have the right to ask that? Did she have any obligation to answer? She didn't understand the code of behaviour that operated in this startling and unforeseen circumstance.

"Yes, I am."

Outside, whistles blew. The carriage, the whole train, began to edge forwards.

"Your first train journey, is it?"

Blushing further, as though she were somehow to blame for this intimacy, she admitted it was. The man smiled. He really had a most engaging smile. His leg moved slightly, rubbing against hers, but perhaps that was the motion of the train, which was picking up speed now, swaying from side to side, the wheels grinding on the track like a blade being continually sharpened.

"Thrilling, ain't it?"

Was it thrilling? Thrilling sounded altogether wrong. And yet it was. The speed. The motion. And this crowding of strangers. Imagination was the curse. Without imagination it would be easy to feel something like shock and repulsion at all this proximity; with imagination, the shock of repeated contact became something altogether rather pleasant, and the repulsion became its opposite – attraction. As though reading her mind, he admitted, "Bit awkward to be squashed up with complete strangers like this. But not unpleasant."

"I think it rather inconvenient."

He laughed. "It'd be beyond measure more inconvenient if you had to go by coach and four. But I have been ill-mannered not to introduce myself. One should not talk to a lady to whom one has not been introduced. Allow me to present myself – Mr. Uriah Owen, Esquire." He put out a hand to be shaken and, in the close confines of the carriage and while the other passengers looked on and doubtless disapproved, she took it daintily in hers.

"Miss Naomi Lulham," she said.

"And may I be so bold as to enquire what Miss Naomi does in life? Is she perhaps in service?"

Indignation. "She is most certainly *not* in service. She is a dressmaker. And Mr. Owen?"

"Is a clerk."

It was a bit ridiculous, all this addressing each other in the third person, as though they were talking about their fellow passengers rather than about themselves. "My brother is a clerk," she said, breaking the trend.

"And I imagine, from what little I know of his sister, that he has a very fine hand."

She blushed once more, glancing down at the hand which had, a moment ago, been in close contact with his and which now lay modestly in her lap. It was, of course, a pleasantry, a play on the word itself. She was pleased to have understood that.

"P'raps," he added, refusing to relinquish his hold on the third person, "if this is her first visit to London, I might give his sister a *hand* in getting to know the city." There was the word again. He smiled in satisfaction at his own cleverness. "You see, London is a dangerous place. Thieves, pickpockets, tricksters, all sorts. And an expensive place. Costs more than a sempstress may earn."

"A *dressmaker*, if you please." Not a "mere sempstress." Naomi had already worked out that, within the bounds of probability, you should elevate your standing as far as possible.

"Even a dressmaker. You need to be careful. Easier to be careful with a man to look after you."

"What are you suggesting?"

"Not suggesting nothing. Just saying what's true. A warning, maybe."

"And you might look after me?" The other passengers stared away out of the windows at the countryside hurrying past, but she knew they were listening, and judging, no doubt.

"Don't want to see a lovely girl like you at risk."

"That's very thoughtful of you."

There was a sudden darkening of the light in the compartment as the sides of the track closed in. A cutting through the landscape. Then an abrupt extinction of all light and a rise in the sound of their passage, the wheels singing and roaring, the racket of the engine thrown back to them. Naomi gave a little shriek. "A tunnel," the man said. "You'll be all right, my dear." As though to reassure her he took her hand, actually took hold of her hand. There was a moment's grappling in the dark, as though her hand were a trophy to be fought over. And then, distinctly, a laugh as he released her. The darkness went on. His voice was close to her ear, loud against the noise of their passage underground. "There's nothing to be afraid of," he said. "It's just that I can look after you. A young girl, all alone in the city. I'll show you the ropes, Naomi Lulham, I promise." Then just for an instant as he spoke, just before the train burst out of the tunnel like a drowning man coming up for air, just before bright sunlight flooded the close and humid compartment, she felt his hand on her thigh. It was so brief a moment that she could barely be sure that he had done it. People in the compartment blinked in the light and looked around, smiling in relief and congratulating each other on surviving the ordeal of the tunnel, while Mr. Owen's hand lay still between his thigh and hers, almost as though it were innocent.

She felt a terrible turmoil of emotion – shame, of course, and embarrassment, but also guilt, and something more disturbing than guilt: a flush of excitement at this encounter with a stranger, the dangerous anonymity of it all, so far from home, trapped in the close confines of a railway carriage. What might happen? She thought of All Saints Street in Hastings, where everyone was known and everything was known and where the familiar extinguished all possibilities. "I think perhaps you have misunderstood me, Mr. Owen," she said, blushing at the lie.

"I'm almost sure I haven't, Miss Lulham," he replied.

What, she wondered, did he know? How could he tell? Was this what her Frittenden aunt had meant about smiling too much? Now he was reaching into his jacket with the same hand that had, just a moment ago, gripped her thigh. "Let me give you my card," he said. "Then if you find yourself in difficulties of any kind, you have a friend with whom you can get in touch. Always useful to have contacts in the city."

She took the little rectangle of card, inscribed with the man's name: *Uriah Nathaniel Owen*, and an address in a place called Clerkenwell.

"And perhaps Miss Lulham, dressmaker, could let me have her address in town? So that if I need a new shirt I will know who to contact."

"I make dresses for ladies, Mr. Owen, not shirts for gentlemen."

He smiled on her. "But surely you could turn your hand to shirts if need be. Imagine how many men there are such as me, who need a good shirt for their work in the city. You must adapt to go forward in this life. Who knows, I may be your very first customer." He took a fountain pen from his inner pocket and another of his cards, and held them out for her to write.

She considered his suggestion. Custom she would need. But followers? And what might her sister say? Yet – looking sideways at the man – he was a handsome fellow, and if truth be told she wouldn't mind walking out with him at all. A city man, with a city man's manners. That secret squeeze of her thigh. The thought sent a shiver through her body, starting somewhere in her knees and coursing up through thighs and hips and belly to her chest and throat. What else might he do, given encouragement? How might it be?

She blushed at her own thoughts and took the pen and the rectangle of card. "On condition that now you leave me in peace to read my book," she said, carefully inscribing in her finest hand:

Miss Naomi Lulham, dressmaker.

And then the address, which she knew by heart although she had no idea where or what the place might be:

9 Church Row, High Street, Bromley St. Leonard.

Mr. Owen blew on the card to dry the ink before slipping it into his pocket as though it were a secret message to be read later and at leisure, or, she thought, blushing further, a love-message. The others in the compartment watched. How much had they understood? Taking out her book, she turned to where she had left her mark and attempted to read while the train trundled on towards London, the countryside changing to suburbs, to rows and rows of houses, to churches and factories and pubs, the train riding above this strange urban world so that, seated by the window, she could look down on streets, down into upstairs windows, down into back gardens with their privies and their vegetable patches. And try and ignore the man called Uriah Owen sitting beside her.

*

66

London Bridge station was a mess of building, a temporary assembly of platforms and staircases and half-built portals, as though a classical temple had been invaded by barbarians, ransacked and pillaged. Steam and smoke clouded the atmosphere. Porters shunted luggage. Ladies and gentlemen from first class sauntered past, their noses turned up at the smells. And Mr. Uriah Owen handed Miss Naomi Lulham down from the compartment as though she were one of the quality herself, and then organised a porter to lift her suitcase down from the roof and tipped him a few pence to bring it along the platform towards the station concourse. That was when, out of the mass of travellers, out of this huge crowd of the unknown and the anonymous, the largest congregation she had ever witnessed, stepped the figure of her sister Mary, almost a mother figure if truth be told, twenty years her senior and now mother of three children. There was a cry of recognition. Mary was waving, hurrying through the crowd.

"My sister!" Naomi cried, turning. But Mr. Owen was gone, an anonymous figure striding through the crowd, distinguished only by his bowler hat and his height as he disappeared towards one of the exits.

"Just a gentleman I met on the train," Naomi explained to Mary. "Most helpful."

"You want to be careful of helpful men in this town. Help themselves more like."

"He seemed very nice. And handsome."

"Specially the handsome ones."

They walked to the exit, followed by the porter with Naomi's suitcase. What was the news from Hastings? How was their mother getting along without their father? And the various brothers and sisters – where were they all living now? Who was married, who was still a spinster? Hadn't William found a wife yet? All that kind of family talk as a hansom cab – an extravagance but worth it just this once! – takes them across the river and through the city. The clatter of the horse's hooves, the hammering of the wheels on paving, on setts, on cobbles, on beaten earth, the universe of the streets sliding past in a bewildering procession of sight and sound. And Mary leaning towards Naomi in the close confines of the cab and telling her young sister the news that she had been keeping to herself, that Naomi must keep secret, tell no one, certainly not their mother when she writes home.

"What is it?"

"Promise me you won't tell?"

Of course Naomi promised, expecting the banal – another child on the way probably, or maybe a move to a larger house. Whatever it was, it would be the kind of news that wasn't news. She thought about Mr. Uriah Owen and wondered whether that was news, the fact that she could cast this spell over strange men?

"We're saving up," Mary said, almost trying to whisper, except there was only the cabman who might hear and anyway the noise of the vehicle's passage drowned anything.

"Saving up for what?" A new house, surely. To *buy* a new house, perhaps. You could do that nowadays, so Mary had said. You could actually *own* the place where you lived.

"Saving up to go to America."

A silence, bridged by incomprehension. "To *America*?"

America. A world apart, a New World about which you heard only rumour. Red Indians. Pioneers. Fighting. Lawlessness. Slavery.

"We've decided. It was Henry's idea but we're all in agreement. Including the children. You can get a grant of land. Hundreds of acres. The possibilities ... " She talked in exclamations, as though trying to convince herself.

"But forever?"

"You could come with us, Naomi! Build your future in the New World."

"You'd not see the family again."

"It'd be a new start."

Bromley St. Leonard

So the happy family group gathers round the kitchen table at number nine, Church Row, just off Bromley High Street: Mary and Henry Watkinson, their three children and the new lodger, Mary's sister Naomi.

Here they are, taken from the 1851 census:

Henry Watkinson and family, census entry 1851,
Naomi Lulham on the bottom row

No doubt the talk would have been about the rest of the family in Hastings but surely it would have kept coming round to America, to the hopes and fears, the excitement and anxiety, the stories and the rumours. They still had to put the money aside for the tickets. They'd already started but it would take time. And in the meantime it was important that every member of the family pulled his weight. Having Naomi as a lodger would help, of course, once she got her work going.

"You can always find work in a factory round here," Mary suggested. But Naomi was stubborn.

"I'm a dressmaker, not a sempstress," she insisted. "I'm not going to sew slops for someone else to make money out of me." She'd even brought swatches with her from Hastings. And some patterns. But she had a good eye – she could copy anything.

"As long as you can pay your rent."

"I'll be earning quick as you like, you'll see."

Maybe she did do all right. Word of mouth, perhaps a card in the window of the local newsagents, maybe even an advertisement in the local newspaper although that would have been a cost. But it wouldn't have been easy in the house in Church Row, Bromley St. Leonard because at best she would have been constrained to share with the young daughter Emma, at worst with all three children.

And then a letter, the envelope adorned with a penny red postage stamp and delivered by that new phenomenon, the postman. A letter with no return address except *Clerkenwell* written at the top above the date. She felt herself blush when she read it. "That man I met on the train. Remember?"

Mary frowned. "Didn't I warn you?"

"What?"

"About helpful men on trains. Or anywhere else, come to that."

Naomi put the letter aside. "It's nothing. He just wants shirts making."

So they talked of other things: the Atlantic crossing the family might choose, which ship of the dozens that made the voyage. "Why not come with us?" Mary asked for the hundredth time. But Naomi was thinking of other things, mainly the possibility of making shirts.

*

Mr. Uriah Nathaniel Owen duly appeared at the house a few days later, suited and hatted, smiling and bowing and raising the ladies' hands to his lips in a most gentlemanly manner.

"Two fine cotton shirts," he explained when he had been shown into the parlour. "That is, if Miss Lulham is willing to turn her hand from dressmaking to shirt-making."

Of course she was. He was easy to please, agreeing to a most generous price, smiling confidingly at her, as though acknowledging that he was paying over the market cost. "It's workmanship that matters, isn't it? I'd not wish to buy from one of those slop-workers."

Mary watched while Naomi measured him up. She wasn't going to let him alone with her young sister, not for a moment. He doffed his frock coat and waistcoat and stood in his shirt and trousers while Naomi took his measurements. "And what is your line of business, Mr. Owen?" she asked.

"I'm a clerk, Mrs. Watkinson. For Messrs. Gold and Lipmann of Cheapside. Two fine gentlemen who give me both Saturday and Sunday off. Saturday, you see, is the Jewish Sabbath."

"I hope you are not a Hebrew, Mr. Owen."

"Most certainly not. A regular churchgoer."

"And which church would that be?"

"St. James's, Clerkenwell, where my father was church-warden and where I have been known to sing in the choir."

That seemed to put Mary's mind at rest. Son of a church-warden and member of the choir, and assuredly not a Jew. So when Mr. Owen came to pick up the finished shirts two weeks later and asked, ever so politely, whether he might call again in order to walk out with Miss Lulham, Mary was quite happy to agree.

The excitement. Walking out with a man! Something Naomi was never allowed to do in Hastings, although she did it just the same, but in secret. This was official, walking down to the banks of the Lea where you could stroll along the towpath and almost imagine yourself in the country. "Do you really go to church?" Naomi asked. Somehow she couldn't quite see him as part of a congregation like Mary and Henry were at Bow Church just round the corner, so stiff and self-righteous, always disapproving of what people said and what they did.

Mr. Owen laughed. He had a strange manner to his laugh, amused but with a hint of sarcasm. "Not at all, my dear. I'm a free-thinker, I am. You know my only belief? Religion is a load of bosh designed to keep people like us in our place. The opium of the people, that's my view."

Somehow this made Naomi happier. She understood possibilities, saw things wrong all around her and considered how they might be put right. And now here was Nathaniel Owen – that was how he liked to be called – having more or less the same ideas but being able to put them into words.

They walked out together quite regularly that spring, strolling along the banks of the river when the weather was fair, getting to know one another.

"Getting to know" is a euphemism for her letting him hold her hand and occasionally kiss her. Later, "getting to know" became other things. One was his hand on her breast, feeling her through the cloth of jacket and blouse, bodice and chemise, all those layers with which a lady encased herself. Then, one afternoon while they sat on the riverbank hidden by willow trees from anyone who might be passing by, something rather more than that – his reaching up under her skirts to explore underskirts and petticoats and drawers. There was much laughter and some degree of coy resistance on her part, but she had to admit to herself that she found the intimacy quite enjoyable. There was also the discovery, almost by chance, that Nathaniel Owen was himself aroused.

73

"You are my dear girl," he assured her and somehow the ordinary words took on a new meaning. *My* dear girl. "Don't you think we should come together properly?" he suggested.

Come together properly. The euphemism, vague as it was, seemed to carry a plethora of meaning. "Perhaps I can visit your place?" she dared to suggest, not knowing exactly where or what his place was except that he took rooms somewhere in Clerkenwell and that there they might come together properly, whatever might be implied. But he didn't think it a good idea. "I'm known around Clerkenwell, see? There'd be no privacy. It'd be so much more convenient here. Problem is your dear sister. She is so careful of you you'd almost think her your mother."

By that time Naomi half thought herself in love, and the half that didn't think itself in love was still driven by the organic fact of sexual desire and an overarching curiosity to discover what this coming together properly was all about. So finally she admitted that yes, there was indeed a possibility of their being alone: once a month, her sister travelled up to the City, to the offices of the shipping agency (Phillipps, Shaw & Lowther at the Royal Exchange buildings) to deposit the next instalment on the tickets that would take the family to America. As Mary's husband was at work and the eldest son was at the print shop while the younger children were at the local church school, on those occasions Naomi had the house to herself for an entire morning.

It was, of course, awkward the first time. It wasn't clear what exactly was expected or what was on offer because such things are rarely discussed in explicit terms in advance. There was a kiss, certainly. An embrace, yes. A move upstairs to her room followed by a bit of fiddling with buttons and tapes. Shyness was disguised as laughter. A display of masculine arousal was greeted with a gasp of amazement. But initial modesty was soon cast off along with most of her clothes, and soon enough, beyond the discomfort and the fumbling, she was making the startling discovery that it was possible for two bodies to be naked like this, bound intimately to each other and unashamed of self. And beyond the initial discomfort, there was pleasure to be had.

Nathaniel Owen was a considerate lover. Considerate, gentle, putting experience to good use. He had even brought a piece of sponge for her to put up inside, to prevent, so he said, "any unwanted consequences." After bidding him farewell she washed herself and washed the sponge and put it to dry on the windowsill along with marine trophies that she had brought from home – a scallop shell, a beautiful and intricate whelk shell, a dried mermaid's purse. An adult trophy beside the childish ones.

Thus, for a couple of months, contentment. It was easy enough to imagine herself entirely in love. But on the third of these visits, in August, disaster did what disaster so often does: it struck. Afterwards it was possible to work it all out – a breakdown on the railway or something, maybe the rails buckled by the summer heat; anyway, no trains running on the up line into Fenchurch Street station and sister Mary returning unexpectedly early to the house in Bromley St. Leonard. But at the time it seemed without rational explanation – a dream transformed into nightmare without warning or reason. They didn't even hear her coming into the house; the first they knew was her standing at the door screaming.

"If you weren't my own flesh and blood," her sister told her, "I'd throw you out on the street." By then Mr. Owen had left of course, his tail, presumably, between his legs, and Mary had lost the scream and replaced it with a quiet calm, as though

75

she were an inquisitor delivering judgement on a heretic. "I do not wish to have someone like you around my children, but I still feel some obligation to you as my sister. Therefore I will give you one week to find somewhere else to live."

"You'll not tell our mother, will you?" Naomi's tone was pleading.

"Tell her that you're little better than a prostitute? Of course I won't. It'd break her heart. And I will not even tell Mr. Watkinson until you're gone. He would throw you out on your ear at once if he knew. And that disgusting sponge thing! I know what that is, don't think I don't. Against all that is natural and good. You can take that out of my house straight-away. I would have thrown it away myself but I couldn't bring myself to touch it."

Naomi never heard from Mr. Uriah Nathaniel Owen again. Somehow she didn't expect to. There was a hard core of shrewdness inside her and once she was over the tears and the shame she discovered that she had never really had any illusions about him. While he professed love and devotion, there was always evasion beneath the open, friendly demeanour and, despite the visiting card that he gave her when they first met on the train, she had never discovered where those rooms in Clerkenwell actually were. When she recalled conversations they had had and things he had accidentally let slip, she was fairly sure that he was married. Gold and Lipmann, the gentlemen in Cheapside for whom he worked? A letter addressed care of them evoked no response.

Yet she felt no anger but instead a strange sense of freedom and a curious gratitude for his having released her from the strictures of virginity and the oppressive grip of Mary's family. For a few days, travelling west towards the city in search of accommodation far away from anywhere she might encounter

Mary or her husband, Naomi felt liberated. She was used to the city by now, the racket and crowds of the main roads, the noise of the pubs, laughter and catcalls, labourers and stallholders calling out to her. She could survive all that. She could be herself.

Mr. and Mrs. Block

Number seventeen, Orchard Row was part of a terrace of modest houses running north from Commercial Road towards St. Dunstan's Church. Naomi had seen the notice in the window of a local grocers.

ONLY RESPECTABLE LADIES NEED APPLY.

She felt a flutter of anxiety as she tugged at the bell-pull. Other lodgings she had tried had already been taken; some were assuredly not suitable for a respectable young woman. Despite her natural optimism, there was a growing concern that she might be cast out of Mary's house with nowhere to go. That – the thought was almost unbearable – would leave her with only one option: a shameful return to Hastings.

The door opened. A middle-aged woman appeared. Her mouth was like a trap, her eyes narrowed in suspicion. "Yes?"

"I've come about the room for rent." Naomi smiled.

The woman looked her over. "You and two dozen others. Maybe it's already gone."

Disappointed, Naomi turned to go.

"No, you can come in. I'll have a look at you." The woman led the way into the front room, a bleak, unwelcoming place of plain furnishings and little decoration. On one wall there was an engraving of a ship at sea which had been taken from an illustrated magazine; above the fireplace another engraving – trees, fields, a river, a cottage. Coals sat in a grate as dead and cold as the woman herself.

"If the room is already taken ... "

"Sit ye down."

Naomi sat.

They confronted one another, an old hen facing a nervous show-pigeon who was trying to look as plain and demure as she could. Lydia Block, née Hales, was forty-four years old, embittered by sterility and scruple. She might well have seen this prospective lodger as a threat – young, self-possessed, attractive and too much inclined to smile, Miss Naomi Lulham was many things that she herself was not. Where, she asked, did Miss Lulham come from? What kind of place was Hastings? What family did she have? What kind of work did her father do? The older woman gave the impression that every question had a secondary enquiry lurking beneath it. "And how long have you been in London, Miss Lulham?"

"Barely eighteen months. I live with my sister, a most respectable woman much older than me. There is her husband and three children, so there is not much room. And anyway, Mary and her family are intending to emigrate. To the Americas. The tickets are half paid already."

Mrs. Block sniffed disapprovingly. "One hears that America is a lawless place. I cannot see the attraction, but I suppose some people hope to make their fortune. You are not going with them? How do you propose to keep the wolf from the door?"

"I work as a dressmaker." Naomi opened her bag to display some of the tools of her trade.

Mrs. Block nodded. "A useful skill to have about the place."

And then, with little fuss, they moved to examine the bedroom upstairs at the back of the house where there would "surely be enough room for dressmaking," and soon they were discussing exactly what Miss Lulham might require in her daily routine: breakfast, of course; a light luncheon daily? A hot supper, with meat of course. Twelve shillings per week in all?

Naomi winced. There was a bit of genteel haggling. Pennies were shaved off the various elements before the deal was struck. "Of course, I expect a month's payment in advance."

And quite suddenly it seemed that Naomi had found somewhere to live.

"We're local folk," Mrs. Block ventured when the deal was done and she was showing Naomi out. "There's just the two of us, me and my husband. Mr. Block is a respectable and hard-working man down at the docks, which can't be said for most of them. A foreman, he is. Most important."

Then, with her hand on the front door handle, she added, "I assume, Miss Lulham, that you have no followers. I don't think I would be happy with a young lady with followers."

"No," Naomi assured Mrs. Block, "I have no followers."

The strange dynamics of contingency: thus, in the summer of 1851, Naomi Lulham, expelled from her sister's house in Bromley St. Leonard, moved into the house on Orchard Row, bringing her few possessions with her. Enough to fill two suitcases.

Abraham Block, Naomi Lulham, these are real people with whom I am playing – their lives, their loves, their innermost secrets. I feel the obligation to place the pieces with infinite care. Each piece placed on the board influences the other pieces, but each piece must also obey the rules ... and the rules are those limits created by document, by the registers of life and baptism, of marriage and divorce, of death. Naomi

Lulham was born in Hastings and moved to London. She had an affair with an unknown man – U. N. Owen (forgive me the joke, stolen from Agatha Christie).* She lived briefly with her sister in Bromley St. Leonard but in 1851 she moved into Isaac Block's house in Stepney. While Abraham Block, Isaac's nephew, was away sailing the seven seas. These things happened.

In Orchard Row Naomi set about making her room into some kind of home. She purchased a picture at a market stall in the Mile End Road and hung it on the wall, a coloured etching of a young couple embracing chastely beneath a tree. Other spaces were taken up by illustrations of various dresses cut from copies of the *Ladies' Cabinet*. Behind the door she hung a mirror that cost her rather more than she intended but would be useful for ladies having a fitting. On the windowsill she placed things she had brought from Hastings, those silly childish things – the scallop shell, the whelk shell, the mermaid's purse – along with that other relic of the sea, a piece of sponge that she used as a contraceptive.

Once settled in she wrote two advertisement cards and had them placed in the window of the local greengrocer and a stationers on the Commercial Road:

Miss Naomi Lulham, dressmaker.
Skilful needlework.
Sensitivity to the needs of the modern woman.
Home visits may be arranged.
Terms reasonable.
Apply No. 17 Orchard Row.

---

* In the variously titled novel *Ten Little Indians*.

Isaac

Isaac Block was a genial man, a loud man, a man who took to Naomi Lulham immediately, and she to him. He smiled on her and her ambition, inviting her to join him and his wife in the kitchen for meals, asking her about her family, and telling her about his own former life in the flatlands of Suffolk, his profligate mother, his various brothers and sisters, his nephew Abraham who had escaped it all by going to sea.

"Miss Lulham doesn't want to hear that nonsense," his wife would say, but Miss Lulham was brave enough not to agree with her. "Of course I do. It's a window on another world."

Sometimes Isaac would knock on her door when she was working. Could he come in and watch her work? He was so used to the crude life of the docks it was a pleasure to see the young girl sewing, her swift, deft fingers working needle and thread with such precision, her oval face bent over the cloth with a frown of concentration that was almost like someone at prayer.

"How's it all going?" he would ask.

She had a transforming smile. "Things are fine, although it's never easy. But there's always work if you know where to look for it."

But her enthusiasm belied the truth. Customers for dresses

were few and far between in this area. Demand was for mending and repair, work that brought little reward because most women could turn a hand to it. She scraped and scrimped but didn't always have enough for the rent at the end of the month. And beneath it all apprehension was stirring within her, apprehension evolving over the weeks into anxiety, coalescing and metamorphosing into fear as she waited hopelessly for her period – her monthlies, her flowers, the curse that would be a blessing if it were to come. But it never did. Instead, standing before the mirror intended for clients to observe themselves during a fitting, she noted the enlargement of her breasts, a darkening of her areolas and a faint swelling of her abdomen. She was a mere nineteen years old, confronting the greatest dilemma a woman of that time could face.

One day she leaves the house and takes the train to Fenchurch Street station from where she goes through the City to Cheapside. For two hours she walks the length of the street, pushing past pedestrians, risking her life crossing from one side to the other, occasionally asking passersby for help. She finds nothing. The city seethes around her, ripe with the stench of horse piss, loud with the rumble of iron-shod wheels. Messrs. Gold and Lipmann, it seems, do not exist.

She makes her way back to Stepney and closes herself in her room, staying there as much as she can, coming down quietly for breakfast and the evening meal, as though quiet might make her less visible. Mr. Block tries to draw her into conversation, while Mrs. Block watches her with shrewd eyes. Eventually – some four months into her dilemma – Naomi informs her hosts that she is leaving.

"Why?" asks Mrs. Block.

"I'm going back home to Hastings."

"But why?"

"Things haven't gone right here."

"That's a crying shame," says Mr. Block. "You've worked so hard. You've been behind with the rent but that's easily overlooked. Of course you'll have your deposit back."

Mrs. Block is watching the girl, her face without expression. When she speaks it is in that flat, matter-of-fact way she has: "You're in the family way, aren't you?"

There is a silence in the small, cold room. Naomi feels the sting of tears. She twists her hands in front of her in the manner of a little child caught out in some silly misdemeanour.

After a long silence, Mrs. Block asks, "Do you want to keep it?"

"Yes."

"Do you know the father?"

"'Course I do." Her voice has an edge of indignation about it.

"Many don't, darling." Before it has always been "Miss Lulham"; but now it's "darling," with an edge to it, a hint of contempt. "Have you told him?"

"No. And I don't want him to know."

"Is he married?"

"I think so, yes."

Mrs. Block gives a small, humourless laugh, no more than a little expulsion of air. "What about your people in Hastings. Have you told them?"

"No. They wouldn't understand."

"Yet you say you are going there. Your sister? Has she gone to America yet?"

"No. But I can't tell her. She wouldn't understand either."

Mrs. Block nods, her face impassive. "So what are you *really* planning to do?"

The Blocks watch her like jurymen in court. Naomi stands helpless before them, wanting only to be away, somewhere in secret where there will be no questions and no accusations.

Mr. Block says, "You'd best sit down, love," and holds a chair for her while Mrs. Block gets up from the table.

"Looks like you could do with a cuppa tea," she says over her shoulder as she goes to put the kettle on. "Mr. Block gets this tea from a friend in Blackwall. Special, so he says. He works at the East India Dock. Knows how to get the best tea, that's what he says. But to me it all tastes like tea."

Is it to give Naomi time to bring her emotions under control that she talks about tea and trivia? She brings the pot over to the table and pours. "You know what Mr. Block and I've been wanting ever since we got married?"

"No," Naomi replies because that is what is expected of her. But she guesses well enough what the answer will be. Mrs. Block stirs her tea, staring at the liquid going round and round in the cup.

"A baby, that's what we wanted. But no baby ever came." She looks up at the young woman with that strange, expressionless face, as though barrenness has drained her of all emotion. "If you want, you can stay here and have your baby. Mr. Block and I have already talked it over and we'd like that. We'll look after you. If you're worried about the shame," a shrug, "you'll learn to live with it. There's plenty of women round here with husbands away at sea, and plenty of others with bastards. People might gossip but no one really bothers."

There is, of course, a further possibility. This would alter the dynamics of the household at number seventeen Orchard Row a great deal, requiring compliance of some kind on Lydia Block's part, perhaps only that she turn a blind eye to the relationship between her husband and the young lodger, or maybe that she is fully aware of what is going on and even connives at it. There is, you see, the troubling fact of the forthcoming baby's given names – they are Isaac Uriah. Names are inherited after a fashion, and often they are passed down with clear intent. Why *Isaac*?

All possibilities must be considered. What is certain is that the nature of Naomi's presence at number seventeen shifted from lodger to ... what, exactly? She still works and still pays the rent as far as she is able, but the obligations have changed from those of tenant to something altogether less clearly apprehended – a moral contract, bound by the constraints of almost familial affinity. Surrogate daughter? Adopted niece? Naomi doesn't really care. She doesn't think of the future beyond the need to work and the need to nurture herself and the child growing within her. The house has become a sanctuary within which this feat may be accomplished. Thus, through the winter of 1851/52 she perseveres with her work while the baby grows, swelling her belly and rendering her body clumsy where previously it has been sharp and neat.

She has heard about Isaac Block's nephew, of course, the young man who went to sea. Almost a fictional figure, he was extolled in his uncle's account as a navigator more or less equal to Magellan or Vasco da Gama. "The last we saw him was more'n a year ago. 'E'd just come from the Baltic and was off to Constantinople, can you imagine? That's Turkey," Isaac added. "You don't hear nothing much once they leave. Sometimes it's in the newspapers, where his ship is, but half the time he might be dead, for all we know. Pitches up here when he's in port, just as he pleases." He smiled and looked at her in that way he had, half laughing, half thinking something secret to himself. "'E's a sailor, that's the fact of it. Law unto 'imself."

But Naomi wasn't much interested because she was subject to other laws, the laws of biology, of her own body and the body of her growing child.

Birth

It's 11 May 1852, in an upstairs back room at number seventeen, Orchard Row.

Mrs. Block is downstairs clearing up after the birth – there are sheets and towels to soak and boil, pans to wash. The midwife – a woman who lives in Back Road and does service as midwife or abortionist as the circumstances demand – has just left, with assurances that she'll be back tomorrow to see that everything is all right. Bleeding is the danger. Watch for bleeding.

Naomi is lying in bed nursing the baby. The axis of her entire world has shifted. Mere hours after the birth and she knows what she wants in life: her ambition, her focus, has become this raw scrap of flesh in her arms. Nothing will be the same after this. The pain of labour and delivery has flowed and ebbed and is fading into memory. Her sexual drive with whoever the father was has found its justification in this crumpled, scarlet face taking her nipple for the first time, clinging to her breast as though clinging to life itself. She doesn't care about the lack of legal father. Life has reason now and for the moment there is peace. The future is irrelevant. The present is this narrow, bare room with a view out of the window of the houses along Heath Street, and this child. She dozes, shifting in and out of sleep, with the baby at her breast or not, as it pleases. The sensation thrills her to the core.

The door opens. There's Mrs. Block, with her strange, impassive face. "You all right, dearie?"

"I'm fine."

The shadow of a smile. "I've brought you a cup of tea."

"Thank you, Mrs. Block."

"What you going to call him?"

"Isaac."

The smile, if there had been a smile, fades. "Is that a good idea, my dear? We don't want people getting any ideas, do we?"

"But Mr. Block has been so kind to me, as have you. If it had been a girl, I'd have called her Lydia. I want him always to remember how good you've been."

Is that how it was? Is that what happened? The truth is, we don't know. All we know is that Isaac Uriah was duly registered in Naomi's name: Isaac Uriah Lulham, father unknown.

Isaac Uriah Lulham's birth certificate*

The baby grew as all babies grow, endearing and helpless at first, bestowing all his love on his mother and taking her milk in return; then curious and individual, reaching out vaguely,

---

* This is the period when Orchard Row was changing its name to Old Church Road, hence the address in the register of births.

smiling and bawling to make his wishes known. Most of his first months were spent indoors. London, and in particular the East End, was not the kind of place to parade babies in the open air. And there was the added fact of Isaac Uriah's irregular birth. Without doubt illegitimate and possibly, if local gossip was allowed its way, Isaac Block's own. Best keep him as far away from strangers' eyes as possible.

Autumn ran into winter. Isaac Block became ... what exactly? A substitute father for Naomi? A grandfather to the child? (That is how he described himself in the 1861 census.) Lydia was a kind of aunt, business-like, practical, helpful but spare with her emotions. She was never a substitute mother, never a grandmother. Naomi knew that in a city where unmarried mothers sank more often than they swam, she was one of the fortunate ones. She began to pick up the threads of her work, just straightforward stuff, mending and darning.

The New Year came and went, with cold, hard days and rain that turned to sleet. The house on Orchard Road was warm enough in the kitchen, chill in the upstairs rooms.

Departure

Surely she would have been there, at the appointed time on the appointed day at Limehouse Dock. Surely sisterly ties would have overcome whatever had torn them apart. Imagine a final farewell at the entry port of the *Ocean Queen* as the crew make ready: a brief, stilted conversation between the two sisters, the children crying and clinging to Naomi, not understanding why she left all those months ago or why their father takes them away across the deck, as though distancing them from contagion. The two sisters kiss a final time, knowing that this is, in all probability, the last they will ever see of one another. An American voice calls for all visitors to go ashore.

"You'd best be gone," says Mary. It is as though she is already across the Atlantic, in a world far away. Naomi moves down the gangway but after a few steps pauses and glances back. "I've got a baby," she says. "A little boy. Your nephew." And then she turns and descends to the quayside, not knowing if Mary has even heard her above the noise of the docks.

Standing among the crowd of well-wishers, Naomi watches as moorings are cast off and the *Ocean Queen* inches away from the quayside. She's a three-masted clipper, sharp-bowed, black-hulled and white-striped along the length of what might once have been the gun deck. The stars and stripes hang at her stern. The Black X Line ensign, almost like a pirate flag, flies from the main top. Passengers line the side waving back at the shore, Mary and the children among them, their faces fast fading into anonymity. A steam tug drags the great ship out into the flow where wherries and barges scatter like sparrows in the shadow of a peregrine. The steam tug belches smoke, a hideous contrast to the clipper which, for all her helplessness in the close confines of the river, promises speed and grace.

There are tears among those watching from the quayside – this is akin to witnessing the passage of souls across the River Styx. These people, emigrants to the New World, are going for good. Naomi watches until the ship slides out of sight down Limehouse Reach, then turns and walks away from the waterside through the narrow streets of the docklands back to her baby and their home.

Dreadnought

In the autumn of 1852, another queen, the *Gipsy Queen* this time, was in Constantinople on her way back from Odessa. By the end of October she had passed through the Straits and crossed the Bay of Biscay, running before a storm and taking shelter at Falmouth before making her way to Queenstown, arriving mid-November. There she had three weeks in port.

Abraham is an old salt by now. A mere twenty-one years old, he has seen places beyond the imagination of most Englishmen. And now he and his shipmates have shore leave and money to spend on beer, whiskey and women. One imagines Christmas and New Year celebrations of a tumultuous nature. They've been working between southern Ireland and the Eastern Mediterranean for two years without a break and now, after Queenstown, they are heading for England. Thus January of the New Year finds the *Gipsy Queen* beating up the Channel bound for London. She passes Deal on 12 January 1853 and docks in London three days later.

It was some time during that passage that Abraham Block discovered an ulcer on his penis. In the shadows of the fo'c'sle no doubt there was a consultation among the crew, the offending organ viewed with a mixture of ribald comment and concern. The ulcer wasn't sore; somehow that made it all the more sinister. "What is it?" Abraham asked.

There was much sucking of teeth and tugging of beards. The more experienced knew well enough: "That's what them doctors call a chancre."

"That's the pox, that is. French pox."

"That'll be that girl in Cobh," said an Irish sailor who refused, as a point of honour, to call Queenstown by anything other than its native name. "She didn't look none too clean. Meself wouldn't have touched her with the end of a barge-pole."

"There's one place for you, my lad," said one of the older men, who knew a thing or two. "That's the *Dreadnought*."

HMS *Dreadnought*, a triple-deck, ninety-eight-gun ship of the line and a veteran of the Battle of Trafalgar, was now languishing at anchor at Greenwich. Shorn of her masts and emptied of her weaponry she was no more than a hulk, a stack of decks serving as the Dreadnought Seamen's Hospital. On 18 January, three days after docking, Abraham presented himself at the hospital with his complaint.

Patients in various states of decrepitude – an empty trouser, a bound head, a skeletal figure dying of cancer – shuffled round the main deck. On the quarter-deck the sick and infirm queued at a desk where an impatient clerk demanded name, age, place of birth and ship, and entered those details in the register, one of those meticulous Victorian registers preserved for posterity.

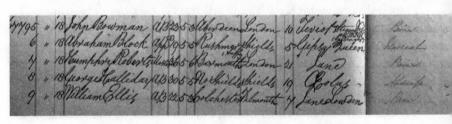

Abraham Block. Admission to Dreadnought Hospital
for Sailors, 18 January 1853. Note the diagnosis –
Venereal – added in a different hand.

Each entry was given a number, running from the very foundation of the hospital in 1821. Abraham Block was thus the 67,796th patient admitted to the Seamen's Hospital.

"Ticket?"

Abraham handed over his apprentice's ticket and his discharge papers. "I'll want them back."

"You'll get them back when you're done. The doctor is through there. Next."

The doctor waited behind a curtain. He was in his forties, whiskered and with the solemn face of a minister, but he examined the offending article as indifferently as a housewife examining fruit at a vegetable stall. He looked up. "How long have you had this?"

"All my life, sir."

"Don't try to be funny, sailor. This ulcer, how long have you had this ulcer?"

"About a fortnight, sir."

"Where've you come from?"

"Queenstown."

"How long there?"

"Since 14 November, sir."

"Before that?"

"Odessa. That's in—"

"I know where Odessa is. When did you leave Russia?"

"September, I think. Not sure o' the date."

The doctor nodded thoughtfully. Maybe he was calculating. "Was she pretty? The colleen, I mean."

"Sorry, sir?"

"The Irish girl. Was she pretty?"

Abraham hesitated. There had been three, one in Queenstown and two in Cork, but something told him that didn't matter, that this was the doctor's joke, ironical but nevertheless a joke. "Pretty enough, sir."

"Well that's your only compensation, sailor." He lifted Abraham's penis to demonstrate the ulcer. "That's a chancre. Your colleen's given you the pox, young man." He let the penis drop. "You can pull your drawers up now."

Abraham did as he was told. It was always best to do what you were told, especially when you had your trousers round your ankles. "What's it mean, sir?"

"It means a dozen things, both in the future and in the present." The doctor took up a pen and began to write. "For the present, we'll keep you here for a day or two just to make sure. Do you have anywhere to go once we release you? Ashore, I mean."

"My uncle, sir. He lives here in Lunnun."

"Good. In a while the chancre will resolve itself—"

"Sorry, sir?"

"It'll go away, man. Get better. Your prick will look like that of a young, innocent boy once again and you'll feel as right as rain. But you're not. You will still have the contagion within you and you'll still be infectious, so you must have no sexual congress with anyone at all. Do you understand? However willing she may seem, or however eager to earn a few pennies from a drunken sailor. Do I make myself clear? You are *infective*. Dangerous to others."

"For*ever*, sir?"

The doctor chuckled, then belied his own amusement: "The pox is no laughing matter, sailor. After a while – maybe a month, maybe two – the morbus will return, but this time you'll not shrug it off so easily. It may present variously. A miliary rash, maybe. Fever, sickness, headaches. Sometimes papules, warts that we term *condylomata lata*. These are signs of the contagion trying to get out of you and find another victim."

"Isn't there a cure?"

"You'll hear talk of mercury. Corrosive sublimate or calomel, administered *per os* or by inunction." He saw Abraham's incomprehension. "By mouth or as an ointment. We medical men are very good at using complicated Latinisms for ordinary matters. It makes us sound as though we know what we are talking about. Do you know mercury?"

Abraham shrugged. "I know quicksilver. In barometers and thermometers. We use them on board."

"That's mercury metal. What I refer to are salts of mercury. To put it bluntly, they are fierce poisons. Calomel is the less harmful of the two and sometimes I prescribe it. But for an otherwise healthy young fellow like you, I think it better to let the disease take its course and let the body fight the battle by itself."

"And then? Once the battle has been won?"

"I'm sorry to disappoint you, sailor, but the battle is never won. The symptoms of the second phase will slowly disappear as your body comes to terms with the contagion. During the second phase you will probably be hospitalised, perhaps here if you are in London when the outbreak occurs. It'll happen in about a month and last for some weeks. Once that is over you are, it is generally believed, no longer contagious and you may resume intimate relations with your beloved wife—"

"I don't have a wife."

"—but my advice is, avoid the pretty colleen or anyone of her kind. Because you may be infected a second time. In any case, the disease remains latent within your body forever. Some time in the future – which may be many years ahead – it may break out again, in the third phase. Syphilis, my good man, is the great deceiver. In the third phase it may attack the bones, the heart, the brain. It may paralyse you, it may drive you mad. One thing is certain: if it does break out in the third phase, it will kill you."

*

Abraham spent two days in the medical ward, in the quiet, with nothing to do but think. It was warm – there were heating pipes running along the bulwarks – the food was good, the nurses were attentive, the doctors sympathetic. His clothes were washed. He even had a bath. So it was heaven of a kind, but a heaven vitiated by the knowledge of the contagion within him. Even though the ulcer on his penis, the chancre, was now fading, that was only the disease hiding away within him. That's what they told him. Never underestimate the pox, they warned.

When they released him it was with yet more warnings about the hazards of infecting others. "You leave the ladies in peace for the moment," one of the nurses advised him. Another shrugged as he took his leave. "See you again soon," she said.

Abraham felt a strange mixture of emotions as he took the steamer up-river: a sailor back from years abroad with freedom in his belly and money in his pocket, but a sailor with corruption deep inside. He shivered in the cold, pulling his pea jacket tight around him but getting little warmth from it. At Shadwell Stairs he got off the steamer and made his way through the chaos of the dockside. Fog skulked around the buildings. Coal smoke stained the air. Among the porters and the lumpers there were tarts, some young, some old enough to be grandmothers, the scrawny, the overweight, the ugly, the pretty, the whole spectrum of womanhood available at a price. And the price was not only monetary but was within him, eating away at him: the pox, French or Spanish, never "English."

He went looking for his uncle and aunt in Orchard Row, turning off the Commercial Road just by the Royal Duchess pub and walking along the terrace of houses as far as number seventeen.

Naomi

At the time you rarely recognise the days that are fateful in your life. That's a matter of retrospect. So when Naomi Lulham, dressmaker, was cutting and sewing in her upstairs room in Orchard Row, she thought little of a sudden commotion below, the banging on the front door, shouts of what seemed like laughter and greeting. The baby slept through it all, of course. After lunch that was always the way, although the nights were more difficult.

She paused and listened.

She recognised Mr. Block's voice all right, and the sharper tones of his wife, but there was a third voice raised above all, an unfamiliar voice, a young voice. She put aside her sewing, closed the door of her room behind her and went quietly down the stairs. The door to the front parlour was open, which was where the noise was coming from. She stood demurely in the open doorway and watched.

"Now here's a thing!" Mr. Block cried, catching sight of her. His wife turned and pursed her lips in that way she had that meant disapprobation even without quite knowing the object of her displeasure. And the young man looked at her and beamed.

It was quite obvious *what* he was – the canvas trousers, wider than any gentleman would wish to wear, the loose shirt and salt-stained pea-jacket, the tarpaulin hat tossed onto one of the three chairs in the room: all spoke of sailor. And the tanned skin and bleached hair told of recent voyages in hot climes. And knowing *what* he was told her pretty certainly *who* he was: Abraham Block had returned home.

"This," said Isaac, "is our new lodger, Miss Naomi Lulham."

There was a moment's absurd formality. It involved bowing and hand-kissing and even a bobbed curtsey from Naomi, along with, "I am, ma'am, your most humble servant," from Abraham, as though they were people of an altogether more exalted class. And in that moment, Naomi Lulham fell in love. That, at least, was what retrospect told her. The truth was probably that she felt an intense sexual attraction, something purely organic, but "love" will do.

"Pleased to meet you, I'm sure," she replied.

He wasn't tall – no taller than her, in fact – and cheerful-looking. His eyes were as blue as the sea and his complexion like oak, weathered beyond his age by wind and sun. Ship-like, she thought. Something small and fast. A sloop, perhaps. She imagined – vaguely, because she had little idea – nights spent under tropic stars and days beneath a burning sun. He saw a slender girl with pale skin and a certain coquettish manner, whom he could surely beguile into bed were it not for the damned curse that he carried.

"You'll behave yourself, Master Abraham," Lydia Block warned him, watching the hand-kissing. Perhaps she saw the signs already. "I'll have none of your mariner's manners in my house."

Abraham laughed and put his arm round her shoulders, a gesture designed to impose affection on a hard and flinty exterior. "Aunt Lydia has no faith in me. She thinks all sailors are the devil's children. Here I am, come back from the Black

Sea – do you know where the Black Sea is, Miss Lulham? – and all my aunt can think of is whether I am going to act gentleman-like when I meet a beautiful lady."

Naomi felt herself blush. "As a matter of fact, I do know where the Black Sea is, Mister Abraham. It is often in the newspapers these days."

"Ah, well. If I'm talking to one who reads the papers then that is different." It was clear that he thought the whole stilted conversation a trifle absurd. "I don't know about all the politics and stuff but what I do know is what I've seen: Turkish men are at an advantage over Russian men. Do you know why?"

"I'm sure I don't."

"Because they are allowed to have as many wives as they wish."

Aunt Lydia gasped. Naomi felt her blush deepen. "Do you approve of that, Mister Abraham?"

"I don't think I would if I were one of the wives. But I'm just a simple sailor, Miss Lulham, without even one wife. I've seen the world a bit and I think people should be left to get on with their own lives."

That was the moment when the baby woke up and started to cry, a thin, piercing sound from upstairs. Abraham looked up in surprise. Naomi turned and disappeared from the room. Aunt Lydia pursed her lips as though whatever had happened was Abraham's fault. "We had no time to tell you," she said. "Miss Lulham has a child. You're not to say anything and you're not to take advantage."

She heard him climb the stairs, go past her room and up to the attic. She turned back to the baby, playing with him to make him smile and feeling that little stir of triumph and love when she succeeded. What did the sailor, Abraham, think of her now? A woman without a man but with a baby. A fallen woman. What was it he said? *I think people should be left to get on with their own lives.* What was his life? The baby was playing contentedly now, gurgling and slobbering over a little bone ring that Isaac had given him. Teething.

When she went back to her work she was conscious of Abraham in the attic above, a thrilling presence moving around overhead.

Abraham had brought things from Turkey – for his aunt a brass dish, chased with geometric designs and the strange characters of the Ottoman script; for his uncle a miniature dagger sheathed in leather. There was also something else, that he only showed to Naomi two days later when she was working in her room. Isaac was on shift at the docks and Lydia was doing whatever she did at St. Dunstan's Church, so Naomi was aware that she was alone in the house with Abraham. She was working, of course, she was always working whenever she could free herself from the demands of the baby, who was sleeping quietly in his bassinet beside her. Abraham was upstairs in his attic room but she heard him come down and somehow she expected the knock on her door.

"Come in," she called and there he was, standing hesitantly in the doorway, with that particular smile on his face. She was kneeling on the floor with material laid out – a dress for a Mrs. Philips whose husband ran the pub on the corner – but she had been thinking of him. That was why she blushed as he looked down on her.

"I've brought you a present," he said, whispering so as not to wake the baby. "I mean, I brought it with me, but I couldn't have brought it *for* you because I didn't even know you existed. But now I do and I want to give it to you."

She put down her needle and thread, sat back on her heels. "That's very kind."

He stepped into the room and closed the door softly behind him. "Here," he said. He held out a small roll of cloth. You could see the colour – blood red, the colour of ruby. And blues and yellows and greens, the whole pattern coiling and writhing as she unrolled it and floated it over the floor. She drew in her breath sharply.

He dropped down to sit beside her, his legs crossed as he surely did on board ship. "Do you like it? Silk. Turkey silk."

"It's a lovely thing."

"Thought you might be able to make it into something. For you to wear."

"It's wonderful."

"Thought you might like it."

"Thank you, Mister Abraham. I could make a chemise, or perhaps, if I can find a suitable lining, a jacket." She held the cloth up, the colours like fire in the dull room. "How kind of you."

There was an awkward pause. "I've been wanting to talk to you alone," he said.

"About what?"

"Just talk." He felt the dreadful burden of not knowing what to say. "I live my life with sailors, you know what I mean? We talk, but it's not the kind of talk I can have with you. I dunno how to do it really, talk with a woman like you, I mean. Perhaps I can tell you what it's like in Greece and Turkey, how the sun beats down, how hot it is, that kind of thing, I dunno."

"Tell me that, then." The child stirred in his bed but slept on regardless.

"It's really the history," he said helplessly. "I forget things, but this place, Constantinople, centuries ago it was bigger than London, did you know that? Palaces, cathedrals, now they're mosques because of the Mussulmans, but before they was churches and before that, temples. There were great battles there – you can still see the walls. An emperor, even an empress. But it's only what I heard and I couldn't really put it into place. But before London, before our kings and queens, before any of us."

"Before the Battle of Hastings," she said.

He didn't understand what she meant but he agreed anyway. "Before that, aye, before that. Roman times. Bezantin. Never heard that word before. That's what it was: Bezantin."

"Why don't you find out about it? There'll be books about it."

The silence of embarrassment. "I can't read." He tried to explain, knowing all the time that he just sounded stupid: "Never learned my letters. Never really went to school, not in our village."

Momentarily she touched his hand. "It doesn't matter. Tell me about that. Your village. Tell me."

So he began to tell her about Kessingland, about the dull, drab land so far from Turkey, and the grey sea that beat for ever against its long beach, and about the dead that they'd found washed up on the beach, he and his brother – also Isaac – the corpse they'd stolen two sovereigns from.

It was then that she took his hand – not just touched it this time, but took it, carefully, as though she might break it – and said, "I can teach you, if you like."

"Teach me?"

"To read. If you want."

Was it pity? That's the question. This simple, illiterate sailor with his muddle of exotic experience – Holland, France, the Atlantic Ocean, the Mediterranean, Turkey and the Black Sea – and his wiry good looks, was it pity that pushed her towards him? Or was it perhaps that motherly feeling that lies in the psyche of most women and has little to do with relative age? Despite Abraham's travels, he must have seemed appealingly naive to her with his lack of reading and his unfamiliarity with the conventions of common social intercourse. And handsome, surely: plain sexual attraction must have played its part. That is the trouble with the usual historical documents: they don't say how things happen, merely when. But this conjunction of Abraham and Naomi must have happened fairly soon for the dates to match up.

Watch her lean towards him. They are on the floor of her small, drab room with the silhouette of a dress all around them and the baby stirring in the bassinet in the corner. She is kneeling and he sitting, and she kisses him. Just a touch on the lips.

He pulled back, frightened of his infection of course, feeling unclean, revolted by his own body. The baby woke. Perhaps that gave him an excuse to leave her alone. Whatever happened, whatever was understood or misunderstood, the facts are that within a few days he was signing on with a collier unloading at Blackwall and in need of a crewman because one of the sailors had been injured. *Elizabeth Young*, the collier was called. Seaworthy enough, doing the usual run up and down the east coast bringing coal from Newcastle, just as the *Bedlington* had done when first he went to sea.

"Going so soon?" Aunt Lydia exclaimed when he announced the news. She seemed curious, as though there might be some hidden reason, and indeed there was. Glancing at Naomi, Abraham felt the insidious crawl of shame through his body. Like parasites inside him, the worms of the disease writhed beneath his skin and in his veins.

"It's ... " he hesitated, wondering what it was. It's just that I want to get away. It's just that I am ashamed of my disease that might infect this wonderful woman I have just met. It is just that I don't understand the constraints and conventions of life ashore. "I just need to get to sea. Find another berth." He reddened, seeing, through his incoherence, the awful double meaning. "That's what we call it on board: a berth."

Standing there with her baby on her hip, hurt and bewilderment on her face, Naomi Lulham watched him.

Escape

On 23 January 1853, the *Elizabeth Young* slipped her moorings and made her way, in ballast, down the tideway towards the estuary and the German Ocean. In the next two months, she made three round trips from London to the North-East, humping coal and returning in ballast. It was the usual humdrum of the east-coast coal trade, a trade that was dying, although few understood it at the time, because of the growing fact of the railways.

On the last passage south, in March, when they were pitching against a southwesterly off Cromer and feeling the first warmth of spring on the air, the spirochaete bacteria – nasty twisted things that had been breeding in Abraham's body for months now – launched their second attack. No mere ulcer on his prick this time but a full-blown storm of rash spreading from his chest. Fever as well, headache, the whole misery. Men looked at him askance as he lay helpless in his hammock in the narrow shadows of the fo'c'sle. They knew that rash well enough. The sailor's disease.

"We'll put you ashore at Greenwich, at the Dreadnought," the mate told him. "You know the Dreadnought?"

Fever hammered at his eyes. Yes, he knew the Dreadnought, but he didn't tell them that he'd been there already. No need to confess to them that he knew he carried the contagion in his body.

*

Abraham Block was readmitted to the Dreadnought Hospital on 24 March, admission number 68,251, with a cross reference to his previous admission, 67,796. Meticulous, the registrar of the Seamen's Hospital, recording for the management committee and for posterity.

Abraham Block, second admission to Dreadnought Seamen's Hospital, 24 March 1853

Once the formalities had been completed they took him down to the medical deck where all was white and breezy, where the gun-ports were open to the fresh air and there were rows of beds where eighteen-pounders had once fired three broadsides at the Battle of Trafalgar. In those active days, when men sweated and coughed and died amid the smoke of battle, all the woodwork of the gun decks had been painted red to hide the blood; now there was this anaemic white, with patients lying in bed, some reading newspapers, others staring at the deckhead, others talking quietly. There were men from Europe, the Americas, Asia, Africa and Australia, all colours of skin, all languages of the world. One of the nurses recognised Abraham from his two-day visit in January. She was a big woman with hands like hams. "Told you you'd be back," she said. "The wages of sin," she added, and laughed.

*

This time Abraham Block was in the Dreadnought for a total of sixty-three days, during which the disease surged like a tide through his body and then, like a tide, abated and ebbed, leaving him weakened and thinner but well enough. "You'll do all right," said the physician at the end, listening to his heart, counting his pulse, flexing his arms and legs, peering into his eyes and down this throat as though somewhere there he might descry the truth about his patient. "A few more days' rest and you'll be right as rain."

"And will I be able to ... "

The question faded away into embarrassment, but the doctor understood. He stroked his whiskers to show the seriousness of the matter. "As far as medical science can tell, once this crisis is over you are no longer infective. The matter is not certain, but it seems that way. So sexual congress is possible without danger. However, young man, you are not cured. The disease is still with you, lying in wait, maybe for decades. When it finally emerges once more, then I am sorry to say, it will kill you. It may be ten, twenty, forty years. You'll probably be an old man, a grandfather who has had a good life, even though he may have strayed in his youth. Nevertheless, that straying will bring you down in the end."

Released from his bed, Abraham walked the deck in the spring air, watching shipping pass up and down the river, thinking of Naomi Lulham. He had had no contact with his uncle and aunt since signing onto the *Elizabeth Young*. It might be that their lodger had left, driven away by circumstance or by his own indifference; or maybe, given the passage of months, she had simply forgotten him.

Once discharged from the Dreadnought he again took the steamer upstream towards Limehouse, got off at Shadwell Stairs and walked away from the river through the maze of half-familiar streets across the Commercial Road as far as the Royal Duchess and the street that led up towards St. Dunstan's Church. At number seventeen he stood, his kitbag over his shoulder, his tarpaulin hat on his head, the sailor back from the sea once again.

He knocked.

Doubts crowded in: all the uncertainty of a sailor's life, all the anxiety of a convalescent. It was four months since he had seen her and then, at the very moment when a barrier between them seemed to have come down, he had walked away. Would she even be here still? And if she was, would she have any regard for him?

He heard footsteps inside, coming from the back, a woman's step, he thought. But he couldn't even recognise her step or know how to distinguish it from Aunt Lydia's.

The door opened.

Shock, of course, on both sides. Abraham was expecting to see the woman of his dreams; what confronted him in the open doorway was the real woman, Naomi Lulham, a mere twenty and attractive enough, but startled, her face pale, her features blurred by anxiety and tiredness, her hair pulled back anyhow, with the child on her hip, its upper lip anointed with snot. Her figure was shapeless beneath a dull housedress that she herself had made out of some bleached calico. She was not expecting to see anyone in particular so in her expression there was a muddle: surprise, something that might have been relief, as though merely by being there Abraham had discounted a whole congeries of doubt and fear, possibly even a glimmer of joy; but then, as suddenly as the other expressions had appeared, the shutters of indifference came down.

"You'd best come in," she said.

There was a moment's awkwardness in the narrow hallway as he went past her. "Ain't you pleased to see me?"

She shrugged, closing the door behind him. "Should I be?"

"You alone?"

"Mr. Block is at work and Mrs. Block has stepped out for the moment. She'll be back soon."

He unslung his kitbag and followed her into the kitchen. There was a sort of cage on the floor for the baby to play in. She put him there and gave him a rattle. "Now don't you grizzle, Isaac," she said. "I've got to talk to Uncle Abraham."

Uncle Abraham.

Isaac.

Was she letting slip a half-truth? Was his Uncle Isaac actually the father? The thought bubbled up like whatever was warming on the stove. Gruel for the baby. She stirred the mess, glancing over her shoulder to talk. "Where've you been, then?"

"Nowhere special. Newcastle, Shields, up and down the coast."

"You don't look so well."

"Been ill a bit. In the hospital at Greenwich. Now I'm fine."

Inconsequential talk, as though between strangers. But they weren't strangers. He'd known her for no more than a few days yet they had kissed – she had leant towards him and kissed him on the lips. Did that mean nothing? All he understood were the transactions of tarts, not the small hints of normal social intercourse. He watched her as she moved. The width of her hips, the hang of her breasts as she turned towards the child and lifted him out of the pen. He could smell her, a warm, mammary smell that filled the room. Naomi sat with the child on her lap and fed him gruel, blowing on it to cool it, presenting it to the little mouth, which enveloped the food, tried to chew it, then pushed it out.

She glanced up at Abraham. "I'm weaning him. He don't understand quite how to do it yet."

He watched the feeding with something like fascination. The baby seemed to spit out as much food as he took and after a while Naomi gave in. "I've got to nurse him," she said, putting the bowl aside. Indifferent to Abraham's presence she opened the front of her dress. He glimpsed a full, white breast before the baby took suck. Naomi was looking back at Abraham with something that may have been a smile, may have been a small expression of irony. "So you've come back," she said. "To grace us with your presence."

"Didn't want to go like I did."

"So why did you?"

"I was afraid."

"Afraid what of? Of me? Of the child?" She winced and adjusted the baby at her breast. "Careful," she said soothingly. "You hurt Mama." She glanced up. "Teething. Sharp little teeth."

"Not afraid of him; of you, p'raps."

"Me? Why were you afraid of me? Aren't sailors meant to be tough?"

"I'm not afraid any longer."

There was silence. He could hear the baby suckling. He wondered what it would be like to suck at that breast, Naomi Lulham's breast, heavy and white, capped with its brown nipple. A strange, exotic fruit.

"I'm here for a while now," he said. "Need a rest from the sea. Got a bit of money so I don't need to work for a month or two."

"And then you'll up and go again?"

"It's my trade. It's what I understand. But ... "

"But what?"

"But a man needs a woman. Even a sailor needs a woman."

"Is that right? But does a woman need a man? Sometimes I doubt it. 'Specially a sailor." She looked down at her child.

"You finished then, you little devil?" She transferred him to her other breast. There was a stillness while the baby settled again. Abraham didn't know how to move the conversation on. There were niceties that he couldn't comprehend so he just said it, bluntly, like a sailor:

"Who's the baby's father, Naomi?"

She glanced up with that look again: half smile, half a little ironical twist. "You're thinking like other people do, aren't you? I call the baby Isaac so he must be your Uncle Isaac's, that's what you're thinking."

"I just want to know, that's all."

"Well, he's *my* baby. He's Isaac Uriah and he's mine. And if I find a man to be my husband, then he'll take my baby on with me, it's as simple as that. Any man what wants me must want my baby."

"What if *I* want you?"

She put her head on one side, looking him up and down. Like a Suffolk farmer inspecting a boar at market, that's what he thought. But if she knew about the contagion within him, what would she think then? The disease might be harmless for the moment as the doctors had told him, but she'd still be repulsed, wouldn't she?

"I'd consider you," she said.

Motherhood

With motherhood Naomi's prospects had narrowed. Her sister's horizon might be the broad sweep of the North American continent but Naomi's had come down to these mean streets in Stepney and the close confines of Isaac and Lydia's house in Orchard Row. Abraham must have seemed an escape of a kind. He was young and handsome, endearing in his ignorance and entrancing in his experience. And he could provide what up to now her son had not possessed, a father. It wouldn't have been long before she had decided that there was no reason why Abraham Block should not become her partner, no great delay before they were coupling on the narrow bed in her room with the tacit approval, no doubt, of Isaac senior and Lydia.

It was about this time that the Blocks moved house, just a five-minute walk across Commercial Road to Johnson Street, at the same time that Isaac changed job, moving out of the docks to work as a gasfitter at the Radcliffe Gas Works on Back Road.* He was edging upwards in the world. No longer the dogfight of the docks, where men battled to get casual work; now a trade with a regular wage and settled hours. This meant they could afford the rent of a house with a few

---

* Variously, Back Lane, Back Street, Back Road; all part of Cable Street.

more rooms, for an extra lodger but also with an eye on the growing family that seemed to be flourishing in their midst. There was even a basement and a bit of garden at the back.

For a while, Abraham was happy enough with his new circumstances. How could he not be? How could he have failed to adore watching Naomi moving quietly about the new house, preparing food for the child, sewing clothes, making things that fitted the baby and fitted her? How could he not have loved seeing her fit the child to her body as tightly as a figure fits a form? How could he not have thrilled to have her fit him to her body as tightly as a woman may fit a man? It was the fitting that was both the lure and the problem. Ask any one of Conrad's heroes: the call of the sea, the wave cry, the wind cry, the vast waters of the petrel and the porpoise were as seductive as any siren call that Naomi Lulham could utter. Casual work around the docks could never be enough for him; ultimately, he had to return to sea.

That autumn he signed on with a schooner plying between Britain and the Mediterranean. Familiar ports and familiar seas. But now it was different. Now he had his woman to come back to and for the moment the disease lay dormant within him. He no longer wanted to go searching for cunt in the Gut of Valletta or the bagnios of Constantinople. He was happy to drink a few glasses of wine and a raki or two with his mates before returning to the ship where he might smoke a pipe and dream about Naomi.

He fancied that the laughter of his shipmates was tinged with envy.

At the start of the New Year he was back in London. As always, it was strange to be back ashore, strange not to hear the motion of the waves and the shifting of the ship's timbers beneath his feet, nor to feel the warmth of the sun on his face and the wind on his cheek. Instead there was the bedlam of Back Road, sour with the smell of the gasworks, and the public house called The Ship where his uncle drank and, immediately next door, St. Mary's Church, where Aunt Lydia made her weekly peace with whatever god she believed in. The Ship marked the turning up Johnson Street, where railway arches snaked over the houses like a sea monster from a mariner's nightmare with trains grunting along its spine, belching smoke and sparks. He walked beneath the arches towards Commercial Road and the terrace of houses that included number three. He knocked on the door.

A shock to see that the natural progression of life had changed matters. As he came in through the front door, the boy – her boy, not his – ran towards him down the narrow corridor, ran, toddled, pitched forward onto his knees, got up and held up his arms to be lifted. Naomi hung back and watched. She appeared subdued, almost sullen. "He's grown," Abraham said, lifting the child to give him a kiss. The boy laughed in his face and pulled at his whiskers. "And he's walking."

"You've been away four months. A lot can happen in that time."

He drew back so he could look at her. "What's the matter? Aren't you pleased to see me?"

She shrugged. The fanlight above the door lit her face, made her look old and worn. "I didn't know when you'd come. Or if."

"Don't be silly. Shall we go upstairs? Will the boy let us?"

"He has a name."

"Isaac."

The little boy laughed and said, "Zak."

"That's what he calls himself. Zak."

"He can talk now!"

"A few words."

With Isaac on one arm, Abraham lugged his kitbag upstairs. Naomi followed them reluctantly. What was the matter with her? Where was the girl who only a few months ago appeared as eager as he? They reached the sanctuary of her room with its narrow bed and the trappings of her work all around. Now there was even some kind of dummy bearing a half-completed dress and giving the impression of a silent and judgemental watcher. He put the child on the floor and turned to face her. "I've dreamt of you, you know that? Every night." There was a hint of accusation in his tone, as though it were her fault.

"And I of you, hoping you'd come back soon."

"Nothing I could do about that. We went to the Black Sea again. Put another month on the voyage. Everything's happening there at the moment – Russians, Turks, Frenchies. There's been fighting."

"I read about it in the papers."

He shrugged, looking her up and down, trying not to touch her, trying to be gentlemanly. "My Naomi," he said. "My clever girl."

Her expression was full of doubt. "Who knows?"

"What do you mean?" He took her face in his hands and kissed her on the lips. She didn't resist, didn't respond. When he pulled away she told him simply, holding back her tears:

"I'm with child."

"You're what?"

"Pregnant, Abraham. Four months pregnant with your child."

"Are you sure?"

"'Course I'm bloody sure. Do you want to see? Is that it?" And then – a strange thing, an act of defiance – she pulled her dress over her head and displayed herself naked and helpless before him. Zak watched. "There you are."

It was the body he remembered, milk white and complex, with curves, declivities and hollows that he had marvelled at. Her breasts were still heavy, her waist still narrow, but now there was a discreet swelling of the belly and a dark line ruled with almost geometric precision from her navel down into the shock of brown hair. He put out his hand, a coarse, sailor's hand, tanned with salt and sun, to feel the peach-like smoothness of the skin, the rough silk of her hair. He knew peaches. The *Gipsy Queen* had carried peaches from Odessa. He knew that within the soft, sweet flesh of the peach there was a hard and uncompromising pit.

He looked at her. "Do they know?"

She shrugged. "Mrs. Block may have suspected something. I was sick at the start but I've been better recently. She's never said anything."

"She will soon enough."

"That's what I feared. That's why I prayed for you to come back. And I had no idea when that would be ... " Which was when her control broke down and tears started to her eyes. "I was so afraid," she said, her voice unsteady. "So frightened you'd never come back, that I'd have another bastard without a father." Her face crumpled and in a moment Abraham Block was holding a damp, weeping waif in his arms, a responsibility he had never had and never imagined ever having. Naomi Lulham. Pregnant with his child. And with another man's child looking on in puzzlement.

Bobby Shafto

Bobby Shafto's gone to sea
Silver buckles at his knee
He'll come back and marry me
Bonny, Bobby Shafto

Bobby Shafto's bright and fair
Combing down his yellow hair
He's my ain for evermair
Bonny Bobby Shafto

Everyone knows "Bobby Shafto." It's the kind of song you learn at your grandmother's knee. But it's a curious song, with its hint of dialect and the precise name of the subject. Not just a generic Bobby but a quite specific Bobby *Shafto*. The song dates from the eighteenth century and, like the most unusual surname Shafto, is of Northumbrian origin. Hence the dialect words – *ain*, *evermair* and *bairn*. Abraham Block spent much of his time on ships out of the northeastern ports – Shields, North and South, Sunderland, and, of course, Newcastle. Did he perhaps hear the song there and bring it back to sing it to his son in London? And did the son in turn sing it to his granddaughter, who became my grandmother and sang it to me? Is "Bobby Shafto" perhaps the one inheritance that

119

Abraham left to his descendants? For sure he left nothing else, except his genes.

Bobby Shafto's gettin' a bairn,
For to dangle on his arm;
On his arm and on his knee,
Bobby Shafto loves me

John Henry Block, Abraham and Naomi's first child, was born sometime in the first half of the next year, 1854. The actual date of his birth is unknown because it seems to have been unregistered, which is strange because Naomi's first child was registered, as was her third. But John Henry's birth doesn't show up in the registry. His date of death is known (6 January 1937) and even where and when he was buried (Chingford Mount Cemetery, 11 January 1937) but his date of birth remains a mystery. And yet he steps out of history almost into living memory: people who knew him spoke of his genial, generous manner – and his tendency to spend the housekeeping money on books. An autodidact, he collected books assiduously throughout his life. He was a great lover of Dickens, which is hardly surprising because he was born and reared in the impoverished parts of London that Dickens chronicled. We even know what he looked like because there is one photo of him in existence. He is sitting with his wife in the garden of their home at Highams Park in Walthamstow on the outer edges of London, the leafy suburbs where the couple moved in their retirement. From this slender piece of evidence you get a feel for them: the photo was taken on the occasion of their fiftieth wedding anniversary and John Henry has a bright-eyed, humorous look that suggests that life has been all right; by his side his wife, Emily Price, is holding a celebratory bouquet of gladioli and carnations. She views the camera with a wry look that suggests she knows more than she is letting on.

Maybe she knows that there is no trace of her husband's birth ever having been registered, that his very existence began in uncertain circumstances as the bastard son of a sailor's woman.

Until the Legitimacy Act of 1926, children born outside wedlock were not legitimised by their parents' subsequent marriage, so although Abraham and Naomi did ultimately marry, John Henry lived with the stigma of bastardy for seventy-two years.

He smiles in the photo; but his wife *knows*.

Was Abraham present at John Henry's birth? It seems unlikely. He was almost certainly at sea, his whereabouts uncertain, his very existence in doubt. You couldn't link your voyages to the vagaries of a woman's pregnancy and once you walked out through the front door with your kitbag over your shoulder, you vanished. Months later, with luck, you walked back in. In between, your loved ones would have little idea of where you were or even if you were still alive.

It's hard to find a modern-day analogy. The crew of a nuclear submarine on patrol, perhaps: three months without contact or communication. But submariners return from their clandestine patrols; in the nineteenth century the dangers of seagoing were vast. Individual accidents were common enough – man overboard, man hit by a swinging boom, felled by a falling block, fallen from the masthead – but entire crews were also at risk: each year thousands of merchant ships foundered and vanished without trace. No radio, no means of communication beyond visual sightings and flags, no mayday, no lifeboats or helicopters dashing to the rescue. Ships that passed one another at sea would report the fact when they next made port – "Spoken with" features often in the shipping reports, with a touching hint of desperation about it: "this ship was sighted then, there; reported all was well." But such happy news would not be read until days later when the reporting ship had made a safe landfall and the news had been telegraphed to London. The blunt fact of such a life was that when a sailor went off to sea you heard no news of him for months and there was a significant chance that he would disappear for ever.

Yet Abraham Block did not disappear. He survived and he remained more or less faithful to Naomi Lulham. In the next three years he came and went like any sailor in a world that was used to sailors, where women would gather on street corners to exchange news and views, like miners' wives during a pit accident. Sometimes it would be to talk of tragedy – an entire ship foundered, perhaps – other times it would be to console the ones whose men had not returned with their ship. More often it was just to find out what people knew, which ships had been reported in the newspapers. Those who could read would pass on the news that had been gleaned from *Lloyd's List* or the *Shipping and Mercantile Gazette* but maritime news only travelled as fast as the ships that carried it, so information from foreign ports could be weeks old. You might be hearing that your man was in Odessa on the very same day that he walked in through the front door in Stepney.

Exactly which ships Abraham served on in this period is hidden from sight among the Crew Agreements held in the National Archives, the National Maritime Museum, or, from 1857, in the Maritime History Archive of the University of Newfoundland. If you don't know the name of the vessel, the port of registration and the port and date of sailing then it is impossible to track a crew member down – at least until the various archives are scanned, digitised and made searchable. Abraham Block's voyages are there somewhere, dispersed through those dusty ledgers, his mariner's life traced out in immaculate copperplate entries. But for the moment they are beyond discovery. Elsewhere, in the documents that illuminate ordinary life, certain facts punctuate the general darkness: for example, Abraham was definitely at home in December 1856 for the simple fact that his sperm is needed at that very month.

Not hard to picture the east London scene: cold fog, a lethal compound of water droplets and coal smoke, hangs like a threat around the crowded streets of the docklands; the homeless are dying of hypothermia and respiratory failure in the yards and in the alleyways; news vendors on the Commercial Road are selling stories of war in Persia and political intrigue at home; and on 5 December in the house on Johnson Street, a celebration marks Naomi's twenty-fourth birthday. Later, once the table has been cleared, Uncle Isaac and Aunt Lydia retire to bed. The two boys – Isaac Uriah is now four and John Henry is two – are already asleep and it is at this fleeting moment of privacy that Abraham and Naomi couple quietly and urgently in her narrow bed. It seems an ephemeral event, an intense but momentary conjunction of flesh and spirit, but it is rather more than that (as are so many such conjunctions) because it will result, nine months later, in the birth of her third and his second son.

Two children in three years by two different men and now, although she wouldn't know it for some weeks, a third on the way. By which time Abraham was once more at sea. This was surely not the life Naomi had imagined when she travelled up to London from Hastings some six years previously, but it was the life she had ended up with: rearing children, sewing clothes and waiting for her man to come home from sea. You put up and shut up. Choice was for the moneyed classes, the quality, not the ordinary people of Stepney and Poplar.

There was, of course, one change that she could effect, and presumably did once she had tumbled to the fact that she was pregnant yet again and he had returned from his latest voyage. "I'm not," you can hear her say, "going to end up a sailor's tart. You, my dear, adored Abraham Block, are bloody well going to make an honest woman of me."

Tying the Knot

How many knots did Abraham Block have to tie in order to qualify as an able seaman? Dozens. Bowlines, reef knots, fisherman's knots, sheepshanks, Turk's heads – a congeries of knots; but this knot, tied in St. Mary's Church, Back Road, the newly opened church just beside the gasworks at the end of Johnson Street, was the most intricate.

They had the banns called while he was away after Christmas. Naomi worried that he wouldn't be back in time because the rector had insisted that the marriage had to take place within three months of the calling of the banns, and who was she to argue with a man like him, Father William McCall, Doctor of Divinity (whatever that was)? And Mrs. Block had warned her of the precedence in the family, of Abraham's grandmother Elizabeth, who had had the banns called but never managed to tie the knot with the man she had chosen as the father of at least four of her children.

"Ten children she had, and all of them born the wrong side of the blanket. You know what I mean, don't you? Wrong side of the blanket."

"Yes, Mrs. Block, I know what you mean."

"And in the end she left it too late to make an honest woman of herself."

But Abraham did turn up. There he was, on 16 March 1857, all spruced up and looking in his prime, with a proper frock coat he'd borrowed from someone and a silk stock and boots so polished you could see your face in them, almost. Even got a watch and chain. And there was Naomi, proudly alongside him at the altar rail, in a grey dress – she could hardly wear virginal white, not with the two boys running round in the background – and a short jacket she had made herself of red Turkish silk. Zouave style they called it. Ever so fashionable. In the shadows of the church she glimmered like a jewel. Abraham thought her the most beautiful creature in the world, and he'd seen a few.

The service was wreathed in the smoke of incense – this was, as it still is, a church in the Anglo-Catholic tradition – and intoned in a voice that might have been happier with plainsong. A plaster image of the Blessed Virgin Mary looked benignly on the proceedings while the vicar, resplendent in his lacy canonicals, hurried the happy couple into that divine state of holy matrimony which they had clearly ignored for a number of years. "What God hath joined," he warned the congregation once the deed was done, "let no man put asunder." And who would wish to, seeing the new husband and wife smiling into each other's eyes as they went together into the vestry to sign the register?

"You can write your name," Naomi whispered to her husband. "Like I taught you." But when the priest handed him the pen, Abraham didn't attempt to write, daring only to make a cross, to which Father McCall added the necessary qualification, *Abraham Block*, and the assertion *his mark*. Then Naomi signed, followed by the witnesses: George Dordon, Sarah Hanham and Mary Elderton, the latter pair being so nervous at the writing that they each made mistakes and the priest had to add their names, written correctly, underneath.

Abraham Block and Naomi Lulham's marriage registration

Formalities over, the wedding party, two dozen or more, went next door to The Ship, where the publican, Joseph Ransom, a Suffolk man himself although from Thurston near Bury rather than Kessingland, had given them a private room for the evening. Someone sat at the piano and played. There was dancing and singing, mainly singing as the beer went down, but still some dancing. No one really knew how to dance a polka or a waltz correctly, but it was fun dancing in couples as you did nowadays. And it was during the dancing, when Abraham and Naomi were much too close for decency and people were cheering and laughing, that she whispered in his ear: "Guess what?"

"What?"

"I'm pregnant again. Three months gone." And then, "You'll stay, won't you? Stay with us for the birth?"

It was easy enough to say yes after a few pints and with the piano banging away and Naomi in his arms and someone – it was her witness Sarah Hanham, who had a fine voice – singing "I Dreamt I Dwelt in Marble Halls" almost as good as you got on the stage.

"When'll it be?" he asked.

"September sometime. If it goes well."

*

127

William Abraham Block was born on 15 September 1857, in the upstairs room in Johnson Street where his brother John had been delivered three years earlier. Unlike those of his two older brothers, this birth was legitimate and, above all, correctly registered. Furthermore, on 1 November, the child was baptised not in St. Mary's but in St. Dunstan's Church.

St. Dunstan's still stands. The sailor's church once, it has been landlocked by changing circumstance: How many sailors still live in Stepney? How many ropewalks survive? How many ships dock in the Pool of London or the great docks themselves? Yet St. Dunstan's still stands, conscious of its past but stripped of its sailors' graves. The death of the Port of London is one of the wonders of the last half-century, transforming this part of the city almost beyond recognition: but on the first of November 1857 – a Sunday, of course, with the church full of worshippers – St. Dunstan's Church was the spiritual centre of world shipping. And there is the proud Block family, gathered round the ancient font, confident in their newfound respectability. They watch in satisfaction while the rector holds the child in his arms and, lifting water from the basin, lets it run like quicksilver over the child's head while intoning the magic formula: "William Abraham, I baptise thee in the name of the Father, the Son and the Holy Ghost. Amen."

A thin bawl of protest sounds through the church.

"That's the devil going out of him," old women in the congregation whisper knowingly to each other. In the side aisle, five-year-old Isaac Uriah, supremely indifferent to the ritual being enacted at the font, encourages three-year-old John Henry to chase him around the columns, and receives a clip round the ear for his pains from Uncle Isaac. Naomi takes back her baby from the priest and smiles lovingly on the tiny creature. People gather, making clucking and cooing noises at mother and child. It seems a perfect little family group, yet there is a shadow cast over the happy moment: Abraham has already signed on with the schooner *Tribune*, even now loading at the West India Docks and soon to be cleared through customs for St. Kitts and Nevis.

The Caribbean

At the end of December the *Tribune* was warped out of the West India Export Dock, through the basin and out into the stream of the river. It was a small departure, insignificant in the general run of things in the Port of London, a small two-master slipping downstream. No steam tug for her, but a careful timing of wind and tide to carry her down from Blackwall Reach and bear round the great meander into Bugsby's Reach. By Christmas Eve she was passing Gravesend and reaching Deal, where she anchored along with dozens of other vessels in the Downs, to catch the tide in the morning and move south into the Channel.

As far as we know, it was Abraham's first transatlantic crossing: an event in a sailor's life as great as crossing the line to reach into the Southern Ocean. *Lloyd's List* has the *Tribune* making landfall in the Leeward Islands on 8 February 1858 after a six-week passage. There is no means of knowing whether or not she stopped on the way. The possibilities are various – the Canaries or Cape Verde islands, perhaps – but no landfall is recorded. What is certain is that from leaving the English Channel she would have sailed due south for a fortnight in order to pick up the trade winds and bear westward across the ocean. For another two weeks they had nothing in sight but water and sky, clouds and stars and sun. Dolphins pitched and rolled in the wake, eyeing them with curiosity; flying fish flashed above the surface; a thousand miles from land, seabirds serenely passed them by. Day after day was like this, running before the wind or sailing on a broad reach, the boat rising and falling in the long Atlantic swells. They had a line out and trolled for fish. Free food if you could catch it, although they were sailors and hankered after meat.

And then came the catharsis of landfall, the call from the masthead of "land ahoy!" and the sight, shouldering over the horizon, of the first fragments of land, followed by frustrating hours while the islands inched nearer to finally resolve themselves into foam-lined shores and jungle-clad mountains. They came under the lee of an island that the master announced as St. Kitts. You could see houses clustered around the harbour and behind them a green mantle rising up into bright cloud. The town was called Basseterre. As they approached, a gust of smoke issued from the fort, followed seconds later by the clap of a distant cannon. The *Tribune* dipped her ensign in salute as she slid through the harbour entrance into still waters.

Landfall in a strange country. Heat and cloud and diamond-bright sun. The first solid ground for weeks, pitching and rolling beneath feet unaccustomed to a world that didn't pitch and roll. Voices all around them, the noise and smell and bustle of strangers, the sheen of black skin. For more than a month the dozen crewmen of the *Tribune* had been battered by wind and salt and sun, fed by ship's biscuit and salt beef, quenched by brackish water; now, in the ramshackle town of Basseterre, they were sated by citrus and coconut milk, by rum and by women.

In a tavern that was little more than a wooden shack, Abraham encountered an Irish sailor who had jumped ship six years ago and now lived on the island. "Paradise," the man

131

told him. "You can fecking live for free here, mate. Never too cold, never too hot." His laughter was like a rasp, sharpened with rum and tobacco. "I mean the weather, not the women. The women? They're hot all right, hot as hell."

"I've got a wife at home, Paddy. And kids."

The man hacked and spat, as though at the very idea. "So had I. And now I've got a dozen or more here." He leant forward, breathing foul, rum-sweetened air across the table and lowering his voice to a whisper. "What's your name, laddie?"

"Abraham."

"Good Catholic name, Abraham. Well, let me tell you this, Abraham. They like white cock, that's the truth of it."

The dank, narrow streets of Stepney, blurred by fog and mired in horseshit, seemed half a world away, and were.

The return crossing, west to east, was always more difficult. You had to sail north first, just the opposite of the outward voyage. No one knew why. It was just the way the winds and the currents worked – east to west in the south, west to east in the north. The trade winds, they called them. One of those mysteries, like the way the sun rose in the morning and set in the evening, day after day, and always would. You sailed north, up the eastern seaboard of the United States, and tried to keep your nerve as the weather and the water grew colder; but if you tried to sail across the middle you'd maybe lose all the wind and stay becalmed. Ships had perished like that, so men said, running out of water and all the crew dying of thirst. Food you could do without for a time, but not water. Of course it would be different with steam ships. Steam ships didn't give a fuck about the winds or the tides.

It was the end of April before they were passing the Lizard and starting the long drag up the Channel into grey rain and grey seas, 3 May before they were once again anchored in the

Downs and waiting for the tide with a hundred other ships preparing to enter the estuary. St. Kitts was no more than a memory now, blurred back into imagination. On 4 May the *Tribune* was cleared through customs; the next day she was in the West India Dock unloading.

Thus Abraham came home once more, the sailor returned, his uncle beaming benevolently, his aunt quizzical, the wife and children happy and excited, the new baby no longer the helpless thing he had left but a sentient being, crawling around the place and smiling at the world when he wasn't complaining. He picked up the child and swung it into the air. It gurgled with delight and puked on him.

"Seasick," he exclaimed, laughing.

The others – four-year-old John Henry and six-year-old Isaac – clung to his legs and begged to be lifted as well. And Naomi, her eyes bright with anticipation, her manner soft and eager (softer than any of the women he had known in Basseterre, who were loud and argumentative and calculating of every penny), watched with a mixture of pride and anticipation.

"I'll tell you all about it later," he said. "But first, I've got one or two things for you."

Presents, of course. Coconuts, limes, a bottle of rum for Uncle Isaac, a bowl carved from a coconut shell for Aunt Lydia, and for Naomi a special gift, something wrapped in a sheet of coarse blue sugar paper. In their room she sat and unwrapped the object; her expression mingled puzzlement with pleasure.

"What is it?" The object lay in her lap like a piece of sculptured pottery. It appeared abstract, a twisted spiral of porcelain about eight inches long and six inches wide, revealed, as she turned it in her hands, to be cleft along its length by an opening, an open mouth with lips of nacre and a throat of glistening rose.

She ran her finger along the undulating border of the lip, experiencing a little shock at the recognition of the shape. His eyes were on her. She felt the thrill of his presence as something physical within her, a shock that centred in her groin and spread up through her abdomen to her chest and down through her legs to her feet. Something like when Abraham touched her, as he hadn't touched her for four months now. And he knew what was happening – he could see it in her eyes, and she in his.

"Conch, they call it," he said. "The islands are famous for them. Put it to your ear, you can hear the ocean."

She lifted the shell to do as he suggested and there it was – the distant roar, perhaps of breakers falling and falling on a coral shore. "How strange!"

"The natives blow notes on them, make a kind of music. I'll show you." He took the shell, slipped his fingers into the opening and put it to his lips to blow. It made a noise, a cross between a strangled yelp and passing wind. He looked at her with indignation. "That's not right."

She tried not to laugh. "I hope not."

"They taught me. Said I was most expert." He tried again, and there, for a moment, it was: a haunting note like the cry of some distant sea animal calling for its mate.

Silence. She wondered what to say that would not bring laughter, the laughter of happiness, bubbling up inside her like milk boiling over. "It's a fine sound." She took the shell back and examined it. "It puts me in mind of something," she said as she turned it in her hands, slipping her narrow fingers into the mouth.

"And what might that be?"

"You know full well, Abraham Block. You know full well."

They had a month together, a month of what passed as family life – playing with the boys, taking them for walks, perhaps down to the docks to see the ships – the steamers, which were the latest thing – perhaps to the park at Hackney Wick, perhaps taking the two older boys to Mr. Brunel's Thames Tunnel and paying thruppence to give them the thrill of walking beneath the river all the way to Rotherhithe: all those little things that a real family might do.

Memories? Six-year-old Isaac Uriah might recall something coherent about his assumed father, a memory of walking with him in the park or watching the shipping at Shadwell or walking among the milling crowds in the tunnel; four-year-old John Henry might perhaps hold one or two episodic memories, without contingency or context but with the presence of his father illuminated as though by the light of a photographic flash; but William Abraham, a mere eight months old, would recall nothing. Of course, Naomi would remember. She would always remember the time when they were just like a real family.

Pactolus

Work was easy enough to find. You could take on a voyage or not as you pleased. For instance, the schooner *Pactolus*, loading for Barbadoes.*

"You got experience of the ocean?" he was asked by the master.

"Been to the Leeward Islands. *Tribune*. Back last month." He had a reference from the master of the *Tribune* that he couldn't read. Naomi had told him more or less what it said: *A goodly, honest fellow, loyal and hardworking. Unlettered but knowledgeable of his trade.* That kind of thing.

Mr. Davison read the letter over. "Years at sea?"

"Eleven as of this year, sir."

Davison nodded, turning the register towards him. "Hired," he said, handing him the pen. "Put your mark."

Abraham took the pen awkwardly and inscribed an unsteady X with fingers that were used to hauling on a sheet not holding a pen. Davison took back the pen and dipped it, frowning. "Abram, was that it?"

"Abraham, sir. Abraham Block." He'd not lost his Suffolk accent. Those long, country vowels. *Abraham Black*, Davison wrote, and, beside the crudely drawn X, *his mark*. "Report

---

* Commonly spelled thus.

the day after tomorrow. Saturday the twelfth, eight o'clock in the morning, sharp. Don't forget. Next."

Abraham Black. How was he to know?

Naomi protested when he told her that he'd signed on, of course she did. It was the subject of their rows – why couldn't he get a job on shore like other people? Or at least something closer to home.

"'Cos those jobs don't pay as well, that's why. You and the children need clothes on your backs and food in your bellies, don't you? I work on a coastal trader and I'll earn pennies. Go foreign, go distant and I'll be back with fifteen quid or more in me pocket."

"If you haven't spent it on all them black women."

"They only cost a few pence." He laughed at his own joke, but she never really knew the truth. They told all sorts of stories, the women did, about what their sailor husbands got up to ...

The *Pactolus* slipped her moorings at Limehouse Dock on 21 June 1858. The family came to see the departure, Naomi standing with the three boys beside her, all waving as the schooner slid away downriver, dragged into the future by a blackened, snorting steamer tossing smoke into the summer air. They watched until the little procession had disappeared round the curve of the river then made their way back to Johnson Street. John Henry was in tears; Isaac was telling him not to be a baby; while the real baby – William Abraham, known as Billy – was indifferent to it all, of course. All he wanted was to suck at his mother's breast, the little devil. Just like his father, Naomi told him.

The next day *Lloyd's List* reported the *Pactolus* at Gravesend, waiting for the tide. That much Naomi would have known. Then nothing more for two months.

You become resigned to it. Your life goes on. The children squabble. The older one goes unwillingly to the parish school and learns his letters. The other entertains himself or plays with other children down the street. Meanwhile, between looking after the new baby there's sewing and mending to be done, which brings in enough money to pay the rent. Uncle Isaac works his shifts at the gasworks and Aunt Lydia keeps house, cleaning and doing the laundry and cooking. And no word comes regarding the whereabouts of the schooner *Pactolus*. Gossip can cross most boundaries, but not the Atlantic Ocean.

Then one day a glimmer of news. Again it was in *Lloyd's List*, the edition of 16 August, a full two months after Naomi had seen her husband off: *Pactolus*, Davison, had docked safely at Barbadoes on 19 July. In truth that didn't tell her much, just that a month previously her husband was still alive and on the far side of the ocean, so far away as to be beyond imagination.

Then nothing more. September, October, November. No news.

People, friends, acquaintances, customers, began to avoid her. A quick smile and a good morning but no more. She told Isaac: "They don't want to talk to me any more, that's the truth of it. A ship's overdue and they don't want to say nothing."

She lay in her bed and dreamt. Of him, his lean, white body with tanned and weathered arms and face. The smell of him, the taste of salt and sweat. His talk of distant islands, distant storms, distant women.

"When's Papa coming back?" asked the oldest boy, Isaac Uriah, who wasn't even Abraham's but thought he was. He was old enough now to guess the answer to his question and know that it would be a lie. "Papa'll be back soon, 'course he will."

On the other hand, John Henry was still young enough to believe what he was told and as a result cried out whenever there was a knock on the door: "There's Papa! There's Papa!" But there wasn't Papa. His absence became part of the daily round. It was Uncle Isaac who played the part of surrogate father, Uncle Isaac who played with the boys, Uncle Isaac who took the belt to them when they were naughty, Uncle Isaac whom they called on to police their arguments. But it wasn't Uncle Isaac who kept Naomi warm in bed at night, not as far as I know. Although there is always the question of the name of her first son.

Autumn dragged on into winter, a chill, foggy London winter that snatched at the back of the throat and clogged up the lungs and killed people quite casually. You waited for your turn to come. The children caught things, of course. Coughs and colds, the usual childhood ailments, but Naomi's were a tough trio from tough stock and they survived. Scamps, the two older ones, running around the streets and occasionally bringing down Uncle Isaac's wrath on themselves.

"If your father were here there's no saying what he'd do. Tan yer hides most likely."

Sometimes that would stop the boys in their tracks. "But he's not here, is he?" they'd retort.

"When'll he be back?"

There was no longer any answer to that.

News finally reached the house in Johnson Street in the New Year, on the last day of January, in the raw cold, when fingers and toes were swollen with chilblains. One of Naomi's friends, Sarah Hanham, a witness at her wedding, heard about it from gossip round the docks. Word always got round, what ship had put in with storm damage, what ship had fouled an anchor, what ship had lost rigging, what ship had run aground or foundered in a gale. This particular item came in *Lloyd's List* of 31 January 1859, a report as bare as a ship's mast in a storm:

> The PACTOLUS, Davison, cleared from Demerara 21st Oct. for London, and has not since been heard of.

> The XARIFA, Bishop, cleared from Demerara 22nd Oct. for London, and has not since been heard of.

Naomi felt the sudden nausea of fear. "Demerara, what's Demerara?" she asked. "It's sugar, in't it?"

"It's a place, you silly. Somewhere in the Indies."

The Indies meant nothing, really. Just what Abraham had told her. Palm trees, plantations, jungle-clad hills steeper than anything she had seen. And the people blackened by the sun. "Two ships," she said, looking at the page that was being shown her. She didn't know what else to say. "No more than a day apart."

"Must have been a storm," Sarah said. "They have them there, stronger than anything you can imagine. Hurricanes."

Naomi knew storms well enough, from her childhood on the coast at Hastings, the waves pounding on the shingle, then drawing back and pounding again and again and again like hammer blows. Fishing boats that never returned. Entire ships that were swallowed by the sea and vomited back as splintered planks and torn canvas and bits of rope thrown up on the shore. And now a storm had destroyed her happiness, fragile though it was, and the happiness of her sons. In its place a great hole opened up inside her, a huge void that devoured her grief and left behind it a strange amalgam of fear and anger. "I told him not to go," she said. "I told him not to go. It's his bloody fault."

Later she found a map and discovered Demerara, which wasn't one of the islands at all but a place on the coast of South America. Which also meant nothing to her. Just a place near where her husband had died, presumably by drowning, some time in October. Now it was January and the months seemed like a gulf, a great yawning chasm into which an entire ship had disappeared.

"You'll be owed money," Sarah told her. "You go and see about it. It's not right that a widow should be left penniless."

Widow. A word that haunted the imagination with images of black bombazine and the odour of destitution. Someone told her the name of the shipping agent, who directed her to an office in the Minories where, so it was said, monies due were being dished out to relatives.

The building was solid and imposing, with steps up to a door like the way in to a church. She was done up in mourning weeds and the doorman inclined his head and called her Madam as he directed her to the second floor. He wore white gloves and didn't smile. On the second floor there were other people waiting in an anteroom, women like herself mainly, a dozen of them talking about what had happened and might have happened to their menfolk and how much money they were due. Naomi stood aside from the gossip and watched. The room was like the inside of a coffin, all wooden panelling and brass fittings with portraits of the dead hanging on the walls. Sir Richard This, Mr. Montague That: grand gentlemen with extensive whiskers and stiff collars. When the women were finally called through, they queued at a desk that was also like a coffin, a coffin within a coffin, with a man behind it who had the look of an undertaker.

"Name?" the man asked when she stepped up to the desk. She stood looking down on him. "My name or his?"

He pinched his lips, as though he had already had enough insolence that morning and was reaching the limits of his patience. "His."

"Abraham Block."

"And you are?"

"'Is wife." She'd brought her marriage certificate, just to be sure. He glanced at it with scant interest, then down at the list before him.

"There's no Abraham Block here."

For a moment absurd, irrational hope blossomed within her. "You mean 'e's still alive? There were survivors?"

"My dear woman, there has been no report of the *Pactolus* since October last year when she left the port of Demerara. No wreckage, no survivors, nothing. In their wisdom, the commissioners have ruled that the ship was lost with all hands. But Abraham Block is not here on the list."

"He must be." She put the "h" in just to be sure she was understood: *He*.

"How do you spell the name?"

"B-L-O-C-K. You can see for yourself on the marriage certificate." She reached forward and tapped the document, just in the right place.

The man sniffed. "There's a Black. Abraham Black."

"Well, that's 'im. Black, Block, what's the difference?"

"A great deal. An entirely different name, an entirely different person. Now, if you'll please stand aside I have other people to deal with."

For a moment her world, her very existence, seemed to hang in the balance. Abraham Block vanished. Not dead but never existed. Cancelled from the world and from memory. She hovered on the edge of tears, tears of misery and tears of anger – dangerous, hybrid tears. Her voice trembled. "Show me," she said.

"This is a confidential document. I cannot show it to any Tom, Dick or Harry who turns up at this office."

"I'm not any Tom, Dick or Harry! I'm a woman who has lost her man on your bloody ship!"

"Madam!"

"Don't you 'madam' me! I demand what is mine. If you cannot let me see your precious list, then I want to see the Agreement. That's a public legal document. He told me all about them. All signed and certified, he said. If not, I'll be back here tomorrow with a lawyer!"

Other men had appeared, like crows gathering at a corpse. The waiting women were muttering to themselves, as though fomenting riot. There was a hasty discussion and a briefcase was produced from which the man at the desk extracted a sheet of foolscap. It bore the printed title *AGREEMENT FOR FOREIGN GOING SHIP* across the top. Below, beneath the preamble, was a list of signatures. The man drew his finger down the column and halted at *Abraham (his X mark) Black*. He turned it towards her.

Extract from Crew Agreement for Pactolus,
10 June 1858, Abraham on the fourth line

"There," Naomi said triumphantly.

"Born in Suffolk. The right age. Served on the *Tribune*. It's all there. That's my Abraham. He was unlettered, see?

Just wrote his mark. How could he know his name had been written wrong? And look at the marriage certificate. Just the same."

The crows debated. Naomi's marriage certificate was consulted, with its near identical signature *Abraham (his X mark) Block*. Heads were nodded. "There will have to be a declaration before a notary public," the more senior of the men said.

"What's that?"

"We cannot just hand out monies to people without some guarantee of identity. You will be required to swear on oath that this Abraham Black and your Abraham Block are one and the same person. Thus the matter will be resolved and the monies owed to you as his wife will be released."

She considered. "How much am I owed?"

The first man, the undertaker, consulted his list. "Sixteen pounds, seven shillings and fourpence."

She looked at the men with a bleak expression, as though her face were braced against a storm. "Sixteen pounds, seven shillings and fourpence," she repeated. "Is that the worth of a life?"

Block to Pain

Whether or not Naomi Block, née Lulham, finally got her 16*l* 7*s* 4*d*, history does not relate. What is certain is that at the age of twenty-six she put her nose to the grindstone of Victorian widowhood. She continued to live at number three, Johnson Street with Isaac and Lydia Block, uncle and aunt of her deceased husband, and she fended for the children – two of them Abraham's, the eldest the fruit of unknown loins.

Now that Abraham was no more, the household had to rearrange itself so that a room became available for a lodger. The first lodger was a certain Ellen Holmstrom, English wife of a Swedish sailor; then, sometime between 1861 and 1863, a young clerk called Philip Pain* took Holmstrom's place. Philip was a local lad from the Mile End Road who had only just left home in order to make way for more siblings in his own family. He was a good-looking boy, about eighteen years old when he came to the house in Johnson Street.

By now Naomi had been four years without Abraham and, with the children to look after, she had little opportunity to meet men. Solitary pleasure in the relative privacy of her own bed was all that was available to her, but now there was this

---

* No relation to the Thomas Pain who was Elizabeth Block's paramour.

fresh-faced young lad close at hand. It wasn't long before she was darning his socks, not much longer before her smile was conquering his shyness and she was inviting him in, at first to her room and then to her bed. It was a pleasant change from what she had known before – instead of the tough, sinewy, salty body of Abraham Block, the smooth emollient of a youthful office worker's limbs and torso.

One can imagine Lydia's disapproval and Isaac's tacit sympathy, but whatever the pros and cons of this liaison, by May 1863 the banns were being called and by the end of June nineteen-year-old Philip and thirty-year-old Naomi were married. The ceremony, graced by eleven-year-old Isaac Uriah, nine-year-old John Henry, and five-year-old William Abraham, took place in St. Mary's, Back Road, the very same church where she had married Abraham six years earlier.

Exactly nine months later their first child, a son, was born.

The new Pain family soon moved out of the house on Johnson Street. They moved to Bromley St. Leonard, where Naomi had been living with her sister when she first came to London and where a few green fields were still holding out against the eastward spread of the city. Cleaner air. Better for the children to grow up fit and healthy. They settled there and had four more children. Philip died in 1884 at the age of forty-one, by which time he'd moved up in the world a bit – *Pain* had become *Payne*. Naomi outlived him by twenty-four years, dying at the age of seventy-six. Eight children by three different men, of whom the third was eleven years her junior? She clearly wasn't going to go easily.

Her two children by Abraham did well enough. By the end of the century, they had worked their way up from illiteracy and illegitimacy into the respectable urban lower middle class. Nothing fancy, nothing pretentious. William became a hairdresser while John Henry started up a small family business supplying paint and building materials. He married Emily Price in 1884 and they had three children: Harry, who emigrated to Canada before the Great War and became a farmer; Frederick, who helped his father with the family business; and finally a daughter named Emily Naomi. Of course, the First World War looms, but these people are survivors. They'll get through that, despite the fact that Fred will be called up in 1917. He went to Belgium with the Bedfordshire Regiment, from training in England more or less straight into the Battle of Passchendaele. He went over the top and survived to tell the tale – many tales – returning to London and the family business. He and his sister Emily both lived into their nineties. Survivors. Survived the Great War, survived the second. And in some sense, they survive still.

Ginger Beer

What about the other two, that sterile couple who were so important in Abraham and Naomi's lives – Isaac and Lydia Block? They stayed on in Johnson Street, Isaac plodding down the road to the gasworks every day but Sunday, Lydia looking after the house and the lodgers. An ordinary London working-class couple of the mid-nineteenth century getting on with an ordinary life, the kind of people who don't come to public notice very often. When they do, it is usually when something goes wrong, which it did in December 1866:

From the London Evening Standard, *Tuesday 3 December 1867*

SECOND COURT
(Sittings at Nisi Prius, in Middlesex, before
Mr. Justice BYLES and a Common Jury)
BLOCK AND WIFE V. WILLIAMS

This was an action to recover damages for injuries sustained by the female plaintiff.

Mr. Layton and Mr. F. Turner appeared for the plaintiffs, and Mr. Bealy for the defendant.

The Plaintiff, Mr. Block, was a gasfitter, in the employment of the Ratcliffe Gas Company, and on the afternoon of the 17th Dec. last his wife left her home in Johnson Street, Commercial Road, and at the corner of the street she stepped into the road to cross. At this moment a van belonging to the defendant, a ginger-beer manufacturer, was being driven round the corner, and it knocked Mrs. Block down, and the wheel passed over one of her legs just above the ankle. The driver instantly pulled up, but in so doing the wheel unfortunately again passed over the injured limb. In consequence of the very serious bruising to the calf of the leg gangrene set in, and for a fortnight her life was in danger. On the 3rd of March she was discharged from the London Hospital, where she was taken on the occasion of the accident; and Mr. Llewellyn, the house surgeon, was of the opinion that she would never have the perfect use of her leg again.

A good deal of evidence was given on each side as to who was in fault, and The Jury found for the defendant.

Even across the years, even not knowing these people and accepting that they are long dead, it is still difficult not to feel anger. Fifty-nine-year-old Lydia Block steps off the pavement into the shit and filth of the Commercial Road and Mr. Williams's ginger-beer cart comes rattling round the corner and knocks her down. The driver pulls up. The horse rears and the bloody cart rolls back over the victim now lying in the roadway. Thus her leg is run over *twice*. These are cartwheels – iron-bound wooden wheels. She is in agony. People rally round, perhaps even lift her onto the ginger-beer cart itself, among the presumably empty bottles (otherwise wouldn't the weight of the cart have broken her leg?), and hurry her to the London Hospital (now the *Royal* London Hospital) on the Whitechapel Road. It's not far – you could walk it in fifteen minutes – so perhaps that's her one piece of luck in this whole sorry story.

In the hospital, in shock and agony, she undergoes whatever trauma treatment they might have managed in those days. No antibiotics and only an approximate idea of antisepsis. Joseph Lister's first clinical use of carbolic acid dates from just the year before Lydia's accident and by grim coincidence he used it on the leg of a Glasgow boy who had been ... run over by a cart. But his seminal papers on antiseptic surgery were not published in the *Lancet* until 1867 and then not all the medical profession took his work seriously. It certainly doesn't look as though the first hints of Lister's work had filtered through to the London Hospital because despite the best efforts of the worthy Mr. Llewellyn, Aunt Lydia's leg became gangrenous.

It is truly remarkable that she didn't lose the limb; indeed, in those pre-antibiotic days, it is remarkable that she didn't die. They would have debrided the gangrenous tissue, cut away the dead and dying flesh from the living. Only rudimentary anaesthetic, of course. But then most of the tissue would have been dead anyway, so that's all right – except for the living bits that you have to cut away round the borders just to make sure.

In all, Lydia Block languished in hospital for two and a half months and yet ...

The jury found for the defendant.

No damage done then. The law says so. No blame attaches to Mr. Ginger-Beer driving round the corner like Jehu and crashing his chariot into an innocent pedestrian trying to cross the road. This is not a criminal case, for God's sake, it's a civil case for *damages*. But no, Victorian concepts of survival of the fittest win through here – and the fittest are clearly not those who step off pavements and get run down by a horse-drawn cart full of ginger-beer bottles.

Lydia Block was a tough old bird. She survived to live with the results of this injury for the rest of her life, no doubt hobbling (her limb looking like a leg of lamb after someone has cut the meat away), probably in constant pain, certainly complaining to anyone who would listen, her old man mainly.

Isaac died in 1871 at the age of sixty-eight, tired, perhaps, of her nagging and all the fetching and carrying he had to do. Left with no income and unable to keep lodgers any longer Lydia was forced to leave the house on Johnson Street and admit herself to the Raine Street workhouse. Oh, yes, you could do that. Many, perhaps most of the inmates were there of their own volition. The reason given, in her case? "Destitute." And crippled, presumably, but that's not mentioned. At least she got a bed to sleep in, three meals a day and some kind of medical provision. It worked, after a fashion, because she lasted a further eleven years, dying in the workhouse at the age of seventy-four.

What is conspicuous is that no one came to her rescue, particularly those who might have been considered the closest thing she had to blood relatives – Naomi or her husband Philip, or any of the children who had been born and reared at number three, Johnson Street. They must have known.

"Have you heard about Aunt Lydia?"

"Oh, don't call her aunt. She was never my aunt. Old sour puss. What's she done now?"

"Gone to the workhouse."

"The workhouse? Well, I hope they're kinder to her than she was to me."

You cannot cast the stones of blame across a century and a half; but still you wonder, what lay behind that indifference? The truth is, you can never know.

Part 2

George Mawer

He's not a hero, nor will ever be. He's a private soldier of the 50th (Queen's Own) Regiment of Foot (known variously as the Glorious Half-Hundred or the Dirty Half-Hundred). It's 1847 and he's getting married in Manchester Cathedral. He cuts a good enough figure in his tight, red coatee and charcoal-grey trousers with their dramatic red stripe down the outside of each leg. Diagonally across his robin-red-breast chest are pipe-clayed bandoleers adorned with a silver regimental badge – the numeral 50 at the focus of a starburst* above a sphinx named *Egypt*. Beneath his right arm is a gleaming, patent leather shako also bearing the regimental badge. To our eyes this is what a toy soldier looks like, something bright and jolly. Harmless enough, the stuff of childhood fables. But this is the uniform he will fight and maybe die in. Now, however, he lives up to his steadfast tin-soldier look, his Hans Christian Andersen image: on his left arm is his bride. She is small and sharp, a white egret against the scarlet macaw (another bird metaphor, but why not?) of her about-to-be-husband. When she follows the priest's words she speaks in the dulcet tones of Sligo –

---

* Technically, a Brunswick star.

"I, Ann, take thee, George, to my wedded husband,
"to have and to hold from this day forward,
"for better for worse, for richer for poorer,
"in sickness and in health,
"to love, cherish, and to obey, till death us do part,
"according to God's holy ordinance;
"and thereto I give thee my troth."

"Mind you," she adds *sotto voce*, "I'm not so sure about the 'obey.'"

She laughs at the minister's frown. She's lippy, her mouth always hovering on the brink of derisive laughter. She has intensely blue eyes, like the sky at the zenith. She looks small and fragile and yet she's as tough as a thorn bush. Those are some of the things that George loves about her. There are others – the fact that she loves him, for one.

They duly sign the register – his careful signature, her mark –

18_47_	Marriage solemnized at _the Coll'l Parish Church_ in the _Parish_ of _Manchester_ in the County of _Lancaster_						
No.	When Married.	Name and Surname.	Age.	Condition.	Rank or Profession.	Residence at the Time of Marriage.	Father's Name and Surname.	Rank or Profession of Father.
319	May 13th 1847	George Mawer / Ann Scanlon	full / full	Bachelor / Spinster	Private in 50th Foot	39 Ryton Street / Ryton Street	Peter Mawer / Andrew Scanlon	Waterman / Gardener

Married in the _above Church_ according to the Rites and Ceremonies of the Established Church, _after Banns_ by me. _W. Wilson_

This Marriage was solemnized between us, _George Mawer_ / _Mark X of Ann Scanlon_ in the Presence of us. _David Anderson_ / _Jane Lambert_

George Mawer and Ann Scanlon's marriage registration, 13 May 1847

and walk out of the church into spring sunshine and a blizzard of rice.

The reception is on the upper floor of an inn opposite the church, where, out of his exiguous savings, George has paid for a barrel of porter to be opened. There is laughter and singing and the distinct promise of drunkenness to come but before that sets in the happy couple retire (cheers and applause), to spend the first night where she's been living, in a lodging house in Ryton Street, off Deansgate.* The room, up narrow stairs, is small and damp – little more than a hutch – but at least it is private. Once they move into barracks things will be different but for now, for this fragment snatched out of the ceaseless grind of time, they have themselves to each other. Their previous sexual encounters have been hurried, shameful things, like thieves exchanging booty. Now they have that wonder of physical revelation unhindered by fear of discovery or shame of transgression. Now it is legal within the context of God's law, her body and his body no longer things to be ashamed of but temples of worship. Didn't it say so in the marriage service – with my body I thee worship? Although neither really understands what that means, still it is with wonder that they undress each other, and surely wonder is good enough. She wonders at the strength of his body, its leanness, its sinews, its muscles; he wonders at the potent fragility of hers, that porcelain-white flesh, that rufous hair – a mane at her head, an insolent tuft at her crotch. In the narrow bed she lies on top of him and looks into his eyes, her blue against his brown, her lips on his, her small body clinging to him like a child clinging to its parent. Yet she's doing that thing with her hips, shifting against him, squeezing him, bringing him to the brink without, for the moment, tipping him over. "George Mawer," she tells him in that lilting Irish voice she has, "I love you. Do you know that? And unlike what I just said back there in church, I'm going to stay loving you even after we both shall live. How about that?"

"How will you do that then?" he asks.

---

* Ryton Street no longer exists, wiped out by the subsequent development of the centre of Manchester.

She giggles. "I'll come back and haunt you."

"And what if I die first?"

"I'll lie on your grave and weep for you."

Again, that little movement of her hips and the momentary grip. He draws in breath sharply.

"Do you like that, George Mawer?"

"I do."

"Well then." And she begins to rock back and forth, back and forth, cleverly, deftly, contracting the whole of his world down to this, her small figure astride him, her eyes like blue china watching him, this motion stirring a tide throughout his body. And then the convulsive moment of release that seems to embody everything that he thinks about her which is subsumed by the single word *love*.

"There," she says, breathing into his mouth. "Do you love me now, George Mawer?"

"I love you all the time, Ann Scanlon. But specially then."

She laughs. Another thing he loves about her – her laughter.

Getting married in a cathedral may sound grand and it is easy to imbue the couple with a certain romantic air – The Soldier and His Wife, another of those Victorian genre paintings, with the man decked out in meretricious finery and his woman draped on his arm like a damsel rescued from the jaws of distress. But in fact the wedding wasn't romantic at all and certainly not grand. Even today, Manchester Cathedral is little bigger than a parish church; at the time of their marriage – 1847, the year it officially became a cathedral – a parish church is precisely what it was. Although the parish had grown out of all proportion and boasted a population of almost two hundred thousand souls, legally it remained a single parish. To get married in a parish church cost three shillings and sixpence; to take advantage of the numerous chapels of ease that had been built to take the pressure off the central parish church, cost a further three and six. Thus, in order to avoid paying double, the poor and the indigent chose to marry in the parish church itself – the cathedral. And Private George Mawer was indigent. The Queen's shilling was literally true – as a private soldier he was paid a shilling a day at a time when a common labourer earned twice as much. So getting married in the new cathedral rather than in the church nearest the barracks was a cost-cutting exercise.

They move into barracks the next day, Ann's scant possessions wrapped in bundles and carried over George's shoulder. He's wearing uniform, of course, and she's in the dress she wore at their wedding, which is the only decent thing she has ever owned. They walk from the town centre out through mean streets to the barracks that lie on the borderline between town and country. The building resembles a prison or a workhouse. The same grim brickwork, the same regimented windows, the same locks and bars. Only that the guard on the gate salutes their arrival, crashing to attention and presenting arms as though the arrivals might be a senior officer and his lady.

It's a joke, of course. The men of the guard are from the 50th. They grin knowingly from beneath their gleaming shakoes, while Ann throws them a sarcastic curtsey. She will be able to survive her new life here. She knows these men, their needs and their fears, their loves and their lusts, because she has been following the troops ever since she has been able to shift for herself; but now, as a soldier's wife, she has acquired a certain status. She has a right to be there because Private George Mawer has married with the permission of the senior officer and so his wife will be "on the strength," entitled to reside in barracks with him, entitled to half rations herself, entitled to share a corner of the barrack room with her husband and make of it what she can – a married corner rather than a married quarter.

Through the gate the parade ground is an empty desert of beaten earth where hours are spent in the regimented tedium of drill. Drill lies at the core of every infantryman's life – the rigour of it, the crash of feet and arms, the *danse macabre* that may, perhaps, save lives in battle. There's a squad drilling now, recruits like George was mere months ago. A corporal bellows commands and the rookies march and wheel, form ranks, form lines, form squares, present arms, shoulder arms, port arms, perform strange geometries like the working of a complex automaton. For a while the newly married couple pause to watch, before skirting the space to reach the offices on the far side.

Beyond a portico that might grace the facade of a bank or a gentleman's club there's an oak-panelled entrance hall hung with portraits of bewigged and caparisoned officers. The Iron Duke is featured, of course. Retired from political life, he is still commander-in-chief of the British Army, which continues to manoeuvre nervously in his long shadow.

A sergeant chivvies Private George Mawer and his new wife into the office of the adjutant ("Step lively now! To attention!"). The adjutant is seated at his desk, with a portrait of the dowager Queen Consort, Adelaide, patron of the regiment, peering over his shoulder like a nanny keeping an eye on her charge. The officer looks the couple, especially the woman, up and down. He is a portly man, no more than forty but already looking ten years older. "So this is the good lady, is it?"

"Ann, sir," says George. "Ann Scanlon as was. Now Ann Mawer."

Ann gives a little bob. Somehow even that half-curtsey is laden with irony.

"I hope she won't make trouble in barracks."

"She's a well-behaved lass, sir."

"But are the *men* well-behaved? That's my point, soldier. We have had this conversation before, have we not? When you persuaded me to overcome my own disapproval and grant you permission to marry. She's a pretty young filly and I don't want any difficulties."

"Difficulties, sir?"

"You know what I mean, man. Jealousy, misunderstandings, that kind of thing. I don't want you having to defend your lady's honour or anything of that kind."

"You mean duelling, sir?"

"I mean *fighting*, private. Duelling's for officers."

Ann pipes up. She shouldn't, of course, but she does: "They won't be fighting over me, Captain. My George has already won that particular battle without a punch being thrown."

The adjutant turns indignant eyes back to her. "Madam, I was not talking to you."

"No sir, indeed you weren't, but you were talking *about* me, which comes to more or less the same thing."

There is a ghastly pause. The officer sucks his teeth and looks at the pair of them standing before him, the brilliant red macaw and the little egret. He might be wondering whether his powers to order a flogging extend to soldiers' women. "Your new wife has a tongue on her, Private Mawer."

"She does indeed, sir. I apologise on her behalf. She doesn't mean to be rude, it's just her Irish manner."

"Irish, is she? Not a papist, I hope. Don't want any popery in this regiment."

"We were wed in the cathedral, sir. Church of England."

"Good. Red hair is not a good sign, though. Temper like a she-devil, I don't doubt. Well, I wish you the best of luck with her. Beat her when she gets above herself and just remember to keep your soldiering first and your marriage second. It's a privilege to be allowed to marry, you know that."

"Yes, sir. Thank you, sir."

"Oh, and there's extra grog this evening, to celebrate the happy event." The adjutant nods to the couple, as though that settles all obligations. "You are dismissed."

They leave the office, Ann struggling with a fit of giggles.

"What a bloody eejit he is," she whispers. "I'll bet he'd love to give me a good hiding, eh? And what about you, George? When I do something wrong are you going to flog me like he said?"

"I might spank your bottom, Annie Mawer."

She laughs. "Just you try."

They make their way across the parade ground to the men's quarters. No wood panelling there. The men occupy a pauper's world of bare walls and cavernous rooms where beds are ranked like coffins in a mortuary, inches between. The rancid smell of unwashed bodies hangs about the place; and the stink of drains.

"Home sweet home," Ann says, contemplating the dormitory.

One of the other wives comes in with a basket of washing. She's loud and blowsy, on her second husband in the regiment, the first one having died in India the previous year. "Once you got your foot in the door you got to keep it there," she explains to anyone who asks. "Otherwise you're out on the street."

She dumps her washing in her corner of the dormitory. "Welcome to paradise, darling," she says to Ann. "Just remember: whatever they tell you, it's not a fucking privilege us being 'ere. They need us more 'n we need them, the single men as much as the husbands. For one thing or another." She begins to distribute laundry round the beds: shirts, stocks, drawers.

George and Ann take possession of their own place, a corner bed where George has already rigged up some kind of curtain to provide a modicum of privacy. They unpack Ann's few possessions, squirrelling them away in a cupboard George has found, or under the bed. Their married life will be lived there, in that corner. They will sleep, live, argue, make love and make plans there. So it was, in that bed, in the fetid heat of August 1847, as silently as they could manage with a barrack-room of men grunting and snoring around them, that their first child, Mary Ann, was conceived.

By the time of Mary Ann's birth the regimental depot had moved to Warrington, and George and Ann were living in a billet on Bridge Street. That is where the new baby was born. She was baptised on 5 May 1848 in the parish church. But it wasn't home – almost nowhere was home. By the summer they were moving across the country to the southeast, to Dover, where the 50th Regiment was regrouping. The ten line companies had been in India. Now they came back, shattered from the fighting on the Sutlej River in the First Sikh War, their nominal strength of 850 reduced by over half to 370 soldiers, ten drummers, twenty-six sergeants.

The task of the depot company had been to recruit and train new troops to replace those lost overseas. It was like feeding a monster, the ghastly imperial dragon that lay outside the village of England and devoured her sons as rapidly as they could be offered up. No appeasement seemed possible; the sacrifice had to go on and on. What no one could know in 1848 was that in a few years the devouring monster would move closer than either India or Africa and that its appetite would increase beyond all imagining.

Dover

A rivalry exists between the veterans of the fighting in India and the new recruits. The new recruits are "lilywhites" – usually, it must be said, "*fucking* lilywhites" – and despised for their innocence. The veterans are "old brownies," an epithet intended as an insult but actually carrying with it a modicum of admiration for their appearance of hardened, weathered wood and the fact that they have done what the new recruits have not – faced an enemy and lived to tell, sometimes at tiresome length, the tale.

Old brownies are invaluable on the range, where the recruits are taught the realities of musketry and the hideous immediacy of bayonet fighting. The veterans can give the reality, the finger-numbing panic as you go through the drill of reloading your musket while the enemy cavalry is thundering towards you, the hint that you don't always have to go by the book when things get desperate, that instead of using the ramrod to settle the ball down in the breech you can just tap the butt of your musket on the ground, tricks like that.

"Saves a couple of seconds," Sergeant Donnelly tells his little group of recruits, "but it may be those seconds that save your life. Just don't you dare do it when the sergeant's watching." Donnelly's Irish like so many of them and he can't articulate "th." Dis, dat and de udder, he says. The recent recruits, from Kent some of them, laugh behind his back. But you don't want to let him catch you laughing, because Sergeant Donnelly's temper is a thing of legend. Now they watch in dumb awe as he holds up a curious device, a small crucifix of steel, one arm of which bears a twisted corkscrew.

"Udder dan your fucking musket," he tells the group, "dis is your greatest fucking friend." He raises the object up for them to see. He might be elevating the host, such is the solemnity and the concentration. "And I can tell you it's not for opening fucking bottles of wine." He looks slowly round his audience, daring them to laugh. "What is it, Private Mawer?"

"It's a worm-and-nipple wrench, sergeant."

"It is indeed, a *worm* and *nipple wrench*," the sergeant repeats with relish. The recruits watch him with the fascination of children watching a snake charmer. (Sergeant Donnelly has told them about snake charmers in India.) "And if you bastard lilywhites don't pay close attention to what I've got to say, I'll stick the worm up your arse and wrench your fucking nipples with it."

How, Private Mawer wonders, is that anatomically possible? He gazes past Donnelly, past the edge of the white cliffs, across the waters of the Channel to where the continent of Europe lies on the horizon like a promised land. Despite being a fucking lilywhite, he is Sergeant Donnelly's assistant, chosen because the sergeant thinks him a little sharper than the rest. He has heard this ritual a dozen times by now and knows it by heart: this is the moment when he hands a musket to the sergeant. Taking the weapon and hefting it in his hand, Sergeant Donnelly continues the litany: "This is the pattern 1842 firelock, which you're already familiar with. The nipple is removed in this manner." He pulls back the hammer to half-cock, inserts the wrench into the breech gives a deft twist of the crucifix and the vital part, the nipple – a small, threaded

165

cylinder – is couched in his palm. "You may now ensure that the fire-hole is open by visual inspection." He holds the nipple aloft and squints through it as though it is a miniature telescope. Perhaps he can see the coast of France. "If you ascertain that the fire-hole is blocked by deposit from the combustion of the priming charge, then you employ the pricker to render said fire-hole open. Once completed, the nipple may be returned to the breech of the firelock, first ensuring that the thread is free of dirt."

A swift twist of his wrist and the nipple is back in place. He holds the musket up for inspection with a conjuror's flourish. "Now, my darling little lilywhites, you've got to be able to do that so automatic that in the event of you having a misfire during an action, while the whole of the rest of the battalion is blasting off around you and half a hundred fucking horses are charging at you with the sole intention of breaking your fucking skull in, you'll be able to clear your nipple and return it to your weapon so that you can continue to blast the fucking hell out of the bastard enemy."

As always, the recruits don't know whether to laugh or cry. They fumble and fiddle, drop nipples on the grass, drop muskets, drop worm-and-nipple wrenches, eventually attain some kind of proficiency in the matter. The lesson continues.

"Next. Next we have hextraction of a jammed ball. Have you ever had a jammed ball, Private Jellicoe? I'm sure you haven't. Too bloody small to get it jammed in anything, I shouldn't wonder."

The litany is repeated, the same jokes, the same threats. The recruits struggle to repeat the next manoeuvre, the "hextraction of a jammed ball," while Private Mawer goes round to assist them. He's content enough. He can detach his mind from the here and now and think of other matters. The baby, of course, little Mary Ann, now two months old, a squalling

166

brat who keeps her mother awake at night. There's a room in barracks given over to wives on the strength, over a dozen of them, most with children. It's a kind of Bedlam, a place of over-wrought emotions and lost tempers; but at least there are occasions when Ann can slip out of the women's quarters and visit him in the men's dormitory. For the moment this is the only way that his fragile family can exist, symbiotically on the body of the regiment. The town itself isn't bad but they can't afford a room there, full as it is with the Navy as well as the Army. Dover, Dovor, with its houses crowded between cliffs that are the last slice of England, is another world from Lancashire. Softer somehow. Lancashire air is sour and harsh, tainted with the smoke of burning coal. Here the air is clear and clean. People even go sea-bathing hereabouts. His company tried it after a route march eastwards to St. Margaret's Bay, grown men as naked as the day they were born, laughing and splashing in the waves. One or two could even swim, which was remarkable. People of the town, southron folk, laugh at the way they speak, these soldiers from the north. Lobsters, they call them. No one likes soldiers much, but the Dovorians are happy enough to take the lobster's shilling off him.

Who knows how long the 50th will be here? The regiments lead a nomadic life, shifting from pillar to post with all accoutrements and materiel, with baggage and wives and camp followers. A new town and new quarters every few months. "Here we fucking go again," men mutter as they pack up their things. Few possessions. Regimental necessities – uniform and one change – and all the other stuff: mess tins; knife, fork and spoon; a few trinkets; a pen if you can write.

"Where the fuck is it this time?" they ask, some with resignation, others with anticipation.

There's method in this incessant movement although the

men usually just accept it as one of the vagaries of military life. But when he's in his cups in the Red Lion, Sergeant Donnelly makes the reason clear enough: "We're the only way they can keep control o' the people," he says. He drinks whiskey, Irish whiskey, chased down with beer. "If they keep moving us around, we're always strangers wherever we go, so they think we'll have no fear about shooting a few poor muftees to keep the mob quiet. That's the truth of it. No different in India. Shoot a few Hindoos to keep the rest under control."

Private Mawer brings his mind back to the present, to Sergeant Donnelly, sober Sergeant Donnelly, coming to the end of his routine instruction on the intricacies of the worm-and-nipple wrench: "And now I'd dismiss you all, except that you are such a miserable shower of lilywhites that Private Mawer will march you back to barracks and give you an hour of foot drill just to drum your stupidity into your thick heads. Do you understand that?"

They bleat back at him in approximate unison: "Yes, sergeant!"

"I don't enjoy doin' this no more than you do," he continues. "So I'm damn well going to make it misery for you, just so I can feel better. Is that clear?"

"Yes, sergeant!"

The baby – Mary Ann – is four months old. As tough and insistent as her mother, she promises to defy the statistics and survive (she does, dying in 1934 at the age of eighty-five). When she wants feeding, she screws up her face and squalls; when she is content, she sleeps and occasionally thrills her parents with a smile like the sun breaking through clouds.

In her old age, Mary Ann would have recalled nothing of Dover in 1848. She might not even have known that she had once lived there. Certainly, she'd have known nothing of Major Petit purchasing his lieutenant-colonelcy and succeeding to the command of the regiment; nor of the King and Queen of the Belgians landing at Dover at the start of a state visit, to be greeted by the band of the 50th Regiment and a guard of honour that included her father; nor that, one wintry day in December, the Duke of Wellington, the greatest Englishman of all time and by then Warden of the Cinque Ports, also visited the town and was similarly received by a parade of the 50th. Nor would she have known anything of the squalor of life in the barracks where she and her parents lived. She'd have had no memory of her mother laundering the men's clothes to earn extra pence. She'd have had no memory of the stench of the latrines and the filth of the washrooms. She'd have had no memory of the smell of meat boiling in vast tubs for the daily meal, the same each day, meat and bread with any vegetables at the soldiers' personal expense.

Nor would she have known that in September, in the grunting, stinking darkness of the barrack room, her younger sibling was conceived.

Georgiana

Mary Ann was a bright three-year-old when the regiment moved from Dover to Portsea, old enough to begin to lay down those memories that might last into adulthood. Did she remember that her mother was eight months pregnant by then? Swollen-bellied Ann endured an interminable journey by train, traipsing across the southeast of England as far as Guildford where they waited while carriages were shunted around and connected to another engine for the journey south.

A small entourage of anxious wives fuss around the pregnant woman. Pains have started, lancing across the dome of her abdomen. The women help her into the carriage. Exhausted but unable to sleep, she lies across one of the wooden benches while the other women tend her, bathe her forehead to cool her down, feed her soaked biscuit to keep her strength up, console her when the pains come. The senior sergeant's wife has taken command. Soldiers' wives pay obedience to her orders just as their husbands do to her husband, the ranking of the men exactly mirrored by the ranking of their women.

"Give me some water. She needs water."

"We don't have water. It's finished."

"I don't care if it's finished. Bring it!"

The same sharp retorts, the same demands, the same manner.

Mary Ann watches the fussing round her mother, feeling a vague, unfocused fear. The train trundles south, the motion somehow absorbed into the mother's body as though rocking her to sleep. But soon enough such temporary relief is cast aside: Portsmouth station is a place of din and confusion, hundreds of troops descending onto the platform, women hurrying round Ann and her daughter. George appears, looking anxious, then goes away on men's business. Baggage is being loaded onto carts. There is shouting, a shrieking whistle, the concussion of steam engines. And then they set off to walk through the streets of the strange town, following the baggage over the bridge and through the Lion Gate to where Anglesey Barracks stands just inside the walls.

The baby is born in a back room in the barracks, a small shred of a thing slipping out into the world in silence. The midwife – the sergeant's wife – cuts the umbilical cord and holds the infant up by the ankles like a piece of raw flesh hung in a butcher's shop. Another girl. Inert. The woman flicks the baby's buttocks, then lies her down, bends over her and blows gently into her mouth. There is faint movement. A quiver of the fragile basketwork of ribs. And then a small mewing.

The sergeant's wife looks up. "Thought she might be gone for a moment but she'll do."

The baby's hopeless wail grows in rhythm. It is like the cry of a distant seabird across the marshes of Portsea and Hayling Island, a plaintive call for help in a desolate world. They wrap her in a towel and lay her on her mother's belly for warmth and comfort, and then, once everything is settled and the child is breathing normally, the father is allowed in to see his second child.

*

A few days later, the baby was baptised in the nearby St. John's Church: Georgiana.

The timeline of Georgiana Mawer's existence on earth:

- January 1851. Travels north from Portsea to Burnley in the train of the 50th Regiment, along with her mother and older sister.
- 30 March 1851. Entered into the national census as resident in the Burnley Barracks – *Georgiana Mawer, one year old, soldier's child, born Portsea, Hampshire.*
- January 1852. Dies aged eighteen months old.

Georgiana Mawer's death certificate

Imagine a cold day in Stalybridge, the very depths of winter. New St. George's cemetery. Trees twig bare; crows circling in the wind; a hint of snow. The gravediggers struggled to break the turf but now their work is complete: a tiny grave gapes open to the air beside its little pile of vomited earth. Around it, mourners, nine of them, stamp their feet and blow on their fingers. Breath rises in clouds like musket smoke. The men – half a dozen – are in uniform, the father proudly sporting his brand-new corporal's chevrons (pay, 1s 4d per week) as well as his five-year good-conduct stripe (1d supplement per week) on his right forearm. Corporal George Mawer is going up in the military world. He looks smart: bandoleers pipe-clayed, brasses gleaming, shako shone. Smart is an alternative to desolation. Beside him, the three women present are uniform in their drabness, in the browns and greys of poverty. The mother holds the hand of her remaining daughter, Mary Ann, three years old. Mary Ann will recall this as a moment frozen in memory, without context or meaning: a group of people, a hole in the ground. Nothing more. No rhyme, no reason.

The tiny coffin is lowered into the grave while the priest intones, "Forasmuch as it hath pleased Almighty God of his great mercy to take unto himself the soul of our dear sister here departed, we therefore commit her body to the ground."

It hath *pleased* Almighty God? But no one questions the words. The Lord giveth and the Lord taketh away; blessed be the name of the Lord. The priest nods towards him and George casts earth onto the coffin, a rattle of stones like the distant rattle of musketry. Then, almost as though he is on parade, he steps back to the side of his wife and takes her hand. Although her loose and shapeless dress more or less hides the fact, Ann Mawer is already six months pregnant.

One dies, another comes along.

George Henry

Movement, incessant movement, as though the Army suffered from some kind of hyperactive disorder. Forever packing up kit and loading it onto carts for transport to the railway. Forever setting off. Long distance was travelled by train but much movement was marching along dusty roads, a great snake of red-jacketed men with the band at the front. Fifes and drums. Colours flying. More circus than war machine. They were in Burnley Barracks in 1851 but by 1852, in time to bury Georgiana at Ashton Barracks in Ashton-under-Lyne. Three months later, when the next child was born, they were at Fulwood Barracks outside Preston. And the new baby was a boy.

Proud, Corporal George? Of course he was proud. Puffed up like a turkey cock, he was. A boy! A boy meant you were a man. A girl was all well and good – a silent, thoughtful creature Mary Ann was, and intelligent no doubt – but a boy! That was altogether another thing. "Congratulations, George," said Sergeant Donnelly. They were in the NCOs' room, drinking beer. George had been pacing up and down throughout the confinement and only now sat down and relaxed. "A boy," he said. "Bloody marvellous."

Later he was allowed in to see Ann and the baby. Ann was looking drained, as though she'd just been on a forced march in the rain, her hair plastered across her forehead, her face drawn, her pallid skin slick with sweat. But her eyes – as bright as ice – shone through all that. She was, as Porrick Donnelly said, a tough one. So too was the baby, another scrap of flesh, but a ruddy scrap, fixed to its mother's breast. "What'll we call him, Annie?" George asked. "Andrew?"

She smiled. "My old devil of a father? I don't want to be reminded of him every time I look at him. Let's call him George, like you." If you cannot have Georgiana you can have George. "And Henry. George Henry."

"Why Henry?"

Those eyes, shining. "So he'll not answer to George alone. So he'll know it's you I'm shouting at."

Thus to the monotony of garrison life was added this small excitement, the birth of a boy to Corporal and Mrs. George Mawer. "A new recruit for the Dirty Half-Hundred," Sergeant Donnelly joked. For Ann the priority became tending to the baby. Cleaning, cooking for her husband, doing laundry for the men – a source of extra pennies for the family – became secondary. The important thing was to avoid a further death. For the father, life continued more or less the same as before: parade, musket drill, foot drill, inspections, more foot drill, running defaulters, more musket drill, more parade, picket duty in the town: all those things that keep active hundreds of young, ill-educated, underpaid men – those whom the Duke of Wellington, the greatest Englishman of all time, described as "the scum of the earth."

It's hard to know what had brought George Mawer down to this life, but there he is with his wife, Ann Mawer, née Scanlon, and their two children, Mary Ann, five, and newborn George Henry, a small family living in barracks, like animals on a giant tree nesting in whatever hole they can find.

Scum?

If the Iron Duke said it, it must be true.

Scum.

No real surprise then that the soldiers of the British Army, often drunk, often whoring, often diseased, trained for violence, were treated like shit and their wives were considered sluts.

A soldier and his woman, and their two brats.

The Wigan Riot

Sergeant Padraig Donnelly, the veteran Sergeant Donnelly, the hardened old brownie that he was, had approved of George's promotion to corporal. Grudgingly, of course, but with agreement. "Corporal's chevrons are all very well, George, but let's see you when it's kill or be killed. That's when you earn your stripes, me lad." He'd taken to George and his wife, almost becoming like a father to them and a grandfather to the children. "I know a good Irish woman when I see one," he said of Ann. "The salt of the earth." Perhaps it was also that Ann cooked for him often and did his laundry for a pittance, perhaps it was that. You always have to unpick the skein of human motives to try and tease out the threads. Donnelly was a rebel, he was loyal; he was tough, he was soft. He'd fought like a lion on the Sutlej, gutted Sikhs with his bayonet, saved the captain's life at the Battle of Ferozeshah, taken up the colours when the colour sergeant was killed at the final assault, all that kind of thing. He had a medal to prove it, with clasps for Aliwal and Sobraon to go with Ferozeshah, and the evidence on his body – two fingers missing, livid scars on his chest; but he half-sympathised with the men he'd killed and hated the Indian government in whose name he'd killed them.

"John fucking Company?" he'd say when he was in his cups. "A load of thieving, capitalist bastards."

Of course, talk like this wasn't welcomed by the officers – he'd earned good-conduct stripes and had them removed, gained sergeant's stripes and lost them once before; but no one could question his courage or his loyalty to the regiment. And there were plenty of others of his kind who didn't hold themselves together so well. Drunks, most of them, one or two deserters, the ruined relics of wars fought far away and out of sight. From time to time pickets were sent out into the town (once all the way to Coventry, another time to Lancaster) to bring them in. Often Donnelly was detailed to help because they respected him and would often come quietly when he appeared.

"The poor bugger's gone off the rails," he'd say, ushering a wretched prisoner into the guardroom. "But at least Colonel Petit's not a flogger, thank God."

Now he was reminiscing with George, swilling beer down and letting his mind wander from the Punjab to his home in Donegal to Preston, where they found themselves now and had been before. "Remember Dover, George? When was it? Two year ago? When you were just a new lilywhite, trying to help out with arms drill. Time flies, doesn't it? That's what they say. And look where we've been since – Portsea, Burnley, Ashton and now Fulwood. And you've had two kids in the meantime—"

"Three."

"Yes, well, of course there was the little one. Mustn't forget Georgina, must we?"

"Georgiana."

"Of course. Georgiana. Bless her. But my point is, we've never bloody stopped moving, have we? All over the bloody country. Did I ever tell you why they move us around like fucking pawns on a chessboard?"

"A hundred times, Porrick."

"And why would that be?"

"To keep us from going native, Porrick."

"Exactly right, George. Always strangers, that's what we are. Always fucking strangers, wherever we find ourselves. Now this place? What's it called?"

"Preston."

"Preston, indeed. Never heard of it. Why do they want us here, George?"

"Because of the Chartists, Porrick?"

"You couldn't be more right. Clever lad, you are. No wonder you got your stripes."

It was then that the colour sergeant burst into the NCOs' room to see who was up. Outside, as though to announce his entry, a bugle sounded.

"Call out!" the colour sergeant announced. "5 and 6 Companies under arms, double quick!"

George got up from his chair and began pulling on his jacket. Donnelly stayed seated. "A call out? At this time of night?"

"The time of night's got nothing to do with it, Porrick. There's a riot of some kind. Now jump to it!"

There was shouting in other parts of the building, footsteps, doors slamming, men shouting and that bloody bugle calling like a strangled dog. Donnelly remained stolidly in his chair. "A riot, you say? At eleven o'clock at night?"

"In Wigan, so Captain Frampton said. The bloody Irish, so he said. Catholics and Orangemen fighting and breaking the place up."

Donnelly stiffened, holding up his ruined hand, the one with the conspicuous absence of two fingers. "Now wait a minute. They're my people you're talking about there. You'll not be asking me to go all the way to Wigan in order to shoot my own kind, will you?"

"There'll not be any shooting, Porrick. Just a bit of sabre-rattling."

Donnelly laughed humourlessly. "I'll bet that's what they told the dragoons before Peterloo. A bit o' sabre-rattling."

"Are you refusing to obey orders? That could get you on a charge. A court martial even. Lose your stripes. Again."

Donnelly took a swig from his beer. "'Course I'm not. I'm telling you I'm feeling poorly, and you're going to agree that poor old Porrick Donnelly isn't quite himself this evening, and that'll be that. Meanwhile my old friend George here is as bright as a farthing. He comes from Lincolnshire, so he doesn't give a damn about the Irish and their troubles."

So it was that, at eleven-thirty at night, two companies of the 50th (Queen's Own) Regiment of Foot formed up on the parade ground of Fulwood Barracks under Major Waddy and marched down to Preston railway station where a special train had been cobbled together to take them to Wigan. It was a deployment of the utmost speed: the *London Daily News* reported that the 50th was drawn up in Wigan's Market Place by half past midnight.*

Although it was the middle of the night, a small crowd of townspeople turned out to cheer the arrival of the troops. 6 Company was detailed off to guard prisoners in the Town Hall and the Moot Hall, while 5 Company was drawn up in the station yard for an address by Major Waddy.

The 50th was there to keep the peace, he explained. It was a noble calling. The 50th fought with honour on the Sutlej. Men died, men were wounded, but they died or suffered wounds in the cause of civilisation. And now they were here to guard that civilisation.

"Kill the fucking Catholics!" an Irish voice called from

---

* *London Daily News*, 10 July 1852.

the crowd. There was laughter, cheering, angry muttering among the soldiers, half of whom were Irish, three-quarters of whom were Catholic. Captain Frampton, hero of the Sutlej, the empty left arm of his tunic pinned heroically to his breast, took Major Waddy's place before the troops.

"We are here to act without fear or favour," he told them. "Neither Protestant nor Catholic, neither Irishman, Scotchman, Welshman or Englishman, but all loyal subjects of Her Majesty the Queen."

There was a bit of a cheer at that. Her Majesty the Queen? Seems all right. Is she anything to do with the Queen's Own Regiment?

Different queen. But similar.

With the colour sergeant calling time, with bayonets fixed and Corporal Mawer as right marker, the company marched out of the station yard down King Street and into Scholes Road. Silence now reigned where, so they were informed, the riot had taken place. Gaslight created pale puddles in the dark. The column tramped its way through the night, immersed in the thrill of the march. However much they might complain about it, they couldn't deny it: the rhythm was in their bones, submerging the individual in the collective until they became the muscles and sinews of a great snaking beast, winding through the Scholes district, stamping the rule of law on the place. Windows opened as they passed by; pale, anxious faces peered out to see what was going on. Someone cheered. Someone else shouted, "We're trying to sleep!" But the column marched on remorselessly, wheeling right into Union Street where the Catholics lived and where the road-way was still littered with bricks and broken tiles. Broken glass crunched underfoot. In these houses no one moved. No candlelight, no lamplight glimmered. The company marched on, turned right and right again and came back on itself. By quarter to two in the morning they were back at the station. Job well done.

"So how was it, George?" Donnelly asked the next morning. They were polishing their kit for parade, pipe-claying belts, blacking boots. "Shoot any Catholics?"

"We didn't see any Catholics."

"I'm not surprised at that. By nine o'clock all good Catholics are tucked up in bed."

"We marched round the streets a bit, bayonets fixed."

"Bayonets fixed, indeed! I'll bet that was old one-arm Frampton, wasn't it? Our pet hero loves the glint of steel." He stood up and fastened his belt and bandoleer.

George watched him. "How long, Porrick?"

"How long what?"

"The regiment's almost up to strength, isn't it?"

The Irishman laughed. "Eager for a bit of real action, are you? Let me tell you, George, best enjoy the peace and quiet while it lasts. Enjoy the comforts of your lovely lady wife. Enjoy your children. Enjoy marching up and down empty streets in England pretending you are tough and brave. Don't wish too hard for excitement or it may come and bite you in the balls."

Excitement would come, of course. If you have a historical bent you only have to look at the dates. Excitement is there, just months ahead. But for the moment, the soldiery in their meretricious uniforms can whitewash over the dirt in barracks and overlay the stench of urine and ordure with coal smoke and pretend that all's right with the world. This is made even more obvious when the order comes for the Army – or much of the Army – to assemble at Chobham Common for the Great Camp.

Windsor

She's lying on top of him. They're in that small space of fragile privacy created by a curtain across the corner of the barrack room. Beyond the curtain lie the double ranks of soldiers, snoring in the darkness. One or two lie awake, listening. George knows what they do. He can hear the grunting begin when he and Ann start, the rhythmic shifting of the beds keeping time, more or less. It made him angry at first, but she laughed at his concern. "Leave them alone, poor boys," she said. "They've got nothing better to do."

Now she just shifts her hips across his in that way she has and breathes her question into his mouth. "How long will you be away?"

"A month. The first night in billet in Windsor, that's the plan. And the next day we march out to the camp. The rest of the time we'll be under canvas. I've already told you this."

"A month." That hint of accusation.

"It's not my fault. Blame the Queen."

"What's it got to do with the Queen?"

"And that German fella she's got. They say it's his idea."

She breathes laughter in the darkness. There is that intense closeness to him. Her words in his mouth, her hands on his chest, her legs astride. "You know what they say about her?"

"What do they say?"

"They say she does all sorts of things for him."

"Like what?"

"I'll show you." She slides down the bed. He can feel her by his thighs. Her touch, her mouth on him. Part of him wonders where she learned these things, most of him doesn't care. But he doubts that the Queen does *this* with that German fella. Doesn't seem very queenly.

All around them the darkness stirs, like an animal half-asleep but aware of what is going on.

They are up early the next morning, bugles blowing reveille and the whole regiment on parade in the thin, morning drizzle, all seven hundred drawn up by companies with sergeants scurrying round them like dogs herding sheep. A small crowd of women and children gathers at the edges of the parade ground to watch, Ann with George Henry clinging to her skirts and four-year-old Mary Ann holding her hand. "Where's Papa going?" the girl asks.

"I told you – he's going to play at soldiers."

"Will he come back?"

"Of course he'll come back. It's just play."

The regiment comes to attention with a rattle that sounds like ragged musket fire. "Fiftieth!" bellows the regimental sergeant major. "By companies, quick march!"

In blocks of seventy men, with fifes playing, drums beating and the regimental colours flying, the regiment marches off the parade ground towards the gate.

"There's Papa!" Mary Ann cries as 5 Company moves off. "Papa!"

But Papa doesn't hear her piping voice, or if he does he takes no notice, looking stolidly ahead from beneath his shako as the company tramps away through the gate and onto the Preston Road.

"Did Papa see me?" the little girl asks, looking up at her mother.

"I'm sure he saw you. He just has to keep looking ahead. That's the rule."

And then: "Are you crying, Mama?"

Of course Mama isn't crying. That's also the rule. "Let's go inside," she says, brushing rain from her cheek. "We're getting wet and they've all gone now."

"When will Papa come back?"

"In a few days. And until then we'll have a bit of peace and quiet." She hefts George Henry onto her hip, takes her daughter's hand and follows the straggle of women back to their quarters, quarters which, for a month, they will have to themselves. With the departure of the men, the rooms are silent, abandoned, tainted only by the lingering smell of male sweat.

At the station a special train is waiting for the men of the 50th. They laugh and joke as they climb aboard. NCOs shout commands. Officers look the other way, wondering how they can get breakfast and where their kit has got to. It is twenty minutes before the train moves off, gathering pace on even ground, rocking from side to side and struggling with its load as it climbs out of the Ribble Valley trailing a long plume of smoke. Throughout the day it traipses across the English countryside with the soldiers' mood slowly degenerating from excited and animated to bored and fractious. "Are we there yet, corporal?" they ask, in the petulant whine of children. By the time they reach Windsor the holiday atmosphere has worn off. It's a relief to climb down from the carriages into the dank evening and stretch their legs. They sling their knapsacks, grab their firelocks and get fell in on the station forecourt. It's still raining. A crowd of townspeople have gathered to gawp, but not many. Familiar enough with the Foot Guards,

185

this is the first time they have seen a line regiment quartered in their town.

> . . . the 50th were objects of considerable curiosity with the multitude. The men had encountered a long journey, but they looked uncommonly well, and would evidently prove very troublesome customers in front of the enemy. Indeed, we have it on the authority of the innkeepers that they were not the most pleasant visitors imaginable when quartered on their friends. Without going into detail, we may say that the conduct of most of them was so unaccommodating and extortionate that the publicans contemplate memorializing the Horse Guards on the subject.*

Some seven hundred men introduced into a town of about nine thousand inhabitants, one for every twelve locals. Not a good idea. Soldiers were billeted all over the place – in the upstairs rooms of public houses, in the empty stables of coaching inns, in boarding houses. They ate, they drank. As the evening wore on, they sang. Later and in the rain, groups of them ignored the curfew and wandered the streets looking for more beer to swill and women to bed. They fornicated in back alleys. They vomited in the gutters. The NCOs spent much of the night leading pickets through the poorer parts, digging men out of beer houses and driving them back to their billets. The more egregious miscreants, a dozen of them, were confined in the railway station under the aegis of Sergeant Donnelly and the dutiful Corporal George Mawer.

---

* *Windsor and Eton Express*, 18 June 1853. In those days "Horse Guards" was used metonymically for Army headquarters.

"Detain them until the morning," was the order, conveyed to Sergeant Donnelly along with the regimental defaulters book. The order came from on high, from the battalion major to the 5 Company commander, from the 5 Company commander to a young subaltern called Dashwood, from Dashwood to the sergeant, down the military pyramid which all too often appears inverted.

"Excuse me, sor," said Sergeant Donnelly with elaborate politeness as they herded the miscreants into the station waiting room. "As we are on detachment, does this qualify as detention in the guard house, in which case there is an obligation to enter the soldiers' names in the defaulters book as guilty of a misdemeanour. Or does it merely qualify as confinement to barracks, in which case—"

"Just do as you are told, sergeant," Dashwood commanded in his piping voice. He had just purchased his commission and hadn't yet understood that running a platoon of soldiers was rather different from ordering the labourers around on his father's estate.

"Of course, sor. I'm just wanting to get everything clear as required in Queen's Regulations. Detention in the guard house or—"

A frantic look came into the lieutenant's eyes. "Are you stupid, sergeant? Just use your judgement, man."

"Yes, sor. Thank you sor."

The subaltern went off to the White Hart Hotel where his fellow officers were billeted and he could expect a glass of brandy as a nightcap before retiring to a comfortable feather bed.

"Stupid bugger," Donnelly confided to George. "Confinement to barracks for drunkenness means they'll be dealt with by their company commanders. Detention in the Black Hole is a battalion offence with a full report to the colonel. You've got to be alert to these matters, George. You know what my old mother used to say? There's none so stupid as them as thinks they're clever. Now you write their names in the good book. You've a better hand than me."

George took the defaulters book and duly wrote across the top of the page, to Donnelly's dictation: *confinement in the Black Hole on the authority of Lieutenant Dashwood.* And beneath it the name and company of each of the now-contrite miscreants. "There," Donnelly said with evident pleasure, "That'll cause the little prick no end of bother."

It was an uneasy night. The men lay on the floor, unconscious or asleep it was impossible to tell. The two NCOs took the dubious luxury of the wooden benches that were the sole furnishing of the station waiting room. Some time in the middle of the night the miscreants in the waiting room were woken from their sleep by the distant sound of drums. Peering through the windows, George could see a rusty glow on the underside of the cloud. "Looks like a fire," he said.

Donnelly turned over on his bench. "Is it nearby?"

"Some way away."

"Then let the bugger burn. Someone else will deal with it." He went back to sleep. That was the capacity of the veteran, to fall asleep wherever and whenever the opportunity arose. George stayed watching until the angry red above the houses died away. Then he too slept some more, but uneasily, wondering whether they should have gone to help.

Outside the windows – grimy, streaked with condensation and coal dust – daylight bled uncertainly into the dark. Curtains of drizzle hung in the air. While the defaulters of the 50th were waking up and struggling to get themselves into some kind of order, a train drew into the station with a flurry of steam and a shrill whistle.

George peered out through the windows. All along the platform carriage doors were opening and soldiers were climbing down. Stretching their legs and scratching themselves, they looked around like animals newly emerged from their nests.

"Bearskins," George reported.

"Guards," said Donnelly.

"Red plumes."

Donnelly joined him at the window. "The Coldstream. Haven't been out of barracks since Waterloo."

Stuff was being handed down to the guardsmen – belts, knapsacks, firelocks. They heaved on their kit, adjusted their ridiculous headgear and moved off the platform into the station yard where they formed up in immaculate companies. From the safety of their temporary prison, the miscreants of the 50th watched, muttering. "Fucking ponces," one of them said.

"Keep your bloody mouths shut," growled Donnelly. "These fellows could eat you alive and not even belch."

The muttering stopped. Donnelly was wearing his medal, the Sutlej medal, with three clasps. They all knew how he had earned them so they listened to him and did what he said, particularly now that the alcohol had worn off and headaches and contrition had set in.

Outside, the Coldstream slammed to attention. Drums beat and the band began to play. Despite the early hour, people had already gathered. The crowd cheered. The band struck up "The Girl I Left Behind Me" and like a giant hairy caterpillar, the battalion turned left and marched away.

That was the moment when the waiting room door opened to reveal, like the devil in a pantomime, the assistant stationmaster. His uniform was almost as resplendent as a guardsman's. His face, set about with whiskers and self-importance, was stern. In his time he had been presented to the Queen and her German princeling, to presidents and prime ministers and visiting dignitaries of every imaginable nature. He was not accustomed to dealing with drunken soldiery. He said, with heavy sarcasm, "You *gentlemen* had better move on. I've got a railway to run. And I'd like to see the place left in a condition suitable for the travelling public, if you don't mind. Otherwise I will have to report the fact to Horse Guards."

Sergeant Donnelly turned to his little gang. "Right, you horrible lot, you heard what this gentleman with the important uniform said. You are going to clear his sitting room up so that his lady wife may come in here and do her knitting in peace. Do I make myself understood?"

The door slammed shut.

"And then me and the corporal here are going to form you up and march you into town. You may have let yourselves down last night but I'll be buggered if you're going to let me down now. So I'm expecting you as sharp and shining as a bayonet, buttons fastened, stocks done up tight. Am I understood? In fact, we'll march with bayonets fixed and we'll look just as good as the Coldstream. Pretend you're the regimental colour guard rather than a load of drunken sots."

Thus, in the wake of the Coldstream, the defaulters of the 50th (Queen's Own) Regiment of Foot formed up and made their way to the centre of the town. Initially they benefitted from the precedence of the Guards – the townsfolk lining the street cheered them as though they might be guardsmen themselves. Bunting was waved. "Hip-hip-hurrah!" sounded out. But quite soon recognition dawned. "Them's the Fiftieth!" someone called out. "Drunken bastards!" These were not gallant guardsmen at all but the shabby line regiment that had disturbed their night's sleep. There were boos and whistles. A stone was thrown, skittering harmlessly over the cobbles.

"Steady there!" called Donnelly to the squad. He might have been dealing with a skittish horse. "They're not firing ball. It's just bloody pebbles."

And then Corporal George had his little stroke of unconventional brilliance. "On the march," he called out, "squad will present arms. Present ... ARMS!"

And they did it. Nothing in the Field Exercise and Evolutions of the Army to suggest that such a manoeuvre might be acceptable but the squad of miscreants from the 50th did what they were told as though they had practised it for days beforehand – they brought their muskets, bayonets flashing, off the slope and up to the present, vertically in front of them as though to salute the onlookers. The crowd cheered. The squad held the present for ten paces before George brought them back to the slope. Applause broke out among the crowd. In the eyes of the people of Windsor, the Dirty Half-Hundred had, perhaps, become the Glorious Half-Hundred.

"A good trick you pulled off there, George," Donnelly said when they reached the Town Hall, where the regiment was mustering.

"Thank you, sergeant."

"Next time you take command of my squad without asking, I'll kick you in the goolies."

"Yes, sergeant."

Around them drums were rattling, a band was playing, regimental colours were flying. Despite the drizzle, there was a holiday atmosphere about the town. Even the castle, looming out of the lowering clouds, was emblazoned with flags and giving a fair impression of Camelot. NCOs marched around like clockwork automatons, stamping their feet and chivvying the soldiers into ranks. The officers stood where they could be admired by the ladies of the town. The band played "The Lass of Richmond Hill." It was all rather like one of those fashionable coastal resorts one heard about – Brighton or Eastbourne.

Donnelly reported to the adjutant and handed over the defaulters book. The major peered at George's entries. "Oh dear, it does look as though Mr. Dashwood has put them all on a charge."

"It does indeed, sor."

"Seems a bit fierce."

"I did warn him, sor, but he thought it necessary. For the honour of the regiment, I suppose."

"I suppose so, sergeant. Well, he'll have no end of a fuss and bother with the paperwork, especially as they all come from different companies."

"Indeed, sor."

He snapped the book shut. "The enthusiasm of youth, eh sergeant?"

"I'm thinking that myself, sor."

Lieutenant Dashwood was detailed off to take charge of the defaulters. He looked furious. "What's this all about, sergeant?"

A bugle blew. The RSM bellowed, "Fiftieth, by companies, get fell in!"

Donnelly shrugged. "The way of the world, Mr. Dashwood, the way of the world. And now, if you'll excuse me ... "

He took his place with 5 Company, giving that sly smile when he caught George's eye. The band struck up "Lillibulero" and finally the order was given to march. The colonel and his staff, mounted on horseback like Wellington's generals at Waterloo and doffing their caps to the applause of the crowd, clattered off down the street towards the Long Walk and the Great Park. Behind them, almost as an afterthought, came the companies of the 50th Regiment of Foot.

There was less spruceness in their gait than the Guards, and not so much splendour in their appointments, but there was more of the rough and ready soldier in their appearance, and the many medals worn by the privates and non-commissioned officers showed that the regiment had passed through the perils of the Sikh war, and won their laurels on the blood-stained banks of the Sutlej.*

The drizzle turned to rain. They marched and they marched and the rain came down. The band played anything from the "British Grenadiers" to "Coming Through the Rye," and the men sang and cursed and still it rained. They stopped to piss in the bushes and fill their water bottles from the water wagon – the *pane wallah* as the veterans of the Sutlej called it – and still the rain came down. "You 'aven't seen the bloody monsoon," the NCOs said, getting them back into ranks. "*Jildi! Jildi!*" they shouted to get them moving again. The lilywhites cursed them for being bloody Hindoos.

And still it rained.

---

* *Windsor and Eton Express*, 18 June 1853, writing of the 50th. The account of the defaulters of the 50th detained in the station house also comes from this newspaper.

The Great Camp

In domesticated southern England, the low, dull heathland of Chobham Common is still what passes for wild country. Although surrounding towns, with their housing estates and golf courses, have encroached on it and the M3 motorway now cuts across it, the poor, acid soil of the heath guarantees that it has never been turned into farmland. Even in the twenty-first century the common still keeps much of its integrity, which is the integrity of the impoverished who have nothing left to lose. In the early summer of 1853, as half the British Army converged on it for the Great Camp, the common was almost a wilderness.

It had already rained for days and was raining still yet much of fashionable London turned out to watch. For the first time, but not the last, the few roads across the common were jammed with traffic:

> Along the road, towards the camp common, and as far back as the eye could reach, was one contin-uous line of pedestrians and equestrians, soldiers and civilians, horses, carriages, and men, all moving slowly but steadily forward. The return from the Derby, though no doubt more numerous, was not to be compared to the aspect which this

road presented. There were carriages and four, and costermongers' carts, donkeys and blood-horses intermixed, squadrons of the 17th Lancers and companies of the Rifle Brigade, with scattered parties of the 50th and 38th Regiments, vans conveying the effects of the officers, carts laden with forage for the horses and straw for the tents, drays of huge barrels of beer for the men, and hampers of wine for the mess-tents, gentlemen guiding mounted ladies out of the press, buglers blowing themselves hoarse with signal notes, to which none seemed to pay the least attention, officers rushing here and there collecting two men and losing three, and calling upon them to fall in or fall out as the necessities of the case seemed to require; all at once combined to form a coup d'oeil of brilliant confusion, such as we have very rarely witnessed.*

It was into this farrago, this combination of military tattoo, circus and street fair, that the Glorious Half-Hundred came. They came from the north, trudging from the Windsor Great Park beneath constant rain and occasional claps of thunder. They had got lost in the woodland round Virginia Water but once they reached the open ground of the common, flags marked the way. The column wound its way up onto the shallow ridge where they were to pitch camp. There were marshals to show the way. Flags marked the limits of each unit's area and tents were already laid out on the ground like rows of shroud-wrapped corpses. Senior officers rode back and forth issuing contradictory orders. The rain came down.

---

* *London Evening Standard*, 15 June 1853.

Why was there always a delay? The men lined up beside the rolled tents, muttering curses. Water trickled down their muskets, dripped off their shakos and into their eyes, penetrated the thin stuff of their tunics and oozed into their boots. A bugle signalled something or other. What was the command to pitch tents? NCOs squelched up and down the ranks, warning, "Wait for it, wait for it."

And then finally the call came and the men could unroll the sodden canvas to open out each tent like a flower on the ground. Poles were hoisted and guy ropes spread out, and almost at once, a kind of conjuring trick, the heathland blossomed into rows and rows of elegant white trumpet flowers into which the soldiers dived out of the rain.

"Thank fuck for that," was the general mood beneath the canvas. And, "How in fuck's name are we going to get dry?" And, "If I'd wanted to bugger about with canvas and ropes I'd have joined the bloody Navy." They groped around in the dank interior twilight and tried to organise their things. Outside, watching from the nearby road, thousands of onlookers cheered and clapped, before climbing back into their carriages and making off to dry houses and warm fires.

The Great Camp of 1853 was celebrated in the Victorian world almost as much as the Great Exhibition of 1851. If the Great Exhibition was designed to proclaim Britain's dominance in the world of trade and manufacture, the Great Camp was intended to do the same for the country's military might. Part military tattoo, part Boy Scouts jamboree, part overgrown town fair, part (a small part) useful military manoeuvres, it was the greatest assembly of the British Army since the Napoleonic War. Eight thousand men, fifteen hundred cavalry, twenty-four artillery pieces, under canvas over a two-month period on the heathland near Bagshot. There were tents and marquees in regimented ranks, pavilions with bunting, flags flying, bands playing, drums drumming, squads of men marching and counter-marching, forming squares, forming lines, building things – a pontoon bridge across part of Virginia Water, hutments, ditches and revetments – firing weapons, charging around on horses, doing all those things that tin-pot soldiers are meant to do.

It seemed a good idea at the time. Look at the date. There were those in high places, the Prince Consort among them, who realised that beating up people with dark skins on the other side of the world might not be the only call on the Army in the near future, that in fact, four decades after the Battle of Waterloo, there was a growing possibility of the British military being once again involved in action in Europe. Furthermore, and contrary to popular prejudice, it wasn't the French who were going to be the enemy this time but rather the Russians, who were even now sniffing round the decaying body politic of the Ottoman Empire. They, these few men who possessed a little foresight, understood that the British Army, with its underpaid and under-appreciated soldiery, with its incompetent officer class, with its piecemeal marshalling around the world to keep the burgeoning empire in some kind of order, was ill-suited to working as a coherent force against a more or less modern European power. It had been forced to do so under Sir Arthur Wellesley in the Peninsula but that was half a century ago. There is an old saw, that generals always prepare for the previous war and, true to form, that is what they did with the Great Camp: for two months, before cheering crowds (over one hundred thousand spectators came to see, the Queen herself on four different occasions, Prince Albert almost daily) they performed what amounted to a vast re-enactment of the Battle of Waterloo.

Sadly, except for the initial skirmishes, the next war was going to be closer to the Battle of Passchendaele.

Travellers

The nomadic nature of Army life astonishes: in the five years of their marriage, George Mawer and Ann Scanlon have lived in six different places. Now, once the 50th abandons the camp on Chobham Common, it doesn't even return to Preston but moves directly on to the next posting, the seventh for George and Ann, in Plymouth. But the regiment is only there for six months before moving again, in January 1854, to Ireland. Another move, another barracks. Another place of soulless corridors and barren dormitories, of long arcades and granite facades, of dusty courtyards large enough to drill two regiments at a time: the Royal Barracks, Dublin, the oldest and the largest military barracks in the world.

"There are those'll call us traitors fighting for King Billy," Donnelly said when they were settling in. "But if that's true then half the British Army are traitors."*

George pretended naivety in such matters. "Who's King Billy?"

Donnelly laughed. "Has your wife not told you about King Billy?"

---

* Almost true. Throughout the nineteenth century Irish made up approximately one third of the British Army.

"Is that your bloody Irish history? The Battle of the Boyne and all that stuff?" George asked. Irish bogtrotter and Lincolnshire yellowbelly, their friendship was built on a mockery of each other's origins. "Annie does go on about it sometimes but I don't take much notice."

"Always best not to take much notice of the wife, eh George?"

"If you ask me, it's always better to ignore Irish history. Unless you want to get into a fight."

The main purpose of the 50th in Ireland was recruitment. An edict from the Horse Guards had demanded that the regiment raise its complement to eight hundred and fifty private soldiers and with it came a rumour that the regiment was about to be ordered overseas. If you read the newspapers this was no surprise. A heady mix of religion and territorial ambition was brewing in the Balkans as the Russian bear sniffed round the dying body of the Ottoman Empire. Rumour finally coalesced into hard fact when the movement order came through on 24 February: the headquarters and six other companies of the 50th were to prepare for departure to the East in early March. The remaining companies were to follow shortly after.

"We've barely set foot here," Ann complained. "And now you're going to be sent away."

But it was worse than that, much worse. The adjutant called a meeting of the married men in order to explain the situation. They assembled in one of those bare, vaulted rooms in the barracks, white-washed like a sepulchre, the men carefully ranked, sergeants at the front, corporals behind, privates making the bulk, all standing to attention as the officer walked in.

He bade them sit. There was a military silence. As so often in the Army, he broke the news under the guise of it being no more than ordinary procedure: "As you know, once we vacate barracks for embarkation women and children will no longer be accommodated on the strength. That means that you must make alternative arrangements for your dependants. Rail passes will be issued for those families who require travel to their home parish. And may I remind you all that you will receive your pay directly in the field; any arrangements to transfer monies to your wives will be on your responsibility."

He let the muttering die away.

"There will, of course, be a small number of wives who may travel overseas with the men. As per regulations they will be chosen by ballot."

It is hard to unpick the full import of that little speech but the few sentences disguise a slow unfolding of disaster:

No longer accommodated on the strength: women and children will be summarily ejected from the barracks that, for better or worse, have been their homes since marriage. Not only will they lose their lodging, they will also lose their board – the half-rations allocated to the wives, the quarter-rations for each child.

Your pay directly in the field: no facilities existed for the remittance of even a portion of soldiers' wages to the wives left behind (this remained a problem that the British Army did not resolve until the 1960s).

Families who require travel to their parish: women unable to earn enough to keep themselves and their children might be obliged to apply for Poor Relief, which, thanks to the Poor Law Amendment Act of 1832, meant, in most cases, the workhouse. Some parishes persisted, against the new law, with "outside relief" for deserving cases. However, all such relief was administered by the Board of Guardians of the union of parishes from where the family originated. The nomadic nature of Army life meant that no soldier ever qualified for residence in a parish other than the one of his birth or upbringing. Parish unions that hosted military barracks were quick to refuse any responsibility whatever for soldiers' families and so the only solution was to return to the place where you spent your childhood.

They will be chosen by ballot: about 10 percent of the wives were allowed to accompany the men on overseas postings. Believe it or not, a ballot was held among those interested, often on the quayside while the troopship was preparing to sail.

When he had finished, the adjutant looked benignly on the ranks of married men, like a farmer looking over his herd of pigs. Fine fellows, really. Not being gentlemen, they were a different order of being, but fine fellows nevertheless.

"Sir," asked one, raising his hand to speak.

"Yes, private. What is it?"

"What if you haven't got no home? No home parish, I mean. Not since I were a kid."

"Pikey," someone said. There was laughter.

"Tinkers, my people," the private admitted. "An' my wife. A traveller."

"Traveller?"

"She's Romany, in't she?"

"What's your name, private?"

"Lee, sir."

"Can't she go back to her people?"

"Dunno where they are, sir. Been lost to them for years."

The adjutant shrugged. There was nothing more to be said really. He looked round for other questions before the RSM brought the group to attention and the officer left.

*

"I'll no go back to Sligo," Ann insisted. She was, of course, stubborn. Those small, knotted fists, that mouth, which could open so generously, now set in a razor line of determination. "What's there to go back for anyway? No work, nothing to eat, just *an Drochshaol*.* That's what I escaped when I came to England. I'm bloody well not going back with the kids."

So it was agreed that she'd go to Lincoln even though Lincoln was no more than a name to her and little more than that to George. He tried sending a letter to his father at his last known address, but had no response. He didn't even know if the man was alive or dead. But Lincoln was his parish, and Annie was his wife and Mary Ann and the baby were his children. If a marriage certificate meant anything, Lincoln was where she would be entitled to poor relief should she ever need it.

"But I won't need it," Annie insisted. "I'll get by. Laundry work, cleaning, something. I'm a good worker, you know that."

"But the children ... "

"We've no choice, have we? You're being sent abroad. I must make do."

They had some savings. They'd led frugal lives in the barracks, kept a few shillings back from his pay, even after stoppages had been taken by the Army. That was all there was and all there would be between her and destitution.

"I'll send money back to you," he said grandly. "Why would I want money when I'm out East? What would I spend anything on? And who knows, maybe I'll make sergeant, which'll mean more besides."

"Of course." She smiled, and touched his cheek, a gesture that he loved, as though someone as small and fragile could

---

* *An Drochshaol*, "the bad times," refers to the Great Famine of 1845 onwards. Approximately pronounced: an droch-heel.

comfort him, the big, tough solider. What she never expressed were the doubts: where was he going? when would he come back? what would happen to him?

"Constantinople, that's where." But Constantinople meant less to her than Lincoln. He might as well have said Cathay or Xanadu or even Utopia. "It'll all be over once we land," he assured her. "The Army arrives on Turkish soil and the Russians just retreat. That's it. All over before it's even begun. There won't even be any fighting, that's what they think."

She shrugged. "Maybe, maybe not. Who knows?"

They went back to what they were doing, which was packing his kit, a miserable process like the laying out of a corpse. George had been issued with a list, each item precisely defined, even down to its weight: two pairs of flannel drawers, two flannel shirts, two pairs of trousers, two cotton shirts, two pairs of socks, one towel. The items lay on their bed in the corner of the corporals' dormitory. She'd laundered them, ironed and folded them: an act of love sublimated into something useful, a means of taking her mind off the reality which was that her man was going away to war.

"You'll have to do your laundry yourself, won't you? Mind you do, though. There's fleas, lice, all manner of things."

"Of course I will."

Beside the clothing were the other items of his kit: one spare pair of boots, his great coat, his forage cap, one pair of mitts, a brush, his paybook, a box of blacking. All of that lot went into his knapsack. And then there was the other gear that he'd have to carry: his firelock and sling, bayonet and scabbard, belts and pouch, and, finally, sixty rounds of ammunition, each round made up of cartridge and ball.

He picked up the musket, hefted it in his hands, pulled it to half-cock. "We're meant to be getting the new one, that's what they say. Minié muskets, they're called. We're meant to have them already." He released the hammer and put the musket back on the bed. "Except we haven't."

"I don't care what they say or what they're called. As long as you come back safe and sound."

It was the first time anything like that had been said. You tried not to mention what you thought or felt. It only brought bad luck. George attempted to change the subject. "You know what else they say? They say that the regiment will be led by Major Waddy tomorrow. They say that Colonel Sidley has been sacked. Drunkenness. He was like that last summer, when we were at Chobham. Half the time he was in London getting slewed. They say he was even in court."*

"I don't care who leads the regiment or what guns you have." She stood on the brink of tears. "I only care about you."

He looked at her. "All you've got to do is not talk about me coming back or not, all right? Just that. Talk about anything but that. Talk about the children. You care about the children – they're the ones you've got to worry about now."

Her own things, her children's things were already packed. Two carpetbags and a small wooden trunk, although how she'd manage those he didn't know. He turned back to his own packing, stowing into a separate box the extra items apart from those he would carry: a shell pocket, a further spare shirt, a further pair of socks, another towel, two more brushes for the cleaning of kit. All was laid out in the directive from Horse Guards: numbers of items, their weight, everything.

Carefully, while she watched, he wrote – a trick she couldn't manage – his name on the package: *Geo. Mawer, Cpl. 50th Regiment of Foot.* She smiled up at her husband. Eyes dry

---

* He was, given in charge on 17 June 1853, in London, and the next day fined "the usual 5s." for being drunk and disorderly.

now. "Never did like that Colonel Sidley. Looked down his nose at everybody."

"But Waddy's all right," George said. "Thinks about the men."

"And I just think about mine."

He laughed. She had that ability, to make him laugh. "And I think about you."

"We'll be all right."

"Of course you will. There's the money for your travel, aside from the tickets." They'd counted it out when the paymaster had given it over: ten pence for the wife and sixpence for each child *per diem*, that's what the paymaster had said. Per diem meant "for each day," he'd explained. The Army calculated two days' travel, which meant three shillings and eight pence for the family. Ann had the money in her purse now, along with the little they had saved. "And you must get a letter to me at the depot as soon as you can," George reminded her, "so that I know you're all right. Although God knows when it'll find me. You've got money to pay for letter-writing but ask around. Get a good price."

"I don't need to be told to get a good price. I'm Irish."

"You've got the address. Mind you don't lose it."

"I can remember it well enough."

"And you must get another letter to the depot commander. You know what the adjutant said: make sure you give them your address so that you can be contacted when they need."

"When will they need?"

"To tell you when we're coming back." He said that despite knowing it was bad luck. Everything was bad luck. The fact that he was going; the fact that she had to leave barracks; the fact that she really had nowhere to go, just the place that he vaguely thought of as home when actually, ever since he joined up, his home was nowhere fixed but whichever barracks it was, and now wherever Ann was with the children; everything was bad luck. But he'd come back sure enough. That's what you always thought. That's what Porrick said. "Believe you'll come back and you will. It's them as don't believe who're done for."

That night, the last night, in the foetid dark of the barrack room, in the narrow bed behind the curtain of blankets, they made slow and intense love, a love that would have to make do for all the time he would be away. "You'll have Turkish girls," she whispered in his ear, giggling. "When you're away, you'll have Turkish girls."

"No I won't." But the thought made him hard again and she felt the hardness and laughed.

Embarkation

The next morning they were woken early by the bugle call of reveille. He breakfasted on bread and butter and a mug of tea, watched by six-year-old Mary Ann.

"Where's you goin'?" she asked.

"To the East."

The East meant nothing. It was just where soldiers went. Sometimes, she'd heard, they never came back. "Will you come back?"

"'Course I'll come back."

It was easier with two-year-old George. When his mother told him that Papa was going away he just laughed and pointed. "Papa," he said.

After breakfast, George dressed in his newly cleaned and pressed coatee, strapped on his belts and bandoleers and then his knapsack. Finally he put on his shako, picked up his firelock and led his family out onto the parade ground. The other women of the regiment were there, along with their husbands and children. The soldiers were assembling in the centre of the square. The bands from three fellow regiments were forming up to march with the Dirty Half-Hundred and give them a real send off. Bugles were calling. Sergeants were shouting. And Ann stood there, her sharp face dry of tears; her mouth set hard; her shock of russet hair somehow defiant, like regimental colours defining her presence and her indomitable spirit. George Henry clung to her skirts; Mary Ann held her hand.

George bent to kiss his son and then his daughter. Then he kissed the mother, on her mouth, something he'd never done in public. Her free hand came up to hold his head for a moment before letting him go. He stood upright, rested his firelock for a moment while he fastened the stock at his neck – the hated stock – then he turned and hurried over to where 5 Company was mustering.

She watched him go, lost sight of him for a moment among the red coats, then saw him again, standing erect, his gaze up and ahead as the sergeant – Porrick Donnelly – brought the men to attention. All around Ann and her two children the other women were waving and shouting, but she just looked. She could see him in the front rank of 5 Company, just there, his profile as the company turned right. The band struck up "The Girl I Left Behind Me." It was Donnelly's voice that called out, "5 Company, by the left, quick march!" And George was there, left marker, front rank. His profile going away, then his back as the snake of soldiers wheeled right towards the gatehouse. And then he had gone and she was on her own, the sole provider for the two children, the sole protector, the sole parent.

While the other women waved and shouted and wept, she turned and led the children back into the barracks.

The progress of the regiment through the city was a grand event: a gala parade with bands playing, drums beating, flags flying, people lining the streets to cheer. Marching along the Liffey the bands played "Auld Lang Syne," which seemed reasonable, and "There's a Good Time Coming," which, with the benefit of hindsight, seems wildly inappropriate. But who was to know? Certainly not the good citizens of Dublin, who braved the February cold in their thousands to watch the Dirty Half-Hundred pass by and seemed delighted at the idea of war, as long, presumably, as someone else was going to fight it.

At the Essex Bridge the 50th crossed the river to the South Quays and Parliament Street while the bands played "Cheer Boys Cheer" and "The British Grenadiers." With drums and fifes going, the column turned left down Dame Street towards College Green and the much-defaced statue of King William III; at King Billy the column wheeled right, then left, down the south side of the College, along Nassau Street, where the students of Trinity, who had stood and cheered at the main gate, now crowded the railings of College Park, shouting and waving. The soldiers tramped on to the station in Westland Row where two trains waited impatiently, steam up, to take the regiment on to Kingstown docks where the good ship *Cambria* waited for them.

Cambria was a hybrid, the product of miscegenation, the off-spring of a mating that was against all that was natural: the conjunction of a sailing ship and a steamer. Wooden-hulled, three-masted, square-rigged and possessing a full complement of sails, she was also a single-funnelled, steam-engined paddle wheeler. On a transatlantic crossing (she was one of the first Cunarders) she would carry 120 passengers to the United States; on this occasion, to the accompaniment of bands playing, handkerchiefs waving and flags flying, she boarded the headquarters and six battalion companies of the 50th Regiment of Foot, comprising twenty-two officers, thirty-four staff-sergeants and sergeants, thirty-one corporals, ten drummers, and 612 privates, a grand total of 709 men, along with the few wives who had won the lottery for the dubious honour of accompanying their husbands to wherever it was they were going.

Thus overloaded, the *Cambria* slipped her moorings. Driven by a twin-cylinder Napier side-lever steam engine – the NCOs were taken below to inspect this gleaming machinery – belching smoke and churning at the water with her paddles, she puttered off into Dublin Bay. Troops lined the railings and watched the coastline slip away. They'd crossed this stretch of water before of course, coming to Ireland a few months ago. They talked and smoked and pointed at this and that – snow on the Wicklow Hills, fish sliding like oil beneath the surface of the sea, seabirds hunting for scraps. The veterans pretended to be ever so much at ease with themselves, going foreign, while the new recruits contemplated an uncertain and unimaginable future.

The paddles slapped the water. The ship pitched a little but the sea was calm enough. Occasionally a breath of wind threw acrid smoke down across the decks, bringing with it the taste of burnt sulphur, familiar from the firing range. Behind the Wicklow Hills, the sun went down in a welter of blood and gore.

Something that the landsman discovers on a sea voyage – that even though he has gone to bed and slept more or less through the night, when he comes up on deck the next morning little has changed. Only that there is a new motion, a pitching and rolling as the ship takes the long Atlantic swell on its starboard bow, lifting, hesitating and sliding, paddles alternately thrashing helplessly in the air, then plunging underwater in the following trough, the ship groaning and shuddering, as though great harm is being done to it.

After breakfast – some kind of porridge and a mug of tea – George went up on deck to take a pipe. There were *No*

Smoking signs below but up on deck a pipe was allowed. He'd heard that smoke settled your stomach. Over towards the forecastle someone was being audibly sick. "Not on the bloody deck!" a voice shouted. "Bloody landlubbers!" A wooden bucket was lowered overboard. Water splashed into the scuppers.

George felt puke rise in this throat. Private soldiers were allowed up in groups to take the fresh air, a few officers were strolling around the quarterdeck, crew members were going about their arcane business with ropes and marlinspikes. Porrick Donnelly appeared. He too lit a pipe and George and he stood together at the rail beside the curve of the paddle-wheel cover, looking out at that great expanse of water. It was remarkable that the horizon was no longer a line but had become a circular thing, a continuous loop around the focus of the *Cambria*, never coming nearer, never moving further away. Disorientating. You never seemed to move anywhere, and yet the paddles thrashed their way through the water and smoke belched out of the funnel and the ship trailed a wake behind it.

"Found your sea legs yet, George?" Donnelly asked. He seemed inured to the motion of the ship, the rise and fall, the sideways wallow, the throbbing of the engine beneath their feet and the smell of sulphur on the air.

"No, I haven't. I s'pose you're used to it, coming back from India."

"Not really. It's just luck. Some of the best sailors suffer. Look at old Nelson. Sick as a dog every time he went to sea, that's what they say." They thought about this for a while, the vagaries of sea legs. Then, "How did Ann take your leaving?"

George felt a pang of guilt. His queasy stomach had quite driven the plight of his family from his thoughts. "Upset, of course."

"What did you decide she should do? Not go back to Sligo, I'll be bound."

"She's going to Lincoln, to find my folk. That seemed the best idea. I guess she's going today. Or tomorrow."

"Doesn't seem right, does it?"

"No."

"But that's the Army for you. You makes your choice and you takes your chances."

"Yes."

Nausea rose within him, relentless, unstoppable and, worst of all, inescapable. Other discomforts you could lessen. Even a broken leg might be rested and splinted so that the pain would fade. But this motion, and the nausea it evoked, was incessant, occupying body and soul, chasing out every rational thought. "I think," he said, "I'll go and lie down."

And so he was trapped in the misery of seasickness until the moment, a day later, and now under sail somewhere off Finisterre – but how could anyone tell? – when the nausea vanished. Like a calm after the storm. For a short while George was ebullient, fascinated, happy, watching the sun – was it rising higher in the sky now? – and the tipping, tilting, glittering waves, and the sudden sleek slipping past of a school of porpoises; then he thought of Ann and the children ...

Lincoln

She's at the ship's rail, with all her possessions at her feet: two bundles tied with string, a wooden trunk and two carpetbags. The Irish coast is slipping away astern. The last time she saw that was when she left Ireland fifteen years ago, for what she thought was forever; but then came George Mawer, marriage and the Army, and this unexpected posting to Dublin. So now, once again, she is escaping her homeland, only this time, clinging to her, she has her two children.

The crossing to Holyhead takes four hours and when they arrive it's dark. Ann finds a room in a lodging house near the station. All night long there's the squeal of girls in neighbouring rooms, the grunting and shouting of men, a coming and going on the stairs. Mary Ann sleeps well enough but George Henry is peevish, whinging and crying whenever he wakes, dozing fitfully. Ann lies awake throughout the night, wondering what will happen to the children, to her husband, to her. She understands what is evident: that she and her little family are walking along the edge of a precipice and mere chance could pitch them over into the void. But she is also determined that she will bring them through whatever happens, that she and they will survive.

Early in the morning they're up, paying for a porter to help with their possessions across to the station in order to catch the early train to Chester. They sit on bare boards in third class and pretend they have somewhere to go, someone to greet them at the other end, some hope, some security. The journey from Anglesey to the mainland takes them through the iron tube of Stevenson's celebrated Britannia Bridge, the sound of the train's passage thundering around them as though in a vast iron drum. They are paupers on the edge of destitution, abandoned by a military that treats its men like the scum that its greatest exponent has claimed them to be, yet here they are travelling through one of the wonders of the industrial age, the first box girder bridge in the world, built high enough – the Admiralty required it – to allow a fully rigged man-of-war to pass beneath.

After the tunnel bridge comes the wild drama of the north Welsh coast before the Dee Valley and, finally, Chester station, where they have to change trains. The remainder of the day is spent traipsing across England until finally, in the late afternoon, they reach Lincoln, a place Ann has never visited, never even knew existed until she met George. They arrive like the first refugees from a war that hasn't yet happened, standing helpless on the platform surrounded by their scant baggage. The girl stares around with wide, tired eyes; the little boy is grizzling with hunger, with discomfort, with something he cannot yet recognise as fear. It is up to the mother, of course, to find someone to help with the luggage that they have brought with them – their life's possessions – and carry them out to the station forecourt where there are hackney carriages for hire to take them up to the old town, the warren of houses that cluster round the cathedral and the ruins of the castle, the place they do not know yet are bound to call home.

Somehow they survive. Ann finds lodgings at number four, West Bight Row, a four-minute walk from the cathedral. The house still stands, just outside the castle walls – a red brick terrace cottage that in those days would have been no more than a two-up, two-down with a narrow yard at the back. Probably she had to share it with another family. She and the children would have had a room to themselves and shared use of the kitchen and the outside privy. The road outside is a cul-de-sac, still paved with the flagstones that Ann would have recognised. The children would have played on those flags, George toddling after his older sister, Mary Ann playing hopscotch with the girls from the neighbouring houses.

Ann found work in the Bailgate laundry. This was something she could do, something she had been trained to do in the barracks, working with military uniforms; and there was plenty of such work around Lincoln Cathedral, what with all those clerics and their surplices, albs, collars, tabs: all manner of vestments to wash and starch and iron. Sweltering in the steam and stench of soap, she was, she discovered, a mistress of the flatiron.

Two months later she discovered something else: she was pregnant.

Malta

Malta, 7 March 1854. Dawn. Corporal George Mawer makes foreign landfall for the first time. He's on deck with other soldiers of the 50th Regiment of Foot lining the rails to watch as the *Cambria* slips through the jaws of the entrance into the placid water of the Grand Harbour. Cliffs of fortification slide past. Bells ring from church towers all around. A cannon fires, the report echoing from the bastions like thunderclaps. At the summit of a casemate the Union flag dips in salute while the *Cambria*'s paddle wheels churn her to a halt alongside dozens of other vessels. Bumboats gather round like lice on a fish. Naked boys dive for coins thrown in the water. All is for sale: fruit, pastries, crucifixes, icons, the boatman's wife, daughter, son. Laughter and jeering comes down from the deck. Somewhere a band strikes up.

A century later, in another war, Corporal George Mawer's great-grandson is on the way to Malta for the first time. The date is 3 June 1941. He is a twenty-year-old sergeant pilot, newly trained on medium bombers. Like his great-grandfather, he has not yet seen action. Like him, he comes to Malta from Gibraltar, but rather than travelling as a passenger in a steam/sailing hybrid ship (the latest technology in 1854), he is flying a Vickers Wellington 1C (the latest technology in 1941). It's a night flight, the aircraft battering eastward from Gibraltar through a black sky. The geodetic airframe, a revolutionary concoction of aluminium, wood and linen, flexes and vibrates as it grapples with the night air. The roar of twin Bristol Pegasus engines drowns out casual thought. The aircraft edges between the hostile coasts of Sicily and Tunisia, the gunners straining to see the invisible Ju 88 that may emerge like a shark from the depths to tear you apart before you even have time to shout.

The voice of the front gunner crackles through the intercom: "Dead ahead, skipper. Is that sunrise?"

George's great-grandson looks up from the glow of the blind flying panel. He has been flying on instruments, watching the faint lights of altimeter, compass, airspeed indicator, artificial horizon. Now he stares ahead through the Perspex windshield over the forward gun turret. There's red light bleeding into the scalpel cut of the horizon. The moon has already set and sunrise isn't until four thirty-seven. He knows this from the flight plan. His watch tells him the time is only two-thirty, so that light is not the dawn. It cannot be the dawn.

"Too bloody early," he replies. Then he remembers the briefing they had in the crew room before takeoff: "You'll find Malta easily enough," the squadron leader had assured them, "don't you worry about that. You'll see it."

Understanding, if nothing else, dawns. "Fucking hell! That's where we're going. That's Malta!"

As the Wellington rumbles eastwards across the Mediterranean, what he and the front gunner are seeing is the light from an island on fire.

Half an hour later they are within the ambit of Malta air traffic control, descending into a shifting architecture of searchlights and a pyrotechnic spray of anti-aircraft fire. Shadows of other aircraft pass overhead. Bombs blossom hotly in the darkness below. But there's no noise beyond the racket of the engines and the calm voice of the controller sounding in the headphones, talking them down like a surgeon explaining that everything will be all right despite all evidence to the contrary. The altimeter unwinds through the hundreds of feet – five hundred, four hundred, three-fifty, three hundred, two-fifty, two hundred. The aircraft rocks and kicks in the hot air coming up from buildings and tarmac. Except for explosions they descend blindly into darkness. And then, as though revealed by some cosmic conjuror, landing lights flash on, drawing converging lines of perspective into the blackness. The Wellington thumps into the concrete of the runway, bounces, hits again, slows and lumbers to a halt. The runway lights go out. Unseen hands throw open the hatches. Men shout. The aircrew scramble dumbly out into chaos. Shadows hustle them down the steps and across a stretch of concrete into a slit trench.

"Welcome to Malta," a voice says in the darkness. No one laughs.

Around the airfield perimeter, lightning flashes outline an alien horizon of flat roofs and church bell towers. Sounds have taken over the engine roar – there are bomb bursts, the crash of things falling, the staccato of anti-aircraft fire. Near at hand a fuel bowser draws up alongside the now empty aircraft and demon figures hurry to attach fuel lines to the machine. High octane petrol pumps into the Wellington's wings while fire burns all around. From his refuge in the ground, George's great-grandson watches in astonishment.

Welcome to Malta.

Agonising minutes later a second crew clambers out from hiding, runs across the hardstanding and disappears into the aircraft. The engines erupt into life and the aircraft taxies off into the blackness. A few moments later it is thundering down the runway, clambering into the air and disappearing off into what is now the very beginning of dawn.

Welcome to Malta.

In 1854 the lead companies of the 50th Regiment of Foot spent a month on the island while the *Cambria* went back to Kingstown to collect the remainder of the battalion. It was a month of idleness and training, the curse of Army life: a month of foot drill, of going through the intricate manoeuvres of musketry, a month of wandering through the narrow streets of the cities when they had free time, of drinking in the narrowest of those streets, the street called straight – *Strada Stretta* – where women plied their trade. Heat and dust mingled with wine, sweat and semen. Men fought for nothing and occasionally died for less.

And then the *Cambria* returned and with it mail, and among the mail a letter from Ann, written in the elaborate hand of some clerk.

Dear Husband,

I hope this finds you well. This is to tell you that I and your children are in good health in the city of Lincoln. We are at 4 West Bight Row which is a comfortable and commodious dwelling. You may write to us there. I do work in a laundry for which I am well experienced.

Be careful of your health and come home soon.

Your affectionate wife,

Annie

her mark ✗

And there indeed was her mark. The ink had spotted at the end of one of the strokes. More than anything else, that brought a smart of tears to his eyes.

Letters

She'd had to find someone to write letters for her. Isolated in the cathedral city of Lincoln, surrounded by strangers, in a world burgeoning with words she felt the fearful burden of illiteracy. For the first letters, the one to the depot giving her address and that first one to George, wherever George was, she paid a clerk: one penny for the paper and ink, two pennies for the writing, two pennies for the postage stamps. But the next letter was more difficult. She decided on the church across the road, St. Paul in the Bail (whatever that meant), and the rector himself, a rather solemn and self-important man but a man who was always polite and always willing to acknowledge her when he passed her in the street. She'd taken to going to church there, and Mary Ann was admitted to Sunday school. After evensong one Sunday she hung back with the children and waited to see him. "Can I ask you something, Reverend?"

He stood over the little group, as black as the devil in his cassock. "Of course you may, my good woman."

"Will you write a letter to my husband for me? I can't write, see? And he's Army, a corporal, away at the war in the East."

The rector was tall and whiskery, in his sixties she reckoned. The Reverend Mr. Richter, that's what people said he was called. Sounded like a foreign name but he was as English as they came and pompous with it. "Well, please God, my good woman, there will be no war. From the newspapers, I understand the Russians have halted at the Danube provinces and are contemplating withdrawal. Surely that means that nothing will come of it all and your gallant husband will soon be back safe and sound to the bosom of his family."

She shrugged, indifferent to his eyes on her bosom. "But still I want to send a letter to him. At best it'll be months before he's back. I don't want any misunderstandings between him and me, see?"

"Misunderstandings?" Mr. Richter frowned. "I do hope not. Perhaps we should talk in the presbytery ... "

She took the children's hands and followed him into a side room off the nave. He shut the door behind them. The presbytery was a wood-panelled room smelling of beeswax and stale garments. There was a desk and two chairs, neither of which the vicar invited Ann to use. "Now, what misunderstandings might there be?" he asked. "Nothing irregular, I hope."

"'Course not. You've just got to write what I want to tell him, which is that I am two months gone. That's all. So he knows."

"Gone?" He looked at the two children, Mary Ann standing at her side and George Henry whom she had lifted onto her hip. "You've *left* him?"

"What?"

"You said, you've gone."

She laughed. That sudden, Irish laugh. "No, not *that* sort of gone. Two months gone, that's what I mean. I'm going to have a baby."

"Ah. A misapprehension. So you wish to tell your good man you are with child?"

"Well, I wouldn't put it quite like that. But sure, in the family way."

"And is the child his?"

"Of course it's his! What do you take me for? He left two month ago and now I'm two month gone."

The man almost seemed to blush. "Well, I meant no offence, but one hears so much about soldiers' wives these days. Temptation always lies in the path of the unwary."

"There's nothing unwary about me, to be sure."

He nodded. "I'm pleased to hear it. So you wish me to be your amanuensis?"

"And what will that be then? It sounds as though it's to do with men. I think I've had enough of men at the moment."

He laughed. He actually laughed. She wasn't sure if he was laughing at her or with her, but laughter was no bad thing. "Amanuensis is derived from the Latin. Nothing to do with men. *Servus a manu*, a servant of the hand. A secretary, one who writes for another."

"Well, I'm not looking for a servant, just I can't write, that's all. I want someone to write for me. Look, it's here. This is where you write." She showed him the piece of paper on which George had written the address of the regimental depot, and his own name.

With the children watching in awed silence, Mr. Richter went round and sat at the desk. "Let us see what I can do." With all the solemnity of a priest preparing to celebrate Holy Communion, he took pen and ink and a sheet of heavy bond paper. Then he dipped the pen and wrote in his fine copperplate hand more or less what Ann dictated, except that he put in words, he said, that made it more mellifluous. She wasn't sure what *mellifluous* meant but she assumed it was a good thing to be:

Dear Husband,

I hope this finds you well. I received yours from the island of Malta but they tell me, for it is written in the newspapers, that you have moved East by now and are

in Turkey. I hope you are well. We are comfortable.
Mary Ann is schooled at the church and does well with
her letters. George Henry is cared for by a neighbour
when I am at work. They both send fond greetings to
their father. George Henry says words now. "Mama"
and "Papa," which I have taught him. "May" is Mary
Ann in his speaking.

I would apprise you that I am with your fourth
child, two months gone, which will please you greatly.
I believe so, in any case. I expect the birth, God
willing, in November by which time I pray you will be
back with me.

Be careful of your health and come home soon.
Your affectionate wife,

The rector looked up. "I'm afraid I don't know your name."

"Annie," she said. "That's what he calls me but really it's Ann. Like it's written here." She showed the paper. "It's Ann Mawer, that's my name."

"With that surname your husband is clearly from these parts, but you are surely Irish."

"Scanlon from Sligo, sir."

"But not a papist?"

She shrugged. "I was baptised a Catholic, sir. For me it's all the same."

He looked her up and down. "Perhaps," he agreed. "Then, perhaps not." He wrote, *Ann Mawer, her mark* and turned the page for her to make an awkward X, then blotted the ink, folded the page into an envelope, copied out the address of the regimental depot, sealed the envelope and affixed a penny stamp to it. "I must congratulate you on your forthcoming addition to the family, Ann Mawer," he said. "You are in work at the moment, I take it?"

"At the Bailgate laundry, sir."

"And when the baby comes? What will you do then?" He sniffed, looking the children over – the girl with her wide eyes, the baby boy with snot on his upper lip. They gave off the sour smell of poverty. "I hope you will not become a burden on the parish."

"I'm sure I won't, sir."

He watched her, considering, while she looked back at him with clear, cold blue eyes. Attractive eyes, but bold, which seemed wrong in one of her class. "Soldiers' wives are becoming quite a problem since the Army went East. I have been reading about it in the newspapers."

"I'll not be a problem, sir."

"I hope not."

She rooted round in the pocket of her apron. "How much do I owe you? For the writing and the stamp."

The rector smiled. "Nothing at all, my good woman. An act of Christian charity."

Malta to Gallipoli

There was a comet. They'd left Malta, left the Grand Harbour, pitched, paddle wheels churning, into a northeasterly which the sailors called a *gregale*, a Greek-wind, and there in the night sky was a comet – a smudge of light three fingers wide against the black. Officers were seen on the quarterdeck observing the phenomenon. A telescope did the round among the troops. George saw a vague blur dancing in the eyepiece. Rumour did the rounds as well: comets were a sign, and not a good one. Pestilence, disaster, war were foretold.

"War's a pretty easy one," Porrick Donnelly remarked as the telescope went from hand to hand. "Because that's where we're going. And pestilence is only what's to be expected if you crowd thousands of men together in a hot climate. So we're only left with disaster. And who knows how to measure disaster?"

When the comet disappeared in the light of the rising moon, men thought it had been engulfed; but it was there the next evening, although shifted in position, and then no more. Cloud or the moon had extinguished it. The voyage continued, with earnest attendance to morning prayers and invocations to the Almighty to look after those in peril on the sea. "Please, lord God, save us from comets," muttered Porrick under his breath.

*

Two days later, land appeared on the port quarter, a great bare spine running down from the north, painted with snow on its summits and stirring the wind and the waves into chaos. Word went round that this was Greece, the cape of Matapan, and the island ahead was Kithera, the birthplace of Aphrodite herself. It looked a bleak place as they approached it, ill-suited to the goddess of love.

Having struggled to round the island, *Cambria* made her way with difficulty and sickness through scattered islands northwards. By 13 April she found herself off what rumour said was the Turkish coast. It seemed an iron, mountainous coastline but as they drew nearer, unexpectedly it opened up like a bay, and the bay opened up like a river and then quite suddenly they were paddling up winding narrows between terraces and hills. The Dardanelles, so the sailors said – the Hellespont, the chaplain called it when saying morning prayers – with Europe on their left and Asia on the right. Finally Gallipoli appeared at the entrance to a further sea, the Sea of Marmara.

Gallipoli

Gallipoli is *Kallí-polis*, the beautiful city – but unfortunately it isn't. It may have been in classical times but it isn't now and it wasn't in April 1854 when the 50th Regiment arrived from Malta. Then it was no more than a squalid collection of stone houses gathered around a small fortress, looking across the strait with eternal suspicion and fear at Asia.

"What shithole is this?" the men of the 50th asked as they disembarked, relieved to be released from the confines of the ship but wondering where they would be spending the night and what they would have to eat. They had been issued with enough bread and salt beef for three days, which didn't bode well. The tiny port was seething with foreign soldiers, idle sailors, sweating navvies, heaving stevedores. The tricolour flag was already flying on the few important buildings in the town and signs in French pointed the way to *Quartier Général* and *Direction du Port et Commissariat de la Marine*. Zouaves and *Chasseurs Indigènes*, beautifully caparisoned and magnificently moustachioed, won the admiration of the locals in a way that British soldiery could never hope to emulate. The town behind the port was a hive of squalid houses punctuated by mosques and minarets from which muezzins called the faithful to prayer. In an impoverished quarter Greek held sway and priests in tall hats and grimy cassocks administered to a surly, resentful population. Nowhere did the usual attractions of a port seem to be on offer.

"Where are the women?"

There seemed to be only men, moustachioed most of them and grim-faced, sitting around smoking pipes and watching this invasion of their territory with apparent indifference.

"They keep their women locked away. They'll cut your balls off if you so much as look at them."

"But you can't look at them, can you? Not if they've hidden them away."

The 50th spent the night sleeping on the floor of a cold and draughty caravanserai and left Gallipoli the next day without regret, marching inland with the band playing, drums beating, colours waving. Anything to stir the people of the town out of their stupor and impress the French. Orthodox Greek or Ottoman Mussulman stared at them indifferently but at least the Frenchmen cheered.

Beyond the town was a dull lowland green with scrub and grasses, devoid of trees but decked out with spring flowers – asphodel, poppies, mullein – and quartered with fields of wheat. Occasional flocks of scrawny sheep grazed the edges. After about two hours the soldiers breasted a rise and there was another sea ahead of them, a smear of distant grey-blue. Which sea it was they had little idea. It wasn't the common soldier's lot to know where or why. Just the sea, and far away beyond that, hills dusted with snow. Shortly afterwards they rounded a curve in the track and something familiar was revealed: a sprawl of white bell tents across the hillside and a Union flag flying. A bugle sounded.

"Just like fucking Chobham Common!" some wag exclaimed.

*

The British Army camp was near the village of Bulair.*
The next month was spent digging fortifications across the
Gallipoli peninsula. The ditch they dug was seven feet deep,
six feet wide at the bottom and thirteen feet wide at the
top. Above the ditch a five-foot-thick parapet was thrown
up using the excavated spoil.† In combination with other
regiments, the total digging was to be seven miles long,
from the Gulf of Saros to the Sea of Marmara. George was
in charge of a squad of private soldiers but that didn't mean
that he didn't dig. Sergeants didn't dig. Porrick Donnelly
didn't dig – or at least he only dug when making a point
about how a slacker of a soldier ought to be bloody well
digging – but corporals weren't so fortunate. You dug just
like a private and at the same time you took responsibility for the digging of the men in your charge. You dug
and they dug.

"What we doing this for, sergeant?"

"Shut up, son, and keep digging."

After a bit of spring sunshine, it rained a cold rain that
sometimes turned to sleet. The dust of the land quickly turned
to mud and once again men cracked jokes about fucking
Chobham Common, jokes that wore thin after the second
freezing rainstorm and the knowledge that after hours of
digging you had little more than a bucketful of water to wash
yourself in, before a meagre supper of salt beef and potatoes
and a miserable night under canvas. What made it worse
was that the beer ration – a quart a day per man – failed to
materialise. What made it even worse was that the French
were rumoured to have vastly superior rations, with wine

---

* Modern *Bolayir*.
† Dimensions from Sir William Howard Russell, *The British Expedition to
the Crimea*, London 1858.

included. Moreover, rumour said that these rations were served by women.

"You heard that, sergeant? Hot meals served on tables by *women*? That's what the Froggies get."

Sergeant Donnelly laughed the idea away: "You got to be joking, son." He was an old soldier. He knew that rumours like that are always a lie.

This particular rumour happened to be true.

Women or no women, George dug. Stripped to the waist, sweating in the cold, feverish at times, sunburned when the sun shone, weathered by the wind, George dug. He dug for the Empire, for Victory or Victoria, it didn't really matter which. He dug and he didn't think of much beyond the digging until there was a pause and then he wondered when he would hear from Annie again and whether he would get news of his son George Henry and his daughter Mary Ann. He thought of them in that order, the younger first because he was the boy, the son and heir, although he was heir to no more than an awkward surname. He wondered how they were, how things were going in Lincoln, how they were surviving. He thought especially about Annie when they turned in for the night and he lay on a thin straw palliasse with a dozen others arranged in a star around the tent pole, with the canvas flogging in the wind and, as often as not, rain thrashing down outside and dripping down the seams of the canvas. He thought of Annie lying naked with him, her narrow body, her slender limbs, the small, sharp figure that was almost as much a comfort to him in his imagination now they were apart as it had been in reality when they were together. Only now he felt his connection to her like a thread stretched across the world, as thin as cotton and just as fragile.

When, how, would it snap?

*

They took to digging naked. Like that there was no clothing to get dirty. It was easier to wash a body than to wash and dry clothes. They dug through April and into May, which was when the next letter came, written in a more elegant, better-formed hand than the first. He wondered about that. Who was this new scribe?

Dear Husband,

I hope this finds you well. I received yours from the island of Malta but they tell me, for it is written in the newspapers, that you have moved East by now and are in Turkey. I hope you are well. We are comfortable. Mary Ann is schooled at the church and does well with her letters. George Henry is cared for by a neighbour when I am at work. They both send fond greetings to their father. George Henry says words now. "Mama" and "Papa," which I have taught him. "May" is Mary Ann in his speaking.

I would apprise you that I am with your fourth child, two months gone, which will please you greatly. I believe so, in any case. I expect the birth, God willing, in November by which time I pray you will be back with me.

Be careful of your health and come home soon.
Your affectionate wife,
Ann Mawer. Her mark: X

He thought long and hard about that. What date was the last time? Easy enough to remember. The night before the regiment left Dublin, 26 February. So, March, April and now it was long into May. But there was the time taken for the letter to travel. The letter itself was undated. Was that a reason for suspicion?

"She's in the family way," he told Porrick. "Annie. She expects it in November."

If it came later than November, he thought, what would that mean? The thread of connection seemed strained to breaking. And even if the baby came on time and truly was his own, how would she manage? She'd not be able to work. The few pence a day that he might send to her would not be enough to keep the three of them and a newborn and no work. She'd become a pauper and have to rely on the parish.

Questions bubbled to the surface. Desertion – that curse or promise in a soldier's mind – occurred to him. But how could he desert from here and be any use to her? How could he get back to Lincoln? He'd seen a map, knew roughly where the regiment was, beached on this spit of land at the very edge of Europe, two thousand miles or more from where and what he knew.

There was the other possibility: the Russkies would withdraw and the Army could go home. He'd get back by summer and he'd have three stripes by then and Annie would be proud of him and he'd be proud of her, what with the two children and a swollen belly to show that the new one was on the way. A fine couple they'd make, a fine family.

When he had the opportunity, he wrote another letter. *How is your health? How are you managing now? How will you manage when the child comes? Here we are safe and do little but dig trenches. Your loving husband* ... and sent it off with the other letters, some of them written by the senders, others dictated by those unable to write. He wrote one or two himself for those who couldn't, even helping out with the words because the poor buggers could barely think what they wanted. Private Jellicoe was one, standing there in the tent, twisting his forage cap in his hands. "Dunno what to say, corporal."

"Imagine she was here. What would you say to her?"

"We didn't talk much. Never been good with words."

"You'd say something, surely."

"Where's my shirt?"

"You can't say that!"

Jellicoe shrugged. Point proved.

"Don't you love her?"

A look of amazement. "I can't say that!"

"'Course you can. I love you and long to see you again soon. How about that?"

A big grin. "I never knew you cared, corporal."

In May they moved camp closer to Gallipoli, where they were brigaded with the 1st Royal Dragoons and the 38th Foot. Spring had come, with sun and growth. The landscape all around seemed rejuvenated and with that came an air of expectation among the troops. Rumour ran through the new encampment like fire through standing corn. Moves were afoot. They were going north, against the Russkies.

They didn't move.

They craved novelty. Boredom followed inactivity, relieved by drill and marching and countermarching and occasional amusement like running competitions against the other regiments. Football. Cricket. A bit of a laugh. Going into the town and drinking with Frenchies. That was a real laugh, trying to understand each other, falling about with laughter. *Je suis*, *tu es*, *il est*, all that kind of stuff. *Ami*, friend. *Vive l'Empereur! Vive la Reine!* And some good songs. There was one, taught by a good bloke who came from somewhere north, so he said.

Quand tu renais à l'espérance,
Et que l'hiver fuit loin de nous
Sous le beau ciel de notre France
Quand la soleil revient plus doux

George learned the song, more or less. The first verse, anyway. The sounds, not really the words. He'd sing it to Annie when he got back. And in return, he taught the Froggie "The Lincolnshire Poacher." There's a thought – him singing some French song about Normandy and a Frenchie from Normandy pretending to be a Lincolnshire poacher. And maybe he'd go back to Normandy and teach his children and maybe it'd be passed down so there'd be a whole lot of Lincolnshire poachers in Normandy. And if George taught the French song to George Henry and Mary Ann, maybe they'd pass it down and there'd be a whole lot of English singing about Normandy. Except he had no idea what the words meant and neither had the Frenchie. Just the sounds.

Minié

On 20 June a momentous event takes place that few see for the revolution that it is: the battalion parades in order to surrender their old firelocks. Here, in a dusty place outside Gallipoli called Chiftlik, a cartload of brand-new weapons has been delivered, to be issued to the men of the 50th.

An armourer from the Royal Ordnance Factory addresses each company. The one for 5 Company is a florid gentleman, sweating in the sun and liberally coated with dust. He's dressed in a manner that might be more appropriate for a Methodist preacher in Enfield than a military expert in the East, and certainly he speaks as though introducing the men to a new religion. The symbol of this religion lies before him on a table that might almost be an altar. It's a weapon that looks little different from the percussion cap muskets they have just surrendered. He picks it up.

"This," he announces, "is the Pattern 1851 Minié rifle-musket." A murmur of awe runs through the ranks of the company, as though they have just been shown the true cross. "Gallant fellows like yourselves have all been trained on the dear old Brown Bess. You know that with Bess you'd be lucky to hit a cavalryman's horse at a hundred yards. Well, because of the magic of rifling, with this new weapon you can" – a pause for effect, the audience hanging on his every word – "knock the rider off his horse at five hundred yards."

An explosion of disbelief.

"Just don't tell the Royals," he adds.

Disbelief turns to laughter. The Royal Dragoons are their neighbours in camp. If you could pick a cavalryman off at that range it would put them out of business.

"In case you doubt me," the preacher continues, "may I demonstrate one of the external features of the new firelock that distinguishes it from its predecessor? Doubtless the sharper-eyed among you have already noted it." He points to a folded hinge of metal on the breech of the weapon. "This here is an adjustable leaf sight such as up to now you'll only have found on a Brunswick rifle." He flips the sight upwards and peers at it dramatically. "This rear sight – you may see for yourselves in a moment – is graduated up to ... NINE HUNDRED YARDS!" Laughter dies away to something like astonishment. "As you know, my good-hearted fellows, only the Rifles have been using Brunswicks. Well from today we are all riflemen!"

Someone calls from the ranks: "What about the rate of fire? That's what matters!"

In an instant the preacher becomes a hawker, with excellent goods to sell. "Of course that's what matters. If it's as good as a Brunswick, does it take as long to load? 'Cos as we all know, don't we, that the Rifles can only get off a round a minute? Whereas gallant lads like you can manage three—"

"Four!" comes a shout.

"Or even *four* rounds a minute. Well, that, my brave fellows, is where *this* little gem comes in." The man lowers the firelock and holds aloft a small slug of lead. It's about an inch long, with a domed head, barely visible between thumb and forefinger of his left hand. "This is the key to victory in the field. Behold, men, the Minié ball."

A murmur goes through the audience. They've heard the name. The usual rumour that does the rounds. Minié. The deadly ball with a girly name. The preacher turned salesman is in full flow now:

"Lady Minnie is as easy to stick up the spout as musket ball, but thanks to the magic of rifling she flies as true as Cupid's dart. She has – you will see it yourselves – a little hollow in her bottom – there's nothing to laugh at, Private! – so when the charge goes off and drives her up the barrel the pressure in this hollow makes her spread her skirts and grip the rifling and she starts to spin like a whirling dervish. You've all heard of whirling dervishes, haven't you, being here in Turkey? So, Lady Minnie grips the inside of the barrel and spins like a whirling dervish and that makes her fly true and far. Together with the rifle-musket, this little lady will turn every man jack of you into a marksman!"

His words bring cheers and laughter. When he is finished, the new weapons are issued. By companies the men march out to the range where targets are set at one hundred, three hundred, five hundred yards. They have five rounds a piece to practise, and it is true – the Minié rifle is as easy to load as the old smooth bore musket. The cartridges are more or less the same – cylinders of paper, twisted closed at one end, blocked with the ball at the other – the biting the cartridge open just the same, the pouring of the charge is the same and the ramming home the ball is the same. Even the recoil is more or less the same. But now the ball flies hundreds of yards ... and hits the target.

Corporal George helps the private soldier standing beside him, flipping up the backsight on the soldier's weapon and showing him how to move the slide up and down the graduations. George has grasped the idea quickly enough. That's why he has two stripes on his arm and why, he thinks, he'll have a third just as soon as they see action and the casualties begin.

On either side men are taking aim and firing. Clouds of smoke scud around them. Mouths are stained from biting open cartridges. Teeth grin through the black. This is just like musket practice ever was: everything is the same with this new weapon, yet nothing is the same. The same noise, the same smoke, the same manipulation of cartridge and powder, of ball and ramrod, of hammer and percussion cap. But with this new weapon the targets are set at distances once unimaginable, maybe even – what did the armourer say and the backsight imply? – half a bloody mile!

There's a strange silence as the men leave the range. They sense, without being able to put it into words, that their world has changed. "If you ask me, George," says Porrick Donnelly, "from now on there's nowhere to hide on the battlefield."

From Gallipoli

Dear Wife,

I am pleased that you are with child and hope that all is well with you and the children. Tell Mary Ann that her father is thinking of her. I'm sure she helps her mother. Tell George Henry not to be a naughty boy but to help his mother as well. I worry that you have enough money. The Church will always help you, will it not? Do you speak to the people who might help?

Here we are at a place called Gallipoli. There is a narrow water that divides us from Asia and in the town are all manner of people from all over the world. There are many Frenchmen who are fine fellows. The Turkey folk are their own people and keep to themselves. The Greeks hate us and wish us gone. But we are here well enough and camped outside the town where we dig trenches against the Russians if they should come here. Of the war we see nothing. It is far to the north and rumour has it that the Russians are stopped. So digging is all we do and maybe when we have finished that we will come home. You will find your husband is quite brown and strong and healthy enough.

*Please write as often as you can and let me know
your news.
Your dear husband,
George Mawer, Corporal, 50th Regiment of Foot*

And then, she is told by the vicar who is reading this letter
to her, George has added beneath in pencil:

P.S.

"This signifies Post Scriptum," explains the vicar. "It means
something added as an afterthought."

*I have this minute, as I seal the letter, been advised by
our good friend Porrick Donnelly that we have orders
to embark. Where exactly we are bound, I know not.
Pray for me, as I pray for you and the children, and the
child unborn.
GM*

On 22 June the 50th strike camp and march down to the
port to embark on the *Cambria* once more. This time, along
with the whole of the allied expeditionary force, they are
going north, across the Sea of Marmara, through the narrows
of the Bosporus and out into the Black Sea. Yes, of course,
there is all the drama of sailing to Byzantium, of passing
Constantinople, of dolphins sliding through the waves, fish
flying, birds diving. On either bank there are buildings older
than Old England herself, domed mosques that once were
churches where emperors worshipped, minarets from where
muezzins call, pavilions where pashas drink sherbet, palaces
where the sultan lives with his dozens of wives and count-
less concubines. But all this means little to Corporal George

as he stands on the deck of the *Cambria* beside Porrick Donnelly and watches the spectacle slide by. Shipping crowds the Golden Horn as they pass. Perhaps one of those vessels includes in its crew list the name Abraham Block, who knows? Certainly, Corporal George Mawer is travelling the same gong-tormented sea that Abraham Block sailed at the same time. But Abraham Block was merely sailing towards storm and shipwreck; George Mawer is sailing to war.

Corporal Forbes at Varna

I am not writing of family, I'm writing of the destruction of family. I'm not writing of enduring love, but of love destroyed. I'm not writing of peaceful contentment, but of disaster, both national and personal. Varna was where it began although not where it finished: as disasters go, this is the long-drawn-out variety ...

Varna is an old town on the west coast of the Black Sea, a port at the head of a small bay. It comes with the usual baggage of classical legend and history, along with an ancient name – Odessos – which, by a case of mistaken identity in the eighteenth century, was given by Catherine the Great to modern Odessa. The twentieth century, followed by the recent grind of communism, has reduced the original Odessos to ferro-concrete and wide boulevards, but in the nineteenth century there was an envelope of ancient fortifications (the French immediately broke open a gap in the walls to facilitate unloading of ships) around a warren of alleyways, a few municipal and dockyard buildings, and a population so oppressed and impoverished by life under the indifferent cosh of their colonial masters, the Ottoman Turks, that they had more or less given up. The language was, as it is, Slav, the script Cyrillic – Varna is Варна – and the religion Orthodox. Yet the people didn't look south to the Greeks for authority but rather to the north, to the Russians who then had crossed the Danube and were at Silistra, a mere seventy miles away.

At first glance the city seemed an attractive enough prospect to the troops who arrived there. There were woods, fields, sunny hills in the background. Behind the town were two freshwater lagoons fed by rivers from these hills; on the north side of these lakes the British Army pitched its tents amid woods and meadows and streams. It was almost idyllic.

The villages along the valley were deserted. If the Bulgars had learned anything from their Muslim colonial masters, it was fatalism. God willing, the French and the English will go; Allah willing, even the Ottomans will go; Bog willing, the Russians will come; and in the meantime, the villagers have disappeared, abandoning their houses and vanishing into the countryside, leaving the French and the British to their own devices and to the devices of a new recruit who is at home in the sullen waters of the lagoons – Corporal Forbes.

George first hears the nickname on Porrick Donnelly's lips. Corporal Forbes. It's a jocular, ironical, bitter name, somewhat facetious and probably with a hint of rhyming slang about it. A typical piece of British Army humour in fact.

Corporal Forbes is *cholera morbus*.

Cholera.

Unlike Covid-19, cholera is caused by a bacterium, *Vibrio cholera*, which made its debut on the world stage in 1817. Emerging from its place of origin in the Ganges delta it spread outwards in successive waves, killing millions. By 1854 the world was in the middle of the third pandemic, which began in 1846 and struck right across Europe from the Black Sea to London. It would blaze on for a further six years while the medical profession argued over the cause – was this plague due to a "miasma," a noxious effluvium from rotting organic matter, or was it caused by waterborne "germs"?*

Such argument was no help to the soldiers camped in their thousands in and around Varna. Had the medical profession resolved the argument in time, through some fairly basic sanitary rules thousands might have been spared. As it was, the disease was so contagious that it spread through the troops like a malicious rumour. At Varna, in the summer of 1854, some regiments were decimated, literally. Eight hundred men? Eighty might die.

Along with the rest of his regiment, Corporal George lived in the company of Corporal Forbes for just over two months. Watch him picking his way between the tents, taking a detail down to the lake to collect water, boiling it because that's what Porrick Donnelly advised all the men of 5 Company to do: "That's what we did in India. Some doctors will tell you there's no need; some will say you should. It can't do any harm, can it? So boil the bloody stuff."

Watch George go about the ordinary life of the camp, organising the distribution of bread and salt beef when it arrives (late, always late) from the commissariat; or leading a party to forage for fruit and vegetables in the fields and orchards around one of the nearby villages or dig a grave in the hard earth above the camp; or taking a group into the

---

* In his seminal paper *On the Mode of Transmission of Cholera*, London: 1855, John Snow cites both the outbreak of cholera in the British forces on the Black Sea in 1854 as well as his famous experiment with the Broad Street water pump in Soho in the same year. 1854 was also the year in which the Italian anatomist Filippo Pacini identified vibrio bacteria in the gut lining of cholera victims and hypothesised that these bacteria were the cause of the disease. His work went unrecognised until 1885.

town – an hour's march away – to collect the post and whatever luxuries they can scrounge.

"Hey, Johnny!" the local traders call. "Look I got. You buy? Good price, Johnny!"

It may be fruit, it may be tobacco, it may be wine, it may be brandy. There's a theory that the local red wine gives you the runs, maybe even cholera itself, while liquor kills contagion. There are many such theories doing the rounds. Some people think the stale rations are the cause of the cholera, some the local fruit. Apricots are in abundance. "Kill-Johns" they're called. Whatever the cause, some men seem immune, or, if they are not entirely immune, lucky enough to get away with no more than a mild attack. But when you get it badly, it's different. Pain, fever, loss of consciousness. Water gushes out of your arse, that's the worst sign. Rice-water, it's called. Stinks of rotting fish. Men who get it badly are hastily removed from their tent in case the others catch it off them. That's another job the corporals are called upon to organise, getting men to move victims into the sick tent until they can be put on a cart and sent off to the hospital in Varna. Those who are still conscious beg not to be sent there because it isn't a hospital in a real sense of the word, it's merely a place to die, a charnel house. The whole place stinks of excrement and death. Once they've delivered the dying, the bullock carts line up at the next doorway to receive the already dead and take them away for burial.

All through July and August, as the temperature rises, the battle with cholera continues. Regiments move their tents to higher ground where they will be away from the miasma of the lakes, but that has little effect. The generals hum and hah and come to no decision about what should be done, either about the cholera or about the Russians, which, after all, is the reason the armies are here. Telegraph instructions come from Paris and London and meet with hesitation and contradiction, while the men go through the rituals of camp life. They cook and launder and try to clean. They drill. They forage for extra food. They drink foul water and cheap brandy. They sit around in the sun, bored into insensibility. They swim to cool off. They play cards. Those who can read share books; those who have someone to whom they can write compose letters home. And all the time Corporal Forbes is there among them, stalking them, killing by day and by night, one or two here, half a tent there. In the mornings the soldiers dig graves in the baked earth to bury their dead companions; at night pye-dogs or jackals dig up the corpses and eat them. The sailors bury their dead at sea (cholera has spread to the fleet, based at Balchik further up the coast) which seems a better idea except that in the waters of the bay, and even in the harbour itself, corpses, inflated by decomposition, rise bloated to the surface and bob around among the vessels like rubber bladders made into the shape of men. Firelocks are discharged to burst and sink them. The stink of putrefaction is everywhere, drifting across the summer sea, gathering round the tents of the Army on the hills and in the valleys, skulking through the alleyways of the town.

This is the cholera at Varna in the summer of 1854.

Lincoln

Another letter arrives, written from somewhere called Varna. She can just make out the name but she has no idea where it is or what exactly it might be. And she has no idea what the letter says. Just his name at the bottom, that familiar signature:

George Mawer

George Mawer's signature, taken from his marriage registration

Leaving the children playing in the street, she crosses the road to the church. The vicar is doing whatever it is that vicars do when they aren't holding services. Praying? Hearing confession? That's what they used to do when she was a girl in Sligo: listen, breathless, to your sins, loving the dirtiness then cursing you for it.

Can he read the letter for her?

Of course he can. He shows her into the presbytery and seats himself behind his desk. "I've been writing my harvest festival sermon," he says, putting on his glasses and then peering at her over the top of them. "I hope you will be there, Ann."

"Sure I will, father."

He seems kind enough, like an uncle or something, with a careful regard for her that is unusual in people like him. Usually people of his kind, the nobs, have little time for you. But not him. "Why don't you come and stand by me?" he suggests. "Then you may see the words as I read."

She stands beside his chair, watching his finger trace the words out almost as though he is writing them himself:

My dear wife,

he reads,

I have not had a letter from you for some time now. Perhaps you have written and it is lost in the post. I hope, and pray, that you and the children are well and that the child that you are carrying is growing well. Perhaps you have heard from reports in the newspapers of the cholera that we have here. Do not worry about me, Wife. I've not had anything much but an attack of the squitters

The vicar gives a small grunt of disapproval. "Squitters, indeed!"

which everyone gets. I am better now but fellows have died. In the poor old Half—

"Half-Hundred?" the vicar asks. "That's what it looks like."

"It's the regiment, father. That's what they call it. Fiftieth, see? Half a hundred."

"Ah. Yes, I do see indeed. Quite droll."

In the poor old Half-Hundred we have lost twenty-one, nine in one night alone, and all of them good

men. Other regiments have done worse. So those
comrades is what we leave behind as we board the
ships to finally get away from this damned place.
I think it will now be quickly over and we will be
home soon.

I will write again when I am able. Greet the
children from me.

Your affectionate husband,
George Mawer, Corporal of 50th

The vicar puts the page down. "There. Not the most effusive of correspondents but it seems that at least all was well
with him at the start of the month."

She doesn't know what *effusive* means, but doubtless the
vicar is right. Probably George is not effusive. The vicar turns
his chair towards her. It's on a swivel so he can turn away
from the desk and face her as she stands there. He reaches out
and takes her hands. His own hands are smooth and fine, like
a woman's. She is ashamed of hers, rough and raw as they are
from the soap. "I'm sure your George is all right, Ann. We
can but wait, and trust in the Lord." He pulls her closer, very
gently, so that she stands between his legs, her belly thrust out,
almost touching him. "You must be brave, Ann. A soldier's
wife must be brave. You are brave, aren't you? Two babies—"

"Three."

"There you are. Three babies. A mother must be brave to
have babies. So you are brave. And you must believe your
husband George will come home and all will be well. And
there is the new baby to think of. How is he doing? Does he
move much?"

"First thing in the morning, yes. Wakes me up sometimes
with kicking." She looks down at the man, feeling brave
enough for a moment. "How do you know it's a 'he'?"

251

He smiles up at her. "What do the women say it is? They always say they can tell by the way you carry it." His eyes, she thinks, are kind. When she first met him he seemed like them all – superior, cold. But not now.

"They say it is thrown out front, so it's a boy. But I think that's a nonsense."

"I'm sure you are right, Ann. A nonsense. May I," he hesitates, "feel him?"

"Feel him?"

"The baby. Like this." He lets her hands go and instead puts his own hands on her, over the taut dome of her belly, very gently as though blessing the baby inside. He seems to swallow something. Surely he can feel her belly-button through the thin stuff of her dress. It sticks out now the baby has grown. Embarrassing to have it touched.

"Which would you like it to be, Ann? A boy, I'll be bound."

"I don't mind. What happens, happens."

"Perhaps we could say a prayer?"

"You can pray for a boy?"

"Pray that it is safe and well." One hand moves down and round. There is a moment when he seems to be feeling for the baby and then a moment when he is feeling for Ann, his hand between her legs, cupping her.

She tries not to move, with his hand there. What would movement mean? Movement forward would mean she wanted it; moving away would be telling him to shove off. He mightn't like that. You never knew with men, how they might act. She could manage well enough in the barracks, and anyway there had always been George around. But now? And with this man, who was a man of God, and kind to her?

He speaks very quietly. "You're a fine woman, Ann."

She stays quite still. She can feel his fingers through her

252

clothing. He has closed his eyes and is murmuring words she can't quite hear. "What are you doin', father?"

"I'm praying, Ann. For a safe delivery. For a strong healthy boy." His fingers move, feeling her. "They come out through here, do you know that? Of course you do. But sometimes, with foolish girls, I have to explain it to them, for they think all manner of things. That the baby comes through their navel, for example. And others think that it is delivered by a celestial messenger. But I tell them that the good Lord, in His wisdom, has the baby issue forth, with blood and water, through this sacred orifice."

"There's no need to explain that to me, father."

"No," he whispers. "No need at all." Slowly, reluctantly, he takes his hand back. There are beads of sweat on his forehead. "My wife, you know, is barren."

"That must be a sadness for her. And you."

"That it is." His voice seems strained, as though it has suddenly become difficult to get the words out. "With not being able to work when the baby comes, it'll be hard for you, Ann, won't it?"

"I suppose it will."

"But I'll see that you are all right."

"Thank you, father."

Does she make the move? There's a pause when neither seems to know what to do or say. "I think I must be going, father. To my children."

"Of course." He rummages in his pocket and produces a handkerchief to mop his brow. "What about answering your husband's letter? Don't you want—"

"Mebbe we can do that later."

"Of course."

She turns to go but he calls her back when she is at the door. "Ann, there's this. For you." He holds something out, a silver coin. She hesitates, then comes back to the desk, takes the coin – half-a-crown – and slips it into her pocket. "I'll look after you," he says. "You know that. You only have to ask."

"Thank you, father," she says.

To the Crimea

On 2 September the order came to invade the Crimea. You might be forgiven for assuming that this was the whole aim of the expedition in the first place, but you would be wrong. The name that posterity has given to the entire enterprise – the Crimean War – is retrospective. At the time the whole allied force, French and British together, was dispatched to the Black Sea without any clear aim in mind beyond the rattling of sabres in support of Turkey. Once the Russian forces that had caused the crisis had raised the siege of Silistria and retired over the Danube there was really nothing more to be done. But by then there was this huge joint expeditionary force camped at Varna on the Black Sea, waiting, like a loaded cannon, to be fired at something. What to do with it?

Truth is, the invasion of the Crimean peninsula was more or less decided on a whim.

Sixty thousand men. Three hundred and sixty vessels, steam-ships towing sailing ships. It was a vast undertaking not to be repeated until the Gallipoli landings in 1915. And, like the Gallipoli landings, it was sailing towards disaster.

The 50th Regiment embarked in four sailing ships, all towed by one steamer, HMS *Sans Pareil*. Launched in 1851, the *Sans Pareil* had originally been designed as a traditional sailing ship, something that Nelson himself would have recognised. It was only during her construction that steam propulsion was added so the completed vessel was neither one thing nor the other, neither a pure steamer nor an efficient sailer but instead a ghastly hybrid, an eighty-gun square-rigged sailing ship with, hidden beneath her skirts, a steam engine and screw.

It was a laborious and chaotic crossing. The fleet dithered across the Black Sea for an entire week before finally fetching up about forty miles north of Sebastopol* offshore of a small port called Eupatoria. By its nature and appearance, the coastline south of Eupatoria might be part of the Suffolk coast, Kessingland perhaps: a long, desolate storm beach of sand and shingle with, behind it, a lagoon of brackish water. At dawn on the fourteenth, the disembarkation of the British Army began, some twenty-seven thousand troops. It wasn't until the afternoon that the 50th went ashore, ferried from the ships, the longboats pitching through the surf, men crowded and jostling, trying to stand upright and keep their firelocks dry, leaping over the gunwales and wading up the shingle. The shouting of English mingled with the sound of beating surf and the call of sea birds. Gulls circled in surprise. A heron took off in disgust and disappeared inland. George and his squad plodded out of the water and up the slope, stumbling across sand towards the dunes, laden down with their kit.

The things they carried: their firelocks of course, bayonets in scabbards hung from their waist belts; fifty rounds of Minié ball; on their backs, their knapsacks with blanket and greatcoat, an extra pair of boots, spare socks and shirt,

---

* Sebastopol was the usual English spelling of the time but it is now more commonly spelled Sevastopol. I have used the contemporary spelling throughout.

a forage cap, three days' rations (four and a half pounds of cooked meat and the same weight of biscuit) and a wooden water canteen; mess tins; and part of a cooking stove, shared with three companions. Then those little things that all men carried that weren't part of the issue. A crucifix, perhaps. A locket (silver-plate) enclosing the silhouette of a wife or a lover. A good luck charm – maybe a rabbit's foot or a sham-rock, maybe a dried merry-thought bone or a shark's tooth. Anything to provide that fragile link with home or person or safety. A Bible, for some who could read. A book of prayers. One carried a mouth organ, another a Jew's harp.

But no tents. They carried no tents.

They went inland, through the dunes to the edge of the lagoon. Orders were being shouted, bugles sounding. No enemy was present. This was enemy territory but no one had been seen beyond a few horsemen eyeing the hundreds of ships and the milling thousands of soldiers, and then disappearing. The sun was setting over the sea, a single eye glaring from below heavy black brows of cloud. The hinterland behind the beach was flat and slack, devoid of people.

The colour party of the Old Half-Hundred was away over to the right, men calling and a bugle blowing. George led his men over to where 5 Company was mustering. The wind had got up and the background noise was the crashing of waves and the seething of undertow. There was a sense of aimless-ness about the whole undertaking, a feeling that this was not where they were meant to be, this desolate sandbar on the coastline of Hades. Somewhere out of sight gunfire sounded and the men stood to, their weapons at the ready, wondering what to do and where to go. Then they stood down because nothing happened, no one came, no enemy appeared.

As darkness hurried on, the whole expeditionary force was ordered to pile arms and hunker down as best they could.

The sun had disappeared behind storm clouds and there was drizzle in the air. The men gathered what firewood they were able to find – scrub and thorn mainly – but soon it began to rain and there was no chance of getting a fire going.

"Where are the tents, corporal?" they asked. But there were no tents. Tents had not been landed. The sea was up, there were drowned horses wallowing in the waves and the ships were standing out to sea in case they should be caught on a lee shore; and no tents had been landed. Rain, which had started as mere flecks on the wind and then progressed to drizzle, was now falling hard.

"Just like Chobham," the wag called. "See what good training we had, lads?"

"At Chobham we had tents."

There was laughter, but bitter, acid laughter. This was nothing like the soft rain that falls in Surrey. This was a cold, hard foreign rain, a vengeful rain with a hint of the Russian steppe behind it. And if that's the pathetic fallacy at work, well, the facts are simple: on the night of 14 September 1854, the first night of the British and French expeditionary forces on Russian territory, it rained as hard and as cold as anyone had known it and there was no shelter. None. The French were all right – they had landed with bivouac tents which gave them some protection from the elements – but the entire British contingent, some twenty-seven thousand of them, were without shelter of any kind on that bleak and miserable shoreline.

George hunkered down in a shallow scoop behind a hillock of grass. His clothes were saturated. The thin sand beneath him became mud. Next to him in the utter blackness Porrick Donnelly muttered and swore. "Should have joined the bloody Navy."

"We'd be a damned sight drier."

"Even if we fell in the bloody sea."

He'd tell his grandchildren all about it, George thought. George Henry's children and Mary Ann's, and the children of the child yet to be born. How the Army went ashore in the evening without their tents and how the weather broke during the night and the rain came, and how it might have been September but in Russia September could be damned cold.

"George!" Annie would say. "Language!"

And he'd laugh and the grandchildren would laugh with him, and he'd tell them: "I'm just an old soldier and I don't give a damn" – that word again! – "about the niceties of polite behaviour, not when I've seen what I've seen."

An old soldier.

What would he be? Regimental sergeant major, perhaps. Retired with honour and a pension, full of memories and covered in medals. Grey-haired, beloved of his grandchildren, respected by the neighbours. They'd do one of those portraits of him, a photograph, in uniform, looking grand.

"Did you fight bravely, grandfather?" they'd ask, but he couldn't imagine the answer to that because he didn't yet know. So far they had barely caught a glimpse of the enemy – just that handful of Cossack horsemen on the skyline watching the chaos of the disembarkation before riding away over the brow of the hill.

By now Ann was – what? – in her seventh month? Was that right? She'd be showing, walking around with her belly going in advance of her. No letter from her in ages. He remembered her full with Mary, and with young George. Ungainly. Walking like a duck. That was their joke. He drifted in and out of sleep. The rain teemed down, oozing through the cloth of his jacket and the thin stuff of his trousers. His feet squelched inside his boots. He felt cold grip him like a fist. He dreamt and he woke, dreamt again, awoke once more, dreaming merging with waking so that it was hard to tell the difference. Time trickled by, as slow as the water down his neck.

Dawn was an apparition, a ghost of grey behind the hills inland. No sun but a thin wash of colour, like paint spilled across a dirty canvas. In the sodden, shivering dawn, George roused his squad into some kind of action. The men's hands and faces were stained red from the dye of their red coats. "Never mind the Dirty Half-Hundred," someone remarked. "Now they'll call us the Bloody Half-Hundred."*

Bitter laughter.

Breakfast of sodden biscuit and cold salt beef. "Not even a mug of fuckin' tea because there's no fuckin' fire because there's no fuckin' fuel in this fuckin' place. Excuse my French, corporal."

"What a way to start a war, eh? If you've survived Corporal Forbes you'll catch your death of pneumonia, never mind the bloody Russkies."

You laughed with them, that was the trick. They were happy enough if they could let off steam. Cheerful fellows for the most part. Put up with anything. "That's enough of that, Private Jellicoe. Let's get on with it."

In the half-light they went down to the beach and battled in the surf to bring the boats in with all those supplies that should have been landed the first day. Tents and stuff. It got some warmth into your bones. Otherwise, as Jellicoe had said, you might die a death of cold.

---

* The nickname the "Dirty Half-Hundred" came from an incident in the Peninsula War in 1808 when the black facing of their uniform jackets ran, giving them the appearance of chimney sweeps.

The Alma

They've halted in double column of companies, in an orchard, amid regimented ranks of trees. They're waiting, arms piled, for the next command. His heart is thumping like the steam engine of the *Cambria*, beating so heavily that it seems to fill his body. Glancing to the left, through the trees, he can see the right markers of the 38th Regiment. To his right, so close he can smell them, are his own companions, breathing heavily, their pallid faces slick with sweat. Some of them have taken apples and are eating them greedily. Ahead, beyond the orchard, in bright sunlight, the land slopes down towards a line of trees that marks the river. The Alma. Down there a village burns. The Russkies torched it, that's what they say. And they cut down some of the trees along the riverbank – stumps like sawn off limbs. Beyond the river where the land slants upwards they've built an earthwork. Smoke belches from a dozen guns and more, the reports coming seconds later almost as an afterthought. Figures swarm up the slope into the teeth of the cannon fire. Red coats. Flags wave like bunting in a breeze.

It all seems strangely remote, happening in another world. Even the sounds reinforce this sense of detachment – distant fireworks, the occasional dull thump of a petard. George had thought that battle would mean noise all around, explosions to rip your eardrums, men screaming, steel clashing, horses thundering. Instead they've waited for hours and the battle is only these distant sounds and distant views. Figurines in the landscape, smoke like fog, rifles like fire-crackers, artillery like maroons going off. Shells bursting in the air, a rocket weaving across the sky. A village burning.

"Ready the Fiftieth!" is the call. Along the ranks men drop their knapsacks and go through the intricate manoeuvres of unpiling their arms. George's stomach churns. Behind him someone is audibly sick. Is that fear or is it cholera?

The company commander stands on a rock to address his men. "We're crossing the river, going in after the Light Division and the Guards!" he yells. "Our objective is the Russian redoubt. Keep your ranks tight. Keep your weapons dry when we reach the water. God go with you!"

The sergeants take over. "Arms at the port. By the left, quick march!"

Drums beat. The columns tramp forward, down through the trees towards the burning village. An approximation of marching. You try to keep the dressing, that's the trick. Anything to focus the mind. George clambers over a wall of mud bricks and jumps down onto a dusty track, the rest of the company with him or behind him, like horses trying to steeplechase. Stumbling, swearing.

"Hold your dressing!"

A riderless horse gallops past, bloody and wide-eyed, the number twenty-three embossed on the saddlecloth. The 23rd Regiment, the Royal Welch Fusiliers. The first immediate witness of battle, like an emissary from hell. The 50th goes on, across the track and through a vineyard, the men dodging around the vines. Grapes. Someone grabs a bunch and stuffs it in his mouth.

"Hands to your weapons!"

The beat of drums and the tramp of boots, in rhythm with your thumping heart. Through the vineyard and onto a road. The clatter of hooves and Waddy is there, Colonel Waddy now, with another of the officers, the one-armed Frampton, as pale as chalk. The column stumbles to a halt. A shell bursts overhead, a white blossom unfolding from the air. Grapeshot rains around them, spent, most of it. The horses buck and rear. Another shot crashes into trees nearby, splintering branches, casting flocks of birds into the air like shrapnel. The colonel struggles with his horse, brings her under control. And then he notices George, grins down on him.

"Remember the Wigan riot, corporal?"

"Indeed I do, sir."

"Not quite as hot as this?"

"Not quite, sir."

"Let's on with it, eh? Job to be done."

"Yes, sir."

That's it. That's how to do it if you're an officer. A good trick of memory. The officers turn their horses down the track towards the river and the men follow. They'd follow them anywhere now.

"He remembered you, George. How about that?"

"He's a good 'un, the colonel."

They go past vines on either side, torn through with shot – grapeshot. At a bend in the track the view opens out into a narrow water meadow. Broken trees at the river's edge. The far bank is littered with the dead and wounded. The slope above is seething with the living, going forward and upward towards the Russian redoubt. The noise comes from there, a gust of noise, the crash of bayonets, the ragged snap of rifles, men calling, men screaming, the noise flooding down the slope like a fall of water. Standing at the edge of the meadow George can see it all, hear it all, recognise the guards in their bearskins, see where they are headed, the hillside of corpses, men at the parapet, gusts of smoke erupting from the guns.

Further down the track there's a civilian on horseback, talking with the officers. A civilian. Men say that the commander-in-chief eschews uniform and instead wears mufti even in battle. Is this him? Is this Lord Raglan? But there's nothing aristocratic about this man's looks – a baggy, disordered-looking civilian, no more than forty. And two-armed. Colonel Waddy turns in his saddle and shouts back to his troops, waving his arm: "Form lines! Form lines!" As they move there's a flash of black in the air, an eruption of stones and dirt between the troops and the horsemen. Something, a moment's presence, streaks past Corporal George and above the man at his side.

Time seems compressed into the tiniest space. That flash of something, that eruption of dirt, the streaking past mere inches from his right ear, so close he can feel the wind of its passage. Beside him Private Jellicoe is standing hatless, his shako smashed and the pieces scattered over the men behind. His face is stark white.

Time is compressed and time seems infinite. It happens in an instant and it's happening still, that manoeuvring on the banks of the River Alma as the Russian batteries up on the redoubt find their range and those desperate men break columns and hurry into lines. Half of them have never seen a shot fired in anger and here they are, drums beating, sergeants bellowing, shot flashing through the air as they open out across the fields and through the vineyards, trying to make parade-ground sense out of the broken terrain.

And Corporal George? He is there on the water meadows, terrified. He's fighting in a place he knows not of, for he knows not what – his companions-in-arms, his company, his regiment, Queen, country, half a dozen other concepts he barely understands. God. Empire. The custody of the Holy Places. The balance of power in Europe. Control of the Middle East.

And Annie. He's fighting for Annie. And his fragile family: George Henry and Mary Ann. And everyone who comes down from them. For my grandfather and father. For me. He's fighting for all those things and none of them. He's fighting just to stay alive, running across the meadow to the position of left marker as the regiment forms lines across the terrain, two ranks deep, firelocks at the port, bayonets fixed, drums beating. Alive for a moment. Up on the redoubt, guns open fire. Shot comes over, streaks of black in the air. But the troops are spread out across the field now so the battalion is less vulnerable. A shot merely brushes one soldier aside, cuts through into the space behind and buries itself in the ground. The line marches on. It's a thin red line (a phrase later coined by the very civilian who was talking to the colonel earlier), and then a ragged red line as they're slithering down the bank and into the water.* Water slides past, with bodies turning in the flow like idle swimmers – Coldstreamers, Grenadiers, the aqueous green of a rifleman. The 50th step over the bodies and wade knee-deep, sometimes waist-deep, to the far side. Then they're scrambling up the far bank, trying to keep their lines, slithering in the mud, clambering onto corpses, knowing that when they reach the top they'll be in line of sight from the redoubt, moving into point blank range.

Colonel Waddy has ridden round by the bridge. He's up

---

* William Howard Russell, correspondent of *The Times* of London, who encountered Colonel Waddy and the 50th at the Alma and warned them of Russian artillery fire from the Great Redoubt. His description of the 93rd Regiment at the later Battle of Balaclava was actually a "thin red streak, tipped with a line of steel." In his subsequent memoir this was changed to a "thin red line tipped with steel."

on the skyline urging his men to join him. "Forward the Half-Hundred!" he shouts. "Show us you're as good as the Guards!" They scramble up and over the lip of the bank, gather into some kind of line and move up the slope towards the Russian fieldwork, towards where the Guards are fighting.

And then there's something new in the soundscape of battle: a sudden silence, a cessation – and a roar, a human roar of triumph, as loud as any weapon. There are guardsmen standing on the parapet up ahead waving their regimental colours. Men are cheering, brandishing firelocks. The line of the 50th comes to a halt. Men sit down, sudden exhaustion overwhelming them. There is distant firing but it is nothing to do with them. The Russians are in retreat, other units pursuing them up onto the top of the escarpment but for the 50th, the Battle of the Alma, begun in confusion, has ended in confusion. The dead are being counted. The living are thanking their god or their good-luck charm or their lucky stars or whatever it is that determines that one man in a line shall be killed while his neighbours live, that one should lose an arm, another a leg, while another should escape unscathed.

Corporal George takes a swig from the stale water in his canteen. He has been fired at for the first time (although he has not yet fired a shot in anger) and his courage did not desert him. Sitting on a barren hillside among the litter of war and the dead of two nations, he wipes sweat from his eyes. Now he's thinking of Annie, longing for Annie, imagining her swollen with their next child, swollen with love for him as he is swollen with love for her. He is going to see her soon, see them all. The Russians are beaten. The allies will go on and take Sebastopol and that'll be the end of it. Back home in time for Christmas.

Porrick Donnelly comes over, picking his way through the wreckage. "How's it feel, George?" he asks.

"A bit flat, in truth."

"Sure, it's always like that. But you did well. Kept your nerve, kept your line. And this time we got away with it." Donnelly looks around the hillside. Abandoned weapons, broken bodies. Some Russians in their grey greatcoats, mainly British redcoats, men of the Light Division most of them. "You know what Jesus said, don't you?"

"He said a whole lot of things."

"Let the dead bury their dead, that's what he said. And that's what we'll be doing, George. The dead burying the dead. Ours and theirs."

They Dig

The slopes of the escarpment are populated by the three states of man – the dead, the living, and those who occupy an intermediary condition between the two. These have smashed legs, broken arms, bullet holes, bayonet gashes. Like souls in purgatory they groan and scream as the living gather them up out of the ranks of the dead and carry them down to the shore, where they wait for boats to convey them to wherever they are bound – to a life ruined or, more probably, to death itself.

Those who aren't carrying the wounded, dig. They dig and they dig and they dig. After the defences at Gallipoli and the graves at Varna, now this digging: dozens more graves, mass graves, sorted for nationality – Russians; British – and rank – officers; men. Stones for markers, lists of names drawn up by the adjutants, a roll call of personal and collective disaster. No coffins, of course. The bodies are stripped of their kit and wrapped in sheets before being consigned to the earth.

Mounds of boots and firelocks grow beside the pits, officers' accoutrements neatly sorted to one side, rank-and-file stuff just piled. The stench of open guts overlays the buzz of flies. Pye-dogs scavenge. Rats dart out of sight. A chaplain recites cursory prayers over heaps of corpses as earth is shovelled back; an Orthodox pope from the village chants and sprinkles holy water. A thurible spews clouds of cloying incense smoke all around. Somewhere a soldier is vomiting.

It's not the battle, it's the aftermath of battle. It's not the terror of the moment, it's the horror of what comes next.

Three days later the survivors leave the site of the battle. They pack up their tents – these are carried down to the ships to be carried round by sea – shoulder their kit and march away, over the hills towards the south. Towards Sebastopol. That is what they hear but they don't really care just as long as they get away from the rotting carnage. In time perhaps the mass graves will become geographical features of the hillside, tumuli from an age long past. Tourists will come and look, consulting guidebooks, taking photos. But for the moment the graves are suppurating wounds in the landscape, clots of earth heaving with maggots, buzzing with flies, scurrying with rats.

"What'd I tell you, George?" Porrick says as they set off. "That's a soldier's life: digging and marching. And occasionally, short moments when some bastard tries to kill you."

News

It's Monday and the bells in Lincoln are ringing. The children have gone off to school and she's on her own in the house, weighed down by the baby that lies couched in her belly and goes before her wherever she moves. The bells are ringing from St. Mary Magdalene. Not from St. Paul's in the Bail, nor from the cathedral itself, but from St. Mary Magdalene.

She goes out into the street to see who's around. Mrs. White next door is cleaning the doorstep, which is what she does all the time. "You could eat your dinner off of our doorstep," her husband claims with pride, as though there are circumstances under which that might be necessary. She looks up from her labour. "Hello, dear. How's it going?"

"The bells ..."

"Oh, that. My Thomas says it's something to do with the Army out East. A battle or something."

There's a pause. The woman scrubbing. The bells ringing. Annie standing in the doorway, anxiety churning inside her, the baby moving, her whole world moving.

The woman looks up. "Oh, of course, your old man's out there, isn't he?"

"Yes. Yes, he is."

Annie closes the door behind her and hurries to the church. Even walking is a trial now, this belly going before her. She has to adapt her gait to it, even her standing. Leaning back, her legs planted wide, her steps shorter. Somehow you forget all about the last time, and the time before that, and the time before that. Every time seems like the first time.

The bells are ringing still.

"It's in the papers," the vicar says.

"You know I don't read, sir."

"I thought you might have heard."

"I have. That's why I've come to see you. I thought you—"

"Of course." He has got the morning newspaper on his desk. "It's all here. Well, some of it. There has been a battle, on the River Alma it says. Reports come by telegraph these days and they don't always contain much detail but it seems that the Russians have been defeated."

"That was the bells ringing."

"Yes, it was the bells of St. Mary Magdalene. The rector is very *enthusiastic*."

"But it's good, isn't it? A victory."

He has that look, a frown, as though it isn't good after all. "Of course it's good. But we do not have the details yet. There will have been casualties."

She feels that sickness, something shifting deep inside her, the baby moving. "Not my George?"

The vicar isn't sure. The reports are vague, he says. The reports talk of hundreds.

Does he know something more and he's not saying? These people know more than they say. They can read. They keep things from the common people.

"The Lord will protect him, Ann," he assures her. "We will pray for him and the Lord will look after him."

"But the Lord didn't look after those – hundreds, you say? He didn't look after *them*, did He? The Lord giveth and the

Lord taketh away, that's what I remember from when I buried my Georgiana. And now you say He might have taken my George as well."

The man seems embarrassed. "God moves in a mysterious way," he says. "His wonders to perform."

"You can't always pretend it's wonders, can you, father? Because sometimes it's not wonders at all. Sometimes it's just misery."

He tries to be indignant. "My good woman! You must not question the wisdom of the Lord God!" That kind of thing. But it doesn't really work.

The Flank March

They're marching in the hot sun, up hill and down dale, across another river and then into the valley of a third. The hillsides are wooded. The villas of the rich are scattered through the woods, emptied of their owners and now emptied of their contents by the passage of British troops. The soldiers have rarely seen such houses before and never so that they can walk in through the front doors and wander through the ransacked rooms. Ornate plasterwork on the ceilings. Heavy drapes hang from curtain rails. In one room, kicking aside a broken chair, Corporal George finds a pendant – an emerald? A green stone of some kind, and on a gold chain. Perfect for an Irish girl, he thinks, stowing it away in his knapsack.

That is the first time he has ever stolen anything in his life; but it's not really stolen, is it? The owners have already abandoned their property and anyway, they are the enemy. Russkies. If he doesn't take it, someone else will. And it's only a small thing – there was an officer carrying a bloody statue out of one place. A whole bronze statue!

So, finders, keepers; losers, weepers.

A plethora of self-justification.

The regiment bivouacs among the trees. There's running water and abundant fuel for fires. Compared with the last days since the landing, this is paradise. Halfway-decent food has been brought up. They can boil water and make tea. Pickets are put out to watch for Russians but there's no sign of them and the general opinion is that they have gone skulking back to Sebastopol to lick their wounds. Yet there's still the enemy within, the enemy that camped with them at Varna, that landed with them at Eupatoria, fought with them at the Alma, stood beside them while they dug the graves of the dead, and now marches with them towards Sebastopol: Corporal Forbes. Cholera. During the night men die, vomiting and squirting rice-water from their arses.

Next morning the two men who died during the night are buried, with the regiment formed up among the trees to pay some kind of honour. Before they move off, Colonel Waddy delivers a diatribe about the dishonour of looting. He is sure that no man of his regiment has done anything so heinous –

"What's *heinous*?" Corporal George whispers; his neighbour shrugs.

– and he warns of consequences if anyone is caught, although there is no explanation of exactly what those consequences might be or why they should be necessary if he is sure than no man of the 50th would have done such a thing. "We are not a gang of damn Frenchies!" the colonel shouts.

The men cheer.

The pendant lies guiltily and undisclosed in George's knapsack.

That day the march continues, over more hills and down more valleys, through forest now, always towards the southeast. They don't know why they are marching or where they are marching because it is not their place to know. They have no idea that they are taking part in the soon-to-be-famous "Flanking March" in which, despite victory at the Alma,

Lord Raglan turns away from a direct assault on Sebastopol and instead marches his army round to the south of the city with the object of laying siege to the place. The soldiers don't know that and they don't know that had Raglan given orders to march directly on the city, Sebastopol would almost certainly have fallen. Indeed, back in Britain the newspapers are almost unanimous in reporting that the city has already surrendered.

If that had happened – if Raglan had attacked Sebastopol directly, everyone would have been able to go home for Christmas, including George with his emerald pendant as a Christmas present for Annie. With the histories to hand one can see it all in context. Hindsight tells us that, because Raglan took the allied armies all the way round the south and laid siege to the city, he was condemning the combatants to a yearlong stalemate in which trenches would be dug, artillery duels would smash defences and blow men to smithereens, in which thousands would die of cold and disease; in which victory, when it finally came, would be as hollow as the conquest of a graveyard. But they know none of this. Specifically, Corporal George knows none of it. How could he? At the time, immersed in the eternal present, he can only see the next step ahead – this boulder to skirt round, that patch of loose gravel to slither across, those branches to duck beneath, this exiguous path to follow through the forest behind men and mules. He doesn't even know which direction is south, merely follows where he is led and stands when the whole column grinds to a halt. His knapsack digs into his shoulders. His boots rub blisters on his heels. Sweat insinuates itself beneath his clothing, down his chest, beneath his arms. Lice, picked up from using Russian bedding straw after the Battle of the Alma, itch in his groin. His firelock is no more than a damned nuisance, a presence that must always be placated, cleaned, cared for, tended like an idiot child that cannot fend for itself. These are the things that concern him now.

By the time they break out of the forests the men are exhausted and racked with thirst. It's growing dark as they stumble downhill to the place called MacKenzie's Farm.

"MacKenzie's Farm? Who the fuck is MacKenzie?"

"Sounds like a Scotchman."

"What's a bloody Scotchman doing here?"

"Scotchmen get everywhere."

"Always trying to escape their bloody country."*

They bivouac in the fields beneath a limestone escarpment. In the failing light it reminds Private Jellicoe of Benbulben.

"Everywhere reminds you of Ireland," Corporal George remarks. "You said Gallipoli was just like Cork."

Laughter.

"Well it was, so."

"Just don't tell me bivouacking reminds you of your old grandmother's bed."

With the night comes the cold. The days are hot and the nights are cold and they have no tents because the tents were sent back on board the ships when they left the Alma. So they wrap themselves in what little extra clothing they have and try and keep warm.

Men die. They die at MacKenzie's Farm just as they died at the river bivouac, of cholera. You can try to run from Corporal Forbes but you cannot hide from him. The next morning they

---

* The name originates with a Russian admiral of Scottish ancestry, Foma Fomich Mekenzi (Thomas MacKenzie), who founded the port of Sebastopol in the eighteenth century. He was granted the estate by the Czar.

bury two more. There are prayers from the chaplain and a salute over the grave, the gunfire cracking out across the plain in the cool morning. Dogs bark. Crows clatter into the air. The survivors pack up and move out, wondering who is going to be next, and how. If the enemy doesn't get you, disease will.

Today's march is across open country, over a river and across an undulating open plain. Wheat fields. Dun-coloured soil. Ahead, a line of hills shoulders its way up out of the plain; further over to the west there's a steep escarpment where the white limestone shows through the earth like bones through flesh. But they're not going there, not for the moment at least. Today is an easy march, almost a rest, a stroll in the sunshine over the nearer hills towards a place called Balaclava. A cushy day, Porrick Donnelly says.

Cushy. One of those words the old brownies brought back with them from India.

They pass scattered farmsteads. Their owners have run away, leaving only the serfs behind. The serfs are slaves really, that's what men say. Chained dogs bark at the marching troops, and there's a great deal to bark at because it looks like a real army now with more than twenty thousand men on the move, cavalry doing what cavalry does best, which is looking pretty, all flashing and jingling like a circus act; the artillery trundling their big guns; and the infantry in massed ranks, grimy and ragged after so many days in the open but at least able to put on a bit of a show, drums and fifes playing and the men moving with a bit of snap. They sing. That makes them feel good. "Look Lively My Lads" and "The Keel Row," songs like that. And they don't forget they have just beaten the Russians. They may be dirty and lice-ridden and half-starved and infected with cholera, but they've seen the fucking Russkies off and now they are going to beat the shit out of the port of – what's it called? – *Sebastopol*, that's it.

But for the moment Sebastopol lies out of sight beyond the distant escarpment and beyond the imagination. Best just to think of today. Today is marching across open fields in the sunshine; a cheerful landscape. Today is cushy marching and a bivouac in a vineyard outside the small fishing port of Balaclava where the Navy has already begun unloading. Today is fresh grapes, if not yet fresh clothing. Today is fuel for heating water so they can wash themselves. Today is warm autumnal air replete with promises – of food, tents, beer, clean clothing, all those creature comforts that will be with them soon. That's what the man from the commissariat assures them, although they have yet to see any of the bounty that he promises.

That night it's another bivouac but at least the weather isn't bad and there's fuel to make fires.

The next day they march up onto the plateau. Colonel Waddy and his officers lead the way on horseback with the drums following and then the companies in order, the grenadier company at the front, the light company taking up the rear. The road runs westward across the Balaclava valley, then climbs up for some six hundred feet through the escarpment to emerge on the high ground. It's a pleasant march in the sunshine. Morale is up and the miseries of the last few days forgotten. Up there on the heights there's open downland that Private Jellicoe claims is just like the Burren. They laugh at that, of course. Only the Irish have any idea where the Burren is or what it might be, but there's nothing like a running joke to keep the spirits up. And it *is* fine up there, marching along the metalled road across the heights, keeping step with the drums, with the wind on your face. Then the battalion breasts a rise and is called to a halt.

Ahead the ground slopes downwards towards the sea, bordered on either side by deep valleys. Two miles away, framed by the valley sides, is an inlet of water, crowded round with white buildings and cross-hatched with the masts of ships.

The men look on in silence. Some of them crane to see. Colonel Waddy's horse stomps on the hard ground, bothered by flies. The colonel's voice is heard indistinctly, snatched at by the wind: "There you have it, men! The city of Sebastopol."

There's a murmur in the ranks. A bit of cheering.

"Take Sebastopol and we can all go home! Is the Dirty Half-Hundred ready for it, lads?"

Of course it is! The cheering grows, becomes united. Yes, the Dirty Half-Hundred, dirty as they may be after eleven days' marching and sleeping in their uniforms, without adequate food, without adequate water, without tents for most of the time, in the cold and the rain, in the heat and the dust, yes the Dirty Half-Hundred *is* ready for it!

"Hip-hip!" A voice calls.

"Hurrah!"

The Sebastopol Heights

The landscape where they find themselves is a complex, dissected plateau shaped like a hand placed down on the ground, a giant, gnarled right hand, fingers pointing to the inlet of Sebastopol harbour. Each finger of land is divided from its neighbour by a valley that begins as a shallow depression between the knuckles and deepens into a ravine as it descends. On that sunny, late September day, the 50th are standing on the leftmost knuckle looking down the two-mile length of the forefinger. Further left, beyond the thumb and curving round the south of the city, are the French lines.

Sebastopol in the far distance, seen from Cathcart's Hill, 1855. Photo by Roger Fenton. The tents probably belong to the 4th Division. The 3rd Division, including the 50th Regiment, were further to the left. The land in the middle ground is deeply dissected by the ravines that cannot be seen in this view.

The officers have telescopes, They stand forward of the ranks, scanning the land ahead as it drops away towards the port, trying to pick out features of importance, looking for defences. Part of the anchorage may be seen between the fingertips.

"Church," one of them says. "Warehouses. Dozens of masts." He points to high ground over to the left, divided from the plateau where they stand by a deep ravine. "Redoubt over there."

As he speaks there's a sudden puff of white smoke from where he was pointing, no more than a smudge in the distance. "They've spotted us."

Someone counts, slowly and deliberately: "One ... two ... three ... four ... " The voice has reached nine when the report reaches them, the sound of a door slamming far away, the laws of cause and effect made elastic by distance.

"Finding our range," the officer says. "What's that? Two miles?"

"Something like."

And then, just ahead and above them, a blossom of fire and smoke magicks itself out of the air, followed a moment later by the crack of a detonation and the patter of shot, like rain falling.

"Better get the men behind cover, sergeant major," Colonel Waddy says. Orders are shouted. Companies turn and march back over the hill and down the reverse side. Out of sight, out of mind. Another regiment is already there on the plain, marking out the lines for the 3rd Division camp.

"Now all we need," Donnelly says, "is fucking tents."

But tents don't come. They bed down for the twelfth bivouac on the open hillside, resigned to misery. It might be hot during the day but the temperature plunges during the night. Wrapped in their filthy greatcoats yet again, the men scratch at their lice and struggle to keep some semblance of warm. George sleeps fitfully in a hollow he has scraped out of the thin earth. Whichever way he turns the hard bones of the landscape press into him, reminding him of being awake. He thinks of Annie. It must be near her time. In snatches of sleep he dreams of her, naked and clothed, available and unobtainable, slender and swollen, all those contradictory things at the same time. Light leaches into the hillside like cold water from a dew pond and brings him back to reality. Whatever she may be, she is not here with him on this bony hillside, in this cold and this discomfort.

That morning they make fires out of bits of scrub and thorn, barely enough to boil a mess tin of water. That morning they bury one of the men who has died during the night. He was complaining of stomach cramps and then he died. Cholera? No one knows, not even the captain-surgeon who is better at sawing off limbs than diagnosing bowel disease. They carry the body away from the camp and bury it where a thicker smear of soil enables them to dig a shallow approximation of a grave. The place is marked with a boulder as a headstone, roughly engraved with his name, Jos. Brown. There will be others.

They had no idea, of course. That's always the problem with any account of the past: how to put yourself into the mind of someone who has *no idea what is about to happen*. But it is obvious that the men of the 50th Regiment have no idea. George Mawer has no idea. He and they are embedded in their present while we watch them through the fog of hindsight. Our view is like the view they will have of the Battle of Inkerman that will be fought on that very plateau in a month's time: they will fight that battle through the fog and drizzle of an early morning; we look back at them through the fog and drizzle of record and memory, seeing figures moving dimly through the cloudy vapour, moving this way and that. Some of the words they speak can be heard, some of the emotion they feel can be sensed. There is the crash of rifles and the clash of bayonets. The details may be wrong but the gist is true enough and with the advantage of hindsight it is possible to know where they are going and what the world will look like when the fog finally clears and the dead and dying can be counted. Yet the men of the 50th have no idea. No one could foresee the enormity of the looming disaster as they looked down on the city of Sebastopol on that bright and sunny day in late September 1854, with skylarks singing in the wind. Disaster only plays itself out in retrospect.

Tents come eventually, brought up from Balaclava harbour along with some of their kit. They pitch them in rows beside the other regiments of the 3rd Division, the 38th and the 4th. It looks almost festive, like Chobham Common. Rows and rows of bell tents, canvas flogging in the wind. Flags flying. Washing flapping like bunting.

Sir Richard England, the divisional commander, inspects the lines and pronounces them excellent. His broad, moustachioed face beams on one and all. "Capital, capital," he says.

Later, a messenger comes up from the harbour lugging a haversack. The pickets stop him. "This the Fiftieth?" He dumps the haversack on the ground. "Mail."

Men gather round eagerly. The quartermaster-sergeant shoves them back. "A bit of order, please!" Letters are doled out like presents at Christmas, the men jostling for position, eager to hear their name called. There's one from Annie, or from whoever writes her letters for her. George takes it and walks deliberately to his tent, refusing to display the emotion he feels. Once inside he scrabbles at the envelope and tugs out the sheet of paper.

She's fine, the baby hasn't come yet, the children are fine, all is fine.

Your affectionate wife, X *Ann Mawer, her mark.*

He looks at the date. Weeks ago; weeks ago and a world away. What is happening to her now? Is he already a father once again – for the third time (or the fourth, if you count poor little Georgiana)? The sting of tears assaults him. He wants the words to have been written by Annie herself, not some damn scribe, so that touching them can be some kind of direct connection with her. How is she? How is her smile? How is the light in her blue eyes? How is the autumnal red in her hair? He recalls how she was when swollen with George Henry, swollen with Mary Ann, swollen and ripe like a fruit about to burst. The drum-taut curve of her belly. The navel curiously everted. How the babies moved inside her, an elbow, a knee, the child swimming like a fish in the strange liquid she had made for them.

When is she due?

They Dig

They dig. Up there on the heights overlooking Sebastopol, forward of the camp, they dig trenches and gun emplacements.

"What did I tell you?" says Porrick Donnelly glumly. "Should have stayed at home and dug railways. For twice the pay."

Engineers appear on the scene, with maps and plain-tables, compasses, rulers and levels. They point out features, issue orders, show officers where earthworks should be, how the main battery will be, where the first parallel should be dug, how the saps should be advanced down the slopes towards the city, where the second parallel should be excavated and then the third. Siege-craft. It is an art and a science, a blend of inspiration and logic. It is also dangerous because the biggest Russian guns in the redoubt over on the left – it has acquired a name, the Flagstaff Battery – have got their range, so while they dig two soldiers are always on watch duty, one to look towards the Flagstaff, the other to the more distant Redan away to the right.

On seeing a gust of smoke, the watcher yells out, "Shot!" and digging stops. The diggers take cover. All goes quiet until the devil manifests itself: either an explosive shell bursting in the air overhead and spraying shrapnel over the trenches, or round-shot that flashes out of the sky and careens across the hillside, scattering earthworks to the wind. Once the danger has passed digging can recommence.

The hillside – ironically called Green Hill – is as meagre as a pauper's back: a thin layer of reddish flesh stretched over a spine of stone. Digging is more pickaxe work than spade-work, levering rocks out of the ground, filling gabions* with earth and rocks, scraping out trenches and building parapets.

While they dig the Navy brings siege guns up for the battery. These are monsters taken out of ships, each one weighing five tons and more, each one dragged up from Balaclava by horses on the road and then a team of fifty matelots up the steep inclines. There's even a pair of Lancaster guns, the very latest technology, capable of throwing a spinning sixty-eight pound shot over three miles.

"Aim it at the fucking Flagstaff," is Porrick Donnelly's comment.

George digs and thinks of Annie. He commands his little detachment of private soldiers grovelling like rats in the shallow soil of the Green Hill and he thinks of Annie. When he gets back to the camp there might be a letter from her. Her time might have come, might already have come and gone. She might be alive, she might be dead. Her own trial, the trial of childbirth, is no safer than his. A baby pushing its way out of her body might kill her as surely as round-shot might spin out of the empty sky and kill him. There's nothing he can do about either, beyond offering up a prayer to a god who seems to have forgotten all about humanity. He digs.

---

* Wicker baskets filled with earth and stones, used to build parapets for temporary field defences. Many of the gabions used had been constructed at Varna, almost the only example of efficient forward planning in the whole Crimea campaign. A soldier was paid a 14d. bonus per gabion filled; more than his entire day's pay.

Birth

Mary Ann watches. She's six years old and she's standing in the doorway, watching. She watches things that will affect her for life – her mother lying on the bed convulsed with pain, face contorted with what seems to be anger, body open like the gaping mouth of a sea monster, bearded and bloodied, vomiting forth the ragged, writhing creature that Mary Ann will come to know as Sarah Rebecca.

It is 9 October 1854.

Mary Ann will come to love and cherish Sarah Rebecca; but the act of childbirth itself she will fear and loathe, loathe so much so that she will never give birth herself, indeed not even marry until she is forty years old and then to a widower ten years older who already has children by his first wife. Of course, six-year-old Mary Ann has no idea about this. She just sees her mother being torn to pieces by giving birth, sees her covered in sweat and blood, sees the way her body expels the little skinned rabbit of the new child.

One of the attendant women catches sight of her. "Out!" she cries. "Out! Out!"

Mary Ann is hustled out of the room back to where she is meant to be, which is downstairs looking after George Henry. George Henry is only three. He will recall nothing, or next to nothing, of the event.

Later, Mary Ann will be called up to witness the baby under less dramatic circumstances, her mother lying on the narrow bed looking exhausted but somehow happy. Her eyes are bright with, it seems to Mary Ann, a kind of insanity. The baby, attached to her breast, seems a different creature altogether from the malicious being her mother's body was expelling only a short while earlier.

"Look Mary Ann, look at your new sister. How proud your father would be."

Mary Ann looks. The baby is sweet enough, suckling at the mother's breast; but Mary Ann's memory cannot rid itself of the means of delivery.

Cannonade

By 16 October the siege artillery was ready: 126 heavy field guns and mortars in an arc around the southern side of the city. What directly concerned the men of the 50th was Chapman's Battery, which they had helped dig: twenty-six field guns and five mortars bedded in just below the crest of the Green Hill, along with a sixty-eight-pound Lancaster gun set further back along the ridge. The plan was that at six-thirty in the morning of 17 October these guns, in concert with the rest of the British and French artillery, would open fire.

However, somehow the Russians had got wind of the allies' plans and *their* guns opened fire half an hour earlier, at six o'clock.

There's nothing like stealing your opponent's thunder, and thunder it was. Barrage and counterbarrage continued more or less throughout the day. The ground shook. Ears were deafened. Smoke billowed up from the city and the surrounding ridges. Parapets and bastions collapsed. Men died, blasted into pulp by round-shot, torn apart by explosive shells. The stench of sulphur filled the air. The whole city and its encircling heights might have been a volcano in eruption.

Throughout this time the men of the 50th did what the poor bloody infantry soon learned to do throughout such barrages: they crouched in their trenches and waited. If they had mind enough to think, they prayed. Common wisdom had it that once the cannonade was complete and the Russian defences had been pummelled into the ground, the infantry assault would be launched, Sebastopol would be taken and everyone could go home.

Common wisdom is all too often wrong, especially in military matters.

At 8:40 a Russian shell from the Flagstaff Battery exploded inside the French no. 4 battery across the valley to the left. The shell not only exploded within the battery, it actually hit the magazine. There was an almighty secondary explosion as the stored powder went up, a great gust of smoke and fire lifting bits – bodies, limbs, splinters of wood, clots of earth and stone – high into the air. Seconds later a mighty concussion clapped the ears of British troops in the trenches on Green Hill. Seconds after that, as dust settled on the silence of the French battery, you could hear cheering from the Russian lines.

After this setback the French guns fell more or less silent, but the cannonade went on from the British lines. Clumsy, brutal destruction, like a child with a hammer smashing toys. Other magazines – one British, two Russian – were blown up by lucky shots. Other emplacements were flattened, other men killed or injured. Seven men of the 50th were wounded.

"They're the lucky ones," said Private Jellicoe as they were carried back to the camp on the other side of the hill. But they weren't really. The regiment had a surgeon and two assistants who dealt with the wounded in the manner of the times. Badly damaged limbs were amputated, the quicker the better. There were rudimentary disinfectants, rudimentary anaesthetics (chloroform mainly), no antibiotics. Gangrene was the great fear. As often as not a smashed limb was a death warrant.

And still the smashing continued. By the evening the major Russian defensive positions opposite the British lines – the Great Redan, the Malakhov – had been more or less reduced to rubble. In the trenches the soldiers waited for an order to advance that never came.

Sarah Rebecca

My dear husband,

I hope this finds you well. Daily I ask for news of the war and I pray that you are safe. My own news is the birth of your child, which is a daughter, in fine health, born on the ninth of this month. My confinement was satisfactory. As I cannot work for the moment we are being looked after by the parish thanks to the kind indulgence of the Reverend Mr. Richter who writes these letters for me. He is as good a Christian gentleman as one could wish to meet and has been like a father to me and to your children. He tells me not to make him write these words and that he is only doing his Christian duty, but I must say what is true and he must write down what I tell him.

The children are well. Mary Ann is a great help to me and cares for George Henry much of the time. George Henry talks of his father. I tell him his father is a soldier fighting for Queen and country and he says that he will fight for his father. Perhaps he too will become a soldier one day, but I hope not.

My husband, we needs must choose a name for our daughter, for her to be christened. With the help of Mr. Richter I have thought of the names Sarah and

Rebecca, both dutiful wives, which I hope our own
daughter may be. If you are in agreement with these
names then you must tell me by letter as soon as
is possible.

  I long for you to come back home safely to your
family, which now numbers four.

  Your affectionate wife,
  Annie Mawer ✗ *her mark.*

The Reverend Richter folds the letter and slips it into an
envelope. While Annie watches he writes the address of the
regimental depot, an address he knows by heart now, and
seals it with red wax. He affixes a penny stamp. "There."

There's a pause, Annie standing by the desk, Richter sitting.
"Is the child well?" he asks. "Healthy?"

"Very strong, father."

"That is good news. Thank the Lord for that. She nurses
well?"

"Very well."

"Where is she now?"

"Her sister is looking after her. I must get back."

Richter looks Annie up and down. She feels his eyes on her
like the cold touch of a corpse. She has no choice but to stand
there before him for he holds the key to her understanding of
the world. He can read for her, he can write for her. And he
holds the purse strings.

"You give good milk?"

"I give good milk, father. Never had any problem with
my others, nor with this one. My difficulty is the older children. Feeding them, I mean. Feeding, clothing. Now that I
cannot work."

He shakes his head. "There is only so much I can do."

"I don't want the workhouse. Not the workhouse."

"No, of course not."

"A soldier's wife and family. It's not right." She's close to tears. She can't help it. Tears welling up inside her, a great pressure of misery.

"Certainly. Perhaps there are monies. I will consult with colleagues. In the meantime ... " He rummages in his waist-coat and takes out a half-crown. "Here."

She takes the coin from him and turns to go but he catches her hand. "Annie," he says, holding her. "Have faith in the Lord."

Up the Line

A new kind of warfare began, one that was destined to carve its name into the collective mind of the whole world: trench warfare. On the Western Front between 1914 and 1915 they perfected it in all its misery, but in 1854 in the Crimea, following the failure to take the city after the bombardment of 17 October, they invented it: the maze of trenches, the troglodyte world of revetments, sandbags, fire-steps, parapets, dugouts, it was all there. The names may have varied but the meanings were the same. Saps zig-zagging from the reserve trenches to the front line. Gabions and sandbags. Raiding parties, snipers, rats. And mud: not the deep and cloying mud of Flanders but rather the thin, calcareous, slippery mud of the Somme. Generals may spend all their time trying to fight the previous war but in the Crimea, quite unconsciously, they anticipated the next one. Add cold, a bitter, continental cold howling down from Siberia into the basin of the Black Sea, a cold more profound than anyone in the Army had ever experienced, and couple that with inadequate food and inadequate clothing – they were still meant to be wearing red coats, for God's sake! – and you have the formula for a misery equal to Verdun or Ypres.

It's a bitter irony that three of the best-known things to have come down to us from the Crimean War are items of warm clothing – the raglan, the cardigan, the balaclava.

In his tent, shared with fourteen other soldiers, stinking of unwashed bodies and stale clothing, rich with undertones of shit and piss, Corporal George reads Annie's letter for, what? The fifth time? The sixth? The seventh? He reads it by the stub of candle he keeps in his pocket. The letter is his only tangible contact with home, with her.

> *I have thought of the names Sarah and Rebecca, both*
> *dutiful wives, which I hope our own daughter may*
> *be. If you are in agreement with these names then you*
> *must tell me by letter as soon as is possible.*
>   *I long for you to come back home safely to your*
> *family, which now numbers four.*

Sarah Rebecca? Sarah and Rebecca are wonderful names! And she is undoubtedly a wonderful child. He can imagine her sucking at Annie's breast. He can imagine Annie's breasts themselves, and her narrow body, her spare thighs, her smooth belly, her flesh the colour of ivory, her hair that russet autumnal colour that surely betrays her Irish blood. Fragile her body may seem, but it is tough when it confronts childbirth. Mary Ann, George Henry, tragic Georgiana and now Sarah Rebecca.

There are times when such thoughts can almost bring him to tears, he who by now has seen, without shedding tears, men with their legs blown off, their bowels opened up in their laps, their heads crushed like walnuts.

All he wants is to see her again.

He tucks the letter away and nips out the candle flame. The others of his tent are already trying to sleep, wrapped in bits of wool and felt and animal skins, shifting awkwardly on the icy ground. He tries to dream of Annie.

Every few days 5 Company go up the line. They're woken before dawn so that they can make it through the ravine in the dark, before the Russian gunners can spot their movement. They've got to be up early enough to allow the men they're relieving to get back before daylight. So it's double early – early enough for you; early enough for them. And it's cold now, continental cold with the wind from the northeast, a cold unlike anything anyone has known, a cold that seems to scrape the sinews from your bones.

George has a secret supply of dry lucifers and has managed to get his stub of candle lit. He goes round his tent kicking people awake, ignoring the protests. "You'll need all your warm clothing."

"We 'aven't got no warm clothing, corporal."

"Well wear it just the same. And forage caps, not your bloody shakoes. Last week someone from the King's Own wore a shako and he got his head knocked off."

There's no time to boil water for coffee. Not enough fuel to light a fire anyway. Breakfast is just dry biscuit and cold water, like every bloody meal. "Why can't they get enough fuel up here for God's sake?"

Why can't they? Why can't they get fuel up from Balaclava? There's all the stuff down there, so rumour has it. Piles of stores sitting on the quayside. Clothing, fuel, food, porter, rum. So why can't they get it the seven miles up the road? Why can't they get decent food and enough of it? Why can't they get warm clothing? The French can, so rumour has it. Why are the British regiments on the front line still living on salt beef and biscuit? Why are they dying of cold and dysentery and cholera more than by shot and shrapnel?

Why?

Cold fingers struggle to light a lamp. When finally it comes, the flame creates a small circle of light like a puddle of piss surrounded by the leathery, bearded faces of prophets: prophets forecasting doom.

"Right, let's go."

Corporal George leads the way, crawling out of the tent. Outside in the dark the company is gathering. A young lieutenant pushes his way between the groups of men, showing that he's in charge. "Ready for the first parallel, men. Sergeant, you take the lead."

"Where's Captain Weare?" asks Porrick Donnelly. "Sir."

"He's not well," the young lieutenant replies.

"Well, we usually go down the valley direct to the second parallel. That's what Captain Weare does. Strictly speaking we're meant to go via Chapman's Battery and the first parallel. But that takes twice as long."

The lieutenant was about to insist, then thought better of it. "Do what you usually do, sergeant."

"Yes, sir. Thank you, sir."

The NCOs make a cursory examination of arms and ammunition and then they're setting off, over now-familiar ground but stumbling over rocks in the dark, cursing and blinding. Corporal George tells his own squad to shut up for Christ's sake. "Do you think the Russians want to hear your complaints?"

In the valley, darkness encloses them like a glove. There's no moon to give light, only a couple of shielded lamps, but they know the way by now. There are markers, of course, and, looming on the right, the familiar bulk of the hill where Chapman's Battery is dug in. You can see the silhouettes of the guns blocking the stars and the luminous black of the sky. They pass the picket's challenge and stumble on down into the darkness. Not even starlight here. Someone christened it the Valley of the Shadow of Death because in one place it's enfiladed by Russian guns and the unwary got blown to pieces. They know the danger now, but the name stuck. It's even there on the maps, as a warning.

The upper part of the Valley of the Shadow of Death in 1855, looking north-northeast. Photograph by Roger Fenton. There is a rather sterile debate about whether Fenton or his assistant Marcus Sparling placed the cannonballs on the track for dramatic effect. They probably did, but does it matter? Whether on the track or in the ditch, the cannonballs were there sure enough. And so was Corporal George Mawer. N.B. This valley is not to be confused with the "Valley of Death" immortalised in Tennyson's poem "The Charge of the Light Brigade." That valley is down on the plain of Balaclava.

Further on, the valley narrows, deepens, becomes a ravine. If you go wrong here and carry on down you'll find yourself at sea level and wandering into the Russian rifle pits at the edge of the city. That's the danger. But just at the dangerous moment, just when the mistake might be made as you're blundering around in the dark, there's a challenge from another picket guarding the path that leads up to the right, up through the cliffs onto the heights and the second parallel: "Halt! Who goes there?"

"Five Company of the Fiftieth," the lieutenant replies, trying to keep his voice down, trying not to alert the Russkies.

"What kept you?" An educated voice. One of the officers, but what rank?

"Nothing kept us. We're on time."

"Aren't you meant to come through the first parallel and the saps?"

"Quicker this way."

A grunt in the darkness. It's not worth debating the point. And the lieutenant has earned a little glimmer of respect from the NCOs for not apologising. Thus is the popularity of officers won, by little things. Keep taking the shortcut and it'll become the approved way. Play the system. And you've got to play it as best you can because if you don't you'll die.

You may well die anyway, even if you do.

The company forms up in single file and begins to climb in the darkness. The covered way is a staircase in places, steps cut out of the limestone, a ramp winding up through thorn and mastic before gaining the high ground and the long, narrow trench of the second parallel. They know it inch by inch because they sweated blood and broke fingernails digging the bloody thing. Four hundred yards across the ridge it runs, with rifle pits and gun emplacements at intervals. Even in the dark you feel you want to keep your head down because the parapet is low and the trench is shallow. At the junction halfway across there's a signpost. Sergeant Donnelly holds up the lamp so they can read it in the halo of yellow light: a crudely carved arrow pointing left to *3rd Parallel*; another pointing right to *1st parallel*. Some wag has nailed a plank to the top of the signpost. It says *Seven Dials*.

"I had a girl at Seven Dials," says a voice in the darkness. Cockney.

"What was her name?"

"Grace."

"How much did she cost?"

There's laughter, some mock fighting, a sharp call for silence. Changing of the guard takes place, people shoving past in the dark, muttering and cursing. Orders are issued – squads to man the second parallel, details to occupy the rifle pits, pickets to patrol the saps, a couple of detachments to repair trenches damaged by gunfire. Corporal George has drawn the short straw – picket duty forward in the third parallel.

"What did we do to deserve this, corporal?"

"Everyone does it in turn. Stop complaining. At least we're going down in the dark."

He gathers his squad, gets them in some kind of order in the narrow trench. "Firelocks charged, half-cock, primed."

They make their way into the sap that descends the front of the hill. The third parallel is sixty feet lower down, cut across the face of the hillside directly overlooking the headwaters of the Sebastopol dockyard, so close that even without a glass you can see people moving on the quayside. But worse than that, the trench is level with the Russian batteries on either flank: the Flagstaff Battery across the valley to the left, the Redan across the valley to the right. Both of them rebuilt after the pounding they received during the first bombardment. A thousand yards from one, seven hundred yards from the other. You live like troglodytes in the third parallel, hunched over whenever you move, skulking behind cover all the time, waiting for the round-shot that comes whirring through the air and smashes the parapet and you to pieces, or the shell that bursts overhead and pulverises you with grapeshot.

This is the most exposed position in the entire British siege line.

Porrick Donnelly has his view: "In the third parallel? You're like a pair of lady's drawers hung out to dry and flapping in the wind."

As they go forward dawn is coming up, leaching a flat grey into the luminous black overhead. The men they are relieving curse them for being late and push past back up the sap. Corporal George gathers his men around him. "I want sentries out on either side, down in the valleys."

There are groans and complaints. He ignores them, detailing names off for the first watch. "Remember, we keep quiet and out of sight. Out of sight, out of mind. Old Russkie's not much different from us. He wants a quiet day just like we do. Don't give him any excuse to get angry."

The chosen men make their way down the sides of the hill, grumbling as they go. Behind them come the others of the detachment, placed along the trench as carefully as a chess player moves his pawns. They settle down for the watch. If you are lucky it'll be no worse than boring and the main danger will be falling asleep.

George peers through one of the embrasures. In the dawn light he can see the inner harbour gleaming like polished pewter. A few ships moored against the quay. Warehouses. A couple of churches with onion-shaped domes. A bell rings, calling worshippers to morning service. If there was any point to it he could set his backsight to five hundred yards and maybe pick one of them off with a Minié ball. But let sleeping dogs lie, that's the motto out here. Don't hurt Ivan and for the moment Ivan won't hurt you.

He wonders, as he wonders every few minutes of his waking day, about Annie. Is she, at this very moment, lying in bed half asleep and listening to the bell from the cathedral calling people to matins? He recalls her early morning warmth, her woman's scent, the hardness and the softness of her, the magic.

The Guardians of the Poor

She has done herself up in her best, such as it is. A touch of starched white cotton at the neck. Starched cuffs. Plain stuff but decent enough. It's important, that's what Mrs. Knowles told her, important that you look good and respectable. "That's lovely," she said, looking Annie up and down. "Attractive enough but not too pretty. You don't want pretty or they'll think you loose. A bit of a frown on you but not aggressive, that's the thing to be. They don't want you answering back." Mrs. Knowles knows what she's talking about, living as she does on parish relief.

So now Annie is standing in the presbytery of the church while the four gentlemen examine her. They are a committee of the Guardians of the Union. Their duty is to disburse monies dedicated to the benefit of the poor and the destitute and to adjudicate on matters of worthiness. "And how old is the new child?" one of them asks. He is whiskered and scrawny, his head emerging indignantly from the carapace of his collar. He looks more like a prawn than a person.

"One month."

"Sir."

"Sir."

"And the father. Do you know the father, woman?"

"Of course I know the father. He's my husband."

"So why is he not here?"

One of the other guardians puts out his hand to touch the Prawn's arm. This man's name, she knows, is Bromehead, Mr. Edmund Bromehead. She has done laundry work in his house. He claims to be an enthusiastic supporter of the Lincoln Volunteer Rifles and therefore sympathetic to the military and their families. That's what he told her when he encountered her in the laundry room. He is youngish – not as old as the others, anyway – and seems impatient to have this whole thing over. "William," he says to the Prawn. "I explained. Ann Mawer's husband is currently serving most gallantly with Her Majesty's Army in the Crimea. While Corporal Mawer puts his life at risk in defence of the realm, his good wife finds herself unable to work because she has just brought into the world the good corporal's child." He adds: "And the Army seems not to take any responsibility for such matters."

"But why should *we*?" the Prawn asks him. "She is a stranger here. Her accent tells me she is Irish. She's probably a papist at heart."

"The father of her children comes from Lincoln. Do you suggest she should have thrown herself on the mercy of her parish back in Ireland, and so join the queues of the starving in that sad island? Surely you are not unaware of the crop failures in Ireland. Our own county is blessed with an abundance of cereals; we can hardly send paupers to Ireland where they cannot even grow potatoes."

The Prawn looks doubtful. "I see no reason we should support soldiers' wives. Horse Guards should be responsible. And when did the husband leave for the East?"

Ann replies, whether or not the question is directed at her. "At the end of February."

The Prawn looks indignant. "*Sir*," he says.

"Sir."

"At the end of February, *sir*," he insists.

"At the end of February. Sir." Annie knows well enough from living in barracks how to make *sir* sound like a term of abuse. She watches the Prawn do calculations in his head and gives the answer for him. "January would be nine months. Sir."

Mr. Bromehead taps the table to interrupt. "I have no doubt that Mrs. Mawer is a respectable woman. She has been taking in laundry since she first came here and, so I am informed by my housekeeper, a very excellent laundrywoman she is. It is most demeaning for her that she should appear before us and appear to ask for charity but clearly, as the Reverend Richter has pointed out, she has little option. Two growing children and now the new baby and the Army washing its hands of her as it washes its hands of all such women."

The Prawn doesn't give up that easily. "And is the child correctly registered?"

Mrs. Knowles warned her of this. "Get it registered proper," she warned. "They're all for that these days." And so she did, walking down to the office with the baby all wrapped up, finding her way to the right desk, inscribing her mark in the box that the registrar man indicated. And now she takes the birth certificate out of her pocket and passes it across the table. "Sarah Rebecca," she says.

Sarah Rebecca's registration of birth

"And baptised?"

The Reverend Richter speaks: "We were waiting for a reply

from the child's father about the choice of names for her christening, but now it seems that the good woman has made the decision on her own." He seems rather peeved.

"Mrs. Knowles told me I must have the child registered ... "

"Is baptism in Our Lord less important than civil registration?"

Once more Mr. Edmund Bromehead taps the table. "Gentlemen, I really think we are going round in circles. Of course the child will be baptised and I'm sure no one here doubts that Mrs. Mawer is entirely deserving. She appears a fine woman placed in a difficult position through no fault of her own. Monies are available from the Central Association for such cases.* Indeed, I myself have contributed to such funds. On behalf of this good woman, I am prepared to make an application to the Association myself and in the meantime, I am sure parish funds can be employed in her favour. I would suggest a sum of ten shillings per week, a sum which I will gladly underwrite. Do we have agreement on that?" He looks round the little group and dares them to object. He nods. "Excellent."

---

* Central Association in Aid of the Wives and Families, Widows and Orphans, of Soldiers Ordered on Active Service, instituted on 7 March 1854. It was dissolved in 1857.

Fifth of November

The Battle of Balaclava, fought on 25 October and so much talked about in the press, was barely noticed up on the plateau. The worst thing about it was the loss of the Voronzof Road because that was how all supplies had come up from the port of Balaclava to the siege lines. The cavalry? Cardigan's precious Light Brigade? A shrug. Who gives a toss about the cavalry being cut to pieces? What use were they up in the trenches? No, what mattered, what *really* mattered, was what happened eleven days later, on Guy Fawkes night.

Remember, remember the fifth of November ...

It was the distant sound of fireworks that woke George in the early morning, pulling him from a dream of bonfires and a guy in flames. The fireworks soon resolved themselves into the crackle of musketry and the heavy crack of field artillery over to the north where the 2nd Division were camped.

He crawled out of his tent to have a look, but there was literally nothing to see. Dense fog had blanketed the hillside during the night and in the pallid dawn the neighbouring tents were mere shadows, vague pyramids seen through curtains of muslin. A thin rain descended, just like bloody Lancashire. The distant sound of musketry rose and fell, rose and fell.

Figures were moving around in the murk. "What's up, George?" someone called.

"No idea."

Buried in the fog were distant bugle calls, the call of regiments to arms. A sound of suppressed panic that turned your bowels to water. And then one close at hand – *their* alarm, the call of the 50th.

"That's us!"

"For God's sake, it's Sunday!"

"It's meant to be a day of rest."

"Bloody heathens!"

The whole division was being woken up, tents giving birth to cursing soldiers scrambling into their kit, grabbing their firelocks, hurrying to the mustering area. There was Colonel Waddy clumping around on his horse in the fog; and Frampton, one-armed Frampton, with that mad look in his eye; and Major Wilton and others. The colours were being uncased, waving around in the murk like a red rag to a bull.

By eight o'clock the 50th had moved off. In open column they stumbled through fog and drizzle, across hillsides that were only half familiar, northwards across the plateau towards sounds that nature told you to run from – the roar of musketry, the detonations of artillery and, through white shrouds of vapour, the shouts and screams of men. The empty tents of the Light Division loomed out of the mist on their left. Ahead a slope rose towards a squat shadow in the cloud – the gaunt, broken windmill, standing like a guardian to the field of battle. Units were mustering around the building, scattered squads emerging from the fog and trying to look like soldiers. Messengers ran back and forth. Horses galloped off into obscurity. Orders were shouted.

The 50th waited. George waited. It was one thing you learned in the Army, to wait. He waited and they waited and the battle went on out of sight, men disappearing off into the fog in response to orders while the 50th, the Dirty

Half-Hundred, waited, listening to the gunfire and the screams, their arms piled in neat pyramidal stacks of four, muzzles in the air. George went along the ranks making sure the muzzles of the piled arms were covered. You stuck a forge cap over them, that was the usual thing. Simple enough. Otherwise rain got down the barrel and, when it came to shooting, half the weapons would misfire. Keep your cartridges dry and your firelock clean. That's what mattered. That's what he told them.

They waited.

"Don't complain," Donnelly said. "Nobody gets killed waiting." Which wasn't quite true but it gave some kind of comfort. Ahead, the storm of battle raged across an unseen landscape called Mount Inkerman. There were flashes in the fog like lightning, the crash of guns like thunder. A man-made storm to go with the fog and drizzle. The talk around the Windmill was of Shell Hill, the Sandbag Battery, the Barrier, the Fore Ridge, of bayonet charges, of hand-to-hand fighting. Rain came down. Bowels churned. Men broke ranks to have a shit, laughter hounding them into the fog.

After a while the wounded began to come back, some walking, others slung in blankets or carried on improvised stretchers. Surgeons began their work under hastily erected tents. The sound of bone saws. The sounds of agony. The stench of blood and, if you were lucky, chloroform. Small groups of soldiers came past, looking shocked. Other units went forward. Mules came up from the rear loaded with boxes of ammunition. Horses clattered by with messages. It was after an hour that orders were finally shouted at the 50th. Arms were unpiled, the men drawn up in companies and the Dirty Half-Hundred went forward.

Home Ridge

At first it was marching in column along a dirt road, then off road and through the wreckage of the 2nd Division's camp, where the first Russian artillery rounds had fallen at reveille that morning and started the whole thing off. Here the ground was ploughed up by round shot, tents had been uprooted and thrown about the place, men's possessions were strewn around. Bodies, bodies still lying there unattended.

A wait, in columns, in the drizzle. Nothing to think but fear. Their world cut down to less than a hundred yards by the fog, the noise of battle loud but disembodied, a constant roar and scream from the primeval monster ahead in the cloud. Finally the order came to move into line. Stomachs churned. Mouths ran dry. A bugle called the advance. Double time.

George? George moves forward as the others move forward. He trips, falls, recovers, marches up a rise following shadows in the fog, not knowing where the hell he is going, except that there are men he recognises around him. Familiarity as a comfort in the unknown. Artillery fire sounding close now, flashes in the cloud to the right – British guns firing blind towards the unseen Russians. Round shot spinning out of the murk from the Russian battery, careering past like skipping stones. Shells bursting in the air like fireworks, like bloody great fireworks on Guy Fawkes night. Ball humming overhead. Shouting and screaming. Up at the top of the rise are shallow trenches where Lieutenant Antrobus is waving the regimental colours like a blithering idiot, as though trying to attract the attention of Russian gunners. Round shot erupts in the earth, showering him and the flag in dirt. A bugle call brings the halt. Round shot flies past, careering over the ground, screaming like a banshee. Men dive for shelter. George lies there, his face pressed into the mud, wondering if the next shell will burst directly overhead and blast him to oblivion. He doesn't think of Annie. He thinks only of the moment, the taste of earth and grass in his mouth, the churning of his gut, the sodden chill of his clothes, the awkward edges of his firelock. For a second he dares glance up. Lieutenant Dashwood is on his feet trying to organise the men into defensive positions. He's waving his arm to show what he wants; then his arm vanishes. It goes just like that, in an instant. One moment the man is standing there waving, the next his entire left arm has been taken off in a mess of blood, flesh and bone. He doesn't even go over at first, just stands dumbly looking with an expression of surprise at what is no longer there. Only then does he collapse. Only then does he die, as men cluster round and try hopelessly to apply a tourniquet.

Others also die, the rank-and-file soldiers who don't get mentioned in the histories but are no less dead. The killing, the shooting, the bursting of shells, the impact of round shot, all goes on until early afternoon, when like two bloodied prizefighters the opposing forces have fought each other to a standstill. The cloud has lifted. The guns fall silent. Under the cover of their artillery, the Russian infantry just melts away down the ravines and gorges to the lower ground. The ridge – Saddletop Reach – between the Russian guns on Shell Hill and British positions on the Home Ridge is littered with the bodies of the dead and the dying: more than ten thousand seven hundred Russians, more than two thousand three hundred British.

Survivors wander through the mess. Russians and British are indifferent in death, lying like ragdolls, their limbs thrown anyhow. Stretcher parties begin their work, searching for the wounded among the dead while two men on horseback pick their way across the high ground. One is dressed in French general's uniform, decked with gold braid and topped with a cocked hat. He has his right arm in a sling. That is General Canrobert, the French commander-in-chief. The other wears a modest black frock coat and might almost be a civilian but isn't. He is Lord Raglan.

"I have been attacked by forty thousand men," Lord Raglan says in astonishment, seeing the number of casualties. His estimation is remarkably accurate. More than forty thousand Russians have indeed confronted his own force of fewer than seven thousand five hundred, making it one of the most uneven battles of the century.* It has also been one of the bloodiest. Overall British casualties run to 32 percent; in the thick of the fighting some regiments have sustained 50 percent killed and wounded. There is no pursuit of the retiring Russian troops because the British forces are simply too exhausted.

---

* Russian numbers: 40,210 with a further 22,444 which were never committed to the battle. British numbers: 7,464 (with assistance from French forces at a crucial time late on in the battle). Figures from Kinglake, *The Invasion of the Crimea*, 1875.

Guy Fawkes

She's knitting. He asked her in his last letter:

*My dear wife, how bitterly cold it is here. I had
thought the East meant sun and heat, but here it is
as cold as the arctic zones we hear about and our
clothes are mere rags. Anything you can make will be
welcomed by your loving husband who knows how
well you knit. In this weather any such thing may
save your husband from a frozen grave! Gloves, mitts,
a woollen cap, anything you can manage would go
towards keeping his body as warm as his heart is with
love of you.*

So she knitted, and set Mary Ann to knitting as well. A
mere six years old yet the girl is a good knitter. She's making a
scarf for Papa. "To keep him warm," Annie tells her. "Because
he's so cold out East."

Mary Ann's expression is solemn. She is a clever girl and
has even managed to read some of her father's last letter,
his own hand being quite plain and simple, so the Reverend
Richter said.

Believe it Wife, we have had men die of cold.

"Will Papa die?" Mary Ann asked. "If we let him get cold?"

"We won't let him, will we?"

"But *if*?"

"Everyone dies if they get too cold. But I'm sure that won't happen to Papa."

"How can you be sure?"

"'Course he's not going to die. But we still want him to keep warm for us, don't we?"

Mary Ann agreed that she did want that. A warm father. So they knit, Mary Ann working at her scarf, Annie doing the more complicated things – a pair of mitts, a helmet to go over his head, with flaps to keep his ears warm, a pair of bed-socks. The sizes she estimates, going by her memory of his body, that dear, lean, hard body for which, now the baby is born, she has begun to ache once more. Sometimes she dreams of him but wakes to feel the dream-memory melt away like snow in the sun.

Sarah Rebecca begins to cry. Annie puts the knitting down, picks the baby out of its crib, opens the front of her dress and presents one marble-veined breast for it to suck. To Mary Ann's eyes there is something vaguely nauseating about this sight, as though her mother were a milk cow. Mother as animal. First the birth, now this.

That evening there are explosions outside the house, the rattle of firecrackers, children running down the street, laughing, shouting. Perhaps the constable is chasing them.

"What's that?" Mary Ann goes to the window, trying to look out.

"Guy Fawkes."

"What's Guy Fawkes?"

"They have bonfires and fireworks. But today's Sunday so they mustn't."

"Why bonfires and fireworks?"

"Why, why, why?"

Knitting, more knitting, by candlelight now, which makes it difficult. Mary Ann is good because she seems to understand, but the boy, George Henry, whinges. Perhaps he is hungry. The baby sleeps.

Next day there is a bonfire of sorts within the castle walls nearby, although the vicar had spoken out against it. But they weren't meant to have a bonfire on Sunday so they're doing it now, whatever the authorities say. Annie and the children venture out to watch. George clutches his mother's hand and toddles along not whinging too much. Mary Ann skips, happy to be away from the knitting. It is the baby's first time outside but she sleeps all through the excitement.

The bonfire blazes in the darkness. Shadows dance round, silhouetted against the flames. Maybe hell is like that. People shout and cheer. There are squibs and jumping jacks. On the top of the fire the figure of the guy looks surprised at all the attention he is getting.

"It's a man," Mary Ann says. "Why are they burning a man?"

"It's not a real man."

"But why are they burning him?"

"He's a Catholic. They burned Catholics then. Long ago."

That silences her for a while. Then she asks, "Aren't you a Catholic?"

Annie laughs. "Once I was. Back in Ireland. But now I'm not."

The bonfire roars on. Balanced on the flames, the guy wobbles and struggles for a moment before vanishing in the blaze.

"I don't want to be a Catholic either," Mary Ann decides.

"Well, you're not a Catholic. You're Church of England. Neither one thing nor the other."

The fire dies down, as fires do.

*

Days later, rumours begin to circulate about a battle fought out in the East against the Russians. It had been on the very day of Guy Fawkes. Annie hears about it from Mrs. Knowles next door, hears the name "Inkerman" for the first time. Weeks later, at the beginning of December, the names of the dead and the wounded come through in the newspapers. She is once more in the presbytery of St. Paul's while the Reverend Richter scans through the lists as she stands beside him at his desk.

"The Fiftieth," she reminds him. "It's the Fiftieth Regiment."

He finds the place, reads the names: Privates J. Daly, J. Slattery, D. Robertson, J. Edge, W. Smith, J. Mooney, B. Cronan, R. Mitchell, J. Bricknell, J. Nagle, William Cooper, William Lavery.

One she knows. William Lavery, Billy Lavery, always in trouble, never rising above private soldier, now in more trouble than ever before. Or maybe not. Maybe he has died and gone to heaven.

In the paper there are even the names of the wounded, other names she recognises, some of them. But nowhere is the name of George. "There," Richter says. "The Lord has saved him, blessed be the name of the Lord." He looks her up and down, as is his manner. "How is the baby, Annie?"

"She's well. Growing."

"Does she take your milk well?"

"Yes."

He puts up his hand and touches her breast, feeling the weight of it. "A wondrous thing," he says quietly. "A miracle."

She waits for him to stop. "I must be getting back to her."

"Of course you must." His hand leaves her. "We'll be seeing you in church soon, I hope. Advent. The coming of the Lord, announced to his blessed mother by the angel Gabriel."

"Of course, sir." She turns to go, but there's the little ritual when he calls her back and gives her a half-crown. And then she's free to hurry back to the little cottage on West Bight and the children.

In the Trenches

Up on the plateau they scratch an existence like Neolithic man following the retreat of the ice sheets. Grubbing around a barren tundra for fuel. Gnawing at salt pork. Pounding dry biscuit with water to make a kind of almost palatable porridge. Improvising clothing out of scraps of cloth and fur. Repairing what they can with whatever comes to hand. Before burial the dead are stripped of coats and boots and anything else of use. Dead horses are skinned to make improvised cloaks. Beards grow, hair grows, stomachs shrink. Dysentery and cholera stalk the encampments, killing dozens. Hypothermia lies in wait, a merciful death among the many alternatives.

As if malnutrition and disease weren't enough, the weather deteriorates. Ice-cold rain beats down on the tents of the British Army. On 14 November the gales boil up into a hurricane that howls across the Sebastopol plateau, smashing down the tents, carrying away equipment, reducing the entire force to a crowd of homeless refugees. Down in the harbour at Balaclava, ships are pulverised against each other or against the quayside. Out to sea vessels are dashed on the rocks or capsized with crew and cargo lost.

The track between the siege lines and the port – the only route through the escarpment since the loss of the Voronzof Road in the Battle of Balaclava – now becomes almost impassable. Carts sink down to their axles and are abandoned. Horses slither, stumble and die at the side of the track. Men on foot might manage the journey, but it takes hours to get down and hours to get back. Yet almost everything goes that way, on men's backs: food, fuel, clothing and ammunition up to the top of the scarp. Some of the dying are carried back down to the living death of Balaclava port but most of them are left to die up on the plateau. Once dead they aren't worth carrying down: they're buried more or less where they die, in pits scraped out of the mud, to be dug up by rats and feral dogs.

As *The Times* correspondent puts it succinctly to the British people:

> It is now pouring rain — the skies are black as ink — the wind is howling over the staggering tents — the trenches are turned into dykes — in the tents the water is sometimes a foot deep — our men have not either warm or waterproof clothing — they are out for twelve hours at a time in the trenches — they are plunged into the inevitable miseries of a winter campaign — and not a soul seems to care for their comfort or even for their lives.*

They forage for firewood, often resorting to digging up roots for fuel to burn. They gnaw at whatever food comes their way. Parties are sent down to Balaclava to see what they can beg or steal. And regularly, almost daily, according

---

* William Howard Russell, dispatch to *The Times* of London, 25 November 1854.

to some rota dreamt up by the officers they form up into approximate squads, to make their way down the Valley of the Shadow of Death and into the trenches to confront the cursed city of Sebastopol.

November shuffles into December. Temperatures fall further. Snow and sleet take the place of rain. The agony is unremitting. The cold brings a whole new meaning to the phrase "stick to your guns." That is exactly what happens: in the Siberian cold fingers do stick to the metal of their gun barrels and if you are naive enough to snatch your hand away you lose the skin of your fingertips. George is there for a while yet, scratching an existence in the camp, sometimes struggling down to Balaclava with a squad to scrounge supplies or going forward into the trenches, down into the second or third parallel to spend sixteen hours or more in ankle-deep water in the freezing cold. He's emaciated, dirty, lice-ridden, beset with fever and diarrhoea. One day he helps bury Sergeant Padraig Donnelly and he doesn't shed a tear. He just endures, having no alternative.

Reports of casualties among the 50th come through in the newspapers, the stillicide of personal disaster conveyed to Annie by neighbours who can read. They come long after the event they record, so that George's world is separated from hers not only by two thousand miles of space but also by time, a month of time, as though he already occupies a different universe. In the reports there is no mention of George Mawer. Does that mean he is still alive and well? Annie has no idea. She longs for his presence but only in the abstract, as one might long for things to be different while knowing that things are as they are – she is here on her own, besieged by the demands of her three children, dependent on charity, scraping an existence because there is no alternative. George and she exist as a couple only in the remembered past and in an imagined future, a world that is no more than fantasy. She doesn't have much time for fantasy.

Surprise

On the night of 20 December the Russians launch a surprise attack on the British lines, a double attack, on Victoria Ridge and the Green Hill simultaneously. The Victoria Ridge attack is frontal but the Green Hill attack is quiet, secretive, a shock: in silence they come up the ravine on the side of the Green Hill trenches, up the Valley of the Shadow of Death down which George has marched so often. It's a flanking move at the very weakest point of the British lines. The sentries in the communication trenches get off a couple of shots before they are overwhelmed but it is probable the pickets were asleep when the Russians made their approach – exhausted, malnourished, diseased men are prone to fall asleep at the slightest opportunity. So the Russians overwhelm the sentries and run up the steep covered-way onto the ridge between the third and the second parallels. The men in the third parallel are quickly overwhelmed. Some manage to retreat uphill to the second parallel, where a desperate stand is made. For a while it seems that the whole of the British left attack might fall to the Russians.

George is there on the ridge. The whole of the 50th is there, between the now-lost third parallel and the first parallel before Chapman's Battery. Like the rest of his companions, he's an emaciated ghost of the man who landed at Eupatoria three months ago and by any normal standards he should be in hospital. But instead he is rousing himself from the semi-consciousness of sleep and stupor to climb out of the trench along with the others, along with Colonel Waddy, who is there urging them on in a counterattack downhill towards the second parallel.

"Fix bayonets!" the colonel is yelling. "Keep tight together. Show them what the Fiftieth can do!"* And they're stumbling down the hillside with muskets and rifles going off all around. Ball whirs past, knocking men down, sparking on rocks, whining off into the dark. And then it's fighting with shadows, stabbing into darkness, trampling over bodies, piling into forms that must be Russian but run and cry and curse like anyone else.

The battle to hold Green Hill lasts over an hour of vicious hand-to-hand fighting. By the time it is over, fourteen of the 50th lie dead and a further dozen are wounded. Two officers and nine men have been taken prisoner.

Christmas, be it of the Western tradition or the Orthodox, came and went before the report of the action appeared in the English newspapers.

"It's the Fiftieth again, love," Mrs. Knowles said, knocking on the front door and holding up a much folded and fingered newspaper. "Here, have a look."

There was no point in Annie having a look, of course there wasn't. "You'll have to read it to me. Come in."

Her two rooms were warmer than the outside, but not much. Coal was scarce and a fire was only lit in the evening. The woman came in, peering round inquisitively, as she always did: at the baby crawling on the floor, at the two older children looking up incuriously from their play.

_____

* Waddy's very words, taken from his letter home of 22 December 1854.

"Tell me," Annie said. "Tell me."

Mrs. Knowles liked to raise the drama a bit. She sniffed and cleared her throat as though she was about to address a courtroom. Mary Ann watched. George Henry had already lost interest.

"On the twentieth a sad occurrence took place," Mrs. Knowles read.

"Sad occurrence?"

"It says: 'a sad occurrence which would almost show that the fatal surprise of Inkerman has not sufficed to caution our pickets against neglect of duty; for to no other circumstance can we ascribe the disaster of that night.'"

Annie's heart skipped. "Disaster?"

"If you're going to keep interrupting dear, I'll never finish."

"I'm sorry Mrs. Knowles, but ... "

The woman continued reading, slowly and inexpertly: "'At midnight a strong column of Russians advanced, without being perceived, upon a portion of the trenches guarded by the 50th Regiment, and took the latter completely by surprise.' Looks to me like they was asleep," the woman added. "The sentries or whatever was asleep."

"Is that what it says?"

"Implies, dear, *implies*. Anyway, it goes on: 'Severe loss was inflicted upon the regiment before the attack could be met. Reinforced by the Thirty-eighth Regiment, the Fiftieth succeeded in repulsing the enemy, and caused him a considerable loss. Our casualties of the night were forty-three killed and wounded, and seventeen taken prisoner. Amongst the killed we regret to say were Major Moller, Lieutenant Clarke, and another officer whose name I am not acquainted with. These unfortunate officers all belonged to the Fiftieth.'"*

---

* From the *Sun*, 9 January 1855.

Mrs. Knowles looked up, tight mouthed. "Gives the names of the officers but doesn't say nothing about the men, does it? Typical."

"It says severe losses . . . "

The woman looked over the rest of the page, hoping, no doubt, to be the bearer of tragic news. "Here they are." And she read through the names: "'Sergeant James Howarth, Corporal Benjamin Inglefield—'"

"I know him. Ben Inglefield, I know him."

"Do you, dear? How sad, eh?"

"And Sergeant Howarth. Well, I know him by sight. He wasn't my George's company."

"The rest are just privates." She read: "'James Carmichael, James Collis, Stephen Connolly, Patrick Cooney, Samuel Dorming, Timothy Keefe, James Mailey, James Moran, Samuel Thompson, Patrick Thompson, Edward Wood.' That's it."

Annie shrugs. "But my George—"

"Not there, love. Nor in the wounded. So that's good, isn't it? Thank heaven for small mercies, I say."

"'Course. But he's still not here, is he? He's still over there."

The Way Men Die

Men die in great numbers and they die in various ways. They die of cholera, they die of dysentery. They die of cold, they die of hunger. Perhaps some of them die of despair. Occasionally, very occasionally, they die from enemy action.

In September 1854, 697 men of the 50th Regiment of Foot landed at Eupatoria on the Crimean peninsula. By the end of January 1855, the regiment has lost well over three hundred men to disease, malnutrition and hypothermia; only a tenth of that number in battle. So half of those who landed on the Crimean peninsula in September are now dead.

One of them is Corporal George Mawer.

A Medal

I regret to inform you that George Mawer, Corporal of the 50th (Queen's Own) Regiment of Foot, regimental number 2524, laid down his life for Queen and Country in the lines before Sebastopol, on the 24th of January in the year of Our Lord eighteen hundred and fifty-five. He died with courage, doing his duty and was buried with full military honours ...

Annie's world collapses. Her whole fragile world, constructed on nothing much – what little she and George had put aside for a rainy day, the money she had been earning taking in laundry, the ten shillings a week that the charity was paying her – all this perilously weak card-house of a world collapses. She's standing in the presbytery of the church – St. Paul in the Bail – where Sarah Rebecca was christened only a few weeks before Christmas,* and the rector Mr. Richter is inviting her to sit down and telling her once again that he's sorry, he's so very sorry. He's holding the letter that has just come through the post from – she could just about make this out from the various stamps and embossed badges on the envelope – the depot of the 50th Regiment in Dublin, and his words ring in

---

* 19 November 1854.

her ears like the aftersound of a musket shot that goes on and on and never seems to stop.

"Do you understand what I have said, Annie?"

He calls her Annie. George used to call her Annie, only George. But Mr. Richter calling her Annie isn't affection so much as his looking down on her. Like talking to a servant. She knows that, knows it by the tone.

"Do you understand what I have said, Annie?"

Does she? Whatever she does understand, it is probably not the truth. The truth is that he did not "lay down his life" or "die with courage, doing his duty" and nor was he "buried with full military honours." He died, hacking, vomiting and shitting, probably of dysentery, maybe of cholera, certainly aggravated by exposure and hypothermia, and his body was subsequently wrapped in a sheet and dumped in a shallow pit somewhere on the bleak plateau above Sebastopol. They'd have fired a salute over the grave, which he probably shared with two others of the regiment who died the same day. They were dying in their dozens by then. And the weather had ensured that the track down to Balaclava port was impassable for most of the time, so all they could do was take the corpses somewhere below the divisional encampment and bury them wherever they could dig into the frozen, stony earth and erect a cross of some kind, probably made out of broken rifle bits because wood, combustible wood, was at a premium up there on the heights above Sebastopol in the depths of winter. Names on the grave? No names. Nothing to carve them on. Let's at least remember them here:

George Mawer, Corporal.
Abraham Brown, Private.
Alexander Hall, Private.

Later, months later, a parcel comes through the post for Annie. She has never received a parcel before, even a small parcel like this, and she can't imagine what it might contain. Indeed, she isn't even sure whether to open it herself or take it round to the Reverend Richter and have him open it, he who might understand the words that will be inside. Eventually she decides to do the deed herself. The children watch as she cuts the string and breaks the seal. Inside the wrapping paper there is a letter and a cardboard box. Within the cardboard box there is a further box, a fine, dark-blue box with a gold crown embossed on it. Lying within the box, bedded down in satin like a miniature corpse in a miniature coffin, is a silver medal with a pale-blue silk ribbon.

The children hold their collective breath. On the medal there's a woman's face in profile. Annie recognises the woman because you see this face everywhere on coins and stamps and things. It is the Queen. She is wearing a crown just to prove it. On the back of the medal is the image of a man wearing a skirt.

"'Im's a Scotchman," says Mary Ann authoritatively. Perhaps she remembers the Highlanders from the barracks in Dublin. This Scotchman, if it is a Scotchman, is holding a shield and brandishing a sword. He is apparently unaware that floating over him is an angel. And there is an engraved word, which Mary Ann can just about read out: CRIMEA.

There is more. Around the rim of the medal are words and figures that have to be interpreted later when she takes the box and the accompanying letter round to the Reverend Richter:

Corpl. Geo Mawer. 50th Regt.

This medal is the final relic of her husband. Except for some clothing he left behind when he left Dublin, this is all she has to remember him by.

*Corporal George Mawer. Crimean War medal with
clasps for the Battles of Alma and Inkerman.*

That week Annie went three months into arrears with the
rent. That week her scant savings finally evaporated. That
week she could no longer put anything but bread and water
on the table for the children, and the child at her breast was
the only well-fed one of the family. That week was when pride
became a luxury she could no longer afford and she went to
the Reverend Richter and begged for help, the very help that
she had assured him she would never need. But at least she
had the medal.

Part 3

A Family Story

What do we inherit besides occasional objects? Besides that Crimean War medal, for example. Photographs, of course. Letters. Postcards. Sometimes names, although that's an uncertain process, always at the mercy of fashion and often skipping a generation just like a genetic trait. And of course we inherit our chromosomes with their cryptic messages from that alphabet of a mere four letters – A, G, C, T – that spell out our genes. But there are other less tangible things that may be passed down, fragile, evanescent things such as memories and half-memories, a shared nursery-rhyme or song, even a turn of phrase ...

Or a story ...

Many families have them, vague accounts of an heir disinherited, a young girl jilted, a fortune lost, a family shame covered over in the way a cat will cover over its shit. The stuff of novels. There's one here, handed down the generations:

Once upon a time in Lincolnshire there was a young servant girl whose family name was Mawer. Her Christian name is lost to history but she was servant in the household of a local family of some importance, called ... Broomfield? Broomhead? Something like that. This servant girl was seduced by the young man of the family and became pregnant by him. When the fact became evident, the young man's family behaved in what might have been considered a most reasonable fashion in those days: they offered to take on responsibility for the child, to give it their name and bring it up as one of their own, as long as the servant girl renounced all rights to the child. She – tough girl – refused this deal. Instead, she ran away to London where she threw herself on the mercy of a religious organisation that took care of unmarried mothers. The child was duly born and christened George. Subsequently, George joined the Army, married an Irish woman, fathered a son named George Henry, and then went off to fight in the Crimean War.

That's the story, passed down the generations like a rogue gene embedded irritatingly within the germ line of documentary fact. Part true, of course. Yes, George Mawer did marry an Irishwoman, he did father George Henry and he did go to fight in the Crimea. But it is clear now that a vital part of this story is wrong: the good corporal wasn't born in London and his marriage registration shows his father's name clearly enough: *Peter Mawer, waterman* (on page 156). And there was no innocent servant girl, seduced by the son and heir of the local squire and fleeing to London to have her baby.

Yet stories don't come from nowhere, and nor does that name with its convincing uncertainty – *Broomfield* or *Broomhead*.

You pick through the evidence, looking for clues, associations, relationships, coincidences. No Broomfield existed in the records of Lincoln city and its surrounds in those years. None. No Broomhead either. But *Bromehead*? Oh, yes, there is Bromehead for sure, there in the city itself, just near the cathedral. In the 1841 census an entire family – widowed mother with three daughters and a son – but by 1851 only the son on his own, thirty-five-year-old Edmund A. Bromehead, unmarried, with a living-in house servant, Elizabeth Wallhead, and cook, Mary Kelsey.

Edmund A. Bromehead and household in the 1851 Lincoln City census

There are times when the sense of curiosity becomes something rather more: the prurience of the voyeur.

The Board of Guardians

They have a uniformly forbidding appearance – black frock coats, starched collars, fine whiskers – their stern aspects relieved only by gold watch chains hung across beautifully upholstered stomachs. They are gentlemen of the utmost probity, determined to clear up the wreckage that was once the edifice of Annie's whole life. "This is for your own good and the good of your children," they tell her. "This is what your husband, God rest his soul, would have wanted."

How, she wonders, do they know what George would have wanted?

"You're sending them away," she retorts. "My children have lost their father and now you're taking them from their mother. Putting them in some kind of orphans' home."

Mr. Edmund Bromehead smiles benevolently on her. "I know this cannot be easy for you. But it is, perhaps, for the best."

The Prawn speaks, glaring at her with protuberant eyes: "The alternative, my good woman, is the workhouse. Not," he adds to make things clear to one and all, "that the Lincoln workhouse is not a very worthy institution. I myself sit on the board of governors and I can vouch for it as a place of Christian decency, cleanliness and good management. However, it is not the place for a family such as yours."

"My brother means that it is for their own good," Mr. Bromehead explains. "For their own good."

Is the Prawn his *brother*? Mr. Edmund Bromehead has always seemed a decent gentleman. But now it appears that the Prawn is a second Bromehead.

"It's a mother should look after them," she says defiantly.

The Prawn almost stamps his clerical foot. "But in your present circumstances, woman, you cannot do that!"

The other men try to calm him down as one might try to mollify a spoiled child – "Now, now," "Tut, tut," all that kind of thing – which only exasperates him further. "It is the profligacy of the poor that drives me to distraction," he exclaims. "I have already encountered this woman. She had barely enough money to feed the children then, and certainly not enough to clothe them. Yet she also had a further child which rendered her unable to work. That is the route from poverty to destitution, can't she see that?"

Annie doesn't know what *profligacy* means, but the meaning of *Bromehead* she can imagine: head like a broom, all bristle and wood. She almost laughs through her misery. She says, "You forget, Mr. Reverend Bromehead or whatever your name is, that I am the widow of a soldier, a brave man who served his Queen and Country and died through no fault of his own or mine."

Her words bring a collective gasp from the gentlemen of the jury, that she should be answering back to such an august figure. She continues regardless: "Also you forget that my baby was conceived" – another gasp, that she should make reference to the facts of sexual reproduction! – "before my man left for the East, and that until that moment the two of us were well able to rear our children to be good, God-fearing folk. It is not my fault nor theirs that I'm standing here before you like a pauper."

There is a terrible silence. The Reverend Bromehead stares, aghast. Some of the others look shamefaced.

It is Mr. Edmund Bromehead who comes to her rescue. "That is exactly true," he says quietly. "Ann's husband died in the service of his country. And may I be so bold as to remind all of my colleagues, my brother in particular, what the correspondent of *The Times* asseverated in yesterday's edition? That the blame for so many wasted lives lies with both the generals and the politicians, and furthermore, it amounts to a national scandal."

Almost they hang their heads in shame at the reminder that in the Crimea the glorious and apparently God-ordained progress of the Empire has met a near insurmountable obstacle. And, even more shaming, that the British Army, allied with the French for the first time in history, has come off worse in the inevitable comparison between the two former enemies. The Prawn looks furious that such matters should be mentioned, especially by his brother.

"However," the brother continues in emollient tones, "that is not what concerns us here, gentlemen. What concerns us is the well-being of this lady" – the suggestion that Annie might be considered a lady evokes a small stir of righteous indignation – "and her *deserving* children."

And Annie is no longer close to tears, she is actually *in* tears. Mr. Edmund Bromehead leaves his place and goes over to comfort her, even puts his hand on her shoulder, which, one or two of the gentlemen agree afterwards, was quite a shocking thing to do and for which his brother, the Prawn, later admonishes him.

"I think perhaps we can stop conducting this meeting as though it is a trial of some kind and understand our obligations to Mrs. Mawer. I would like a moment or two in which I may talk to her in confidence, if she is willing to retain my services as her legal advisor. I am certain that thereby she will understand what is best for her and her children."

340

Bromehead

There are documents to be signed, documents that she cannot read and, when the contents are read to her, can barely comprehend. This happens in Mr. Bromehead's offices which occupy the ground floor of a house in James Street, just by the cathedral and separated from his home by a private garden. The offices consist of a suite of rooms where books and ledgers dominate, where clients come and go, where a clerk scribbles on sheets of foolscap and affixes solemn and important seals to elaborate documents.

"This must be very confusing for you," Mr. Bromehead says. "I fully understand that. But I really do believe that we all wish to help you and your children. Even" – he gives a tired smile – "my elder brother. I'm afraid William must always temper generosity with a little self-righteous anger."

The conference room to which he shows her is like a grander version of Mr. Richter's presbytery, wood-panelled and leather-bound but in this case lined with books, hundreds of books, great tomes in tooled morocco hide. Down the centre, like a coffin at a funeral, lies a long table, polished to a mirror shine. A maid brings in a tea tray and Annie sits at the table and drinks – sips – from fine bone china for the first time in her life; while Mr. Bromehead, seated at the head of the table, turns the documents towards her for signature. He must be, she guesses, about forty years old. A good-looking man, without those heavy side-whiskers so many of them affect. Rather shy. Inclined to blush slightly when he talks.

"I don't write," she tells him when he hands her the pen to sign.

"That is quite all right. You may" – he points – "merely make your mark and I will append my own signature as witness." His tone suggests there is nothing to be ashamed of in not being able to write. Some people can, some cannot. Like whether or not you are able to sing in tune or play the fiddle. "Thus," he adds as he signs alongside her mark, "we two are bound together in law."

"Like being married."

A laugh. A faint blush. "Associated perhaps, if not exactly married. You will, of course, receive letters from the children once a week. They will be sent here and I will pass them on to you. Or, if you would rather, you may come here and I will read them for you. And write replies for you if you wish."

"The Reverend Richter—"

"I'm sure Mr. Richter would be pleased to do the same, but my offer is there. In case you are worried, any costs – my professional fees, for example – are entirely covered by the monies we have obtained on your behalf from the Royal Patriotic Fund."

He pauses and seems confused about how to proceed. Annie wonders whether she should make to leave, but Mr. Bromehead is looking at her as though he is about to say something. It would be polite to stay, wouldn't it? She sips tea, trying not to make a noise.

"Mrs. Kelsey tells me you used to work at the Bailgate laundry."

"I did, sir, until the baby came. Then they found another woman, so now I just take laundry in when I can. And help out with Mrs. Kelsey when she needs. That's why it's difficult to get by ... "

"Yes, of course." The very tip of his tongue, curiously pink and innocent, emerges for a moment to moisten his lips. "If it would be useful to you, I could offer you more work here in the house. At number four. Not just laundry, although I understand your starched collars are second to none." A smile at his little joke.

"Thank you, sir. When you've had to do soldiers' chokers you can do anything."

"I'm sure Mrs. Kelsey could use some help around the house, although I am on my own now my mother has passed away so there's not much to do, but still ... How do you feel about that?" He looks at her quite steadily. His eyes are blue.

"That's very kind, sir."

"I daresay you could bring the baby as long as it behaves itself. Is it a girl child? I'm afraid I don't remember."

"A girl. Sarah Rebecca. And she's generally good as gold."

"Then that would be fine. Your hours we can arrange with Mrs. Kelsey. What about payment? Does a shilling a day sound fair? It's what a soldier earns, is it not?"

"That is very generous of you, sir."

"It is just ... " He pauses, as though searching for the word. "It just seems to me that it is most unfair, the hand that has been dealt you. If you see what I mean. A ... " – hesitation; a search for the right expression – "a fine-looking and intelligent young woman like yourself. Your husband torn from you, leaving you to fend for yourself and your three children." He shakes his head. "Unfair." And then, quite unexpectedly, he reaches across the table and takes her hand. "If things work out well, we can even think of raising your wage." Then his hand is back on his own side of the bargain and he is sorting

343

the papers into a neat pile and calling for his clerk to come and take them away.

He smiles quickly at Annie, blushing faintly. "So that's settled, then." And when she rises to leave, he stands too and shows her out. No one has ever done that before.

The sum total of all the tides and currents of all the moments and all the interrogations and all the decisions is this:

On 14 October 1857, at the age of nine, Mary Ann is sent away to the Royal Victoria Patriotic Asylum in Wandsworth, a school founded specifically for the daughters of soldiers who died in the Crimea.

Ten months later, on 24 August 1858, at the age of six, George Henry is admitted to a similar school for boys, the Orphan School at Barnet, run by the Reverend William Pennefather, whom the Reverend Bromehead could recommend most heartily.*

And Annie herself moves less than two hundred yards, from West Bight, which lies just outside the castle walls, to Angel Yard, the courtyard of a former coaching inn.

The Angel Inn is long gone now and replaced by shops, but part of the yard itself remains tucked in behind buildings near the cathedral. There, in her own little apartment, number three (the rent covered by Royal Patriotic Fund), she settled in with the last child to remain in her keeping, Corporal George's final contribution to life on this planet, her two-year-old daughter Sarah Rebecca.

*

---

* William Pennefather (1816–1873), perhaps not entirely coincidentally a cousin of Major-General John Pennefather, the effective commander of the British troops at the Battle of Inkerman.

344

Time doesn't heal, but like an ill-used whetstone it dulls the edge of pain. That seems a suitably Victorian metaphor. The pain of saying farewell to her two older children recedes, and perhaps the sense of guilt fades as well. Annie grows resigned to her lot. Yes, there is the ache of separation and the deep-seated sense of desolation at the death of her husband, but at least her immediate affairs are settled. The threat of destitution has receded and the fear of the workhouse faded; life, after a fashion, can restart.

Every morning she feeds the baby, washes it, dresses it, then washes and dresses herself. There's food for breakfast – bread, an egg, some porridge, milk delivered fresh to the inn with a jug filled for her – and after that the walk with the baby through the gardens and alleys behind the Angel building and into the garden of number four, James Street, the house of E. A. Bromehead Esq., Proctor, Solicitor, Attorney-at-Law, immediately adjacent to his offices at number three.

There is already a maid who comes in to help the housekeeper, so there is little work for Annie to do. Some laundry, some polishing of silverware and dusting of oddments and ornaments – most of them relics of Bromehead's parents, who lived here before him.*

"Can't for the life of me think why he employs you," Mrs. Kelsey remarks. "With only Mr. Edmund to cater for, and him so easy." She looks Ann up and down. "I suppose he's taken pity on you. He's soft like that. Always giving money to lost causes. And people take advantage of him for it."

"D'you think I'm taking advantage of him, Mrs. Kelsey?"

The women shrugs. "You're Irish, aren't you?"

It was, of course, arguable who was taking advantage of whom. Was it the man who, in that signal moment when

---

* His father died early in 1832; his mother, at the age of seventy, in 1850.

Annie was making her mark on the documents to send the children away, reached out from his natural reticence and took her hand? Or was it the woman who, at the same moment, looked at him through her tears with a smile that stepped across the barriers of class? In the uneasy arena of personal transactions, who gains and who loses? And how are understandings reached? But for the moment Annie dusts and polishes assiduously, hoping that this labour justifies her employment.

It's the first time she has been in a household of the gentry. What astonishes her is the amount of stuff there is, the sheer abundance of possessions. She owns almost nothing outside the realm of the useful – some pots and pans, a few plates, bowls, knives and forks, that kind of thing; the Bromehead family possess vast amounts of stuff – pictures on the walls, objects under glass domes, clocks, ornaments, souvenirs, mementoes. More than that, there are items which have a use but are never used – occasional chairs, side tables, cabinets – and what look like precious objects that have no obvious purpose.

"Perhaps," Mr. Bromehead suggests one day when he finds her scrubbing an already well-scrubbed floor in the main house, "it would be better if you were to take on number three. The office maid is getting married and will be moving to Gainsborough. And I think you might be more comfortable with such an arrangement than here in the house."

Ann looks up at him, wiping hair off her forehead with the back of her wrist. "Very well, sir."

"I will inform Mrs. Kelsey." He considers her for a shade longer than one might expect. "And ... "

"Yes, sir?"

"It might be, ah, better if you did not wear ... " – he appears to search for the right term – "scullery maid's clothes. Because of clients."

"I can wear my best, sir."

"Your best will not be necessary."

"It's all I have otherwise."

That faint blush. "Then your best will be fine. And I will provide you with money to purchase another suitable dress."

He turns away. She continues scrubbing.

Thereafter it is at the offices of the law firm, *Edmund A. Bromehead, Solicitor, Proctor, Attorney-at-Law*, that Ann works. Mr. Bromehead crosses from the house to the offices at ten o'clock every morning, always immaculately dressed – striped trousers, frock coat, cravat with gleaming tie pin – and trailing behind him the faintest scent of Cologne water. He greets his clerk with a polite but indifferent enquiry about his and his wife's health, he nods to Annie if he happens to pass her, and then shuts himself away in his private office. She has no idea what he does there. It is all papers and documents and occasional meetings with those clients who, apparently, would be offended to see her wearing scullery maid's clothes. The clerk, a Mr. Hatchet, spends all of his time writing. Annie spends all of her time polishing already gleaming furniture and dusting already dust-free books. But she is entirely presentable in her best, which is, as mourning fashion dictates, a full-skirted, tight-waisted, black bombazine dress. She also moves up to making and serving tea or coffee in those very same fine bone china cups that she encountered when dealing with Mr. Bromehead in his professional capacity for the first time.

"Mrs. Mawer," he explains to clients, "is the widow of one of our gallant soldiers who gave his life for Queen and Country."

Client faces are drawn in sorrow and admiration. "In India?" they ask because by now India – the Mutiny – is the current imperial slaughterhouse.*

"In the Crimea."

"Oh, the Crimea." The appalling Crimea, the shameful Crimea, the Crimean disaster, pushed to the back of the imperial mind. "Not in the cavalry, perchance?" They are thinking, of course, of the slaughter of the Light Brigade so ably memorialised in the famous poem by Mr. Tennyson (whom some of them knew in the early days, before he moved out of the county). Was her husband a trooper? The Hussars? The Light Dragoons? What a thing to tell people!

"The infantry," she replies softly. "He was a sergeant in the Fiftieth regiment."†

A disappointment – the infantry, and only a regiment of the line, not even the guards. "How sad. But then again, how noble."

"Indeed."

At which point Annie has learned to curtsey and retire to the kitchen at the back of the house, which is where Mr. Bromehead has taken to finding her in the afternoons, after his clerk has gone home and he is on his way back to number four for his evening meal. "Mrs. Kelsey will be waiting," he says as he comes into the kitchen. "I must go, I must go." But he doesn't always do so, taking apparent pleasure in staying to talk with her.

He is a shy man, a solitary man, a man who has lived with his parents all his life. These things he explains to Annie over

---

* The Indian Mutiny was an uprising against the rule of the East India Company. Now known variously as the Indian Rebellion and the First War of Independence, it lasted from 1857 to 1858.

† He was never more than corporal, although in a number of instances it appears that Ann may have "promoted" him.

the weeks and months. How the early death of his father made him the effective head of an otherwise female household, two older brothers and an older sister having already married and moved out. Thus Edmund, an idolised eighteen-year-old, was left to be worshipped and spoiled by his three remaining sisters and his doting mother. "Then my mother died and the sisters left, one to get married, the other two" – he shrugs – "just to get away. And I was left alone." He seems to wear this loneliness like a badge of honour.

Annie says, "To be sure, that's your own choice. A man like you could find yourself a wife easy enough. I'm thinking" – she looks at him sideways – "I'm thinking Mr. Edmund Bromehead enjoys his independence. Don't say you don't!"

He laughs. "You are very good for me, Ann, do you know that? You take me out of myself. All the others, my family, my friends, acquaintances, treat me with a solemn respect, as though I'm some kind of paragon. Mr. Edmund, they think: so good, so benevolent, so keen to do good works. But they never ask themselves what goes on inside my head."

She raises her eyebrows. "And what does?"

He blushes. "All manner of things."

It is a slow and awkward process, this overcoming of solitude, this edging round barriers of class and education and morality. Following a reading of her children's letters – this is a weekly ritual – there comes a comforting, masculine hand on a distressed lady's shoulder and her hand put up to cover his. There are other, lesser missteps – a hint here, a shared smile there, a look exchanged, a passing encounter on the stair or in the corridor that leads to unseemly proximity and unbecoming laughter. These things take time in that world of euphemism and shame, of prudery and moral rectitude. Clothing has something to do with it, the full skirt and tight waist, the high, choking collar and the bastion of a buttoned waistcoat. And sound, the rustle of underskirts, the creak of hand-stitched boots. And chance, the shock of interrupting her while she is in the kitchen at the tub, taking advantage of the piped hot water to wash herself after cleaning. He makes a rapid retreat but she calls him back. He stops and turns. From the doorway, momentarily, as she lifts a towel to cover herself, he sees her naked from the waist up, the curve of a pale breast glistening with suds, the glimpse of a nipple.

"I'm sorry, sir."

He watches her, for a moment unable to find words.

"There's nothing to be afraid of," she says.

"Your modesty ... "

"My modesty?" She laughs. "I used to live in barracks. Can you imagine?"

The sentence *there's nothing to be afraid of* remains in his mind for days afterwards, as though it were the utterance of an oracle. Of course he is afraid of what is unknown and hidden from decent gaze; indeed, his whole existence is as hidden from the raw facts of life as it could be, except for bizarre occasions when reality intrudes. For example, when he attends the annual ball of the county lunatic asylum,* of which institution he is a board member. To see these poor creatures going about their weird and aimless existence, trying to dance, trying to show some semblance of normality while the head physician – after the French fashion he calls himself an alienist – explains that most of them suffer from morbid and excessive sexuality, the state that is normal in animals. That makes Bromehead realise the fragility of the civilised human condition and how easily one might step over the border into the world of the animal, a subject that so many

_____

* 30 December 1854.

350

are talking and writing about these days, that all animal life is connected, and that we ourselves are mere animals.

So are the feelings that he discovers within himself for this woman merely animal and therefore something to be cursed and despised and ultimately dismissed? Therein lies a conundrum, because it seems to his stunted mind that his feelings are both animal and spiritual, the two blended together. He longs to touch her, to know her; but he also longs to raise her above her lowly status – that of an ordinary soldier's widow, rescued by circumstance from destitution – and place her on a pedestal so that he might kneel down before her and worship her.

Sacrilege? Blasphemy?

He has been foolish enough to utter the words, "They never ask themselves what goes on inside my head."

To which she was brazen enough to ask: "What does?"

He wanted to tell her the truth, that is the terrible thing; but he dared not. "All manner of things," was all he could say.

Annie understands most of this well enough. She's had too much experience of men not to know what is going on inside Mr. Bromehead's mind. The way he breathes when he is near her. His heightened colour as he addresses her. The manner in which he looks at her or avoids looking. The things he says and the way he says them. But her own motives? Her own feelings? They are, presumably, as muddled as his. Her need for affection, for male presence; but also the physical attraction of a man who may not have the raw masculinity of George but instead possesses an endearing vulnerability. For all his educated self-assuredness, she knows well enough that Edmund Bromehead is still innocent. She might be ignorant in many things but in that strange dynamic between men and women she can outmatch his innocence with her own instinctive knowledge and her understanding of the power that her small, fragile womanly body may exert over his physical strength.

When it actually happens it is surprisingly easy. The wall of class and morality between them has been undermined over the weeks without their really noticing it: a piece of mortar here, a brick there, a weakened pillar of rectitude elsewhere. It is when he comes into the kitchen at the back of the house, as he has taken to doing every afternoon, and stands beside her as she prepares a pot of tea, close beside her so that he is almost touching her. And, when she turns towards him to see what he wants, rather than backing away he remains standing there, looking down on her as she looks up to him. Her hair is drawn back in a modest bun. She knows that the shape of her face, the angle of her jaw, her sharp nose, her blue, Irish eyes, all seem to arouse him.

"Mr. Edmund," she says. He might step back at that point, but he doesn't. "Do you want to tell me something?"

He does. She can see that. She can see the way in which he swallows, the unsteadiness in his breathing.

"Annie," he whispers.

She smiles up at him. "Mr. Edmund, it will be a secret between the two of us."

She doesn't say what might be a secret but she doesn't need to. He puts his hands on her shoulders. Just that is enough, but having done so much makes it easy to do the next thing, to stoop towards her and kiss her on the lips. For a moment they are like that, mouth to mouth, her head thrown back, his hands on her shoulders, before he draws back in something like panic, mumbling things – this not being right, how he holds her in high regard, he must not take advantage of her, a whole congeries of nonsense. "Annie," he says, his voice thickened by emotion, "this is improper."

"Don't be soft." Her hand goes up to stroke his cheek, as you might comfort a child. "Whatever happens, Mr. Edmund, no one will ever know."

And she was right: we'll never know precisely. What goes on behind closed doors is not the stuff of documents; it's the stuff of novels. But something like this must have happened, something like an awkward exchange of kisses, of touching and feeling coupled with an unspoken agreement that down here was not right, not comfortable, not suitable, either in the bare kitchen at the back of the building or among the desks and the tables and chairs, the ledgers and tomes of the offices. Upstairs was much better.

It would be an afternoon when an appointment for Mr. Bromehead had been cancelled and the clerk, Mr. Hatchet, had left early because his wife was unwell. Upstairs at number three was largely unused, a floor of empty bedrooms, some now housing client records but one at the back left empty – a dusty room with an iron bedstead and a bare mattress, two bedside tables with marble tops, a washstand complete with water jug and ceramic bowl. It was there, with curtains drawn to let in only a sliver of daylight from the garden, that it happened, that first coupling.

Awkward, certainly. Never before has Bromehead seen a mature woman naked and the sight is a shock. Her skin might have a luminous, marbled whiteness but that is the only resemblance to the classical statuary or academic painting that has until then been the limit of his knowledge; instead the living creature is flawed, marked by child-bearing and suckling, smudged with rufous hair in groin and armpit, possessed of angles and declivities he has never imagined. Yet she is also suffused by a new and quite overwhelming power. When he lies down beside her he is shaking.

"Are you afeard of me, Edmund?" she asks.

It is almost as great a shock to hear her call him by his plain Christian name, unadorned with title, as to have her naked against him.

"Well, you mustn't be. It's just loving, that's all. Just loving." And she shows him how to do it, guiding him with deft hands, talking quietly to him, reassuring him, telling him that things are all right, that he mustn't worry, that, no, she is quite happy with him there, in there, that she – whisper it – enjoys feeling him inside her.

Remorse the next day, certainly. Shame and embarrassment when she appears in the morning, bringing coffee for some important clients. Bromehead reddens and looks away as she enters the office, the first woman he has ever seen naked now demurely clothed, skirt to the ground, bodice to the throat, sleeves to the wrists. Her eyes, those eyes that looked into his own mere inches away, now downcast as she settles the tray on the table and makes to pour.

"Thank you, Mrs. Mawer. We'll see to it ourselves."

Quietly she leaves. Just the rustle of her underskirts.

"Mrs. Mawer's husband was in the Crimea," he explains to his clients as the door closes behind her. "A sad story."

But surely, he thinks, they can all tell. They can read the shame in my face.

The day passes in that way, a kind of silent tension, looks not exchanged, words not spoken. Finally, after Mr. Hatchet has left early to see how his wife is doing, Bromehead calls Ann into his office.

He is pale and anxious, as though he's ill. When he speaks, his voice is uncertain, not the voice she is used to, with the lawyer's authority and the educated man's assurance. There are apologies, of course. Shame expressed, blame apportioned, his tongue tripping over words. "I'm sorry. I am so very sorry. About what happened yesterday." He shakes his head. "Unforgiveable. It was unforgiveable. It must never happen again."

She uses the softest of her Irish voices: "There's nothing to say sorry for, Mr. Edmund. You made me happy, don't you see that?"

He appears surprised at the idea of her happiness. What little he knows about sex is that it gives the man physical satisfaction while bringing the woman only discomfort and revulsion. "And I think ... " she seems to be searching for the right words, as though she possesses a wide and complex vocabulary; but the only words she knows are words she has heard spoken. "I think you were being honest with me."

"Honest?"

"A woman can tell, you see? What's natural and right. It was natural, really. Two lonely souls, comforting each other. Very natural."

"There's nothing natural about committing sin. A sin is against nature."

She smiles, her head on one side, those blue eyes laughing at him. "Is that your brother speaking? It sounds like the priests in Ireland. What we did *was* nature, d'you not see that? A natural thing between men and women. How can that be a sin?"

"It was outside the bonds of holy matrimony."

She shakes her head. "Sin, holy matrimony. It's all what's written in books, isn't it? That's not natural – it's just words."

It is absurd, this argument with an illiterate servant. "Words lift us above the animal, Annie. You don't understand, not reading or writing yourself."

"Well, it's sure I understand things you don't seem to. I understand the heart. Yours and mine."

He shakes his head. "You're just a servant, Annie. I hold you in high regard, but something like this just cannot go on. It cannot."

But things have changed in the balance between them. Now it is her turn to come round the desk, to stand beside him and turn his head towards her. "Of course it can go on, Mr. Edmund, just as long as we wish it." She bends towards him and touches her lips on his, and as soon as he opens his mouth and feels the insidious softness of her tongue, he is lost once again.

Or

Or maybe this ...

She never gets taken on to work in the office at number three. She never progresses beyond the laundry room at number four, a place clouded with steam and strewn with soap suds, up to her elbows in hot water. She's got Mr. Edmund's underwear and shirts to wash, which is all straightforward enough, and then shirt collars to starch, which is a bit more tricky but nothing when you've learned to do soldiers' chokers. She's been working there a couple of months now and it's all right as a job. Easier than the commercial laundry and Mrs. Kelsey doesn't mind having the baby in the servants' quarters as long as she behaves herself and doesn't cry. Of course it's better when Mrs. Kelsey goes out, as she has now, and Annie has the place to herself more or less, the maid being off today for some reason.

The door opens. Unexpected. She jerks round to look but it's only Mr. Edmund standing there. Wants something, perhaps. She shakes suds from her hands and wipes them on her apron. "Sorry, sir," she says. "Are you looking for Mrs. Kelsey? She's just stepped out."

He flushes slightly. "What? Mrs. Kelsey? No." He's looking at her, at her eyes, then down. She knows that look, saw it often enough in barracks, men looking at you like that and envying George. A sort of focus. A breathing, as though there is a shortage of air and it has become something you might treasure, air, something you needed to hold on to, let go with reluctance. Sometimes they made an offer when they were like that. Some wives accepted but it was an uncertain game with all sorts of consequences you could never be sure of. Yes, there were some husbands who turned a blind eye because the extra money was always welcome, but often enough it ended in violence.

"So, I'll just get on . . . " She hesitates, holds out wet hands to make her point.

"Yes, of course, Annie. Don't let me disturb you – just get on with what you're doing. Go on." He waves a hand as though to turn her round, and she does as she is bidden, turns back to the washing, conscious of the fact that he is still there and still watching her.

"Where's the baby?" he asks.

She answers to the sink and the hot suds. "Playing next door, in her pen."

He has come nearer. She can sense him standing just behind her. "Would you like to earn some extra, Annie?" he asks.

She continues with her washing, not wanting to confront him. "And how would that be, sir?"

"A guinea on account." He reaches out past her and places a shiny gold coin on the draining board. She doesn't know what "on account" means but she knows a guinea well enough.

"That might be welcome, sir."

"You'll have to be good to me. And it'll have to be our secret."

She takes the coin and slips it into the pocket of her apron. "I'm sure it can be that, sir."

The deal is done. She waits for him to make the first move and there it is, his hands on her backside, lifting her skirts. She's wearing no stockings or hose; she never does at work. Nor drawers. That makes it easier, although whether or not the choice was deliberate even she cannot tell. She moves only to shift her legs apart, feeling his fingers probing and his breath on her neck.

"Don't turn round, Annie," he says.

"Sure I won't, sir."

She waits, knowing what he's doing – that scrabbling with his clothes, she recognises it: undoing his trousers, pulling down his drawers. Then he's touching her again, handling her, lifting her up and forward over the basin so that she's looking down on the suds and at one of his shirts floating in the cloudy water. He pushes against her. There's a moment of hesitation and then he's inside her, filling her, not roughly but with an urgency that she remembers well, although it has been a few years now. Men are like that. George was like that, Mr. Edmund is like that, making noises like a dog panting or a man running; and then those convulsions – one, two, three, four – that dying away to stillness. Slowly he withdraws, letting her down but holding her head with one hand so that she cannot turn round.

"Thank you, Annie," he says quietly. Ever the gentleman, Mr. Edmund. "I only ask that you keep this as our secret."

"Of course, Mr. Edmund."

"And ... we'll see about it again. In a day or two, when there's a suitable moment."

Then he has gone and Annie is left standing at the sink with a thin trickle of liquid running down the inside of her thigh. Now she understands what "on account" means.

The baby is crying in the room next door.

Or this

But maybe it was even less personal. One has to contemplate the possibility of Ann Mawer, soldier's widow, laundress and charwoman by trade, receiving gentlemen by appointment in her house at number three, Angel Yard, between the hours of, say, half past two in the afternoon and six o'clock in the evening, offering a discreet personal service at a reasonable price. But that rather moves it out of the ambit of Edmund Bromehead, Esq., and there is that family story to take into account:

Broomfield, Broomhead, something like that.

Thus you scrape away at the surface and uncover things, lumps, objects, fragments that you don't at first recognise but which you carefully put aside so that when the time comes they may fall into place like pieces of a jigsaw, or reveal themselves like a crossword clue suddenly resolved. The narrative has to fit in with the facts, and the facts are that these things happened that winter, the first one being the most significant and incontrovertible:

In November 1858 Ann Mawer conceived a child.

Also, at some point Mrs. Kelsey left service in number four and a younger woman, Eliza Scarborough, took her place.

And as always, Edmund Bromehead Esq. conducted his life in his usual, even manner. Apart from his legal practice there were meetings of the Choral Society, of the Hospital Board, of the Lincolnshire Law Society, of the shareholders of the electricity company and the Lincoln Waterworks. There was also the Twelfth Night Ball at the Assembly Rooms.

And all the while, beneath the surface of these quotidian things and beneath the surface of Annie's belly, the baby grew.

Gestation

So how long *did* it go on, this relationship of whatever kind? In the slow march of documentary evidence, not long. A maximum of about four years, from 1858 to 1862. In the turmoil of human relations it must have seemed little more than an instant, and at the same time an eternity. Different things to each partner, of course. For Bromehead, an education, a revelation, an adventure. Perhaps he had a King Cophetua complex. Annie was, after all, little more than a beggar and at least in one sense, a maid. Maybe it was through this imbalanced relationship that he could confront his own sexual longings which had been so long suppressed. For he *was* an innocent, his upbringing barricaded by the strictures of the Church of England (the cathedral towered then as it towers still over the houses in James Street), his youth blinded by the dry dust of legal practice. Dutiful in his pursuit of good causes, above all he would have been fearful of the sins of the flesh, that they might be used in evidence against him, because, as a good lawyer, he surely believed in the forthcoming day of judgement when, like a prisoner in the dock, he would stand before the throne of God and have to give account of himself. In the dusty upstairs room at the back of number three, James Street, maybe Annie Mawer overwhelmed that fear. At least for a while.

An unbalanced relationship, of course. In the first few days and weeks perhaps it was tipped in Annie's favour. She might have been ignorant and illiterate but she was also bright, sharp and funny. And she *knew* things. She understood the ways of men, their lusts and their loves, their physical needs. She was also an adept teacher, showing him what he could not have imagined and yet contriving somehow to make those intimacies, those indecencies something natural and rather marvellous, a joy that could, at least for a short while, overcome the terrifying gulf, dug by education and class, that yawned between them. And from this relationship she could have the prospect of some kind of security, and maybe a memory of the kind of love that George had shown her.

Then came the moment when she told him she was pregnant. This would have been in late 1858 or early 1859. What would she have hoped for by the confession? The impossible? Maybe. It's common enough to believe the world might be yours, even if you are the penniless widow of a soldier. Perhaps for a while he believed it too. Perhaps shock and shame was mollified by affection, even love; maybe consternation was mingled with absurd elation, euphoria fighting with dismay and, for a while, winning. Annie was carrying his child? Wonderful! The alternation of emotions. It was the greatest gift, the gift of life; it was a disaster, the wages of sin. He'd be ruined. He'd be fulfilled.

"What'll we do? What *can* we do?"

Ridiculous promises might have been made, to be undone in an instant: they could escape, go away, away from Lincoln to somewhere they wouldn't be known. To the Lakes, maybe. Bromehead's younger sister was planning to move there. Her fiancé had just become curate at Patterdale and was surely destined for good things in the Church.

"Would we marry?"

Marry? The idea was absurd. "You'd be my housekeeper. We'd be respectable. A retired solicitor and his widowed housekeeper."

For a few minutes that didn't seem beyond the bounds of possibility.

"And my children?"

Ah, her children.

Ultimately, of course, common sense took over, mediated no doubt by a serious talk. I imagine that Edmund Bromehead was good at serious talks, probably better than he was at frivolous ones. Doubtless, in that legalistic way of his, all such talks would have ended with a conclusion expressed as a product of the utmost logic. I can see him standing there, ever the advocate, his hands grasping the lapels of his frock coat, his watch chain hanging like a smile across the dove-grey face of his waistcoat, while she sits demurely at the coffin-table dressed in black with white lace at throat and cuffs, looking every bit the client rather than the lover.

"If it gets out that this child is mine, my reputation is ruined," he explains. "And if my reputation is ruined, then so is my career. My clients trust me, Annie, both legally and morally. The two things are inseparable, don't you see? The law is merely the expression of society's morals, and if I am seen to transgress the morals then how can I be expected to uphold the law?"

She wouldn't have known the term *sophistry* and so can hardly accuse him of it.

"So, I am afraid I see no alternative. Once your condition becomes evident you will have to leave my employ. However, I am prepared to continue to pay you during that period and I will, of course, support you through your confinement.

When the child is born – and assuming all is well – there is a permanent solution which seems entirely reasonable to me. I have spoken, discreetly of course, with my brother."

"Your *brother*?"

He sighs. "I know you have ... " a hesitation, searching for the right way to frame it, "crossed swords with him in the past. But beneath his manner he is a most devout and decent man. Naturally, I presented the problem as belonging to one of my clients and I most certainly did not mention you by name. A servant girl, I said. A respectable but unmarried gentleman and a servant girl."

"And you think he'd not guess?"

"I'm sure not. He came up with this idea, that you should – the servant girl should give up the child for adoption. He can arrange such matters through his ministry, and I, of course, can provide the necessary legal help. Or ... " he hesitated, "there is the possibility of my own dear sister, Jane. She has always longed for a child, and now she approaches her fortieth year ... "

Annie feels the baby inside her. Even though this talk may be before the quickening, she can still feel it there, growing like some kind of sea creature within her, her flesh and his, accepting its lifeblood from her. "Your family takes my child from me?"

"Annie, you already have one child—" as though children are fungible goods and may be exchanged one for another.

"Three. I have *three* children. Your brother and those other men took two of them away."

"Yes, yes, of course. But you know what I mean. One child to care for directly. Three in total, but that is the very point I am trying to make: you are not able to look after all three. You struggle even to deal with your current child. You depend on charity for help."

"It isn't charity. It's what rightly comes to a war widow."

"Of course it is. But that doesn't alter the fact that another will be too great a burden."

"And you want to take it from me. And give it to your sister!"

"I am endeavouring to discharge my responsibilities."

"You'd be kind Uncle Edmund, wouldn't you? But I'd not see it again." She shakes her head. "It's the way men have children, isn't it? That is the problem. You have a quick fuck—"

"Annie!"

"—and that's it. But with us women it takes all the months that follow, nine of them, and all the years that follow that. You men can just wash your hands of the issue – even pretend it wasn't yours in the first place—"

"I am not doing that!"

"—but the mother has no choice. She has to love the child she has created. That is her burden. My burden. So, Mr. Edmund Bromehead, I will have my baby – *our* baby – and I'll bring it up and love it with the same love that I bear for my other children, both the ones you took from me and the one you left me with."

"Now you are just being stubborn. That's the Irish in you. Well, there's something else, Annie, something you clearly have not considered." He looks pleased with himself, as though he's in court and about to reveal the key point in a litigation. "If the administrators of the Patriotic Fund should get to know that you are pregnant, that you have had this child out of wedlock, they will, I am afraid, revoke your eligibility on moral grounds."

"What does *revoke* mean?"

"They may cut your pension and expel your children from their institutions."

"Throw us all out on the street?"

366

"You'd become a burden on the Lincoln Union.* They'd send you to the workhouse, Annie. And your children. Separated, of course. Although you'd be able to visit them in the children's quarters on Sundays."

The shock is palpable, like a physical blow. Suddenly, she feels that she is drowning, she and her child are drowning in this sea of words and the pitching, suffocating waves thrown up by society and the law. "What have I done to deserve this?"

"I am being logical, Annie."

"That's the law, isn't it? Logic to tie common people in knots."

"I'm not trying to tie you in knots. I'm trying to do what is surely best. You have the child as quietly as possible—"

"Have you ever *had* a child?"

He ignores her sarcasm. "And we pass it over to the new mother immediately. Yes, my sister Jane if she is willing. It is she who will register the child as a foundling." What, he must surely wonder, is he doing? Proposing to break the law? Conniving to destroy everything that, up to now, he has held sacred? "That way you will not appear in the records as the mother, and perhaps the administrators of the Patriotic Fund will not find out."

She's gasping for breath, struggling to stay afloat. "So that's it, is it? Either you take my child from me or you take all my children from me?"

"It's not me, Annie. It is simply what will happen."

She holds up her hand as though to ward off another blow. "I'll go away," she says. "I'll go away from here and take your shame away with me. I'll go somewhere I can be with the other children. But you, Edmund Bromehead, will have to assist me."

---

* The local Poor Law Union of parishes, responsible for administering poor relief.

Ann Gleeson

Excavation of the past continues, the careful scraping away of the dust of centuries, uncovering relevant facts as an archaeologist looks for potsherds. There's this, from the *Stamford Mercury*, 7 October 1859:

> **A young Irish woman, named Ann Gleeson, was apprehended on Sunday in Angel-Yard (at which place she was lodging), and charged with deserting her child, 2 years old, by which it had become chargeable to the parish of St. Mary, Islington. She had been up to the last few months in the service of Lieutenant Massey, of Lincoln; after which it appears she lodged in London, where she left the child. On Monday chief constable Mandley delivered her into the hands of the parochial authorities of Islington, whose intention it is to forward her and her children (she has two) to her own parish in the sister isle.**

The Lieutenant Massey mentioned in the newspaper report had been recruiting officer in the Lincoln district for the 30th Regiment; quite what he was doing moving around the country with a young woman "in his service" is open to question but the fact is that in July 1859 he was posted away from Lincoln to act as recruiting officer in Nottingham.*

At that time in Angel Yard there were five separate households totalling about a dozen people: two families of three or four; a childless couple; two older women living in single rooms;† and two young Irish women, both with children of uncertain fatherhood, both with connections with the military, and, rather significantly, both in the late stages of pregnancy – Annie Mawer and Ann Gleeson.

In life, unlike in novels, things happen like this: people just turn up, intersect with your own story for a while, then disappear. Ann Gleeson is one such. Waving and shouting, she emerges from the fog of the unknown and just for a moment she is visible to history – indeed, cursing in her broad Irish accent and calling down a dozen saints as well as the archangel Lucifer onto the head of Lieutenant Massey, she is unavoidable. She's loud, she's young, not unattractive when she's sober, and she's pregnant.

Inevitably she turns to her neighbour in Angel Yard, Annie Mawer. "Will you help me, Annie?" she asks. She's pissed. She's often pissed. Most evenings she's round the back of the Angel begging for a jug of porter and the potboy usually gives her some just to get rid of her. And then she turns to Annie for a shoulder to cry on and an Irish accent to talk to.

"Will you help me, Annie? You're a lovely Irish *cailín*. You'll understand."

"I'm hardly a colleen – I've had four children and I'm waiting on a fifth."

---

* *Lincoln Chronicle*, 8 July 1859.
† Census of 1861.

"Well dat's amazin' 'cos you don't look a day over twenty."
Ann Gleeson laughs to show it's not true. But she doesn't
laugh at the thruppence that Annie gives her, which is what
Ann Gleeson means by "help."

Apart from begging, she has two topics of conversation: her
daughter, Mary, and the treachery of her erstwhile employer
Lieutenant Massey. Mary is conspicuous by her absence in the
squalid room Ann has rented in Angel Yard. She might even
be a figment of the woman's imagination. Or perhaps Mary
is dead. Lives are fragile, children die, stories are easy enough
to make up. "Me lovely little girl," she cries. "So beautiful,
so much her mammy's little angel, *macushla machree*. So
defenceless and innocent."

"What happened to her?" Annie asks. "What happened to
your Mary?"

"I left her," the mother admits tearfully.

"You *left* her?"

"I ran out on her. Me own flesh and blood."

"Where was that, Ann?"

"Up Islington way. Left her with a woman, I did. Said
I'd be back."

"You just *abandoned* her?"

"Don't *do* dat, Annie! I can hear the feckin' priests in your
voice, all morality an' dat. Accusin' like."

"I'm not accusing you of anything."

"I know you're not. I know you understand. He led
me on, see."

"Who did?"

"Feckin' Massey. Told me he'd make an officer's wife of me."

"And you *believed* him?"

"'Course I believed him, the feckin' bastard. Wasn't he an
officer? I lift my skirts for him and then he throws me out
for a tart."

"Well, you *are* a tart, aren't you?"

Ann Gleeson roars with laughter. "Sure I'm a tart, Annie. An' aren't we all?"

In moments of relative sobriety Ann Gleeson talks about London. "Have you never been to London, Annie? It makes Dublin look like a feckin' village, I tell you. You can live there. I was that sad when Massey said he was leaving to come up here. Lincoln's a city, he says. You'll be all right. Another feckin' lie. Lincoln's a city like Dublin's a city: it's got a bloody cathedral and loads of priests with their hands on their cocks. Just that these priests here have wives. But they still want to tickle your twat. But London! Dozens of cathedrals yet no feckin' priests that I ever saw. Instead there's theatres and public houses and all manner of things. You can live in London. You can earn a good wage. And there's men in London who appreciate a good-lookin' girl, even one as old as you, Annie." More laughter. "Just stay away from Islington, that's all. It's cheap enough for lodgings but it's full of bloody Irish." Yet more laughter. "Full of bloody Irish, Annie. It's just like being at home."

When she is sober they compare their pregnancies, how they are going, whether they are carrying a boy or a girl, who will give birth sooner, that kind of thing. Annie explains her problem, the danger of the Patriotic Fund finding out she is pregnant and taking away the little they give her. And throwing her children out of their schools.

"They're bastards, all o' them," Ann Gleeson says. "What I'd do is this. You register the child, bold as brass, but you give yourself whatever feckin' name you like. They won't check up. You could call yourself Victoria MacQueen and they'd not say anything." She laughs. That is the thing about Ann Gleeson – she is either laughing or weeping. There's no in-between.

*

Ann Gleeson has her baby on 4 July, sweating in the heat and screaming like a banshee while delivering herself of another baby girl. Once the umbilical cord has been cut and the baby wiped down and handed back to her, she declares with a certain sense of drama that the child shall be named Hannah. "It means *grace*, did you know that? Like her mother." And through the sweat and tears, she looks up at the midwife and at Annie. And she laughs.

Charles Scanlon

Annie Mawer's child, her fifth (we must include the tragic Georgiana), was born on 20 August. Who attended the birth? Possibly Dr. Sympson, the general practitioner who lived at number two, James Street, next door to the legal office of E. A. Bromehead. Young Sympson (a mere thirty-three) was surely just the kind of man who would be tactful about it all.

"A woman I used to employ," Bromehead explained to him. "She lives just round the back, in Angel Yard. Maybe you know her?"

"I think my wife mentioned something . . . "

"Husband died in the Crimea. Sergeant in the Fiftieth. Of course, once I discovered she was with child I had to let her go. Can't have that sort of thing going on in the practice. But I want to do my best to help her."

"I'm sure you do, Bromehead."

Bromehead felt himself reddening. Was there a knowing tone to Sympson's voice? "She's had a difficult time, you see . . . "

"Of course."

"And I know childbirth is hardly a physician's business but I thought you might be able to help. Recommend a good midwife, that kind of thing. And maybe be around in case there's any difficulty . . . "

But there was no difficulty. Physically slight Annie may have been, but she was a good bearer of children. The midwife performed her ancient art and Annie sweated and screamed but Dr. Sympson was not required to do anything more than bring the news of a successful delivery to Bromehead. "A male child," the doctor announced as he came in. "Hale and hearty to judge by the noise he was making."

"And the mother?"

"Oh, the mother. Yes, she's well enough. This is her fifth, so she said. Well used to it by now."

Bromehead seemed uncommonly relieved to hear that all was well. Appeared quite overcome for a moment. But he steadied himself and cast around for something appropriate to say. "Will you have a glass of port wine with me, Sympson? To celebrate?"

So they toasted the birth, a little awkwardly – why exactly *were* they celebrating a servant woman's bastard child? – and talked about matters of family, of Sympson's pretty young wife and their own hopes for the future. "Between you and me, Bromehead, Caroline may already be expecting. It's nothing definite so don't breathe a word to anyone. But it will be wonderful to bless our marriage so soon."

He downed the remainder of his port and made to leave. "Of course, the infant must be vaccinated," he said as he took his hat and cane. He was talking about the servant woman's child now. "The law demands it. I can do it myself if she wishes. Maybe you can tell her. And registered," he added. "These days it is all most officious, as I'm sure you know."

What on earth was he implying by that? Bromehead opened the door. Sympson paused on the doorstep. "I take it there is no acknowledged father? I thought it indelicate to ask the woman herself."

"Apparently not."

"Aren't there two other children in institutions?"

"Indeed. The Royal Patriotic Fund."

"And now she has another child, and a bastard at that." He shook his head. "The Patriotic Fund was hardly set up to encourage such incontinence, was it? This could make her ineligible. Midwives are usually beholden to the registrars, so there's no way round registering it."* Shaking his head, he stepped out of the front door into the warm August evening. "Will such people never learn?" he asked of no one in particular.

Nine days later Annie registered the child.

Is it possible to conjure up the emotion she felt as she stood with her newborn son before the same man who four years previously had registered her and George's fourth child? Panic? Fear? Shame? Defiant pride? Who knows? Emotions aren't inscribed in the registry of births, which the registrar, Mr. Henry Holmes, opened in front of her. A leather-bound tome like a Bible, the book of life itself.

Mr. Holmes looked at her over his spectacles. "The name of this child?"

"Charles."

She watched him write.

"Date of birth?"

"The twentieth."

"Of this month?"

"Yes."

"Place of birth?"

"My house."

---

* According to the 1836 Act, the onus was on the registrar to register all births and deaths in his district. He was paid accordingly per year: the first twenty births and deaths, 2s 6d each; each subsequent birth or death, 1s.

"Where is your house, woman? What *address*?"

"Oh, yes, to be sure. Angel Yard."

He glanced down at a paper on his desk and nodded. "I registered a birth there only a week ago. Irish, like yourself."

"That'll be Ann Gleeson's little girl."

"Indeed it was. And the number?"

"The number?"

"Of your house."

"Ah yes, the number." Her heart was beating. She could feel it. Maybe the baby could feel it too: the drumbeat of panic. "Four."

She was wrong. Number four was where she lived previously in West Bight; four was also the number of Bromehead's house in James Street. But it was not the number of her house in Angel Yard. Yet Mr. Holmes duly wrote *4, Angel Yard* and thus, across a century and a half and through the cold fact of an official form, communicated Annie's anxiety and confusion.

He moved on to the question that was uppermost in Annie's mind: "Father's name?"

She swallowed. Against her breast the baby slept, unconcerned. "I don't know the name of the father," she said quietly.

"Do you not?"

"No."

"You have no idea who the father is?"

"No, I don't."

Mr. Holmes thought for a moment, then nodded – "Neither did Miss Gleeson" – and passed to the adjacent column. "Your name?"

Her mind raced through possibilities and consequences. This was what Mr. Edmund had suggested. This was what he had *advised*. As her solicitor. This would mean that the officials of the Royal Patriotic Fund would not have George

Mawer's widow's promiscuity staring them in the face. "Ann Scanlon," she said.

The man tapped his pencil, as though uncertain how to proceed. Finally he said, "Forgive me, but I have to remind you that, under the 1836 Registration of Births Act, to make a false declaration in the register is to perjure yourself. Do you understand the meaning of the word *perjury*?"

"No."

"It signifies lying under oath. It is a criminal offence that may be punished by imprisonment. Furthermore, I personally, as registrar for the city of Lincoln, am bound by law not to make any entry in the register that I know to be false … and I happen to know that you are the widow of Sergeant George Mawer. Isn't that correct? And that your husband died, when was it? Fifty-four or fifty-five? Very sad story, I'm sure. I remember registering your previous child. I am, you see, required to enter the mother's name, surname and maiden name."

"My name is Scanlon. That's how I was born and baptised. Ann Scanlon. Just that."

He looked at her. "And is that how you wish to be known?"

She nodded. "Scanlon. And that's Ann without an *e*." Over the years she had learned that much.

Mr. Holmes grunted some kind of acceptance. "Very well." He wrote *Ann* alongside the surname as she seemed to say it: *Scanlan*. Then he turned the tome towards her and pointed to the eighth column. "Your signature here."

"I can't write."

"Your mark, then. Leave room enough for me to write, otherwise we overrun the allotted space and make a mess of the whole register."

She duly made her X and he duly wrote beside it: *The mark of Ann Scanlan, mother, 4 Angel Yard Lincoln*. And finally,

377

in the last column, signed his own name, *Henry Holmes, Registrar.*

| 412 | Twentieth August 1859 Angel yard Lincoln | Charles | Boy | | Ann Scanlon | | X The mark of Ann Scanlon Mother 3 Angel yard Lincoln | Twenty Ninth August 1859 | Mary Holmes Registrar | |

Charles Scanlon, registration of birth, 29 August 1859

She waited while he copied out the entry for her to take. "There," he said, handing over the form. His smile was pinched. "Your child is now an official subject of Her Majesty the Queen." And then, as she went out, he added, "And give my warm regards to Mr. Bromehead."

Fleeing to the Lakes

On Sunday 2 October there is a disturbance in Angel Yard. Men in navy blue uniform and stovepipe hats are banging on one of the doors. People emerge to see what's happening. There is an argument, the waving of papers that half of the onlookers can't read even if they want to. "Orders of the Chief Constable," one of the officers says.

After some time and much protesting, Ann Gleeson, clutching her baby to her chest, is marched out of her lodgings. Accompanied by jeers and whistles, the police officers solemnly lead her away.

Perhaps Annie immediately went round to Bromehead's house and demanded that he do something. Maybe he did make enquiries on the younger woman's behalf, but it all happened with remarkable dispatch and there was nothing to be done: Ann Gleeson and her daughter spent Sunday night in a Lincoln City Police cell and Monday, with an escort, on a train down to London. In London she passed a few days in police detention but by 8 October she and her baby daughter were admitted to the Islington workhouse *"for passage to Ireland."*

It was in the workhouse that Ann was reunited with her two-year-old daughter Mary, who had herself been admitted in June, having been *"deserted by her mother."* By 12 October Ann and her two children were discharged by order of the Magistrate: *"passed to Ireland, her legal settlement, with her two children."**

And then the fog closes around her and she disappears. Her daughters vanish too. Ann may be any one of a dozen Ann Gleesons in the Irish records, most of them admissions to prison for drunkenness and petty theft or vagrancy. Like so many of the "undeserving" poor in the middle of the century, she was tossed onto the scrapheap of history. When she first appeared in this story she wasn't waving a greeting, she was warning of impending disaster. How easily Ann Mawer might have gone a similar way.

The incident of Ann Gleeson is soon forgotten but other occurrences in Angel Yard are not so easily dismissed. For example, the occasional, discreet but irrefutable visits of E. A. Bromehead. Almost weekly he takes that walk that commences at the garden gate of number four, James Street before threading its way through a winding alley to emerge in Angel Yard. It might be construed as a shortcut through to Bailgate and on to the County Court, a journey that Mr. Bromehead is constrained to make often enough in the course of his legal practice – that is, indeed, what he tells himself it is – but all too often he stops on the way at the rooms of the soldier's widow.

There is speculation. Of course, there are other things to gossip about – for example Dr. Sympson's wife, who by Christmas is most evidently with child – but such matters are nothing compared with the visits of Mr. Bromehead to the

---

* All dates and quoted passages from the admissions and discharges register of Islington Workhouse, 1859.

soldier's wife, and the debated fatherhood of her most recent child. Even the other child, the little girl, was born when the woman's husband – poor man – was away at the war, so who knows? But this child, the little boy, was born *four years* after the noble soldier's death so it's plain as the nose on your face that it's a bastard. For all her airs and graces, the mother is no better than that Ann Gleeson – little more than a common prostitute.

And if the soldier's wife is no better than a tart, is Mr. Edmund Bromehead, the single Mr. Bromehead, the upright and decent Mr. Bromehead, nothing more than a whoremonger?

Tongues wag. There he is, forty-six years old, living on his own but for the housekeeper, in a house which twenty years ago was home to five family members and three living-in servants. Nothing out of the ordinary about that, of course. Family members die or move out. And being alone with a young, living-in female servant means nothing because Bromehead is a man of the utmost moral rectitude. A solicitor and notary public of importance in the city and the county, Steward of the Courts Leet and Great Court Baron of the Duchy of Lancaster, receiver of tenths on behalf of the Archdeacon of Lincoln, board member of the city hospital, board member of the Lincoln Gas Company and the Water Company, a keen supporter of the Royal Patriotic Fund (contributing two guineas at the initial public meeting), a committee member of the Lincoln Choral Society, trustee of the Lincoln Savings Bank, secretary and treasurer of the Lincolnshire Law Society, ardent supporter of the Lincolnshire Volunteers, the list goes on and on.

And yet ...

It has to be admitted, Ann Mawer is not typical of her kind, despite being Irish. Soft-spoken, polite, quite unlike that Ann Gleeson. You could always hear that girl's voice and usually see too much of her when you were face-to-face. Easy enough to understand what men saw in her. But Ann Mawer? A small, thin stick of a thing. Tough, yes. Doesn't take cheek and doesn't take any nonsense from anyone. But not the kind who would attract a flock of men. They say she receives regular letters from her two elder children and dutifully replies, although as she cannot write she is forced to dictate. Which is why Bromehead visits her from time to time. Of course it is.

Of course it isn't.

In the early spring of 1860 Mrs. Caroline Sympson, the doctor's wife, gives birth to a baby boy.* What a happy event! The doctor is popular enough – prepared to treat for free people who really cannot pay – and his wife such a pretty young thing. He went all the way to Devon to find her, and who can wonder! And now here they are with their first child – the perfect happy family.

On 27 March Caroline Sympson is dead of puerperal fever.† The funeral is held in the church of St. Mary Magdalene, with the good doctor chief mourner, his hirsute upper lip magnificently stiff. His siblings gather round him for support; as does Mr. Bromehead.

Personal tragedy is always good for gossip.

"Such a shame."

"The good Lord wanted her for His own."

"And their little boy now wanting for a mother."

"And yet the soldier's wife, she's quite all right with her new child."

---

* 22 March 1860.

† *Lincoln Chronicle*, Friday 30 March 1860.

"It doesn't seem right, does it? Not fair."

"And whose child may he be?"

Whose, indeed?

Life around the cathedral goes on. And life goes on between Bromehead and Annie and the child. There is no means of telling exactly what took place, but one thing is sure: E. A. Bromehead was tiptoeing along the edge of disaster. At the Twelfth Night Ball at the Assembly Rooms, which he attends, he appears a somewhat stuffy bachelor watching the dancing with a glass in his hand – but people whisper about whom he might have invited as a partner if such things were possible.

"That soldier's wife!"

"You think so?"

"I'm told he's always round there. And she with that baby ... "

"That would be disgraceful ... "

"If it were true ... "

He attends meetings of the board of the Lincoln Hospital, he advocates the building of a lifeboat on the Lincolnshire coast, he dines with the Volunteer Rifles at Hackthorn Hall, he attends the opening of the Lincoln Exhibition of Arts, Science and Manufactures as a member of the organising committee. He is most regular in his attendance of Sunday services at St. Mary Magdalene and, on auspicious occasions, in the cathedral itself, where he commissions a stained-glass window in memory of his parents.

Meanwhile his visits to the small house in Angel Yard continue, as does the conflict in Edmund Bromehead's head. Not only does he face judgement in the court of society but he also faces the prospect of judgement in the court of law. For he has connived – it would take a good advocate little time to demonstrate the fact before judge and jury – at the deceit committed by Mrs. Ann Mawer when registering her recent child. Moreover, he has done this with the clear intent to defraud the Royal Patriotic Fund of the monies it disburses to the said Mrs. Mawer for the upkeep of herself and her legitimate daughter and the maintenance and education of her two elder children at the expense of such fund in the institutions where they are currently enrolled, *viz.* the Royal Victoria Patriotic Asylum, Wandsworth, and the Orphan School, Barnet.

He can hear the outraged tones of the counsel for the prosecution tearing his reputation to shreds: "And, as if this were not enough, m'lud, it seems likely that Mr. Bromehead actually fathered the bastard child on this wretched woman."

"Annie," he tells her, all too often, "this cannot go on."

Annie agrees with him. "Of course it can't. All things, good and bad, come to an end."

"And this is bad."

"Is that what you think?"

"At times, yes I do."

She smiles. It's her smile that disarms him. "And is now one of those times?"

"Of course not now."

"So why don't you just stop frettin'?"

"I cannot stop, except when I'm with you. Then it all seems easy."

And it is. Standing at the table she lifts her skirts for him and he finds it very easy, that sight of things forbidden and barely imagined, the grasp of her narrow waist, the sensation of her against him, the heat of her, the liquid slide into her and the momentary annihilation of self.

"There," she says, wiping herself and settling her clothes.

He sits heavily on one of the chairs, as exhausted as if he had run a mile. "What if the girl should come in?"

"Sarah? She knows not to."

The girl is seven years old. Does she know what is happening? Does she understand what her mother does? In the aftermath of such visits he is consumed by self-disgust, as though Annie is nothing more than an addiction, his laudanum that he cannot control and cannot put aside.

And Annie? What are her motives and her feelings? Comfort and security surely, and the recovery of her children from the institutions where they are boarding. But she must have felt affection for Bromehead, enough to mention his name to at least one of her other children (which one? Stories are not inherited in the same determined manner as genes), through whom it mutated and slipped back a generation.

Broomfield? Bromehead? Something like that ...

Or was Annie just indulging in a bit of casual prostitution to make ends meet? One must consider all the possibilities, examine all the fragments to try and work out what is going on. Yet whatever the motives and motions, there is an event that will pin everyone down in place like so many butterflies in a Victorian lepidopterist's cabinet.

1861 Census

In the spring of 1861, the national census took place, when all men, and occasionally women, were called to register their own existence and the existence of any other person or persons staying within their household on the night of 7 April. The census is like that parlour game called "statues," when the music stops and everyone freezes in the midst of what they are doing: the butcher, the baker, the candlestick maker; the vicar, the tart, the man with a cart; the banker, the lawyer, the pauper, the sawyer; the merchant, the actor, the labourer, factor; all written down, from beggar to Crown.

So, in this lightning flash of stillness, E. A. Bromehead Esq. is still safely there at number four, James Street, along with the housemaid. Naturally, he would have completed the census form himself. On the other hand, Ann Mawer, householder of number three, Angel Yard, would have needed the assistance of the census enumerator because she was, of course, illiterate.

This is the entry for Ann Mawer's household in April 1861:

Extract from the Lincoln census 1861,
showing Ann Mawer's household

Address	Name	Relationship	Status	M (Age) F		Profession	Birthplace
3 Angel Yard	Ann Mawer	Head	Widow		34	Charwoman	Ireland
	Sarah R. d°	Daur			6	Scholar	Lincoln St. Paul
	Charles Scanlen	Boarder		1			d°. St. Mary Magdalen

Charles Scanlon (*Scanlen* in the register), one year old at his last birthday, born in Lincoln St. Mary Magdalene and registered as her son on 29 August 1859, is declared on the census not as her son but as a *boarder.*

It is almost as though in Annie's world there are two Anns – Ann Mawer, respectable widow of Corporal George Mawer (deceased), mother of three children, two of whom are in orphanages under the aegis of the Royal Patriotic Fund; and Ann Scanlon, of dubious moral standing and mother of Charles Scanlon (father unknown) who, at the time of the census, has been given as a boarder into the care of the other Ann.

Of Annie's two elder children, at the time of the census George (nine) is still in the Barnet Orphans Institution while Mary Ann (thirteen) has apparently progressed from the Royal Victoria Patriotic Asylum in Wandsworth. Now able to read and write, she has been taken on as a "pupil teacher" in the nearby Wandsworth Lunatic Asylum for Pauper Lunatics.*

Yet these people, apparently so permanently preserved and pinned to the board of the census, are actually on the move. Where they were for that moment, they will not be very soon. The signs are there: by December 1860, Bromehead has already resigned from the board of the Lincoln Waterworks

---

* Subsequently successively known as the Wandsworth Asylum, Springfield Asylum, Springfield Mental Hospital, Springfield Hospital and now Springfield University Hospital under which name it still operates as a mental health hospital within the National Health Service.

and later from the board of the Lincoln Gas Company. In early 1861 he goes into partnership with a certain Henry Kirk Hebb, to become Bromehead and Hebb, Solicitors. In October of that year he retires from the board of the Solicitors' Benevolent Association. These small fragments tell of seismic changes to come.

In March of the next year the Bromehead house in James Street is put on the market to rent:

CLOSE of LINCOLN

TO BE LET, at moderate rent, a convenient and commodious DWELLING-HOUSE, in James-street, Lincoln.—For particulars apply to

BROMEHEAD & HEBB.

Lincoln, 19th March, 1862.*

A decision has been made. Discussions and arguments are surely at an end.

"We just cannot go on like this, Annie. People are talking. Hebb himself is complaining about damage to the firm. My reputation is being ruined."

Reputation is a thing that only the middle classes cherish. The lower class, the poor, cannot afford the luxury; the upper classes don't care. But Bromehead has noticed passersby in the street looking at him askance. He perceives acquaintances hastily changing the subject when he approaches them at the annual general meeting of the Midland Insurance Company

---

* *Lincolnshire Chronicle*, Friday, 28 March 1862.

of which he is a shareholder. He hears officers make jovial innuendos during the annual dinner of the Lincoln Volunteer Rifles: "Mr. Edmund Bromehead, the greatest supporter of the military – who sets an example to us all in both his public and his private life!" (*Applause, laughter.*)

Or is he imagining it all? That's the problem. Imagination plays slave to his shame, guilt whispers accusations in his ear. He cannot separate himself from Annie and his own son so the only solution is to get away. In June he formally dissolves the partnership with Henry Hebb. He has his eye on the Lake District as a refuge, an exile where he can do his penance. In choosing the Lakes he is almost certainly following his younger sister who, in 1859, married a cleric and went to live in Patterdale where her husband was curate of St. Patrick's Church. So now, through her, Bromehead makes enquiries in the area and finds suitable accommodation near Keswick: a pleasant house on the road towards Braithwaite with views of the fells and Derwentwater. Woodlands Cottage, it is modestly named.

And Annie?

"Where will you go?" he asks. They have talked of this vaguely. Not back to Ireland, certainly not that; perhaps to Preston. Lancashire is where she met George, where they got married, where they first lived, days that seem happy in retrospect but at the time were hard, living in barracks, living a public life.

No longer are there fantasies about her going with Bromehead as his housekeeper.

"London," she says. "Islington."

"Do you know Islington?"

"There are Irish there. Ann Gleeson – you remember her? – she said it's a good place."

"I can help with that. Somewhere to live. You cannot just go there hoping to find lodging."

"Of course I can."

"I'll not let you."

Now it is serious, a negotiation, the harsh realities of money and survival. Where she will live, how much support for the baby, how the money will be paid – a weekly allowance paid through solicitors in Cannon Street.

Does she know where Cannon Street is?

She'll find it.

The solicitors are Reyroux and Bromehead.

Bromehead?

A distant cousin. He has done work with them in the past so they know him. He'll write them a letter and they'll do what they are asked. She can rely on them. He writes down the name of the firm for her and shows her the letters, explaining about French pronunciation: Ray-roo, watching her as she frowns at the letters, trying to read them properly, like a child. And something seems to break inside him, spilling out a flood of sympathy and an emotion that approaches love and is certainly physical desire. This woman who appears so strong yet seems devoid of those skills necessary for survival in the modern world. "I don't want your pity," she has said to him in the past. "I don't need it and I don't want it."

And now he wants only to do that thing with her that has brought about the very difficulties that they are facing; just when he is attempting to put all emotion aside as they set about making the arrangements needed to break apart a union that should never have been, he wants only to lie down with her. Which is when the baby, their baby, wakes up and issues a thin cry of protest.

"He's hungry," she says, pulling away from Bromehead's grasp and lifting the child from his bassinet. She unbuttons her bodice and puts the baby to her breast, while Bromehead distracts himself with practical matters. "I'll get Reyroux and

Bromehead to find you lodgings. They'll do that for me, put down a deposit, whatever is necessary. And we need to contact the Patriotic Fund as soon as you have a change of address ... "

"I want a place that's big enough for all the children."

There's that grim determination about her – this is why she's doing it, moving to London. Perhaps she could have agreed to go to the Lake District with him, just she alone, with Sarah Rebecca and the baby. A housekeeper. A quiet, self-effacing scandal deep in the countryside. But she wants her older son and daughter as well, the ones who were taken from her. Perhaps all she retains from the Ireland of her childhood is the sense of family.

"Write to them for me," she tells Bromehead. "Write to them and tell them – their Mam is coming to bring them home."

Bromehead has moved to Keswick by mid-1862 but comes back to Lincoln regularly, to "tie up loose ends," to see friends and family. In October he is in the city for the dedication of the memorial window to his parents in the cathedral but he is soon back in the Lake District where he has become an honorary member of the local Volunteer Rifles known as the Skiddaw Greys. On the anniversary of the Battle of Inkerman he plays host to these stout fellows at his house outside Keswick, addressing the assembled troops at the end of their manoeuvres and finding it a thrill to be able to talk about Annie without the fear of laughter and innuendo:

"A lady of my acquaintance is the widow of one of the heroes of Inkerman. She is now left alone with his three children to care for. It is over those, the ones left behind, that we must cast the blanket of comfort and concern."

He bathes in the men's warm applause.

Christmas

Before Christmas Bromehead is back in Lincoln, taking rooms in the White Hart Hotel hard by the cathedral. One evening after dinner he makes his way round to Angel Yard. He has come from the deanery and is dressed appropriately: stiff collar, stiff shirt front, waistcoat, tailcoat, looking every inch the gentleman emerging from one world – the world of gaslight and laughter – into the dark and cold reality of the streets, the cobbles brushed with snow, the streetlamps occasional and inadequate. Yet Annie's kitchen is a small hub of warmth in this darkness, lit by candles and a single oil lamp, warmed by the range. The little boy – *his* little boy – is a toddler now, cared for attentively by his half-sister Sarah Rebecca, who explains that he must shake hands with the nice visitor.

Bromehead takes off his overcoat and bends awkwardly to talk with the child. "Hello, little chappie," he says and the boy stares at him in something like astonishment.

"He's not seen such a grand gentleman before," says Annie.

"Doesn't he remember me from my last visit?"

"'Course not. Life's all confusing to him at the moment."

The boy looks round at her, as though to confirm to himself that his mother is still there and so things are all right with the world.

The little girl says, "He can say words now, can't you, Charlie boy?"

Charlie boy looks at her and smiles. "Mama," he says, and waits for his women to respond with laughter, which they duly do.

"I'm Sarah," the girl says, and points at her mother. "That's Mama."

"Mama," Charlie says pointing at Annie.

Bromehead feels in his waistcoat pocket and produces a sovereign, holding it out to the child. The boy reaches out and takes it. His sister watches with wide eyes. Perhaps she's never seen such a coin.

"Is that a present?" Annie asks.

"Of course it's a present."

"Say thank you, Charlie," the little girl says. "Thank you to the nice man."

The boy looks at his father and makes some kind of sound that might be "thank you": "Ancoo," something like that.

Sarah laughs, as though the triumph is hers. "There you are." She takes the coin from Charlie and slips it in her apron pocket. "Else he'll swallow it," she explains, taking the toddler's hand and leading him towards the door. "Come on, Charlie. Time we left Mama alone with her man-friend."

Man-friend. Bromehead wonders about the little girl, how sharp she is, how aware. "What does she know? About me, about Charles."

"Sarah? She's clever. Reads already."

"That's no answer."

She shrugs. "I don't know the answer. She's only a little girl, loyal to her mother. There are many things she doesn't understand but she keeps them to herself."

There's an awkwardness between them, exaggerated by the disparity of appearance: he in his dinner clothes, looking smart and affluent; she in a drab, brown dress, that dress she was surely wearing when he spoke to her all that time ago, when she was cleaning the floor and he suggested she come to work in the office. One of those moments that turn a life, two lives, the whole world.

"She called me your man-friend."

"Aren't you that?"

He feels himself redden. "Are there others?"

Annie smiles. There's a hint of distain, as though he is the one importuning her. "Don't be soft. She just doesn't know your name, that's all."

For a moment they look at each other across the great gulf that still lies between them, that gulf of class, of education, of knowledge and understanding that they managed to bridge through the powerful but fragile medium of sex.

"When are you planning to leave?"

"In the New Year. Will you visit before then?"

"I don't think so." He lights a cigarette, as a distraction as much as anything. "You know the house has been taken? It's to open as a girls' school."

"I heard about that."

"Miss Becket's Academy for Young Ladies."

They talk for a while, perhaps aware of the strange incongruities of a sexual relationship, that once they had lain naked in each other's arms and their intimacy was of mind and body, and now they have come to this – clothed and modest and barely able to converse except in conventional terms.

"Will you be all right?"

"I've managed so far, haven't I?"

"Of course you have. If you want for anything you must get a letter to me, through the solicitors." He pauses to draw on his cigarette and examine the glowing tip. It is as though he is trying to make all this just seem a thing of little consequence, an afterthought. "And I'd like to know how the boy is doing, Annie. So perhaps from time to time you can let me know how he's progressing. Maybe one day ... "

He lets the thought hang in the air like the smoke from his cigarette.

Maybe one day.

Maybe one day a descendent four generations down will come poking around the scraps of evidence to put a story together. Maybe it will come somewhere near the truth.

London

Ann Mawer did indeed leave Lincoln in the New Year. She took the train down to the newly opened King's Cross station. Perhaps she stopped off at Barnet to see her son, George Henry. What is certain is that she reached London safely with her two younger children – the eight-year-old Sarah Rebecca and the three-year-old Charles. And there to meet them off the train would have been her older daughter, Mary Ann. Surely so. There may be no documentary evidence of such a meeting but the Wandsworth Asylum is only a two-and-a-half-hour walk away and it is hard to imagine that Mary Ann – fifteen-year-old Mary Ann, an adult in those merciless days – would not have been there to greet her mother and the two children on the platform, the London girl greeting her family from the provinces. Wearing a hat. Her smartest dress. Standing on the platform and waving as they come towards her, the two children holding hands. A porter behind them with their luggage.

Two children?

Can you see her astonishment? They'd not only taught her to read and write at Wandsworth, they'd also taught her arithmetic. Surely she'd have asked the question as soon as she was out of the earshot of the children:

"Mother, *who in God's name is Charlie?*"

Was she told the lie, that Charlie was Charles Scanlon, a cousin of some kind? Maybe that's the story she'd already been given by letter. But how long would that story have held up? After all, Sarah Rebecca knew. She had seen her mother pregnant; she had been there at the birth of her little brother whose hand she holds so responsibly.

Perhaps this was when the story about Bromehead first saw the light of day, in undistorted form, the mother explaining – not really a confession because Annie wasn't the type to carry guilt on her shoulders – about the realities of love and lust: "There was this man, and a good enough man he was too. I worked for him, you know. Cleaning, laundry, that kind of stuff. And one thing led to another ... "

But beside the evident fact of Charlie, there was another revelation coming that Annie herself was unaware of at first, but which she would not be able to dissimulate for long. On her visits from Wandsworth, Mary Ann would have had vague, unspoken suspicions. She'd have noticed those slight changes – the way her mother held herself, a certain modification of her gait and her manner, a thickening around the waist, perhaps a tendency to be tired in the afternoons. A woman of Annie's slight build could not hope to hide things for long. Soon enough suspicion would have coalesced into certainty. I wonder, would Mary Ann have phrased it as a question? Or perhaps she'd have waited long enough to frame it as a statement, brooking no denial:

"Mother, you are pregnant! In heaven's name, who is the father *this* time?"

Caledonia Street is an undistinguished lane leading from the east side of King's Cross station through to the main artery of the Caledonian Road. In those days, just as today, there was a pub at either end. It was in this street, at number six, that

Annie and the children lived when she first came to London. Here, in an upstairs room, her sixth child, Eliza, was born on 17 September 1863. Who was at the birth? A local midwife, no doubt; perhaps a neighbour to assist. But surely Mary Ann would also have been there at her mother's side during her delivery, just as she had been present for Sarah Rebecca's birth. Once again she'd have seen the head of a baby emerge from between Annie's legs, seen the damp scribble of hair, the screwed-up face, the rubbery shoulders twisting their way out like a bird from a burrow. She'd have heard the thin wail of protest, seen the blue-grey snake of the umbilical cord and heard the midwife announce the arrival into this sublunary world of "a lovely little girl, bless her."

She would have witnessed her mother's expression of exhaustion and triumph as she took the little girl to her and said, "Eliza. She'll be called Eliza."

Eliza

This time, Annie changed tactics when registering the child. She did not register Eliza as fatherless, as she had Charles, nor did she use her own maiden name. Perhaps she was reassured by the anonymity of life in London. Whatever the reason, this is what she declared:

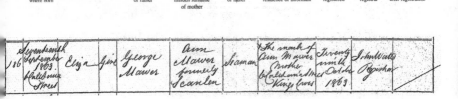

When and where born	Name, if any	Sex	Name and surname of father	Name, surname and maiden surname of mother	Occupation of father	Signature, description and residence of informant	When registered	Signature of registrar	Name entered after registration
Seventeenth September 1863 Caledonian Street	Eliza	Girl	George Mawer	Ann Mawer formerly Scanlen	Seaman	The mark of Ann Mawer mother 6 Caledonian Street Kings Cross	Twenty ninth October 1863	John Watts Registrar	

Eliza Mawer's birth registration

There is something triumphant about George Mawer being invoked as father of this child. And there is even a neat trick to account for his current absence. Occupation of father: *Seaman*. Apparently George is away sailing the seven seas, far over the horizon and out of sight of any registrar in Islington.

What was Mary Ann's reaction? She'd had obedience and certainty ground into her by her education at the Royal Victoria Patriotic Asylum. How did she react when her

399

mother came back from the register office with a copy of the registration? You can imagine the horror in the girl's expression as she reads. "Mother! Father is *not* Eliza's father. He has been dead nine years! You cannot lie on an official form!"

And you can hear Annie's laughter. It has a strong Irish accent.

Within a short time the family has moved from the cramped quarters in Caledonia Street to better accommodation on the Caledonian Road itself. Number forty-four. Thus, for a few years, Annie's family is complete. With few resources beyond her native wit she has battled against the harsh world of mid-century Victorian England and gathered her flock around her – Mary Ann and George Henry from their Patriotic Fund schools, Sarah Rebecca and Charles who came with her from Lincoln, and now Eliza. Five children crowded into the narrow terrace house. George found work as a warehouseman; Mary Ann began life as a governess; Sarah and Charles were still at school. At first Eliza was at her mother's breast; later, she toddled around, clinging to Annie's skirts and begging to be lifted. A happy family.

It isn't going to last. Nothing ever does. For a while, for those few years, Annie's triumph against the odds may have seemed complete, but whatever hope she may have had for the family she had so courageously gathered round her, it was going to be dashed soon enough. That's the trouble with being human, isn't it? We are born in hope and die in tragedy; the only difference between us is how long we can string out the gap between the two. For Eliza it wasn't very long. Soon enough she contracted that universal curse that has been with humanity since prehistoric times – tuberculosis. Perhaps the older members of the family had developed natural immunity because none of them seemed to have suffered from the disease then or later, but Eliza was cursed.

Annie nursed her through her decline, through the wasting away, the hacking cough, the bloody sputum, through the fear. She was there at her daughter's death on 14 July 1873; six days later she buried her in Finchley cemetery. In between the little girl's death and her burial was the bureaucratic ritual of registering the death, a distorted mirror-image of the registration of her birth fewer than ten years earlier.

Death certificate of Eliza Mawer

You can hear the thin scratch of time as the registrar writes. He writes what he is told – the child's name, her sex, her age – and what the doctor's note says about cause of death: *Phthisis Pulmonalis*, which is consumption. And dates, always dates. Dates are the business of registration, the whole Victorian world being entered and certified and dated: the date of death; the date of registration: *14 July 1873; 16 July 1873.*

The registrar glances up at the woman standing before him, the nib hovering over the final empty column. "For minors we put the father's name and occupation."

"Why not the mother's?"

"It is the procedure."

"He's dead. Her father's dead."

"We note that fact."

She shrugs, and lies once again. "My husband. George Mawer."

The pen scratches. "His former occupation?"

"What does it matter? The man's dead."

The registrar sighs. "It is the procedure."

"Plumber," she says. "Put plumber."

Thus having been born into the fiction that her father was "George Mawer, seaman," Eliza is now registered in death as the daughter of "George Mawer, plumber (deceased)."

Is it a joke? At the moment when she is recording the death of her daughter, is Ann Mawer *making a joke*? Otherwise, why not "seaman (deceased)" or even: "soldier (deceased)?" Why, in God's name, make George a *plumber*?

"Why not? We could do with a plumber about the house."

Charles has no such memorial and no such bitter joke. How he met his end is unknown. In the 1871 census he was an eleven-year-old "scholar"; thereafter he just vanishes, as though into a kind of documentary limbo, neither alive nor dead, although apparently dead to the family. Except that, poignantly, Sarah Rebecca named her first child Augustine Charles, surely in memory of her half-brother. And Eliza's name was similarly handed down to George Henry's first child, christened Mary Eliza. That's remembrance of a kind, I suppose, even though neither of the recipients may have understood the reason for their naming.

So it was that ultimately only the children fathered by George Mawer survived to make the hesitant steps from incipient destitution to lower-middle-class comfort – Mary Ann, George Henry and Sarah Rebecca.

It's impossible not to wonder how the family story about a Mr. Bromehead threaded its way down through the generations, picking up details and shedding others on the way. It would have been through Mary Ann, of course. You wouldn't confide in your son about this, and certainly not in George Henry who, apart from working in the warehouse, was studying the Bible in the evenings and forever reproving his mother for not attending church. He would hardly have lent a sympathetic ear. And Sarah Rebecca was still a young girl and anyway about to go into service at a big house in Kent. It would have been to Mary Ann. Perhaps it was in the spring of 1868, when Eliza and Charles were still alive. They'd have been at school, and Annie would just have come back from one of her monthly visits to the solicitors in Cheapside, those mysterious visits that resulted in money to be spent on the housekeeping.

"He was called Bromehead," she told her daughter. She felt quite settled about telling someone now. This seemed the right moment, what with the news she'd had at the solicitors. "Mr. Edmund Bromehead, if you want to know. You and George were both away at school and he helped me with writing to you, that kind of thing. And he was company."

Mary Ann disapproved, you could see that. That stubborn, acute look she gave to the children in her care when they misbehaved. "Rather more than just company, Mother. I really find it hard to believe. And Father only a short while dead."

"Four years, Mary. Four years."

"But still."

"And he was a good enough man, Mary. A kind man."

"Oh, I'm sure he was. And married, I expect."

"No, he wasn't."

That little sarcastic laugh that Mary was so good at. "So he was good but not good enough to offer to marry you. You a respectable widow and he a bachelor. It wouldn't have been difficult."

"It wouldn't have been right, Mary. He was an educated gentleman so he couldn't have married me – him a lawyer and me a soldier's widow who can't read or write."

"Then he was taking advantage of you."

"I think we took advantage of each other, Mary. He offered to have his sister adopt Charles, d'you know that? But I wouldn't have it. I wanted you all – you and George as well as Sarah and Charles – around me. The poor man couldn't be expected to take on the whole tribe!" She tried a laugh, one of her bitter, Irish laughs, but Mary didn't react to it. So Annie turned back to whatever she was doing, some darning, mending George's shirt, the one he wore for church. "Anyway, it doesn't matter any longer, does it?" she said, trying not to make too much of it. "Because he's dead." And to her surprise as she uttered the words she felt a small pain, something physical like a hollowing out of her chest. And a stinging in the eyes, like the smart of wood smoke.

"Dead?"

"They told me today at the office." She put down the darning and handed Mary Ann the letter the solicitor had given her. "That's what this says, so he told me. He read it out before sealing it. It's from Mr. Hebb, who was Mr. Edmund's partner."

Mary Ann opened the envelope and unfolded the single sheet of writing paper. The letter was written in the immaculate copperplate hand of a trained clerk:

We regret to inform you that Mr. E. A. Bromehead, previously of 3 James Street, Lincoln, late of Woodland Cottage, Above Derwent, Cumberland, passed away on 2 May. During his illness he had expressed to us a wish that regular payments made to your good self in regard to your son Charles be continued . . .

It was signed *Henry K. Hebb, solicitor.*

Mary Ann looked up. "This Bromehead is the man?"

"I said so."

Mary Ann shook her head, finding it difficult to breathe. The shock of so many things hit her, among which was that there was money involved, that there was the persistence of an illicit relationship and then the most squalid thing, a vision of her mother coupling with this unknown man – her naked legs thrown open, as blatant and shameless as when she was giving birth. It was a kind of counterpoint to birth, wasn't it? The injection of seed becoming, in the fullness of time, the ejection of a bloodied mewling creature such as she, Mary Ann, had witnessed issuing out of her mother's body when Sarah was born. And Eliza.

How could her mother bring all that upon herself? *How?*

"I don't understand you, Mother," she said when finally she caught her breath. "I really don't."

Annie managed a smile. "Do you not, though? I was, you see, in love with him."

"It is not a matter of love, Mother. It is a matter of what is right and proper."

Annie still smiled, although she was close to tears. "You sound like George. Is that what they taught you in those schools?"

"It is what I learned."

"Perhaps learning is not the same as understanding, Mary. Maybe one day you'll understand."

Maybe. Maybe not. The story certainly filtered down, mutating as it went, becoming, in its final form, that story of an innocent servant girl in Lincoln getting pregnant by the young master of the house. There followed the offer of adoption. The refusal. The flight to London. The mercy of some charitable institution. And in the telling, there came that neat leap backwards over a generation so that the servant girl becomes Corporal George's *mother* rather than his *wife*; and thus Ann Mawer is sanitised. Or perhaps sanctified. And her three children by the good corporal – Mary Ann, Sarah Rebecca and George Henry – can take their places in the rising, respectable lower middle class of the latter half of the nineteenth century.

But to modern sensibilities, Ann Mawer doesn't need sanitising and certainly not sanctifying. To us she is merely a remarkable woman who was carried along by the tide of events beyond her control yet did not drown. Illiterate and ill-educated she may have been, but she was shrewd, imbued with a native wit and a determination to swim against the current. Those years at forty-four Caledonian Road with all her living offspring around her were a personal triumph.

Ann Mawer, née Scanlon, aged fifty-four, Easter 1881

Epilogue

There's a family photograph, taken in 1928, showing a cheerful, prosperous middle-class group gathered outside a weatherboard house in Essex. Looking at it, one feels the uncanny mystery of photography: a century ago these people stood in that particular configuration for an instant and had their images trapped for ever in silver salts on a photographic emulsion. Today they are all dead, yet there they are in the photo. We can almost feel the chill wind that has blown across the Essex flats from the North Sea. The young women seem indifferent but the men are wearing overcoats and the old lady at the focus of the group has been wrapped in a shawl. We can almost hear the laughter and the chatter, the cries to hurry up, the desperate call of the photographer to "please keep still, ladies!" (An earlier shot, also in my possession, has already been ruined by the woman second from the left turning her head.)

This photograph is significant in the context of this story in so many ways. One is that it draws the two threads together: the story of the wayward sailor Abraham Block and his wife, Naomi, and the story of Ann Mawer and her husband, the dogged soldier Corporal George Mawer. Because the woman standing second from the left with the tightly crimped hair, the woman who spoiled the photographer's first attempt, is

Abraham and Naomi's granddaughter, Emily Naomi Block, while the man standing second from the right is her husband, Gordon, the second of Corporal George and Annie's grandsons. My paternal grandparents. The young fellow seated on the ground bottom right is their only child, my father (he's the one who, in 1941, will be landing his Wellington bomber through the flak and bombs of a Luftwaffe raid on Malta).

Mawer family photo, 1928

And the old lady in the centre? Bound up in bonnet and black bombazine she looks like a time traveller from another age, which in a sense is exactly what she is. This family gathering is to celebrate her eightieth birthday (although to modern eyes she may look considerably older). She is the principal witness to the story of Ann Mawer: she is Annie's elder daughter, Mary Ann.

She *knows*.

Annie's other daughter, Sarah Rebecca, was still alive at the time of this photograph (she died in 1935) but there's no means of telling why she wasn't present at this family reunion, centred as it was around her older sister. The man standing on the right, looking slightly out of place and watching the laughing women with faint bewilderment, is the older of her two sons, Augustine Charles Randall, known as Gus. He seems something of an outsider. Indeed, thirty-five years ago, when my father named as many of the people in the photo as he could, he was uncertain who this "Gus" was. Now it is too late to tell him.

Most of the others are children or grandchildren of Annie's son, George Henry. He had two sons, including my grandfather Gordon, and three daughters. From his modest start as a warehouseman, George had found his true vocation: a devout student of the Bible, he ultimately became secretary to the Country Towns Mission Society, espousing low-church, no-nonsense Protestantism. Considering that ever since that dreadful business in the Garden of Eden, Christianity has been concerned with man's relationship with God, it is hard to believe that George did not from time to time wonder about his mother's relationship with her Maker, and his own relationship with his two half-siblings, Charles and Eliza. What conclusion he came to is, of course, unknown and essentially unknowable. As he died in 1923, even at the time of the photo he was beyond asking.

This happy photograph – they'd have called it a snap – was taken at a moment of confidence in the future. The Great War has claimed no victims here. My grandfather served in France with the Royal Naval Air Service without coming to harm. Now he is secretary of a company on the Baltic Exchange in the City of London. The Great Depression is yet to happen; the Nazi party is little more than a footnote in the foreign press. He, like all the others, is looking forward to a world of peace and prosperity, none more so than his older brother Allen, the tall, genial man in the centre. Allen is an Anglo-Saxon scholar of renown, founder of the English Place-Name Society and about to be (next year; maybe he already knows?) appointed Provost of University College London. In 1937 he will be knighted.

Sitting on the ground next to the youngest of his cousins, my father is not yet seven. He couldn't care less about the future but he won't be able to avoid it: in a mere twelve years he will join the Royal Air Force, train as a bomber pilot and, miraculously, survive six years of war; in nineteen years he will beget me; and almost a century on from that happy family gathering in Essex, I will root through document and record to unearth this family's barely known ancestors – George Mawer the doomed soldier and Abraham Block the hapless sailor, but also their wives, Annie and Naomi.

Ultimately it was the women who won through, the women who swam doggedly against the tide of history and dragged their children to the shore, thus saving them from destitution and setting them on the path to middle-class prosperity. Yet by the time of this photograph these women had been largely forgotten. They are the real dispossessed, surely emblematic of thousands of others in the nineteenth century and before. They had no voice, often because they could not even write; they left few artefacts because in life they possessed so little. Rarely, until the advent of popular photography, do we even know what they looked like. It is only through those remaining fragments – an entry in the census, a birth or death certificate, the occasional relic passed down through the generations – that they can be perceived. Yet they lived and loved, cried tears of pain and laughter, slept and dreamt, awoke and ultimately died. We know that because those are attributes of being human; the rest is intuition.

Acknowledgements

Firstly, I must acknowledge the contribution to this book made by my second cousin, the late Frances Macartney. Over half a century ago she told me the family story of a certain "Broomfield or Broomhead" who, by seducing a servant girl named Mawer, fathered the future Corporal George. Frances even sketched out an approximate family tree with this irregular liaison included. I still have it. Long before the internet brought open access to digitised census and registration records, this story awakened the interest of an embryo novelist into his family history. I am sorry that she is not alive to see the result. Finding out that the story was wrong, yet at the same time how it almost certainly concealed a hidden truth, was part of the fascination of my subsequent research. This research was largely a personal exploration through the archives but details about the 50th (The Queen's Own) Regiment up to and during the Crimean campaign I owe to Colonel Arthur Evelyn Fyler's history of his beloved regiment (published in London in 1895). I must also thank Professor Valerie Burton of the Memorial University of Newfoundland who offered useful insights into the nineteenth-century nautical world; members of the Crimean War group at Groups. io who provided small but vital details that fitted like jigsaw pieces into the puzzle of Corporal George Mawer's family story; and Dave Randall, another second cousin but in this case twice removed, who sent me a photo of the 1928 family group taken a few moments after one already in my possession. In Dave Randall's version my grandmother has ceased chatting with her neighbour and is, for a moment, still. That is the image you see in the Epilogue.

As always, I am indebted to my wife, Connie, for her patient acceptance, over forty years and more, of being married to a novelist. My final acknowledgements must be to less immediate family members – my ancestors in the nineteenth century and the scant records they left behind. Without them a story like this would have been an entire fiction; with them I hope I have come somewhere near their truth.

Credits

SIMON MAWER was born in 1948 in England. His first novel, *Chimera*, won the McKitterick Prize for first novels. *Mendel's Dwarf*, his first book to be published in the United States, was long-listed for the Man Booker Prize and was a *New York Times* Book to Remember. He is the author of the Booker short-listed *The Glass Room* (Other Press, 2009), *Trapeze* (Other Press, 2012), *Tightrope* (Other Press, 2015), and *Prague Spring* (Other Press, 2018).